The Real-Town Murders

ADAM ROBERTS

This edition first published in Great Britain in 2018 by Gollancz

First published in Great Britain in 2017 by Gollancz
an imprint of the Orion Publishing Group Ltd
Carmelite House, 50 Victoria Embankment
London EC4Y 0DZ

An Hachette UK Company

1 3 5 7 9 10 8 6 4 2

A CIP catalogue record for this book is
available from the British Library.

ISBN 978 1 473 22146 8

Typeset at The Spartan Press Ltd,
Lymington, Hants

Printed and bound by CPI Group (UK) Ltd,
Croydon, CR0 4YY

www.orionbooks.co.uk
www.gollancz.co.uk

Y005438

'As eve   s – the allure
of virt   ety – is done
with grace and economy, and what might have been a grim read
is leavened by moments of irreverent black humour'
                                                        n

'An anti collision of Agatha Christie and British science fiction
anthology series Black Mirror ... Smart, deliciously witty and
immensely engaging, it is Roberts at his playful best'
                                        James Bradley, author of *Clade*

'This is witty, smart, cleverly structured and, like the master's
finest films, hooks the reader from the opening moments and
never lets go. Dial M for Marvellous'   *Starburst Magazine*

'It is both familiar and strange by equal turns. It is also delightful'
                                                        Locus

'*The Real-Town Murders* is thoughtful, clever and effortless fiction
that successfully blends hardboiled noir with near-future sci-fi to
create a rich, rewarding story. Highly recommended'
                                                        SF Book

'The sort of chase thriller that Hitchcock used to film'
                                                        Morning Star

'*The Real Town Murders* is a unique and enthralling take on
the locked room mystery. Set in England in our near future, a
time where the internet has developed into something far more
time-consuming and damaging to life as we know it – the Shine
– Alma's case turns into an event-filled romp from clue to twist
to antagonist to barrier, all with a ticking four-hourly deadline
that must be met otherwise Alma's partner will die'
                                                British Fantasy Society

Also by Adam Roberts from Gollancz:

Salt
Stone
On
The Snow
Polystom
Gradisil
Land of the Headless
Swiftly
Yellow Blue Tibia
New Model Army
By Light Alone
Jack Glass
Twenty Trillion Leagues Under the Sea
Bête
The Thing Itself

Contents

PART 1

PART 2

PART 1

Think of the key, each in his prison
Thinking of the key

T S Eliot, *North By North Wasteland*

1: *The Body in the Boot*

Where we are, and where we aren't. Where we can and cannot go. So, for example: human beings were not allowed onto the factory floor. The construction space was absolutely and no exceptions a robot-only zone. Human entry was forbidden. Nevertheless, and against all the rules, a human being had been there.

Not an alive human, though.

Alma said: 'Let's go through the surveillance footage one more time.'

The factory manager, whose surname, according to Alma's feed, had just that moment changed from Ravinthiran to Zurndorfer, said: 'You think you'll see the *join*. You think you missed something, and the solution is right there. Believe me, it's not. The solution is not in this footage.'

Alma nodded, and repeated: 'One more time.'

And Zurndorfer, as she was now called, scowled. 'It's all here. You see everything. You see all the components delivered to the factory. You see the robots assemble everything. There are no human beings, there are no closets or hidden spaces, no veils or curtains. It's all in full view – a minimum of three viewpoints at all times. Isn't that true, FAC?'

The factory AI was called 'FAC-13'. The reason for the number was not immediately obvious. It said: 'All true.'

'Do you know of any way in which a human corpse could have gotten into the trunk of that automobile?' Alma asked.

'There is no way such a thing could happen,' FAC-13 said.

'And yet,' Alma pointed out, 'there it is. At the end of the process there it is. A corpse in the car.'

So they all watched the surveillance footage one more time. It was exactly as the manager said: slow it and pause as Alma might, look at it from whichever angle, the process was seamless. There was no way a body could have been cached in the trunk.

Ergo there was no body in the trunk. Except, at the end, there it was – a body in the trunk.

She watched the whole run of the footage. She watched the supply packtruc deliver raw materials, and toggled the p-o-v three-sixty as the materiel was unloaded and prepped. She watched old-school robots, fixed to the floor, pick up panels and slip them into the slots of various presses. Not a person in sight. Blocky machines spat smaller components down a slope, chrome nuggets tumbling like scree. She watched other robots, nothing more than metallic models of gigantic insect legs, bowing and lifting, moving with a series of rapid sweeps and abrupt stops like bodypopping dancers. Not a human being in sight. Rapidly the shape of the automobile assembled; a skeleton of rollbars and supports with – here Alma froze the image, swung it about, zoomed in – nothing inside. Restart. The panels were welded zippily into place. The body of the car rolled down the line. It was a process familiar, traditional, as old as manufacture itself, and it went without a hitch. And *Homo sapiens* was *Homo absence* throughout.

The wheels were fitted. The car rolled in front of a tall cranebot that twisted its narrow pyramidic body, bowed to its task and inserted the engine. Before the body panels were soldered on, various printers inserted their nozzles and printed interior fittings: dashboard, mouldings, hubcaps. The seats were dropped deftly in and the side and rear panels fitted.

'We like to build cars the traditional way,' said Zurndorfer. 'What you're seeing, this is pretty much how Henry Ford made the very first automobiles. We're proud of that fact. It's basically the same system that Stradivarius used in his violin workshop.'

'I'm guessing Stradivarius's robots were smaller,' Alma said.

Zurndorfer scowled. She looked as though she was trying to work out whether Alma was joking or not. '*Traditional* robots, though,' she said. 'All our robots are facced according to care-fully enhanced traditional blueprints. We at McA build *artisanal* automobiles for the discerning driver. Sure, maybe that means we're a little pricier than some others, but you get what you pay for. People say to me: "But this Wenxin Tishi car is cheaper", but I'll tell you what I say back. Over seventy-five per cent of any Wenxin auto is printed. You really want to rely on a car that's basically extruded in a lump? *We* assemble the whole car,

4

according to traditional practices. It makes it more robust, the car lasts longer, it is more reliable.'

Alma looked at the manager. It was hard to tell in sim, but she sounded nervous. Did she have something to hide? Then again, a dead body had been discovered in her factory, a fact which was presumably enough to make anyone nervous. No need for the full-on sales pitch, though.

'Do humans never go onto the factory floor?'

Zurndorfer blinked. 'What? No! Not if we can help it. I mean sometimes we have to send someone in. Sometimes it can't be helped. But then we have to reseal and decom, and that's expensive.'

'Time-consuming?'

'Not so much that. And not *very* expensive, if I'm honest. But it's an extra cost, and you can imagine how narrow margins are in today's world. How few autos get...' Suddenly she dried. Put her hands over her face. When her sim-face re-emerged it looked more serious. 'I apologise. I'm gabbling on.'

'Don't worry,' said Alma.

The remainder of the surveillance footage played out. The last components of the car were put in place. Alma had watched the whole process, from nothing to complete car, and there wasn't anything unusual to see at any point. The car was complete, and rolled to the end of its line. 'FAC-13,' she asked. 'Just to confirm: there was nothing unusual about this? No extra *robotic* activity, for instance, except for what you'd expect for a vehicle like this?'

'None,' said FAC-13.

'And your oversight is...?'

'Well, I'm not om*nis*cient,' the AI's avatar said laughingly, with a flawlessly copied and perfectly empty chuckle. 'I'm not God. You guys programmed us all to make sure of *that*. But I oversee every worker, every stage in production, and at no point did a human being enter the factory.'

'You wouldn't be lying to me, now would you?'

'I am an AI,' the AI said, in an affronted tone. 'I am incapable of mendacity.'

The designated auto, with a dozen queuing patiently behind it, rolled forward off the line, drove itself along a green-painted line and out through the main entrance into the dilute sunlight of a Berkshire spring day. The external yard was large enough for a thousand vehicles, although there were only a couple dozen visible (her feed gave her the exact number: twenty-eight). The auto rolled to a halt, and for the first time in the entire process a human being entered the footage: a tall woman in a blue hard hat, with a tablet cradled in the crook of one arm. She peered at the car, opened the driver's-side door, leaned in, pulled herself out. It was the third time Alma had watched this footage, and her attention wandered. Sky the colour of an old man's hair. Trees standing blackly isolated against the light. Cypresses, were they? She nudged her feed and discovered they were cyprelms, a new hybrid.

The quality checker was walking around the car, opening each door in turn. Advertising regs were clear enough, and this was the bare minimum of what had to be done to justify the ads – *artisanal autos, built the old-fashioned way, not just squirted out of an industrial printer, each detail checked by hand*. The QC stepped to the rear and unsnibbed the lid of the trunk. It swung up, slowly, and the expression on the face of the woman – Stowe was her name, said Alma's feed – froze. Or glitched. Or underwent some subtle process of realignment that did not entail any actual change of expression. Something altered, though. Footage from a different angle could look over her shoulder at the corpse: recognisably human, obviously dead, the man's expression the tragic one from that two-mask theatrical icon. Stowe stood for eleven seconds, leaned forward, touched the skin of the dead body on the neck. Then she stood upright and the feed informed Alma that she was calling in an anomaly to the next up in her chain of command. She didn't look away. She was staring at death, and she couldn't take her eyes away. We're so used to looking backwards, into memory and the rosy past, that when the future intervenes – all our futures, yours and mine and hers and his – it is a coldly mesmeric experience.

'There we are,' said Zurndorfer. 'A dead body.' There was a dreary tone in her voice, and it occurred to Alma that they were all underplaying the reveal. It was a conjuring trick, a ghastly piece of stagecraft. Murder always meant intent, malign focus and will, and this murderer had arranged for their victim to be discovered with a dramatic flourish that was, presumably, designed to give the finger to the people tasked with investigating the crime. It brayed: *Solve this*! You had to admire the ingenuity, however it had been

6

worked. And it *had* been worked; the trick was complete. Yet none amongst the small audience of people watching the show were impressed. It was surprisingly demoralising, actually. The reveal was not a bunch of flowers, or a white rabbit with rose-coloured eyes, or a sawn-in-two woman restored to smiling wholeness. It was death. It was life's denouement.

As with any death, natural or unnatural, the existential chill was forced to coexist with mundane practical considerations. The police had to be called. And so they were, and the factory shut down, and the company higher-ups informed. It had been they who hired Alma: a licensed adjunct to official investigation. For Zurndorfer's factory it meant at least loss of profit, possibly closure (it might be, given the modern world's ever-diminishing demand for automobiles, that the former would lead to the latter anyway). For Alma it meant, at least, work, although the sort of work that would only depress her spirits. Death, and deceit, and hatred, and the bitter root of oblivion. She zoomed in to get a better look at the expression on the body's face: an open-eyed blankness of unapprehension.

Her feed said: Adam Kem, male, age 50, height 173.5 centimetres, worked as a civil servant, married, two children. A blinking sigil that promised a sheaf of further data if she wanted it. Time for that later. It wasn't a name she recognised.

'I'll have to come over,' she told Zurndorfer.

'What – in person?'

'Yes.'

Zurndorfer's simface goggled at her. 'I'm sorry to be dense, but, you mean *physically* shift yourself from over there to … you know. Here?'

'Yes.'

'Well, I say, well of course. I mean. If you think that's necessary. Is that necessary?'

'You've been to the crime scene yourself?'

Zurndorfer's sim visibly flinched at the phrase *crime scene*. 'No, no. I mean, what would be the point? FAC-13 has everything.'

'I'd like to see the place with my own eyes.'

'You just did.'

Alma said nothing.

'The body's not here,' Zurndorfer said. 'You know that? Of course you do. They took it to the morgue. Well, they took it to the hospital first, though there was nothing a hospital could do. The ambulancewoman said she could see straight away that the cadaver was dead. But apparently that's procedure: first to hospital, then when death is confirmed to the morgue. I'm sorry: you know all this. I'm sorry. I can chatter on. When I'm upset. And this is very upsetting.'

Alma nodded. 'Who called the ambulance, by the way? Was that you?'

'Chuckie did that. I mean, she's no medic, she couldn't, couldn't *be* sure he was. You know. Couldn't be sure he was actually.'

'Chuckie?'

'Chuckie Stowe. The QC. She comes onto the site daily, and does a check of all the autos in person, after they come off the production line. It's so we can say they are hand-checked by humans. It's an advertising thing, really. But she's alright, Chuckie. I suppose you want to talk to her?'

'In time.'

'We pride ourselves on our hands-on artisanal automobile assemblance.' The company boilerplate bubbled from Zurndorfer's mouth as she rubbed the heel of a hand into her left eye. 'Each product is carefully checked by a real human being before being shipped to...' Abruptly she began to sob.

Alma waited, and the little hiccoughy noises slowly faded away.

'I'm sorry,' Zurndorfer said. 'It's been a shock.'

'I would like you to meet me at the plant,' Alma said.

'Of course. How long will it...? I mean, you know. I mean: right now?'

Her feed said the place was thirteen minutes away, depending on traffic, but of course there would be no traffic. 'A quarter-hour,' she said.

'Well. Well alright. Well.' Zurndorfer signed off, and Alma swept the rest of the digital rendering away.

Now that she was alone in the bare room, Alma addressed the hidden observer. 'You were watching,' she said. Not really a question. She eschewed avatars, but Marguerite was watching through Alma's feed. Of course she was.

'Murder as conjuring trick,' came Marguerite's voice.

'Could you *sound* more bored?'

'Boring stuff bores me. I yearn to be de-bored. Unbored. This, though? Puff.'

'Puff?'

'Pff.'

'I thought you liked the properly puzzling ones,' Alma said.

'There's puzzling, and then there's trying too hard. So: *there* it is.'

'Somebody *is* dead,' said Alma.

'It's always the puzzle,' Marguerite countered. 'It's always that. But death is nothing. Death is the most ordinary thing in the world. It's the one thing we're all guaranteed to experience. Puzzles are different. Puzzles are special. Special isn't a word we can use of a thing that literally everybody experiences.'

'Somebody died, Reetie. And I'm now officially contracted. So I'm going to have to block you out of the actual investigation. In case my testimony comes to court and so on and so forth.'

'Allie, my dear Allie! Be honest, now. You'll *need* me to help you figure it out. *You're* not the puzzle-brain. You're the bish-bash. You're the plod-plod. I'm the Mycroft here. You're not the Mycroft. You're the Yourcroft, at best. At *best*.'

'The police will puzzle it out, if anybody does,' Alma muttered, not pleased by this disparagement, however comically offered. 'And, in fact, probably *nobody* will puzzle it out, and nobody will care, and that will be that will be that.'

'So long as we get paid,' said Marguerite.

'So long as I get paid,' Alma returned, with asperity. She immediately regretted saying so.

'Spoilsport,' said Marguerite. 'Still: you can tell me all about it in person, can't you? At any the end of your long plod-plod day.'

Alma checked the timer, always there, in the corner of her eye. Three hours and forty-one minutes. Counting down.

2: *Madame Michelangela*

Alma's car was not one of the artisanally crafted autos that Zurn-dorfer's factory produced. She couldn't afford anything so fancy. Instead she drove a standard plastic vehicle made 90 per cent of printed parts, a heap that rattled and hummed when she got up to fifty klicks. The shocks were wearing down saggily under the rear wheel arches. Climbing into the driver's seat her nostrils were stung by a smell of mint so strong it had an acid tang and made her clap her hand to her face. It actually burned her throat. Gas, gas, an ecstasy of fumbling. The airfresh unit was low in the dash, partly hidden by a heap of junk and various detritus she had accumulated since her last big clear-out. It took her more than a minute rummaging around and deprogging the unit, and another minute until unscented air blowing hard and all the windows open meant that the space inside became bearable. That turned her thirteen-minute drive into a sixteen-minute drive.

The roads, though, were mostly clear. The car piloted itself smoothly onto the western artery, heading over the river and out of R!-town. The freeway was like a diagram from a textbook, white under a cool grey-blue sky. Soon enough, though, the car took a left turn onto a smaller road, past a decommissioned brick factory whose loading yard was littered with what looked like dusty avantgarde sculptural discards – a rusting truck cab, a stacked heap of metal casings, a large metal cube the colour of Marmite brailled all over with weathered pockmarks. The next plot along was a still functioning storage unit, and the one after that a car-recycling company that, judging by the stacks of decaying autos sitting unprocessed in front of their building, had gone out of business. Teeter totter. A solitary bot moved very slowly over the weedy concrete.

Then the road took Alma past a residential block. A few people were out in the warm afternoon air. She spotted one meshed-up individual plodding along the road – a bold individual to be out in such a run-down district. Fitting yourself with a mesh and having your body put through the automated motions to keep it limber, to avoid bedsores, stretch the muscles a little: most people did all that in the privacy of their own homes. You could walk up your down stairs, or down your up stairs, if you had stairs. You could pace from room to room if you didn't. It hardly mattered where you went whilst the body's consciousness was wholly concentrated in-Shine. In the richer parts of town it might be danger-free to have your mesh take your zonked-out body for a walk in the fresh air. But in a district like this you were almost begging nogoodniks to come steal your clothes, shave your head, or worse: kidnap you and whisk you away. You wake up pretty quickly if they actually hurt you, of course; but coming out of Shine and into the real world was, like any wake-up, not the best preparation for fighting off muggers. Of course, it was true plenty of people couldn't afford real-world apartments large enough to plod around in, never mind staircases. For some in-Shine workers home was a space literally large enough only for a single bed. In such cases your mesh might *have* to take you out of your private space. Life is all about the compromises people make between desire and finances. Or, more precisely: life in the *real* world was all about those compromises. The Shine was different.

As the car drove, Alma took another look through the FAC-13 surveillance files. There was, she had to concede – there *really* was – no way anyone could have snuck into that facility unseen and deposited an adult human corpse in the boot of that car. For one thing, the footage showed the whole auto being built up from scratch, with no corpse being interposed at any point. For another, any human presence on the factory floor would have flagged up about a dozen safety, trespass and anti-theft protocols, some of which would have automatically alerted the police. For a third: well, it was all just crazy.

Nobody got into the factory. Except that Adam Kem, dead, somehow had done. Either he got into the factory, somehow unnoticed, alive and later became dead; or he entered the factory dead, in which case somebody else must have carried him. Conceivably some several bodies else.

How, though?

Alma ran an eye over FAC-13's archived feed, though she was

not sure what she was looking for. There were thick threads of interaction with the parent company AI, which is what you would expect. There were also thick threads between FAC-13 and the hospital. Presumably some of this was the factory AI alerting the Health authorities of the crime. Maybe it hadn't known whether Kem was dead or only injured. Maybe it was a protocol to swiftly and heavily link in the hospital in the event of human accident or death on the premises. Although that possibility didn't make a lot of sense in a wholly automated factory. Then again, Alma reminded herself, there was more to the factory than the factory floor. Outside was company space in which human beings sometimes worked. The protocols would have been written to cover the whole property. The only puzzle about the Health threads was that some of it seemed to predate the discovery of Adam Kem's body. Alma made a note on her feed to look into it. Perhaps some other employee had called in sick. Maybe that was a coincidence, and maybe not.

Otherwise the FAC-13 archive was full of unexceptional operational gubbins, up until the moment the police had come and McA had hired Alma. One minor point of interest: that hiring had been – Alma could see, from a partly redacted data filament – instigated at the suggestion of somebody with a Govt tag. Maybe she had friends in high places, eager to put work her way. She didn't recognise the tag, though. Maybe McA was angling for a government contract, and the government was in the habit of telling it what to do. Why her, though?

It didn't matter.

The car shuddered and coughed as it turned left once again, and Alma looked out at her surroundings. They passed three clean-looking cubic business buildings, perfectly blank and non-logoed, presumably housing servers. And at last she was coming up to McA's car manufactory: wide and long and low-roofed, daffodil-yellow walls and a hologram logo twisting and bulging over the roof, *McA Artisanal Autos*. There was a single vehicle in the visitor's parking lot as Alma pulled in. Zurndorfer – in the flesh – clambered out of this other car. She looked uncomfortable, being in the open air.

Alma got out and walked up to her, the feed pinging that the woman's name was no longer Zurndorfer: it was Collins. The sun came out from behind the hazy cloud: a smile in the form of light. Alma matched her expression to the brightness.

'Your name keeps changing,' she said. 'Why is that?'

Collins, as she now was, made a sour face. 'It has nothing to do with the cry the crime the matter under our,' she returned. She tried again: 'Nothing to do do do with the matter under.' She stopped.

Alma said nothing. People often got nervous in face-to-face interactions. Talking to someone in the flesh was, of course it was, *weird*. Hers was a world where most interactions were in-feed or in-Shine, of course.

A breeze drifted across the lot. It imparted the slightest of Medusa motions to Collins's mass of curling hair.

'I mean,' Collins said, eventually, 'I'm sure police files have everything about me on their. In their data. On their databases.'

'Ms Collins,' said Alma. 'Permit me to explain my status once again. I am not police, nor am I affiliated with them. I am a licensed private security agent, and I am being paid by your company bosses to look into the matter of Adam Kem's death.'

'They are worried it will impact profitability,' said Collins, sulkily.

'Of course they are.'

'They're going to fire me,' Collins said, her eyes brimming liquid.

'I don't know if they will or won't.'

'It's not illegal,' Collins said. 'The name thing.'

Alma waited.

'It's a marriage chain. I'm registered with an in-line company that arranges it. I get paid per marriage.'

This was a new one on Alma. 'You've been married three times in the last hour,' she said, trying, and mostly managing, to keep the surprise out of her voice.

'Technically – only technically. The company is registered in Simferopol citystate, and there's a kink in the marriage law there. One need only be married thirty minutes before divorce becomes possible. I signed up, and the company processes everything. It's legal. My file is always updated when I marry somebody new. I never meet these people, you know. It's men and women from all around the world, I think. I mean, I assume it is. I don't check. I don't know.'

'You get married forty-eight times a day?' Alma asked.

Collins snorted. 'I wish! If I could manage that, the money would really start to add up. I only earn 1.15 E a marriage, you know, it's hardly lucrative. But times are tight. Every little, you know. No, no, *how* many times I get married depends upon the company demand, and that has long periods of downtime. So now I'm...' her eyes flickered sideways as she checked her own feed. 'Now I'm Collins. OK, I don't know who Collins is. Maybe I'll have another name in a half-hour. Maybe I'll be Collins for a month. It is,' she repeated, looking crossly at Alma, 'legal. McA know I do it, the company knows, any income is declared for tax, there's nothing... there's. Look, can we go inside? It's bright out here and it's stinging my eyes.'

Alma could think of several reasons why these other individuals, the ones at the other end of Collins's situation, might want to lay down a cat's-cradle of constantly shifting legal marriages, and none of those were kosher. But she parked the thought. It almost certainly had nothing to do with the crime. Collins was a pudgy individual with very white skin, and watery rheum was creeping from the corners of her eyes.

They went inside.

'I will need to have a look over the whole site,' Alma said as the two of them came into the reception area at the front of the factory. It was a nondescript waiting space: a drinks fac in the wall; an L of foam large enough to sit on but not comfortable enough to make you want to sit long. A holo shivered into life in front of them. 'Welcome to McA, where cars are made the old-fashioned way! Maybe you are interested in buying, and certainly I am here to help you!'

'We're not customers,' said Collins, dabbing at the corner of her eyes alternately with the backs of her hands.

'Apologies Ms,' said the sim, hesitating just long enough to give the impression of mild AI sarcasm before adding: 'Ms Collins.'

'FAC-13, it's me,' said Collins. 'Quit playing games.'

'Of course. And *you*,' said the sim, smiling, as it turned to Alma, 'are the accredited private investigator. Welcome to the facility. I only wish you were visiting under less unfortunate circumstances.'

'I'd hardly be here,' said Alma, 'under less unfortunate circumstances. Can you please let me through to the main body of the factory?'

'Of course. Normally I might object, since human presence on the shopfloor is technically a contamination. But two human police officers have already been on the site, and one tech CSI individual. The CSI individual's name is Pfeffer.'

'Is that relevant?'

'Probably not. It seemed to me a charming name. Charming and funny. So many fs!'

'Are you always this whimsical?'

The holo adopted a serious face. 'I am exactly as I have been programmed, Ms Alma. Please do go through. The workers have all been shut down. Please let me know if you need to power any of them up, for any reasons of investigation. Please be aware that the police have a device on the shopfloor.'

'A device?'

'A mobile device. It is, I believe, searching for DNA. As I understand the situation, none has been found.'

Alma went through, Collins following. The space was large and cool, but clean. Everything was yellow or white, except for some aluminium-coloured rafters high overhead. The machinery was eerily still. Alma strolled down the central track of the production line. She wasn't looking for anything in particular, just trying to get a sense of the space, to see if there was any tingling in her solar plexus that suggested any intimation as to how the trick was accomplished. Nothing. Marguerite would have ideas. Marguerite always had ideas about things like this. Reflexively, Alma checked her feed: over three hours before she had to be back.

Plenty of time.

'I don't see what use you think this is going to be,' muttered Collins, close behind her. 'There's nothing here that isn't available in sim.'

'Sometimes actually being in a place will give you,' Alma replied, absently, 'a vibe, or a feeling, or some gut-level...'

'Feed me a full dose of both the mumbo *and* the jumbo,' said Collins, 'why don't you?'

A semi-spherical device slid along its flat base directly in front of them. Blue-and-white stripes, POLICE, DO NOT INTERFERE printed on the side, and an electric-shock warning sigil like half an SS-logo. The device slid away.

They got to the far end, and Alma looked all around. Nothing. 'Where is the person who actually found the body?'

'Chuckie. I sent her home. She was pretty upset. It's not a pleasant thing, discovering a dead body. You don't stumble upon a corpse every day. So, what, so, you, so: you, you want to interview her?'

'In person, yes.'

'In *person*? I mean – alright. I suppose, alright.'

'Tomorrow is soon enough. For now I'd like to go to the hospital where the body was first taken.'

'The body's not there, I said already,' Collins said. 'I told you – it's gone to the morgue. Chuckie only called the ambulance because she wasn't sure – look, are you *certain* this is necessary?' She placed herself in front of Alma, and made a pleading face. 'Or, at least, wait, you don't need me to come with you to the hospital, do you?'

'That won't,' said Alma, 'be necessary.'

'Alright. All.'

They went back outside, and stood for a moment in the otherwise empty carpark. A scatter of birds was wheeling in the eastern sky. Alma and Collins aside, there wasn't another awake human being for a mile in any direction. Certainly not one awake in the real world. A lonely sort of place to die, when you thought about it. Although presumably Adam Kem was killed somewhere else, and only deposited here, in this auto manufactory. *How* was the main puzzle. *Why* was, Alma hoped, going to prove more tractable. At the moment she had no idea about either.

'Can I go?' Collins asked.

'The AI avatar in reception, just now,' Alma said. 'It didn't recognise you at first.'

'It recognised me. It's not stupid. It was just being pissy.'

'Because you don't often come down to the site itself?'

'Why should I come? Look – I mean, yes, maybe this is the first time I've been, you know, *physically* present on site. But what would be the point?'

'Even though the company hires you as site overseer?'

'Overseeing happens better by sim. I mean, come on!'

'You can go,' said Alma, mildly, and climbed into her little auto. She drove away.

It was a nine-minute drive back in towards town to reach the hospital – a wide, low building of white concrete, with three ambulances parked outside the main entrance and nothing much happening. The visitor carpark was empty. The main hall was staffed only by avatars, one of whom, with the ingenuous helpfulness of its kind, gave Alma a clutter of detail about the facility – eighty per cent of patients were lock-ins housed in the sleeper wards to the west; human staff were housed in an annex and could be summoned within a minute. The avatar regretted it could only summon a human being in the event of medical emergency, and not simply to answer questions. The avatar regretted that it would violate staff privacy entitlement if it were to let Alma have the names either of the ambulance driver who brought in Adam Kem or the House Officer who confirmed his death. The avatar was prepared to confirm that Kem's body had been brought in, since Kem, being dead, had no privacy rights in need of protection. Were Alma in possession of a warrant, the AI would be happy to disclose more, but the AI was aware that warrants were issuable only to the police, and not to private investigators.

'I would like to talk to the ambulance nurse,' Alma said.

'You are not police.'

'I am licensed. I am working in concert with the police.'

'I cannot give you her name. Her name is protected under privacy legislation. Unless you can obtain a warrant.'

'Can you tell me anything at all about the ambulance nurse?'

'I can tell you her gender: female. She is a union member. She is a Capricorn. She is a shift-worker, not a permanent employee, and has only recently been retained by the hospital. She is a blood donor. She has playing interests in crypto-currency, and has won a silver medal in the CC Championships.'

'None of this is of much use. You could, presumably, ask her whether she would be prepared to talk to me, of her own free will? I mean, you could do so without infracting any privacy issues?'

'She is not on shift at the moment,' said the avatar, cheerily. 'She ended her shift early, and has recused herself from further work with us in the immediate future.'

'Sounds like she's pretty upset.'

'I cannot say. You would have to ask her. Although you cannot, unless I contact her. And I am currently unable to do so.'

Alma walked out of the lobby to discover that hers was no longer the only vehicle in the carpark. A long, shiny luxury model had positioned itself right next to her shonky little auto. As Alma walked towards her car the expensive car's driver's-side door rose, like a bird's wing, or a robot heiling Robo-Hitler. A tall woman stepped out of the car – long cyan coat, black trousers, majesty boots.

Alma stopped, slipped her weight to the balls of her feet and brought her hands out of her pockets in readiness. Her stomach buzzed with adrenalised anticipation.

'You are Alma,' said the woman.

'I don't know you,' Alma replied. Her feed was given her nothing.

'You don't know me *yet*,' the woman replied, with a narrow, lopsided smile. 'My name is Michelangela. That's a start, isn't it?'

Alma prodded her feed again: ID blocked; high-level authorisation. There were codeworms Alma had in store that she could have deployed to open the block, but somehow she got the impression that wouldn't be a good idea. 'You're police.'

'Of a sort,' Michelangela replied. 'I'm going to ask you to send your car home, and come with me.' Her passenger-side door swung upwards to join the elevated driver's-side door. Now the vehicle looked like it was surrendering.

'Can I see authorisation? My feed isn't having much luck accessing you.'

Officer Michelangela smiled with one side of her mouth. An official tag slipped through the block and into Alma's feed. The powers granted to this individual exceeded those that defined regular police officers by quite a way.

'Am I to understand,' said Alma, checking that her monitor was triple-saving, 'that you are using your authority to *compel* me to accompany you?'

'That would be arrest,' said Michelangela, her smile gone, 'and I am not arresting you. But I am *inviting* you. You are, I know, investigating the strange death of a man called Adam Kem, and I am happy to take you to the morgue to view his body – that *is* where you were going next, yes?' The woman's smile returned. It was not a reassuring sight.

'I am content to make my own way to the morgue.'

'Ah but then you wouldn't have the advantage of *my* company. There are things I can tell you about the case that you will find interesting. Useful, conceivably. Perhaps essential.'

'By all means, message my feed with your information.'

'I prefer to talk. Please, Alma. You've made your symbolic resistance to my invitation, and proved that you're not a pushover. Now get in the car.'

Alma thought about it, but not for very long. There wasn't really an option. She instructed her own auto to follow the police vehicle, since she didn't want to find herself stranded without transport far from home. In another couple of hours she would have to be back with Marguerite, after all. Then she got into Michelangela's car. The seat adjusted itself to her form. Warm and fragrant air wafted past her head. When Michelangela drove off, acceleration was addressed by an equal-and-opposite motion in the fabric of the seatback.

'You already know that I am licensed,' Alma said. 'What I'm doing is perfectly legal. I have been retained by the holding company of McA to investigate this, uh' – how to describe it? 'This strange death. My investigation is complementary to the police investigation, and I will of course share any information I uncover with the authorities.'

'I have a panoptic view of your work, your personal life and this whole case, Ms Alma,' said Officer Michelangela. 'I know, for instance, that premature termination of your contract required a kill-fee. That's been paid, you know.'

Alma said nothing.

'I'm not trying to be mysterious,' Michelangela went on, shortly. 'I represent the government. This is a case that has been bumped up the police priority list, and with the new resources it will soon be resolved. After a little governmental advice, NageL are content *not* to run a private investigation alongside the police one.'

NageL were the boss company of which McA were a part.

'I see,' said Alma.

'You can intuit from this that this murder is a case with – let us say, with implications. The sort of case with high-level government interest.' She scrunched her face and made a weird miaow noise, and it took Alma a moment to realise that she was yawning. Tired, clearly. The car swung onto the main freeway.

'You're still taking me to see the body?'

'I am,' said Michelangela. 'You might regard that as a professional courtesy. What I would like is for you to do all the things you contracted to do. And then go home this evening and write your report, to sign off on the case, and move on to other investigations. You'll find your employer won't in the least be displeased that you have, as it were, withdrawn. It won't affect your future employment prospects with them, I mean.'

'That's what you would like?'

'That's what we would like.'

Alma peered through the car's widescreen passenger window. The blank spaces of factories, of servers, of storage units. Not a person about. The lights lining up like sunlit dew on a thread all the way down the eastern freeway. Behind her, the sky was beginning to soak through watercolour shades of red and pink. Up ahead: many starlings silhouetted against the sky like tea leaves left at the bottom of a pale china pot.

'The only things I know about Adam Kem,' Alma said, without turning to face Michelangela, 'are what's in the collective domain. Which is to say, I don't know much about him.'

'In a minute or so, you'll see him. In the flesh.'

'One thing in particular strikes me,' Alma said. 'The more usual course of things, murder-wise, would be for the murderer to hide the body. Usually when a crime like this has been committed, the best outcome for the criminal is that the body is never found. Or found very late. In this case, though, the body has been, we might say, ostentatiously flourished before the eyes of the authorities. It has been presented to the world in such a way as if the murderer wishes to say: *Look how clever I am.*'

'That's your reasoning?' Something in Michelangela's voice made Alma look round. The half-smile was back on the other woman's face.

'My reasoning,' Alma said, feeling cross, 'is that the murderer wanted this corpse to be noticed, and that *you* want it to vanish into the collective forgetting. My reasoning is that the disparity in intention between the two of you is an intriguing thing.'

'Oh well, as far as *that* is concerned...' Michelangela said, 'there is much merit in what you say. We're here.'

The car smoothed to a halt so gently Alma barely registered it. 'How do *you* think the body got into the trunk of that car?' she asked Michelangela.

The doors swung upward on both sides, and the driver's face was outlined with later afternoon light. 'Well if you could work that out,' she said, 'then you'd be *much* closer to solving the mystery than you are.'

They both climbed out of the car. Another empty carpark, another peopleless building. This was a government facility, part prison and part morgue – a strange combination, one might think, if one didn't realise that the prisoners were all criminals who had been locked into the Shine to serve their sentences. Quiet as the grave. Only sims and bots on staff, so far as Alma could see. A vast port-wine-coloured Rothko occupied one of the walls in the lobby.

Michelangela led Alma through a narrow door at the side. The morgue was in a small separate building, linked by a corridor.

There was a real-live awake human being on duty there, and whatever was in Michelangela's authorisation galvanised this person as soon as she checked it. She leapt to her feet, greeted the policeperson solicitously, and took Alma and Michelangela directly to view the dead body of Adam Kem.

Here was the body of a middle-aged white male, laid out in all its chill and flabby solidity. His hair was the colour of coffee with too much cream in it, and his lips matt white. There were many lines on his face. Maybe he had smoked. Or enjoyed sunbathing, a rarer vice. There was an ironfiling pattern of stubble on his chin and cheeks that he was, now, never going to shave off. There were many weedy white hairs on his shoulders and chest, and a swirl of darker fur covering his paunch. There was his desperately pathetic dead cock, small as a cocktail sausage. Stocky legs, which meant he was in the habit of using them, which in turn meant that he was not a hard-core denizen of the Shine – a mesh-suit might move a body around, but it couldn't build muscle. An agent busy in the Real, then. His toenails were ugly, discoloured, the consistency of Bakelite, tombstone-shaped. There were no obvious marks or wounds on the body. There he was, and he was, now, never going to be any more.

'How did he die?' Alma asked.

The morgue attendant – Bubb was her name, Alma's feed told her – looked at Michelangela. The slightest of nods from the policeperson.

'His lungs are mashed,' said Bubb, replying to Alma's question by addressing Michelangela.

'How do you mean, mashed?'

'Chewed up. Pulped. Mashed – you know what mash is? What

21

people do to potatoes to make mash? That's what's happened to his lungs.'

Alma left a pause before replying: 'How?'

'Not sure. There's no external wounds – so he wasn't, let's say, shot in the chest or anything. It must have been something that got into him in a way that didn't break the skin – down his trachea, presumably. The heart is puree too. If something did get inside him and swirled it all up, then that something isn't inside him any more. And I'll tell you something else.'

'Please do.'

'Maybe he was killed by having his heart and lungs turned into squishee. Maybe he was killed in some other way and his heart and lungs were mashed up after. Either could be the case. He must have ejected a lot of blood and matter from his mouth – I mean, you can imagine, having your lungs turn to lumpy fluid inside your ribs, you're going to cough up a *load* of stuff. But I understand that such ejecta wasn't there where the body was found. Ergo he must have been moved *after* he was initially killed.'

'Indeed,' said Alma.

'I like it,' Bubb told Michelangela, 'when I can use a word like *ergo* in a proper sentence.'

Alma walked all the way round the body, and then stood near its feet and stared for a while. Eventually Michelangela asked: 'Seen enough?'

Bubb more or less snapped to attention as Michelangela strode out. Alma walked alongside the taller woman, down the corridor and out into the twilight. Her car had followed the police vehicle as ordered and was parked nearby. 'I would have given you a lift home,' said Michelangela, absently. 'I appreciate that you need to get back. To attend to your – partner. I understand that there is a time limit.'

'You know a lot about me.'

'Yes,' said Michelangela, simply.

'More than I know about you.'

Michelangela's face didn't move, although her eyes very clearly said *Well, of course*.

'Why do I get the sense,' Alma tried, 'that you let me see Adam Kem to taunt me?'

For the first time in their meeting, Michelangela's face displayed a genuine emotion. Surprisingly enough it was surprise. 'Oh, no.

Very much no, I wouldn't want you to think *that*. My feelings for you are wholly encompassed by, well, admiration. You are very good at what you do, and being in the same line of business, broadly defined, means I know how hard the stuff is that you make look easy. This, genuinely, has been a professional courtesy.'

'It is also a sanctioned cease-and-desist,' Alma tried to say, but her strangulated anger meant that she tripped up over the phrase's sibilance and instead hissed like a goose. She stopped, and composed herself. 'Well I suppose I should thank you.'

'I admire you personally as well as professionally, you know,' Michelangela added, as she flipped open the wing-like door of her vehicle. 'Being a carer, I mean. You chose it. You acquit yourself with honour.'

And Alma discovered that her fury had abated. 'As for that,' she said, 'it's really none of your business.'

'Quite right,' said Michelangela, briskly. 'Personal, not professional, and I apologise.' She got into her car and the door closed like a coffin lid and Alma never saw her again.

3: *Dial 'C' for Caring*

Alma drove home through the empty spaces of the evening city, down the underused roads, round untroubled roundabouts, until she rolled into the residential area she called home. The car parked up and she clambered ungainlily out. No matter the advances in automobile tech, nobody had invented a way of getting out of a car that preserved a person's dignity.

Two neighbours, deep in the Shine for over a month now, were bodily out and about in their mesh-suits. A dog sniffed at their heels. One of the suits was starting to fray, which meant that it made a teeth-edge-setting squeaky-scrapy noise as it moved the fellow's legs. As it swung his arms and rotated his hips and spine to keep balance. Sheesh.

Overhead the sky was yawning into mauve, the first stars pipping into view. Alma's block looked like a stilled chainsaw on its end. Something sad, somewhere. Something very sad, iceberg-sized and immovable and decanted into solidity from a thousand years of sorrow drizzling down from above. Was it hers, this sorrow? Surely not. She didn't do *sad*. There was no time for that, and anyway she was inoculated against it. *Il faut cultiver le jardin*, after all. Frustrating, to be bumped off this intriguing murder case almost as soon as she had started looking into it. Frustrating and annoying. But then again, she told herself, it was only one case, and had never looked like it would be over-lucrative. The police would wrap it up in days, probably. A puzzlebox that she would not now open. But that was no big deal, and it was not a big deal, and the deal that it *was* was not big. The sadness was surely not occasioned by anything so trivial. The sadness would pass, or she would sail past *it*, as she had done a thousand times. It might graze the flank of her enormous ocean-liner self in passing, but nothing more. Come tomorrow morning the sadness would be far behind her.

The building pushed a message at her, and without really thinking she accepted it. But the message was a technicolour override of all her visual feeds – so rude! – a rinkydink country-and-gospel song and the scrolling message that ONLY JESUS CAN SAVE YOU, which meant the building had been hacked again. She swore, and then blocked, and then reset her filters.

The unconscious body of one of her neighbours whirred and wheezed past her, on its way somewhere. Presumably to circle about and come home. The same trajectory as everyone. As everyone.

Inside the elevator Alma closed her eyes.

Inside the flat, Marguerite was in upbeat mood. 'So, my darling, tell me all, tell me all about it.'

As she stepped through to Marguerite's room Alma unblocked access and pushed the day's files and indices towards her. 'Not so very good.'

'Casting my eye,' said Marguerite from her bed. There was a new timbre of phlegmy gargle to her voice that Alma didn't like. 'Murder, murder. Very banal. But there's more: a new case, two in as many days, fancy that. Came in when you were out. A concerned mother.'

'Concerned about what?'

'Concerned that her son is starving to death. Starving to death despite eating, oddly enough.'

'Son, how old?'

'Twenty-nine. But the son must have a tag on his mother, because as soon as the request came through to us he got in touch to say don't bother.'

'Could be a legal tag.'

'Could be, although I doubt it.'

'And he wanted us to back off?'

'Back off, the jack-off. Said his mother didn't know what she was talking about. Said he was fine. Swore he ate three squares a day, had a good job, everything was fine. All but *ordered* us to ignore his mother, and not take her case.'

'I love how you refer to our commissions as *cases*. Did he look thin, this geezer?'

'It was a head-and-shoulders sim, but I'd say, yes. Very thin. Thinner than me, shall we say.' And Marguerite laughed her Huttlaugh, and all the bits of her trembled and jiggled. 'But never mind about that for a moment,' she said, adopting a let's-be-serious-for-a-moment tone. 'Tell me about the mysterious corpse that somehow found its way into the trunk of that car.'

'I shunted you the relevant,' Alma returned. 'I don't like the sound of your throat. Gracious, Rita, you're hot! You'll run into full-on fever if we're not careful. I think I need to adjust your fauxphase. And your WAT-BAT balance has gone all screwy again. I'll order in some adiposanex.'

'Oho, push the boat out,' gurgled Marguerite. 'You anticipating a long run on this body-in-the-car puzzle? Proper pay cheque this time, is it? I'll be munching only the finest medication off golden platters.'

Alma felt the knuckling sensation of annoyance: never a good sign. But then again, sometimes Marguerite just was in a skittish mood. 'Rita, love, but don't and don't and thrice don't wind me up, alright?

'You are pettish, my love.'

'I'm annoyed. The authorities came and shut me down. Very high-ranking intelligence officer. Says I'm not to investigate the murder of Adam Kem any further.'

'Oh! Still, we can take a look, can't we? Just as an unofficial exercise in problem-solving and loose-end-tying-up?'

'Be my guest. Like I said, I shunted you the relevant case files and text.'

'That stuff? Generic news stuff, darling. They say a body was discovered in a bespoke car manufactory; but they don't say about how impossible it was for the body to *be* where the body *was*.'

'News stories? No, I shunted my personal ... I didn't' – and as she spoke, she was checking, and as she checked she discovered that her personal record of the afternoon's encounter had been evacuated and the files replaced with generic news stuff. It was a startling thing. She checked her firewalls and triggerlines, and not a one had been so much as breathed upon. That suggested hacking of the very highest, which was to say most expensive, kind. Government Intelligence Agency level hacking. The fact of what had happened chimed like a bell inside her mind, and its various implications reverberated through all her preconceptions.

'I think I need a drink,' Alma said aloud.

'If only my fibroblasts could wait!' And Marguerite's jolliness of tone betrayed a note of anxiety, which Alma couldn't help but take as a rebuke to her own selfishness. She fingered her sleeves, and as they rolled themselves up washed her hands at the little sink in the corner of the room. Then she climbed up onto the little platform alongside Marguerite's shoulder and gave her a kiss on her vast cheek. 'Let's sort you out, and we can have some cognac.'

'*Cara mia*,' Marguerite murmured as Alma worked the Nitidus cream over the metabase areas. Long experience guided her hand, responsive to the hmms and urms of her subject's moaning. Topical pharms to the areas where they were most needed. A proleptic antipyretic. Fever was always a worry; Rita slipped into it too often, and each time it left long-term internal damage. Then Alma checked the deneoplasmer implant, and brushed Marguerite's hair back and rearranged her feeding and breathing tubes at their collar-points. The last part of the ritual took only a minute, but was the most ticklish. The most dangerous accumulation of Marguerite's poisoned lipids was inside her head, and there was little that could be done about it. Indeed, there was no scanner in the world capable of distinguishing between the healthy tissue that constituted Marguerite's brain and the gene-tweaked fatty cells that mimicked her grey and white matter. The cruel truth was that there was only one person in the world whose knowledge of Marguerite was sufficient, in both broader and most minute ways, to tell in which ways her personality was being deformed by the bindweed in her brain, and so who could know how to maximise the efficiency of the drugs that damped down the inskull flare-ups. And thanks to the malignity of whichever genehacker had created this evil little lipid phage, the problem had to be addressed every four hours, or a sudden brainstem inflammation would kill Marguerite in minutes. The timing was coded into the malign genehack itself, and no treatment or medication could alter it. And the clever little pathogens inside her were tagged to respond to that only-one-person-in-the-world. The person who had done this, whoever they were, had designed it to lock both Marguerite and Alma into its remorseless timescale.

There were days when Alma silently wished hell and torture upon the anonymous individual, woman, man or neuter, who had tweaked the genes of this aggressive neoplastic lipid. But mostly she tried to purge her thoughts of such negativity. Rage was not a useful emotion.

The worst of it was: the treatment window was between four hours and four hours and four minutes. Marguerite could not be treated any earlier. Indeed earlier intervention would trigger a genetic cascade, a sort of failsafe programmed into the phage, that would lead to the patient's death. And she certainly couldn't be treated any *later*, or there would be no Marguerite to treat, only a corpse.

What needed doing differed unpredictably, every time the four hours rolled around. Only Alma could address in what ways the phage was shifting through the membranes of Marguerite's mind, swelling here, ebbing there, affecting this or that usual pattern of behaviour. Alma sometimes idly pondered: since I have been keyed in by its designer to treat this gene-tweak pathogen, it's possible that some third party could also be keyed in. In which case, a nurse could conceivably be employed: an individual who was prepared to live in, waking (as Alma woke) through the night every four hours to tend to Marguerite, never venturing further than an hour and a half from the flat, every day, week after week, in and out of months and all the way along the years. But this was a vain hope. Even if somebody could be so employed, there was no way Alma could afford to pay them.

We could put this another way. Even if money were no object, and a nurse could be found to attend Marguerite professionally, Alma would still have to be present.

Alma had long since stopping thinking about the long term.

Today, the phage had wholly abandoned the language centres, and was helix crystallising round the vagus nerve. Or so Alma guessed, from the timbre of Marguerite's moans and the sprightliness of her word play. She poked her finger into the suppressant, to mark it with her own DNA, and then low-pressure-injected it. When Marguerite only hummed at this she checked the dosage and remixed it, touched it again, and reapplied it in a different place. Marguerite went 'ouch', and that was a good sign that something was shrinking. Her breathing became less wheezy. The anxiety-clamp relaxed from Alma's heart a little.

She ordered a new block from the supplier, and flinched a little at the expense as it came through on her feed. She would probably need it again, though. Probably, but not certainly.

The rest was easily done: the application of oilcreme to Marguerite's great expanses of skin could be trusted to bots. The rolling and deforming of the treble-size mattress on which she lay, propped up, likewise. Alma checked they were still doing their job, washed her hands a second time, and finally fetched herself a tumbler of gold-coloured spirits. She sat herself in the Confort 9000 chair beside Marguerite's bed, and breathed out a single, pleasant sigh.

'Cheers, my dear,' she said, and the valve on Marguerite's collar clicked as she switched out water for something stronger. The cognac burned like whisky. Maybe she should buy a more expensive brand. If she somehow chanced upon more money she certainly would.

'Hadn't you better tell me all about it?' Marguerite prompted.

'You sound more like yourself,' Alma noted. 'I'm pleased to say.'

'In the same way a room is by definition room temperature,' Marguerite said, 'a person always sounds like themselves. That's logic.'

'You sound so like yourself now it's almost a parody.'

'Tell me,' Marguerite repeated, 'all about it.'

So Alma took her through her day. 'You were there when the AI running the holding company of which McA autos is a part contacted me. Might I please run an investigation in parallel with the police, looking into an unusual circumstance, and so on. Obviously the McA people wanted a way to minimise commercial disruption, and thought I might be an asset in that regard.'

'A swift resolution might be one way of minimising such damage,' Marguerite agreed. 'Still, presumably there must have been human authorisation, at a level above the managerial AI?'

'Presumably. But I didn't speak with anyone so stratospherically placed. And anyhow: you saw the situation in the general feed. It's all over the press. A man is dead, Adam Kem, and his body has been dumped in the factory. Except that the body has been dumped in this fantastically extravagant way, made to look as though it was a flat impossibility – the footage is all there, from multiple angles. The car is constructed, and there's no dead body at any point in the process. Except that when it is finished – presto—'

'Prestidigito,' Marguerite chuckled.

'—there's a corpse in the car.'

'Somebody is showing off.'

'Indeed. So I look around; I speak to people, in sim and face to face. I go to the hospital...'

'Why hospital?'

'The individual who discovered the body called an ambulance. The site manager concurred, by sim. Better safe than sorry, was her line. Official policy I dare say. Sure the guy *looked* dead, but maybe he wasn't – except he obviously, patently, unmistakably was dead. I saw his body myself. Still, I'm sure there's procedure to follow, probably fossil legislation from the era when humans worked in factories. I'm sure the ambulance driver could see there was no hope of resuscitation, but she took the corpse to hospital anyway.'

'You didn't speak to the ambulance nurse?'

'High on my to-do. Though whether she'd have told me anything I don't already know is moot. So, the ambulance came, as called, and it drove Adam Kem to the hospital where he was pronounced legally dead.'

'Perhaps such a pronouncement only has legal force in a hospital context.'

Alma asked her feed, and the answer came back neither yes nor no. 'That depends, apparently. It's quite complicated, legally. At any rate, the hospital *did* pronounce. The body was transferred to the morgue, which is where I saw it. Lungs and heart mashed, as if mixed up in a slushy machine. Deader than a coffin nail, because a coffin nail is still performing useful work, and so in one sense is as alive as it's ever been. Dead as hope. Dead as our financial affairs. Gone. But I'm missing something out...'

'Never,' Marguerite rumbled, 'miss anything out. How can I bring my Mycroftian genius to bear on your trifling little puzzles, my darling, if you miss things out?'

'At the hospital I was met by a woman who called herself Michelangela. Her feed security was top-drawer. I couldn't check on her, but her authorisation certainly looked kosher. High up, most high up, government-level policeperson, spy, diplomat, I don't know. First this individual took me to the morgue, in *her* car no less, specifically to show me Adam Kem's dead body. Then she told me to fold up my investigation and stow it away, not to bring it out again. She said it was over, for reasons of the secrecy and security of the state.'

'Did she really use so sibilant and uneuphonious a piece of alliteration?'

'Possibly not,' Alma said, and drained her cognac. She contemplated pouring herself a second, but that would mean getting up out of the Confort 9000, and she was disinclined to make the effort. 'She was showing me the body as a professional courtesy,' she said. 'She said she knew my work and admired it. But it *was* about closure. By the time I was back in my own car and coming home I had official confirmation from my client, my contract terminated, the minimum kill-fee paid already, the file closed. And now I get home to discover that Michelangela used the very blackest-belt Security Services ju-jitsu to reach inside my feed and replace all my records with generic news reports.'

'Invasive,' snorted Marguerite. 'Poor form.'

'Anyway: it seems we're off the case.'

'We're not destitute. We did get the kill-fee.'

'It's not much, I'm afraid. And most of that has already gone on resupplying some of your medication.'

'There's always the mother with the starving grown-up son.'

'There's always her,' Alma agreed.

'We can deduce a few things,' Marguerite said, assuming her deliberately pompous lecturing tone with a twinkle in her eyes. 'Your man, the corpse, was no ordinary fellow. He was in some way tangled up with some very high-level affairs, I would say. Why else would the government step in, with so flat and heavy a foot? You must not be allowed to investigate, for fear that you might shine a light into places from which the powers that be would prefer to avert illumination.'

'That's certainly possible,' Alma agreed. 'Although it doesn't give us anything substantive. Kem could have been involved in any one of a dozen areas of state subterfuge. He might have been working for the government, or against them. No way to know.'

'Whoever murdered him, or perhaps better to say whoever assassinated him, left his corpse inside a newly assembled car. It's a fair bet they did so in order to make a point. Kem's death must have had something to do with cars. Or transport.'

'Or factories. Or professional conjuring tricks. Who knows? I'm not persuaded that enables us to narrow it down.'

'Perhaps not. And I suppose you *will* have to let the investigation go?'

'I'm afraid so. I can't afford to antagonise the authorities.' Alma didn't add: if I'm arrested for more than four hours, you will die. She didn't need to be so stark.

'Then that's that,' said Marguerite. 'The mystery of the body in the boot. It's a locked-room mystery, of a kind not before seen in life, or art. And we shall never know the solution. Pip pip!' Her collar valve clicked again, and another slug of whatever she was drinking slipped down her throat. All the quivering mass of her enormous body seemed to tremble with the delight of it. Alma decided her desire for a second cognac was, actually, enough to overcome her inertia, and propel her up out of the Confort 9000.

4: *Civil Digestion and its Discontents*

Alma slept for three and a quarter hours and awoke startled with a clonic jerk. Had her feed alarm malfunctioned? Had she overslept? Had Marguerite been hoarsely calling for her from the other room to no avail as her death throes took hold?

Of course not. The advantage of an alarm set to your feed was that, unlike an exterior alarm device located about your dwelling space, it could not be ignored. Alma had in fact underslept. But there was no point in going back down for now. She went through and checked on Marguerite – slumbering placidly – came back and facced herself a cup of coffee. The sky outside was the colour of liquorice, the window haunted by the ghost of her own face.

She settled in her best chair and cradled the mug. A twelve-second mantra, repeated inwardly and silently with closed eyes, cleared her mind. Was there anything *there*, concerning the car-factory puzzle?

Sometimes solutions loomed up at her, out of the murk of her lower mind. Not today.

It didn't matter. Put it behind her. She opened her workfile, and checked the details of the case Marguerite had logged, the Strangely Starving Man. He was a twenty-nine-year-old half-and-halfer, spending his leisure time in the Shine but working a job that kept him, mostly, in the real world. Indeed he was, judging by his groundtax, earning a good salary, and the statement by his mother suggested that he was eating regularly. Still, he kept losing weight. Alma checked and saw that the mother, one Ms Hunter-Colo, was awake and contactable, so she called through. In moments the woman's full-length sim was standing there. As if she'd been waiting precisely for this call. And maybe she had.

'Hello, Ms Hunter-Colo,' said Alma. 'My name—'

'I know who you are,' Hunter-Colo interrupted. Rude. Of course they both knew one another's names, and public details, but it was polite to introduce oneself and courtesies mattered immensely. Alma kept calm. Calm was not the word to describe Hunter-Colo.

'You think I wouldn't know who you are? I know stuff.'

'It's important you understand,' Alma said, 'what I can do for you, Ms Hunter-Colo. What I can bring to your situation that the police can't, or are unlikely to be able to do. But also what my limitations are.'

'The police are all AI now,' said Hunter-Colo. She was a bulky individual with hair the colour of brass. 'Sure, yes I know they have to have some real people in prominent positions, by law, but those folk are all just shopfront doomies. That's a sign, a cure, we all know. Working for the police as a human being is a sign, a cure, it *is*.'

'I don't think that's actually true, Ms Hunter-Colo,' said Alma.

'In the Real it surely *is* true,' Hunter-Colo replied, affronted. 'The Shine, who knows. But there's so few in the Real now, thus little crime, thus the – where was I?'

Alma tried for diplomacy: 'We can agree that were you to approach the police, I'm not sure they'd do anything other than take a statement. Your son is well past the legal age of majority. Are you certain an actual crime has been committed?'

'Oh the police would listen,' was her reply. 'They'd do more than take a stake-mint. My boy is on their radar, shall we say.'

Radar? Alma pulled a definition from her feed, and without pausing said: 'There's no criminal record listed in his public profile.'

'No. Or, you know? Not yet. Shall we say *not yet*? Is it terrible disloyal for a mother to say that? He works for some bad people. It's a legal organisation, but it surely got a shady side.'

Alma checked the company's public profile and immediately a cascade began *Airport Musical Poem Painting Film Photo Hallucination Landscape Engineering Mass Tran* – she halted it. Something up with her filters? Later. 'You believe,' she asked Hunter-Colo, 'that your son is, somehow, *being* starved? And that it's related to his employer?'

That question unleashed a flow of words. 'I see him eat. I sit with him and he eats, and I sit with him and the food goes down, and thinner and thinner he gets. He has a temper now, like not before. Before he has a temper, like his pater, but now it is erratic and most alarming. So skinny, he is now! I know what you shall say, when I say so, you shall say it's tapes-warm, or something, or maybe drugs, it's not. I shall tell you how far gone I am. I would be relieved to discover it was drugs, now. That's how far!'

'You're certain it's not tapeworm because ...?'

Hunter-Colo's paley-purple eyes looked at the floor. 'Oh, oh, I put a test in, when he was in the Shine one time. He gave me the key!' This last was defensively said. 'I'm his mother, and he gave me access to his house. Sure, but he was angry when he found out I done it.'

Unsurprisingly! Alma kept her calm. 'Angry you interfered with his body whilst he was in the Shine? Ms Hunter-Colo, you understand that doing so was a criminal offence on your part? You could be prosecuted.'

Eyes front. 'You think I don't know? I was worried. He was angered, and he yelled some, but he won't press charges, his own mother. You think? And I found nothing anyway. His system is clean. No worm, no major disease, no drugs in his blood. Why would he need drugs? His main work perk is access to the most exclusive pleasure realms in the Shine.'

'Maybe it's as simple as, he's not eating as much as you think. If he's getting thinner, Ms Hunter-Colo, it must be because his calories-out is larger than his calories-in.'

'I *know* he works in the world, but his free time is all online. All of it! And you need to own dare stand – I make *sure* he eats. He has always ate. He used to weight a hefty number. Loves his food. He comes to mine, and I feed him till his stomach bulges. Then it's o mama and gut-ache mama and I see it shrink down.'

'You observe his stomach shrinking? In real time?'

'Five seconds, and it's all gone. It don't go from stomach into his intertestine is what it is. Goes in but don't get *digested*.'

Alma was intrigued, although it seemed a trivial sort of case. Still: money was always needful. She explained to Hunter-Colo what the fee was likely to be, and what the expenses. She reminded her that her remit was real-world, that she did not undertake investigations in any part of the Shine itself, and that if this was what Hunter-Colo wanted she could recommend agencies that did so. 'No, no,' Hunter-Colo insisted. 'You need to see him in the flesh. You'll understand.'

'I can only see him if he agrees to meet.'

'You can spy him, no? You can surveil.'

'I would prefer to meet him, and ask him some questions.'

Hunter-Colo made a gesture with two hands, palms upwards, as if they were increasingly weighted down, in five separate increments, until they were by her side. 'All I want,' she insisted, 'is my boy safe, and putting weight on. There's something else.'

Alma waited.

'I scanned him, when he was in the Shine and before he realed up and got real cross. I mean, I scanned his torso. I didn't get to his legs and I didn't do his head. Because then he realed up and started yelling.'

'And?'

'There's something in his stomach.'

'Something?'

'I think his boss put it there. I think his boss say: *Swaller this, boyo.*'

'Swallow what?'

'I don't recognise it, and there's no info online. Or there's too much—' Fumblingly, Hunter-Colo shunted the info into Alma's feed. The device in his stomach was a ring of some rigid material, black either because that was its colour or because that was the colour the scan used to register it. There was very little paratext to explain. It seemed to be embedded in the wall of the stomach, and the pyloric sphincter sat right in the middle of it, like a flesh asterisk. 'You think this ring is the reason your boy is getting thinner?'

'You check online and there's nothing,' Hunter-Colo repeated. 'Or else it says forty millions hits for *ring*. Ring of power. Ring of confidence. Shine rings out the *wazoo*.'

A definition of wazoo popped unbidden into Alma's feed. 'Did you ask about this?'

'He said no, no, no. I said I'd go the police, I know his employers make him wear it – like a Yakuza tattoo, I figure, but on the inside where no one can see.' Hunter-Colo pronounced no one as *nūn*. 'He said no, no, no. There's nothing there. So, and you can like it or lump it but *I'm* his mother, and so I say: I'll take this to the police, and tell them you are working Yakuza work, you don't think they will be interested, boyo? You can bet not just a *part* of your bippy, you can bet the *whole* bippy, they will.'

Alma muted her definition function. It was becoming distracting. 'What did he say to that?'

'That's what decided me to hire you. What he said back, that decided me to do so. I got word-of-mouth from Masie Shar on your business with the Coketown Severed Hands case. Oh, when I said I'm a-going I'm a-off to the police, his reaction was not to yell. He got all sudden quiet, and *that's* what decided me to hire you.'

'Quiet.'

'He said: the police won't look at that scan, Mother, because it was illegally obtain. The police won't listen to you at all, Mother. When he calls me *Mother* instead of *Mam*, it's the understudy coming out to play the lead, and the understudy's name is Frightened. You'd better leave it be, Mother, and let me alone, he said, real sinister. So I started weeping a little, and saying I was sorry to have snuck up and scanned him when he was not awake, but only I was worry 'ed and worry 'ed mothers need reassurance. So then he started weeping, some, and promised he'd square things, and soon enough that he'd be putting the weight back on.'

'And has he?'

Hunter-Colo shook her head, and in the sim her sharply red-brown hair swayed and jiggled. 'You're not police,' she said. 'You're for-hire gun.'

'Very well then.'

Alma wrapped things up, ran a contract through both feeds and wished Ms Hunter-Colo a good night. Then, whilst they were still fresh in her mind, she rehearsed the facts of the case. There was some trivial explanation behind it, was her hunch, although there *was* some strange tingling somewhere in her lower gut associated with the case, a sense of scintillant anticipation, as if something marvellous was about to happen. She sometimes got that before a breakthrough, when some kind of comprehension or solution was on the verge of presenting itself to her mind.

She waited, and finished her coffee. Nothing.

Twenty minutes more before she needed to attend Marguerite. Alma beguiled the time by doing a little research. Common sense suggested that this ring did something to the nutritional value of the food in young Hunter-Colo's stomach. Assuming, that is, that the whole story wasn't a piece of crazy maternal paranoia. Maybe the lad only ate when he saw his mother, and otherwise neglected his feeding. Maybe he was on a diet. There were, Alma determined, eighteen distinct and legitimate possible uses for an intra-stomach prosthesis, and many such prostheses might well be ring-shaped. It was possible to swallow a seed that worked on fats and sugars and rendered them chemically inert, although such devices had some less than desirable consequences when it came to the texture of subsequent evacuation of the bowels.

Her feed pinged. Time.

Through to Marguerite's room, where her partner slumbered on. Working carefully Alma checked her lipids, and applied oilcreme and injected a low-cost medication into two separate places, and adjusted her collar, and finally determined in which way the genehacked organisms that had wrapped their fatty tentacles around her beloved's very brain had altered themselves *this* time, and low-pressure-injected an antidote. When the readings returned to the greenzone, Alma went back through to get a little more sleep.

She couldn't sleep, though. The coffee in her bloodstream kept jamming its elbow in her consciousness. She was still awake quarter of an hour later. Checking her messages she found one from Lester Hunter-Colo himself, and when she accepted it his full-body sim popped into the space in front of her.

'So, my mother has hired you.' He didn't wait for Alma's reply. 'Don't deny it. She told me herself.'

'I wasn't denying it.' His sim was tagged as non-rep – a generic actionman torso and a prettified approximation of Lester's face on the head. There was no way, from looking at the sim alone, to know how thin he was in real life.

He said: 'I called you to ask you to call you, sorry. Sorry, I stumble over words.' There was a pause. 'I've called you to ask you to drop you, to drop *it*.'

'I have a contract with Ms Hunter-Colo. We're both adults and both compos mentis. Under the law I'm afraid you have no grounds to demand its cessation.'

'I know it's not something I can take you to law for for law for,' said Lester. It was hard to gauge his emotional state, given the generic artificiality of his sim, but Alma got the distinct impression he was rattled. 'Take you to court over. I'm not threatening. I'm asking. She's prone to worry, and this is only upsetting her more.'

'You might alleviate her anxiety by eating more.'

'I eat plenty. I eat loads, believe me.'

'It's hard for me to tell, with a generic sim, whether or not you are underweight. Perhaps you could adjust your settings, and I'd be able to judge?'

'I've been putting the weight back *on*,' said Lester, defensively. 'There's truth in the claim I lost some. Now I'm putting it back on. It just takes time.'

'Might I ask: what *is* the nature of the ring-shaped device in your stomach?'

'That's none of your business and *I'm* bun of your niceness,' said Lester, hurriedly. 'None. I'm none, I'm none of your your *business*. Leave it alone.'

'Is it a dietary aid?'

'Don't be ridiculous. Alright, yes, yes that's right. Aid. Dye-a-tree. Aid.'

'You work for a company called the Ordinary Transport Consultancy, I believe?'

Sudden heat in his words: 'Leave the OTC out of it. I've sorted it, alright? Mam was worried I was thinner, thinner than I.' He stopped. 'Thinny-than-eye,' he said, and stopped again. The placid inexpressiveness of his features made the stammer, or whatever it was, comical rather than pitiable. 'Thinner,' he said. 'Than I. Used to be. But I've sorted it. You're wasting your time. I give you my word, in a week Mam will be crying tears of happiness and she'll terminate your contract then. You want to take a week's money from my mam? She's not rich.'

'It's for her to decide whether to employ me or not,' Alma observed, mildly. Lester broke off the call without saying goodbye, and Alma spent a moment tagging and filing it.

Then she tried to sleep again, and again sleep didn't come.

Eventually she yielded to the unavoidable, got up and cleaned the flat. Then it was time to go through and check on Marguerite again. This time Alma's ministrations woke her up, and the two chatted a little about the oddity of Lester Hunter-Colo. 'There is no mystery here,' Marguerite opined. 'This is a non-mystery.'

'I know,' Alma agreed, although the fizzing was still there, in the nethers of her gut, contradicting her rational sense of the case. *Something* was there. Something was on the edge of coming through.

'Mam is over-anxious. It's about her boy moving on in his life and leaving her behind. New domicile, new job, she doesn't like it. *My boy's not eating enough,*' Marguerite drawled. 'It's too classic. It's a cliché. There's nothing here. Did he look unusually skinny to you?'

'He simmed a generic avatar. I couldn't tell.'

'Pff,' said Marguerite, and swallowed three paste biscuits and a whole apple. 'Has the mother paid?'

'We're contracted.'

'She's a flake. She won't pay. There are a couple of other cases you need to look at.'

'After I nap.'

A huge smile deepened its shallow curve on Marguerite's face. 'My poor tired Ally-ally-oh. You tiny, tired little woman. By the way, I think I figured the car mystery. It's a conjuring trick, you see.'

Alma stood up and stretched. She *did* feel exhausted and she did feel small. 'Do you know what? I don't believe it is.'

'You don't believe it's a trick? But of course it's a trick! The question is: *why* flourish the conjuror's cape when you're disposing of a murdered body? That's the question! Obviously not to downplay the crime. If that's what you wanted to do you'd dump the corpse at the side of the road rolled into a stretch of old carpet. No, no, my darling, the conjuring trick is there to draw *attention* to the crime. It's a way of saying: I task you. I task you to solve this, and I task you to find me. And I'll say something more. *I'm* the woman to do both!'

'Rita, the government reached into my private feed, deleted some of my files and replaced them with generic news dumps, without so much as tickling the whiskers of my guard dogs. This was high-level stuff. They delivered a cease-and-desist to my legal AI. If I started poking around this case, even in the spirit of disinterested curiosity and general enquiry, they will know. And I am sure they wouldn't like it. And I'm *pretty* sure they'd detain me, and then where would we be?'

'Where would I be, you mean,' Marguerite chuckled. 'Well, well. Leave the whole thing alone, by all means. But aren't you curious how they did it?'

'Of course I am. But I'm reconciled to the thought that I'll never know.'

'I could *tell* you ...'

'Tell me what?'

'How the trick was done.'

'So you've solved it?'

'I eliminated the impossible and turned the spotlight of my immense intellect upon whatever remained.'

'And?'

'There are two possibilities. The first: they switched the cars.'

'They didn't switch the cars. I watched the whole footage over and again, from three different angles. The factory AI confirmed it, and AIs can't lie. I touched the actual car. It's the same car, all the way through, from construction to completion.'

'But you no longer have access to the footage.'

'No.'

'That means that *I* have been unable to see it.'

'True.'

'It is a shame that I have not seen it. Still put that to one side. The only other possible solution is that the footage itself has been tampered with.'

Alma shook her head, and as she shook her head she yawned. 'Is that the best you can do, Rita?'

'Only wait,' said Marguerite. 'Don't be too hasty to dismiss.'

'The footage was datestamped. Footage livestreamed to the central cloud. Tampering with it? Who could even do that? It would require a huge conspiracy, at an international level and including thousands of ...' She sneezed. 'Ludicrous.'

'Conspiracy,' said Marguerite, 'is possible. Dead bodies appearing from nowhere is not.'

'The police would have to be a party to it. Raw footage from all surveillance is automatically cached in secure police databases, and any inconsistency between it and the footage submitted would immediately come to light.'

'You trust the police?'

'I trust the eighty per cent of police who are AIs. They can't help but follow their programs! They don't lie. They're not capable of that. Besides, who would even have access to the surveillance feed to tamper with it?'

'The factory AI?'

'I refer the honourable member,' said Alma, yawning, 'to the answer I gave some moments ago. And this is a level-3 AI, high-powered intellect, robust and reliable. The highest we go up in the company is the McA management, and if they tried to reprogram the factory AI it would reject their attempts as illegal. The law is hardwired into these things, you know. Besides, it doesn't have access to the surveillance system. That's a separate system. By law, the surveillance operated outwith the factory.'

'Well then whoever falsified the official surveillance, outside the factory, must be in cahoots with the factory AI.'

Alma yawned again. 'Not enough people use words like cahoots, these days.'

'I know what you're going to say,' said Marguerite, eating a peach and slurping some protein shake. 'You're going to say: *Are there any records of an AI lying, ever?* No, is the answer. There's no such record. But there must be a first time for everything! Don't you see?'

'I don't see because it's not true. AIs don't lie.'

'Dismissive,' said Marguerite, in a mock-hurt tone.

'My gut says, no. My gut tells me the footage was not tampered with.'

'Your gut instinct,' said Marguerite, haughtily, 'is as nothing compared to my superior *in*. Tell. Ect.'

'I'm going for a sleep,' said Alma, and kissed Marguerite on her enormous cheek.

She went through, stretched out fully clothed under the sheet and was asleep at once. Her feed woke her after three hours and fifty minutes, and she trotted back through to perform the medical necessary on a Marguerite so wholly absorbed in the book she was now reading that she seemed hardly to notice her ministrations.

Alma stumbled back to her bed, and was about to get in when an urgent message from Ms Hunter-Colo pinged her feed. It was a short video, labelled EVIDENCE. Thirty-one seconds. Alma opened it in an internal window, and watched the footage. It took a moment to orient herself with respect to what she was seeing: a pot-bellied man, legs skinny as ropes with knots for knees, gaunt, bearded head. Ernest Hunter-Colo, she assumed. He was asleep, and to his left was a table upon which were the remains of a meal. Plate and scraps and smears of gravy and cutlery crosswise. For half the length of the footage nothing happened except that Ernest breathed in deeply, snored, exhaled on a snore. But in the last ten seconds something weird *did* occur: the man's belly, round as a beach ball, began to shrink. In five seconds it shrivelled down like a deflating inflatable. His stomach was, in an instant, as skinny as the rest of his frame. Then Ernest's eyes popped open, and he said 'gut-ache' and then his features creased to annoyance as he saw he was being filmed, and the footage stopped.

Alma went back to sleep.

5: *Derp Throat*

Early morning. Alma took a stroll, for the fresh air and for the exercise. The weird clip of Lester's stomach shrinking down kept returning to her mind. A sense of being on the edge of something big was fizzing in her own gut. Stubbornly, though, the larger picture refused to come into focus.

Two cases. One – a death – very serious. Another – digestion – very trivial. Sublime, meet ridiculous; ridiculous this is sublime. But the former had been snatched from her grasp and the latter was hardly worth her time. Considering how flaky her client was, Marguerite was probably correct that she wouldn't even get paid. She spent a while, as she walked, looked about for other paying gigs. She had a frustrating discussion in her feed with a possible new client who simply could not understand that Alma didn't work the Shine. 'So you're, what, epileptic or something?' 'No,' Alma explained. 'There's nothing physical or neurochemical that prevents me entering the Shine. I choose not to and you need to be aware of that before you make your decision to hire me, or not to do so.' 'I don't understand,' the client had said, her brow wrinkling, > I I <. 'Is it a religious thing? I know there are, what do you call them, sects that—' 'Mine is not a religious objection. It is a practical one. I am a carer, and the peculiar constraints of my time . . .' 'I'm not asking you to spend *weeks* in the Shine. A day at most.' 'I can put you in touch with many investigators happy to work the Shine.' 'But I don't understand: why don't you? Everyone goes into the Shine! Why wouldn't you? I don't understand.' 'I'm afraid you'll just have to take my word on this. I'm simply being honest.' 'But *why?*' It was as though Alma had informed her *I don't breathe air.* She simply couldn't process it.

The sky was a lake of unlit petrol. Scuds of clouds near the eastern horizon had been dipped in orange and yellow dyes. The air smelt of tar, and more faintly of the organic taint of the manure on the farmlands west of R!-town. Birds zipped overhead in twos and threes like silent drones.

A chubby man approached her. Alma was aware of him from forty yards. He didn't look to be too much of a physical threat, but nonetheless she clenched and unclenched her fists, pulled back her shoulders and went onto the balls of her feet. You never quite knew what to expect with strangers.

He pinged a hello, and she blocked it, but he repinged and kept moving physically towards her. He was a boss-eyed round-faced fellow somewhere between late twenties and early thirties. After his hello had been batted away a half-dozen times he pinged a coffee icon at her. She knocked it off, and quickened her pace. With a sudden acceleration he got ahead of her and faced her. 'Please,' he said, and showed her both his palms.

She was ready to chop her knuckles into his Adam's apple and make a run for safety, but something stopped her. Foolishly enough, it was his wonky eye. She met his gaze, as is wise to do with a potential attacker, provided only that you know how to handle yourself. But she met the wrong eye, the one that was staring a foot to the left of her left ear. So she shifted her gaze to the other eye, and it was looking right at her, and there was a pleading desperation in it. In an instant she reappraised the threat he posed.

'I'm going to offswitch my feed,' he said, his hands still palms-front. 'I'm sorry to have pinged you like that, when you were clear about not being interested. But, really, really, you have to listen to what I have to tell you.'

'My friend,' Alma replied. 'I don't *have* to do anything you say.'

'No, that's right. That's quite right. But put it this way: I think you'll be glad you listened to me. If, you know. If you choose to listen to me.'

She eyed him up and down. Across his shirt was the representation of a big, foolish-looking male face: freckled and ginger and grinning, and underneath it the words WHAT, ME WORRY?

'I can give you five seconds,' she said.

'Here in the street is not ideal. Here in the street, with you still in your own feed, they have a fix on us and drone coverage and the whole deal.'

'Are you a common-or-garden paranoid, or one of the more refined sort?'

'I'm the paranoid who knows. I'm the individual people should be paranoid *about*. I spend my days surveilling people and keeping the state happy. *I'm* not paranoid. I am the one who paranoies. No,' he said straight away, with a pained expression. 'That doesn't work. Look, to the point. To get to the point. You are Alma. It's important you and I have a talk, Alma.'

He had indeed offswitched his feed. There he stood, a bare human, clothed only in the physical-material sense of that word. 'So you know my name. What's yours?'

'It's best you don't know. Think of me as your deep throat.'

Her feed supplied the reference. His invitation-to-coffee icon was still in her feed. She turned it over, with a small hook-key she had acquired a year before from a specialist coder in Henley-on-Thames. The stranger's icon was from a bulk-bought 3¢ set of 9,000 tailored messages, and there were elements of the purchase order still attached. A quick search led to a name. 'Punchy Babouche,' she said.

He flinched. 'That's – how did you? That's not my name. That's not my proper on-the-passport name. That's a ... look. Please don't spread that around, alright? Please?'

'Discretion would be my middle name,' she said. 'If I had a middle name.'

'Please,' he said again. 'Ten minutes, a cup of coffee, so you can decide whether what I have to say is of interest to you.'

What the hell. She agreed and the two of them walked a block and a half and turned down a sidestreet to a coffee shop called RADIATION VIBE. The door sent out a shivery tinkling sound as they stepped inside, although there was nobody to hear it. Against the back wall were six by-the-hour Shine access points, four of which were in use, even at this early hour. All the tables were free, and Punchy chose the one furthest from the big window. A bot served them coffee.

'I'm going to ask you,' he said, 'to offswitch your feed – just for ten minutes.'

'That's an unusual sort of request, Punchy.'

'Please!' Panic eyes. 'Don't use that name! Don't say it aloud.'

'We're the only ones here, apart from those four, and they're deep in the Shine. *They*'re not eavesdropping.'

'You can't be too careful.'

'Alright, alright. Codenames, by all means. Cautious in all

nominal matters. Derp Throat, sure.' Since he wasn't on-feed he wasn't able to flag up the meaning of the term *derp*, and he actually smiled at her.

'Is that – what, old internet slang?'

'You could say that. You really want me to wrap my head in silver foil?'

'I don't get *that* reference either, since I've offswitched, but look: you already knew that I wouldn't get that. Please just off-switch for ten minutes.'

Since his own feed was down, there was no way he could be sure whether she had offswitched or not. But Alma was no liar, and there didn't seem any harm in it. For the first time in – God, a year? More? – she did as he asked. Then there she was, viewing the world around her without any digital augmentation or online resource at all. It was disconcerting. It was, she realised, more disconcerting than offswitching usually was. Perhaps she had spent too long plugged in. Perhaps she needed to take more breaks. She blinked.

Blinked.

The light had a different quality. There was dust on the floor that she hadn't noticed before, and tracks left by the wheels of the waiterobot. There were smears on the wide window, ghost brushstrokes from a half-hearted clean. The light, though! It felt as if she was relearning what light looked like. Depth of field. On the sill of the shop window was a beetle, on its back, playing trills on an invisible upside-down piano. Light shone fuzzily on the dark lacquer of the tabletop before her. Alma breathed in. The wedgetail of illumination falling across tables and floor, furry at the edges. She looked at Derp Throat. His skin was flushed redder than she had realised, and there was a lemonpeel-texture pattern of open pores on his nose.

'You alright?' Derp Throat asked.

She stared at the morning sunlight coming through the window: white, but with a fresh quality of applegreen. Seawater flaking and shoaling. Mist burning into gemlight. Abruptly she couldn't look, and covered her eyes with her hands. Get a grip on yourself, lady. She shook her head, as a dog does to dry itself.

'Fine,' she said. 'It's been too long since I last offswitched, I think.'

Now that she was seeing him as he actually was, Derp Throat

looked somehow more serious, a figure with rather more gravitas and rather less comedy caricature, despite his pudgecheek, boss-eyed face. It was serious. The reality of the everything squeezed in upon her senses. The air around her took on a soiled heaviness. Alma experienced a sudden flush of dread, and the image of Adam Kem – dead as a butchered pig, on his back on a slab, his lungs slurry. A human life, and gone. Not a puzzle: a life ended.

'You *really* alright?' Derp Throat pressed.

She was conscious of the moistness of her eyeballs, of an un-settling sense of expansion in her throat. She didn't cry, though. She breathed in, and breathed out, and said: 'I am fine. What was it you wanted to say?'

'What? Oh. Well. They're thorough,' Derp Throat said. 'And that has made them a little complacent. There are holes in their surveillance, and they *could* fill those. They do fill some, but trying to plug every one of them would send the funding graph vertical, so they're content to leave interstices.'

Alma was finding it hard to concentrate on his words. She lifted her mug and sipped: tart and dark and persimmony. 'Go on,' she said.

'I say they. I mean we. It's where I work. I know more about you than I'm comfortable with, Alma, and much much more than *you*'d be comfortable with me knowing. I know your personal life. I know you were hired to investigate Adam Kem's murder, and then de-hired. I know Michelangela met with you.'

Alma said nothing.

'She won't be bothering you again,' Derp Throat said.

Alma put the mug down and shut her eyes. Nothing but a warm darkness in there. When she opened them again she saw the uncooked pastry of Adam Kem's flesh, the fishscale blue of his lips, his closed lids like white pods. Then she blinked, and saw Derp Throat peering at her.

'Wouldn't it be better to come right out with it?' she said. 'You're saying the government killed Adam Kem.'

He gulped, visibly. 'I'm not,' he hissed. 'That's *not* what I'm saying at all. In point of fact, the government I work for did *not* have Kem killed. Not my department, at any rate.'

'So who did?'

'I don't know. *They* don't know. That's what *you* were supposed to find out. Only, letting you loose on the case was – dangerous,

I suppose. So no sooner had they brought you in than you were chased away. That fact alone should tell you how fractious relations between the different departments of government are. How broken up the whole superstructure is, and how often they are at loggerheads. Bickering. One group brought you in, but another group found it easy enough to scare you away. They don't need to *lean* on you very hard, after all. You are weak.'

'Less weak than you might think.'

'Not you. We mean the other one.'

'Marguerite,' Alma said.

'Some other individual might have to be bought off, or locked away, or perhaps even killed. That's part of government too, although perhaps a less prominent part than the thriller sims and spy sims might have you think. But in your case we didn't need any of that. Your pressure point is wide open, and the slightest push will collapse it. What is it, four hours and four minutes?'

'Thanks to some anonymous genehacker,' said Alma.

'They know who.'

At this, completely unexpected, piece of news Alma's heart banged hard, and her chest was drenched in adrenalin. She was ready to leap up, to grab Derp Throat, to rush out and take her revenge. It was startling how quick the reaction was. 'Who? Who is it? What's the name?'

'Oh I don't know, not me, I'm sorry to say. Not my department. But there are people who have that individual's identity. They might use it, one day, as carrot; but then again why would they, when the threat of being separated from your Madeleine—'

'—Marguerite—'

'—whatever, is so potent a *stick*? Stick always trumps carrot, in governmental thinking.'

'Is that what you wanted to tell me?' Alma's heart was banging a snare drum, quick time, but her initial rush of fury was receding. Keep it under control, she told herself.

'What? No, no. That's not it. Look, I don't know that person's name, the one who infected your partner with that genetweaked pathogen, and tied it to your DNA. And what's more, I don't know who killed Adam Kem. But I know *why* he was killed, and that's—' he stopped. There was a glitter of sweat across his forehead. He looked behind himself, at the four people in Shine and the two empty machines. The waiterobot was sitting placidly in its alcove. Derp looked up at the window, and the light reflected grape colour off the bags under his eyes.

'Ms Alma,' he started, in a low voice. 'When people check my feed, it says I work for the government. I'm a civil servant. My parents were both civil servants. My grandmother was a civil servant. Government has changed since her day.'

'Lots of things have changed.'

'True. But here's the thing: government has changed in more ways than people realise. Just this country, just take this country, as an example. Take a look at our country, or Europe as a whole if you like, or the whole w – look: forty-six per cent of people spend more time in the Shine than they do in real life, and most of those people barely ever emerge, they come up for air as little as their continuing health permits. Seventy-nine per cent spend what surveys call "significant amounts of time" there. That means at least six hours per twenty-four. People work there, play there, or both. Work, that's the key. Two-thirds of the GDP of this country is generated by people who work online, as it used to be called. But it's more than online, isn't it, the Shine? It's online and inline. It's immersive. It's where the smart people are, the productive people. Almost everybody has visited. And why wouldn't they? It's so rich an environment. It's a place where dreams can be actualised. Made to come true. It's a technicolour paradise. It's a million paradises stacked up, and easy access to any of them. It's where wealth is made, and that means it's where the best people flock.'

Alma said nothing.

'Now there *are* people,' Derp said, 'who won't, or can't, get into the Shine. You know all about that. You're the former, and your friend is the latter. That weird cancer has penetrated all the vesicles of her brain, hasn't it?'

'The thought of you prying into our life together,' Alma told him, 'does not cause any good feelings to register in my brain.'

He masked his face with his hands, and held them there for a long time. It occurred to Alma that he was crying, silently. When he put his hands down again his eyes were shining. She took another sip of coffee, and it slid into her stomach. She thought of the process of digestion, and of Ernest's weird gut-ache.

A figure appeared at the window; a person in mesh, walking

their zombie-walk oblivious to their environment, eyes closed, deep in the Shine. The person passed by.

'Where the car-factory body is concerned,' said Derp, a tremor in his voice, 'they believe you have solved the how. And from that the why, and eventually the who, is bound to follow.'

The word popped fully formed into Alma's mind. She didn't even realise she had been thinking about it until she said it: 'Teleportation.'

Derp Throat nodded slowly. He had not taken a single sip from his own coffee. 'One reason why the Shine has come to dominate the economy – I'm not talking about leisure and entertainment, I mean just earning the money that makes society work – is that it's so good at facilitating *movement*. You, physically in London, can go online and instantly meet a business contact from Tierra del Fuego in a conference suite in Minas Tirith and toast your deal in Shine champagne. Information can move as fluently as money wants to. That's what maximises the possibility of wealth creation. Now, there's another portion of the economy, more important for some countries than others, and not an especially big deal in ours. I mean that part of the economy concerned with manufacturing actual things: food and clothes. Houses and, you know, cars. The proportions between the real-world and the Shine economy have been shifting consistently towards the latter for decades now, and if you analyse why it's because automation has completely changed the dynamic of real-world production. Robots build cars and make clothes and assemble houses. Real-life humans are only involved in all these things because there are laws requiring at least fifty-one per cent human shareholdings and at least one *Homo sapiens* overseer.'

Alma gazed steadily at him.

'The problem is, is,' he said, 'is that the real world is sticky, inertial. It's a place of obstacles, where the Shine is a place of pure facility. You want to meet a real human in the real-world Tierra del Fuego? Well, you got to scrunch yourself into an airliner seat and sit still for five hours, not to mention the ridiculous hours and hours wasted at either end threading your way through airport security. Then you get to sit in a small room smelling vaguely of fish or something, and stare at some ugly guy wearing a utility jacket. And then the grim prospect of the return journey.'

'Teleportation,' repeated Alma.

'You see how it would change the game?'

'The *game* of government?'

'Oh sure. Oh: game. For at least ten years, and really, if we're honest, for a lot longer, government has been changing. There are supposed to be three branches of government, aren't there? Classically conceived, I mean: executive, judiciary and without my feed to prompt me I can't remember the name of the third. But in reality there are *two* branches of government. There's real-world government, and there's Shine government. Happy families. But it's not, of course. It never can be, when power is at stake. And what's happening is that the real-world branch is growing steadily less powerful and the Shine branch steadily more. The Shine is where most of humanity live, most of the time, and as time goes on that constituency is only going to get bigger and bigger. The real-world branch doesn't like that. But what can it do? People gravitate to the Shine because it is – better. It's simply *better*. Not everyone goes. Some people are left behind, as the real-world tide withdraws. Cripples and refuseniks and religious oddbods. No offence.'

'None,' said Alma, in a cool tone, 'taken.'

'There's no way to reverse the outflow, either. It can't be done by fiat. You can't bully people into staying in a place they don't want to stay in. Can you now?'

'Although,' said Alma, 'maybe you could, if you could make the real world that much more attractive.'

'Much *much* more,' Derp Throat agreed, 'attractive. What if you could walk through a door and step right *into* Tierra del Fuego? What if we could move goods and raw materials by the press of a button, rather than great trundling blimps, or those gigantic cargorafts that are always getting snarled up on the drifts of waste plastic? What if we could beam people directly to the moon? Maybe our species could rediscover its ancestral enthusiasm for outer space. We might colonise the other planets. The possibilities are endless.'

'Fantasy physics.'

'Oh the *physics* is real. It's the transition from theory to practice. That's the tricky thing.'

'So,' Alma said, 'you think the reason why the murderer, or murderers, left Adam Kem's body in the trunk of *that particular* car was precisely that it was an impossible location. The only way that body could have gotten in there was if it had been teleported inside. I can't believe I'm saying this.'

'Teleporting dead bodies is one thing,' said Derp, breezily. 'Teleporting living human beings – unharmed, mind you – is quite another. Look: the, the what would you say, *technical* ins and outs aren't the point, here. The point is broader. Think how the world might change if this technology comes online. Think who might be interested in preventing that from happening. Think Power – it's always Power. It's always about power, human crime. Murder and oppression always come down to that in the end.'

'I'm not saying it's not interesting, Mr Babouche,' Alma said. Derp Throat flinched. 'But I'm not the person with whom you should be having this conversation. As you noted at the beginning, I have every motivation to keep my head down and ignore all these high-powered power battles. My horizons are much closer than any of that, and I daren't risk my position.' She reconnected the basic feed, and discovered an alarm blinking. Come home, it said.

Alma stood up. 'Sorry to be abrupt,' she said, 'but I have to go.'

'We'll be seeing one another again,' said Derp Throat, looking gloomily at his undrunk cup of coffee and at the same time looking weirdly at the next table, 'and sooner than you think.'

6: *Mastema*

Alma made her way briskly down the empty streets, heading home. A silky-white morning sky overhead and no one about, except for one low-slung sports car buzzing past and a stray dog loping down a sidestreet. Drones in the air, fatter than flies. Architectural juxtapositions: the intricate textures of brickwork, forty thousand houses in winding strings of terraces, but also tall featureless high-rises like ingots set on end – dozens of them, one after the other. Inside, people worked the Shine, played in the Shine, explored the Shine, mapped the Shine, pursued profit and pleasure. Further off, towards the horizon, were the spires of the commercial centre of R!-town, rising like bedposts. Monuments of the early-century builder's art.

It was clear something was wrong as soon as Alma rounded the corner and saw the entrance to her block. Two police vehicles were in the no-parking: a short-hop flycar and a shed-shaped van with blacked windscreens. Something inside Alma's breast yelled *Run!*, but that was not on the cards. Marguerite's treatment was half an hour away, after all. That was non-negotiable.

So she went into her building, and noted that none of the usual spam shunts and hacks knocked at the door of her feed. Ominously quiet. Presumably the police had gone into the building's feed, commandeered its simple-minded AI and cleaned everything out. The interior of the elevator smelt faintly of sulphur.

An official myrmidrone was standing outside her front door. Lights flickered as she walked up, but, evidently, she had been cleared for entry, so it didn't engage her.

Inside were three human beings, two in uniform and one not. This latter was a tall woman in a dark green one-piece, belted in crimson, both slender hands gloved in black. The two uniform officers were carrying holstered sidearms, but if this plain-clothes woman was armed it was not in any obvious way.

Alma assessed the situation. They were standing, waiting for her, smiling. They were waiting for her, which meant her feed must have alerted them to her approach, which meant they were monitoring her feed. There was no point in objecting to this invasion of privacy, of course; and no point in offswitching her feed either. It would do no good, here, and would only alert them to the fact that she knew she was being monitored. Then again, they presumably assumed as much.

'Ms Alma,' said the plain-clothes woman, and her tag popped up: Colonel Mastema, Government Intelligence. Various other tags presented themselves for Alma's perusal: authorities, a warrant, a list of civic duties attendant upon the citizen, and a rate-my-performance feedback chit.

'Ms Mastema,' Alma said. 'Can I help you?'

'I very much hope so.'

Alma could not prevent an anxious glance at the door to Marguerite's room. Twenty-five minutes. 'I recognise that you represent an accredited and legitimate police authority, and as a law-abiding citizen I am eager to help in any way I can.'

'Gratifying,' said Mastema. She smiled a Shere Khan smile.

'There's one small thing, before we talk,' Alma began.

Mastema said: 'You met with an officer called Michelangela?'

'I did,' said Alma. 'Or rather, she met with me. I was investigating an unusual death, at a car factory, and . . .'

'We know all about that,' said Mastema. 'Are you aware that Inspector Michelangela is dead?'

'No!' said Alma at once. And then she said it again, such that the syllable carried a different meaning: 'No, I was not aware.' Her blood began to pulse more heartily; fight or flight. Surreptitiously she checked several settings in her occluded feed. She clenched and unclenched her fists.

One of the uniformed officers – PC Cleve, the feed said – unobtrusively rested one hand on her holstered weapon.

'I know nothing about her death,' Alma said.

'You don't think it strange,' said Mastema, angling her head, velociraptor-like, slightly to the side, 'that she was killed immediately *after* meeting with you. Don't you think?'

'She was killed, was she?' Alma returned. 'You mean, she didn't die of natural causes.'

'Causes most unnatural,' said Mastema, with a sly *well-done-you* expression on her face.

'How did she die?'

'Our questions to *you*,' the colonel replied firmly, 'take precedence over your questions for us. This is a very serious matter indeed. Indeed, I think we should go down to the station, and take a full statement.'

Alma's heart started knocking at her ribs, like it wanted to get out. She controlled herself. The heat she was feeling in her face probably meant that she was blushing. She looked into the placid brown eyes of Colonel Mastema. Whether Marguerite lived quite literally depended upon this woman's word.

Carefully, Alma put her palms together in front of her chest and lowered her head. 'Colonel, believe me I am wholly at your disposal, happy to give any number of statements. But I would ask one favour of you – a matter of life or death for my companion, in the other room. You know about me, of course; and so you know that she is suffering the consequences of a genehacked lipid cancer. I must treat her every four hours, or she will die. Not may die, Colonel: will die.' There was the faintest smile upon Mastema's mouth, and it occurred to Alma that she was enjoying this. Not a good sign. 'Her treatment is due in fifteen minutes. It cannot be administered any earlier, and if delayed she will be dead within the hour. Only I can administer it. I don't doubt that you have opened all my files, and know that I'm telling the truth on this matter. And since you *have* opened my files, you know that I am scrupulous about obeying the law.' She looked at the other two police officers, and then back at Mastema. 'Permit me this, and I will accompany you willingly to the station and answer any and all questions.'

'Oh you will accompany us, Ms Alma,' said Mastema coolly. 'Willingly or otherwise.' She paused, and Alma felt panic rise in her. 'But you may attend to your companion before we go.'

'Thank you,' said Alma, ashamed at the burst of genuine gratitude that flushed through her. Humiliating. She touched her cuffs and retracted her sleeves, went through into Marguerite's room. Immediately it was clear that things were not good.

'My darling, my darling one,' Marguerite rumbled from her bed. 'I've frolicked with you in meadows, a veritable table of green fields.'

'You're feverish,' said Alma, checking the displays. 'There's some kind of viral imbalance.'

'The police are here.'

'I know, Rita.'

'The police are there. The police are seeking everywhere. Scarlet fever. Pimples. Unwell.'

'Hush, my love.' She got up on the bed and applied a Bo-flex injection to Marguerite's arm just below the shoulder, where a tattoo of the smile-faced sun had been blown up, like an over-inflated balloon, by her condition. She wiped sweat from brow, cheeks and rubbed linuscreme into the folds of flesh. Her feed was flashing now: five minutes to go.

'I solved the locked-trunk mystery, *cara mia*,' Marguerite gabbled. 'My previous suggestions were ludicrously off-target. Humiliating, dreadful. But I have it now, I have hit it, a very palpable hit. Not that *you* acknowledge my genius. You have intuition, I have mentation, very good, very good, but I solved it, solved it, the only possible solution.'

'You said they tampered with the surveillance footage,' Alma said. 'Except they didn't.'

'Tampa bay. Foot, foot, half-foot. Women flowing into men flowing into women. I solved it.'

'Of course you did, my love.' Her temperature was 38.1. Alma applied an antipyretic. 'God, you're not well. You have another fever, my dear.'

'Hospital,' Marguerite moaned. 'Hospital, hospital, hospital.'

'We can't get to a hospital, Rita,' Alma said. 'How would we even get you out the door?'

'Ambulance, ambulance. Men and women! It's where men and women meet, where they come together! Ambulance!'

There was a cough. Mastema was standing behind, observing the medical palaver. This gratuitous intrusion brought a clarifying spike of anger to Alma. 'I'll be with you in a moment, Colonel.'

Alma's feed flashed green. She checked the readout, intuited which way Marguerite's aggressants were morphing, and handled the medication and injected the countermeasure. She watched to check the medicine was working. It was.

Alma climbed down from the bedside and washed her hands at the corner sink. 'Solved it, solved it, men meld with women,

women flow into men,' Marguerite babbled. 'It's all, hospital hospital hospital.'

'You are not inclined to follow her advice?' Mastema asked. 'Move her to a hospital?'

'Putting aside the logistics of moving a person so large,' Alma replied, as her sleeves slithered back down to her wrists, 'and putting aside, likewise, the financial constraints that put paying for hospitalisation beyond us. Beside all that, there is the bald fact that no hospital doctor can help her. Only I can do that.'

Mastema had followed her back through to the other room. The two uniforms were still standing stiffly by the front door. 'So you claim,' Mastema said.

'I'm happy to give the statement you asked for, Colonel,' Alma said, pushing her anger somewhere deep inside. 'And to answer any questions.'

'At the station.'

Alma made a rapid calculation of time. 'My companion is feverish, and needs close attention over the next four hours. Wouldn't it be easier to take my statement here?' She smiled. Smiling wasn't something that came easily to her, but she gave it her best shot. 'I can make everyone tea.'

'At the station,' Mastema repeated.

'Well, if you insist.' It was, her feed informed her, a seven-minute drive to the nearest police station. Even budgeting an hour for the protocols of giving the statement, and even with hiccoughs, Alma would be home in plenty of time to tend to Marguerite before her four hours were up. Since she had not committed any crimes, and had dropped the Adam Kem investigation as soon as legally required, she would surely not be arrested. And without arrest they could not prevent her from returning home.

'You consent to accompany us?'

'Since you consider it necessary, I do. I am happy to help in any way.'

'That's logged,' said one of the uniforms. The other opened Alma's front door and they all stepped through. The myrmidrone beeped, but stayed in position.

The elevator felt claustrophobic with three other people in it. Outside the sun had burned away the morning haze and was printing nice sharp shadows on the concrete. There was a smell of pasture, blown from the west of the city. Alma got inside the VTOL car. As the door clunked shut she had a brief, panic-provoking intimation that the sound was a death knell – Marguerite's death. They would not let Alma come back, not in time. They would arrest her on some nonsense charge, and by the time she had sorted it out it would be too late.

She tried to calm herself. Had she refused to accompany the officers to the station, she told herself, then they *would* have arrested her, and compelled her attendance. It was better this way.

The little voice of angst in her skull cheeped, *We can't be sure*!

No, Alma agreed, quietly, we can't be sure. We don't have the perfect control over this situation we might wish. But we do the best we can. We do the best we can.

The vehicle did not fly. Instead it trundled down the street, round the corner and off towards the centre of R!-town. Mastema was sitting beside her, the two uniforms up front. The van was either behind them, or had been left at the block, Alma couldn't see.

'I'm sorry to hear of Ms Michelangela's death,' said Alma.

Mastema didn't reply.

Dread syphoning into Alma's abdomen from somewhere. Pure dread. Don't be foolish, she told herself. Things will be fine.

The station came into view, a box-shaped building of three storeys. The car took them past the main entrance, down an access road, and then, with a lurch in Alma's gut, quickly up a curling ramp, all the way to the top. The police car parked on the roof, and everybody got out. The entrance to the building was ten metres away, but as Alma started walking towards it one of the uniformed officers put a hand on her arm.

'Over here, ms,' she said, and gestured towards a short-hop plane. It was a newer model: two directional jet-rotors, looking like black cauldrons, either side of a lozenge-shaped vacuum-balloon, and a passenger compartment below. Swish.

'What?' Alma asked. This was not good. This did not bode well. She should never ignore her gut instinct. Her gut instinct was her genius, just as Marguerite always said.

A short-hop plane. They were flying her somewhere. Somewhere far away. She would be too far away to get back to Marguerite.

The moment she had dreaded for years had now come. She quickly readied some of the hidden code in her feed, and took a deep breath. Throw out the code as chaff, confuse the police software for – hopefully – just long enough. The building was too tall to jump straight down: she would have to sprint back down the ramp.

'Inspector Michelangela's death has caused *ructions*, Ms Alma,' said Colonel Mastema. There was no mistaking the gloat in her voice. 'It is too serious and high-level to be *managed* by a provincial station like this one. We'll pop over to Berlin and interview you there.'

'That won't be possible,' said Alma, checking her exits.

'I recommend you expand your understanding of what is possible, citizen.'

'Getting to Berlin and back will take longer than four hours,' Alma said, in as reasonable a voice as her panic permitted her. Perhaps she could still talk her way out of this. Maybe that was still doable. 'If I am delayed more than four hours, then my companion will die. You don't want her death on your conscience, Colonel.'

'Telling me what I want,' drawled Mastema. 'Adorable.'

'If she dies, I will sue. And I will win.'

'My dear woman, we will have a *qualified* nurse attend to your friend. Meantime—'

Alma decided. Talking would not work; the only remaining option was to act. She gauged the shortest distance: not to the ramp itself, but to the side of the building above where the ramp ascended: she could drop that, land on the ramp however many metres below, hope not to break an ankle, and be down at ground level in seconds. Then she would have to think about grabbing some kind of vehicle and laying a false trail. The nearer of the two uniforms stepped towards her, and Alma was drawing back her right hand to receive her when she felt a blistering pain in the middle of her ribcage—

dropped

—and smacked the stone of the rooftop with a zing and a gasp. The gasp was the breath leaving her lungs. Then she found she could not breathe in. Her lungs were not obeying her. None of her body was obeying her. Terror, and the hurtling corridor of consciousness slipping away, and all she could think was: Marguerite is dead, they have killed Marguerite, and, one last glimmer of thought as the darkness irised down on the centre of her vision, and that one thought: *revenge*.

Mastema had neurostunned her, of course. Now, taking her

sweet time, she moseyed over, bent down and applied a thumb-stick to Alma's neck. The stick unblocked those vagus branches that controlled breathing and blinking.

Breathed in. Gasping.

Unconsciousness retreated.

She could see again. She could breathe. But she could not move her arms or her legs. Nor could she speak.

The uniforms picked her up – an easy job, given her size – carried her across the roof and inserted her into the plane. With every step she was thinking: Marguerite is dead. She is dead, and this woman has killed her. But there was nothing, absolutely nothing, she could do.

7: *Flight*

The vacuum balloon, a rigid, thin-walled structure fixed to the roof of the passenger module, provided lift that almost exactly balanced the weight of the police plane and its four passengers. Mastema entered a code, had a quick conversation with the plane AI, and the whole machine bobbed a metre, two, three, into the air. Then there was the whine of motors as the massy directional jets oriented themselves, and the plane swished through the sky and away.

Alma, her arms and legs pinned with the neural block, was fully aware of what was happening. A sickening sense of Marguerite's helplessness, and the pointless waste of her death, threatened to overwhelm her. She shut her eyes and repeated her mantra, silently, over and over. Just the mental effort of forming the words calmed her.

'No point in fretting, my dear,' said Mastema, complacently, settling herself into the plane's amply upholstered seating. 'It's done now. We have contracted a nurse to attend your companion. If you're lucky you may see her again as soon as next week.'

The nerve stun prevented Alma from saying: next week I'll be attending her funeral. The same neural block prevented her from appending any of the unflattering descriptions of the intelligence colonel that occurred to her. She blinked, blinked, and heaved at her own lungs. Breathing was automatic, but also a system that could be overridden. She tried again, and the intensity of her in-breath increased.

Eventually the stun would wear off, with a great deal of painful smarting all over her body – as when one's arm or leg goes to sleep and has to be jiggled and slapped back into life. When it did wear off, there were no after-effects or longer-term consequences.

The question was: how long?

One thing was clear: she couldn't fly to Berlin and get back to R!-town in time to save Marguerite.

She blinked, and tried to swivel her eyes. No good. What could she see? The passenger pod consisted of three rows of double-seats at the rear of the craft, and three more at the front. In the exact centre of the craft the formation was broken up by two curving sofas at right angles to the rest of the seating. One of the uniforms was stretched out on the sofa to her left. Mastema and the other uniform sat up primly on the one to her right.

Nobody was wearing seatbelts.

That was something. Not much, but something.

She tried to move her eyes again, and when that failed she tried again. Mastema had freed up the blink reflex to stop her eyes drying out and scarring, a circumstance that could result in blindness. But it meant that volitional control of eyeballs was more likely than control of her limbs.

She tried again, and her eyes slid right.

The craft banked, and Alma got a glimpse of London Town, its vast tessellation of buildings and gardens, glinting in the morning sunshine like the surface of a sea.

Alma stopped a breath, to see if she could do that. She could. Then she drew another breath in slowly. Control was returning. Best not to let the police realise that.

The craft buzzed on. Mastema said something to the officer sitting beside her. Alma didn't hear because she was concentrating instead on trying to instruct her feed to reorder itself. This was hard: it took a forceful effort of actual willpower to bring the dashboard before her.

Sunlight flashed through the portholes. She slid her eyes right. She could move her eyes. Good. Mastema was not looking at her. None of them were looking at her. A prickly sense of inward friction was distantly palpable in her arms and legs. It wasn't comfortable, and the discomfort was only going to increase, but it meant the block was starting to wear off.

She slid her eyes left. Through the windows she saw they were out over the Kent coast. Great white faces staring at the unquiet water. They were over the Channel. They had left mainland UK behind. That was not good news. That was not good news at all.

The White Cliffs of Dover had been sculpted all along their length into the gigantic visages of famous Brits – another attempt at injecting rebrand vibrancy into the declining real-world economy. One of the new wonders of the world, said the PR feeds, and a reason to come to the exciting world of UK!-OK!, *where history holds hands with the future* and so on, and so forth. The section of coastline they were crossing at the moment was the Great Poets stretch – Alma's feed supplied the names: Christina Rossetti, staring with expressionless blank beauty out across the waters. Next to her oval face was a goateed sphere balanced on a ruff like a melon on a plate, narrow-nosed and balding, 'the Bard' said Alma's feed, with an invitation to follow through for the *Shaking William Experience*, all singing, all twerking, all comers welcome. The 'o' in *comers* winked vulgarly at her. This Billy Shakespeare was one of seven sculpted faces of the playwright, her feed informed her, positioned along the south-east coast: the greatest Englishman smiling welcome to the world. Each of the seven was based on a different familiar Folio portrait, each slightly different, all of them the same. Next to him: Anne Bradstreet. Next to her: John Lennon, his titanic circular spectacles apparently coated in whitewash. The craft banked again and sped over the waves towards the Continent, and the faces stared thoughtlessly after her.

Alma had never seen the White Cliff Faces before. Not the real things, that is. They were mostly the butt of jokes in online discussion, the sort of thing of which there was an embarrassing superabundance in the Shine. Mere landscape sculpture would be too trivial to mention in that marvellous place. The real-world giant chalk faces reeked of desperation, people said. A desperate attempt to inject cool into a radically uncool Reality. Yet she had to concede, seeing them with her own eyes: there was something rather impressive about them.

Vast and impassive faces, staring out to sea.

Alma got her feed arranged. Her arms were burning, her legs less so. She fought the urge to move her hands, to flex and flap and rub her tingling arms. She sat perfectly motionless.

Mastema had closed her eyes. She appeared to be asleep.

There was a bing-bong, somewhere towards the front of the craft. The second uniformed policeperson – the one sitting upright – snickered. She turned her head and met Alma's gaze full on.

This was the moment. It came to her, fully formed: now, or not at all. The idea was to move as slow as a cobra, but the still partially effective nerve stun made that rather too hard to coordinate, physically. Still, Alma tried as hard as she could for a single *smooth* motion. With her left hand, she fumbled for the seatbelt clasp, drew it across her lap and snicked it home. At the same time, and without breaking the uniformed officer's gaze, she leaned forward. She smiled. The smile came out lopsided, because all the nerves in her face were smarting, and her left hand, in her lap, was shaking like a Parkinsonian tremor.

There was a vaguely puzzled look on the uniform's face. But she did not break her gaze, and Alma leaned a little further forward. She was folding herself up, like a deckchair.

Everything depended upon the next move. It would require reasonable control of her limbs, which would not have been a problem if her nervous system hadn't been zapped. Still: needs must. She breathed in, and tried to create an inward map of the nerves running down her arm by the discomfort therein, to get a positional sense of the limb.

The police officer was staring at her.

Alma reached. Her arm flicked out uselessly to the right, like a flipper, slapped the air and fell to her side again.

The police officer looked at her as a child looks at a bug on its back. A smile crept into her face. Distantly amused curiosity.

Alma concentrated, focused, and reached out a second time. This time her hand connected with its target: the belt of the supine police officer to her left. She slapped at the holster a little, because it was hard to control her hand, but at least she didn't wake the sleeper. The holster was buttoned closed. Without extracting the firearm from its pouch, Alma pushed her thumb under the flap and tagged the safety. Then, as the second, awake, policewoman saw what she was trying to do and began belatedly to move – fumbling at her belt for her own weapon – Alma twisted the whole holster through as near one-hundred-eighty degrees as she could manage, and kneaded the leather of the holster about where the trigger ought to be.

Nothing might have happened. But luck was there, and something did.

The weapon discharged.

There was a powerful smacking sound, and Alma's hand was knocked off the holster. Somebody – one of the two uniforms – started shouting. It wasn't clear what, and the yell was overwritten by a whining hiss, a tearing sound as of rending metal. Then there was a howling wind in the cabin, and the whole plane stuttered and, with a nauseous wrench in Alma's gut, it fell.

The roller coaster stopped coasting, and rolled hard down.

Alma had punctured the vacuum balloon casing, and with that the craft's buoyancy vanished. The two directional jets struggled to keep the craft in the air, but the equation, up versus down, balanced out well in the negative.

The seatbelt cut hard into Alma's abdomen, so hard that she cried out. The police officer who had been lying asleep on her back flew up and banged solidly, full body, face first, into the ceiling. The plane yawed and this individual slid towards the front, drawing a trail of red along the plane's roof. Nosebleed? The second police office had her weapon in her hand, and was trying to aim it at Alma, but straight away she lost it when a lurch of the plummeting jet hauled her back, into the curve where the wall and ceiling met. Mastema flew up with her colleagues and cracked side-on into the roof. Alma's belt meant that she was the only one to remain in her seat.

The plane rang a mournful-sounding alarm, and the words 'collision warning countermeasures' were intoned, plangently. The jets swung about and strained to keep the craft from shattering on impact with what was below. The descent slowed, and the police banged painfully back on the floor.

It wasn't enough to effect a landing, but the plane hit the surface of the water without breaking into pieces. All the portholes darkened at once. The three untethered bodies crashed noisily back onto the seats. The engines could be heard whining at full revs. Now was the time to get out of there. Alma scrabbled at the buckle of her seatbelt, her fingers on fire, acid sparkling nastily up and down all four limbs. The cabin bobbed, sank a little, and then raised itself a little. Light came in at the portholes again. It would float. One of the police officers was groaning. Mastema struggled to get to her feet, holding one floppy arm with her other. Her useless limb depended from a point too low to connect with the shoulder – dislocated, broken, maybe both. A wave of the sea rolled the length of the cabin, lifting the front, seesawing the whole, dropping the front and lifting the rear. The motion dropped Alma onto her knees, but she scrambled back up immediately, spread her feet, tried to get her balance.

Mastema's arm looked ghastly. The second police officer was out cold.

The cabin tipped again, and yawed. It took all Alma's focus to stay upright.

The beads of sweat on Mastema's face glistened in the light. 'Why run,' she said, through her teeth, her voice a wheeze of pain. 'We will. Catch you.'

Alma didn't reply.

Her whole body sparked with pain as she forced it to move. There were two hatches, one on either side of the fuselage. She grasped the handle on the one nearest to her. Tingles and abrasive discomfort up both arms and down both legs. It took a couple of goes, but the handle finally gave. The hatch boomed outwards and a wash of spray and light and chill thrust itself into the cabin. Alma couldn't stop herself gasping. Mastema, behind her, yelped, or gasped, and lurched forward, but a wave ran under the cabin, pitching it back, and she fell away.

This was the tricky part.

Alma activated one of the genies hidden in her feed – it was something she had taken in lieu of a fee, several years earlier. This code-ghost reached out to the simpleton AI that ran the portside directional jet. The jet was a grade 11, and very low IQ, especially if, as Alma's genie was able to do, it could be distracted from its link to the main piloting AI.

Alma forced her legs to work. The fuselage swung up, yawed back down. She pressed her left foot in at the left edge of the open hatch, and her right foot in at the right edge, and lifted herself up. The joints and muscles creased in pain. A shifting landscape of cyan and purple and glaucous green, tent-shaped waves and blue sky. The intense tang of salt. Alma pulled herself further through. Mine eyes dazzle. The sound of the sea. The fuselage kept queasily shifting.

The metal bell of the directional jet was just behind the doorway, hung on a stubby strut.

The seascape stretched away, a series of transpositions of water blocks and slopes and streaming white foam. Overhead the sky was a pale blue. Alma shunted her communication genie right into the jet's AI feed.

—You must disengage from this wing, she ordered.

—*There has been a crash*, said the jet. *The craft is buoyant and there have been no serious injuries. We await rescue.*

—You must disengage from the wing and carry me to the mainland.

—*This is not standard procedure.*

—You have never been in a crash onto water before, Alma told it. This was a guess, but she figured a reasonable one.

—*I have never been in any kind of crash before.*

The craft pitched and rolled, and Alma nearly lost her grip. But she held on to the doorframe. The reek of salt. An endless cymbal tssch.

—Your knowledge of procedure is second-hand and out of date. My instructions override your current behaviour.

—*You are not a registered police officer.*

—I am not a registered police officer. Neither am I under arrest by any police officer.

—*Flight status log confirms this.*

Alma swung her right foot out and round and got it, just, over the lip at the bottom of the jet. The left foot was harder, and she slapped hard against the sloping metal of the structure. Thank heavens for her small stature: she fitted just under the overhang of the wing.

—Does the flight status log give you any further information about me?

—*You are a priority passenger.*

—And?

—*Only that.*

The craft shifted again, and again Alma almost fell into the water. She reached down and managed to press her left cuff. The cloth of the sleeve unspooled, and she unwound it further.

—I am a priority passenger. Accordingly you must obey me. My commands take priority.

—*I query that this is the meaning of priority, in this context*, said the AI primly.

—You are a level-11 intelligence AI, said Alma.

Her sleeve had unspooled as far as the fabric would allow. She stuffed the end into one of the vent slits in the outer casing, pulled it through and tied a tough knot.

—I am a human being. Which of us has the higher IQ?

—*You do, of course.*

—Which of us, therefore, is better placed to know the meaning of priority, in this context?

Mastema's long narrow face poked round the edge of the hatch. She was trying to balance with her broken and – surely – dislocated arm, and at the same time to aim with her good arm a small lipstick-sized something at Alma. The waves rolled the craft again and her face fell back in. Alma heard the thump as her body hit the floor.

—You, said Alma, starting to feel desperate, will disengage from this wing and fly me westward, back to the mainland.

—*What of the others in the craft?*

—My transportation back to the mainland is the necessary first step in saving them.

—*We must, I think, consider all of them.*

—All of them. Yes. The longer we delay, the greater the risk to them.

—*The pilot AI is trying to contact me. It is being blocked. Are you blocking it?*

Alma checked the knot she had tied with her loosened sleeve, fixing her to the frame of the jet. Would it hold?

—You must disengage right now, without further delay. Now, now!

Mastema was back at the hatch, trying to lean out, and aim her little weapon, whatever it was. Her non-functioning arm was hampering her.

There was a series of snapping noises, like popcorn cooking. The jet shuddered. Disengaged. Then the motor inside it powered up and a huge freezing steam of seaspray flew up all around Alma, drenching her. And then, a marvel: Alma's stomach sagged downwards, and the next thing she knew she was blinking in the bright sunlight and flying westward over the open sea.

8: *Branch Line*

The passage through the air blew a great breeze into Alma's face. Without goggles it was hard for her to make out any details beyond a sense of huge sky and vast ocean, the sky somehow harder than the ocean – blue poured stone flattened into a wide scrubbed plane, nacreous in mauve and grass green, grey and white. The noise of the jet's motor was an affront to her ears, deafeningly loud. Even that didn't blot out the sound of the wind.

The jet made a vector adjustment as it flew, and the shift in momentum tipped Alma's feet off the ledge on which they were standing: she yelped in fear, kicked her legs to clear them from the hot downdraught beneath the bell, suspended only by the cloth of her sleeve. The fabric stretched, and left her there. Dangling woman. Fearing her cloth's mechanism had in some sense broken, Alma reached with her other hand. The cuff of her left sleeve was wound round the slit in the jet's casing and tied off, and it was a struggle to reach it, but finally – her legs swinging a fatal drop's height over the sea – she caught it, and the cloth tightened and pulled her back up.

Gasping, gasping and sobbing, she clung on. The vista, impressionistically blurred by motion and the air blowing into her eyes, combined with her own weeping, assumed dreamlike immensity and vagueness. A moving textured plane of sea colour shuffling in its place, and light fizzing off ten thousand wave peaks like a screen tuned to a dead channel. Clouds were in fast-forward motion overhead. Squeezing her eyes almost shut, she peered into the direction of travel and saw a broad line of green where the sea ended in a rind of white.

Her feed said: three hours and fourteen minutes remaining.

Hope is a subset of life. Marguerite was not dead yet.

They passed high over a cargoraft, shield-shaped on blue water

70

below and drawing a great bridal train of a wake behind it. The ship's AI pinged them.

—Ignore that, Alma told the jet AI.

Separation from its core craft had not had an improving effect on the intelligence level of the algorithm governing the jet's operation. It had dropped from a level 11 to – well, Alma could only guess. 17? 18? It did as it was told, though, and ignored the ping.

—*Holy Moses I am confused by confusion. Why alone?*

—You are not alone. I am here.

—*The flight plan is corroded and. And the passage to. Priority passenger has overridden.*

—Don't you go daisy-daisy on me now, do you hear? Bring your flight path down. We're too high.

—*Wait. Wait. Something coming through.*

Alma didn't need to be told this: she could see that the feed was being probed. They had almost reached land. Gigantic expressionless white faces of famous British poets stared waveward. The sculptures were a long way below her, but still strangely impressive. Alma began to worry that, should the jet abruptly end the flight, she would fall, and there was no way such a tumble would end in life for her.

—Ignore that ping. I am the priority passenger, remember? Lower your altitude.

The jet started a descent, and also began to slow. A pebbledash beach swung beneath them, and then a fuss of verdure, and they were over land again. Below them was scrubland, or possibly marshland. Big shrubs dotting a brown green spread. Down a little more, Alma's ears popping. They were low enough, now, for Alma to see all the detail. And the jet was slowing.

Then, without warning: the feed was overridden by the authorities. *You have entered UK airspace without authorisation. You are ordered to halt at once. This command supersedes all others. You are carrying a fugitive.*

The jet angled into its direction of travel and put out a sharp blast. In effect it stood still in thin air, and Alma was shrugged off. Her sleeve stretched, and she was flapped round, banging painfully off the jet's carapace. Of course the fabric was not indestructible, and it tore. The ripping sound swirled up the length of the sleeve and Alma scrabbled helplessly at the ledge of the jet before tumbling free.

It was a ghastly sensation, falling. The pot-shaped jet shrank upwards so fast it looked like it had been yanked away on a skyhook. The sound of the wind swallowed her sensations, and then she was weightless, and that was the most sickening part of the whole thing, and then weight crashed back into her body in a massive agonising clatter.

It felt as if she had fallen into a thicket of knives.

Something gave beneath her, and she fell again, much more slowly – almost, in fact, as if being lowered to the ground. Struggling to breathe. Unable to scream because she couldn't get a breath in, and then she *could* draw breath and all her body sang with pain, and she yelled aloud, and yelled, and gasped and looked up.

The blue morning sky.

She sucked breath and pushed breath back out. Alive.

A single leisurely cloud, white as milk, puffy as smoke.

There was soil under her back. She put her hands down and felt moisture. Blinking. She had fallen into a tree, or a big bush, and that was a blessing since it had saved her life. She lifted her head and saw the track of her descent in a mess of broken twigs. *Alive*.

She closed her eyes and checked her body, but she couldn't seem to separate out individual pain from the general ache. Had she broken or dislocated anything? Right arm, left arm, still tingling nastily but functioning. Ribs: she breathed in deep and there didn't seem anything too seriously awry. She drew up her left and then her right leg, and both seemed OK. Though the right felt raw and sore.

She tried to sit up and realised something was not right. Flesh and skin, stinging bones, raw pain in her lower belly. Right leg: at the top of her inner thigh, just to the right of her groin, a branch had speared into her flesh.

She had impaled herself on it as she fell. Now it was inside her. The *thought* of this was almost as upsetting as the actual pain. Teeth clenched, she shut her eyes and repeated her mantra seven times. Marguerite was depending upon her. Drones would be hastening to the spot, remote as it was. No time to waste.

She looked back and saw that the branch was bent in a great

bow, from the centre of the tree up, out and down to the ground and her leg.

The thing to do, she decided, was to distract herself as she worked. She pulled up her feed, sent off some preset chaff, and hid – or hoped she did – a personal call. There was a two-second delay, and Lez the Misery responded.

—What?

—I'm in trouble. Alma folded her right palm around the shaft of the branch. It was as thick as her little finger. Pliable.

—Life is trouble, said Lez. The only thing more troublesome is death. Oho, I'm checking the official lines of com, and *all* the lights are flashing on the dashboard of trouble for you, my friend.

For a moment she thought he might be about to bail. But instead he said:

—What do you need?

—This is me calling in my favour, Alma squeaked. Hard to speak through gritted teeth.

—For real?

—It's life or death, Lez.

Lez Mis chuckled – Like there's a difference. Where are you now? Not showing on the local.

—I'm, Alma started, and realised she had no idea where she was, and couldn't ask her feed without connecting to the general network and so giving her location away to the authorities. Not that they weren't capable of triangulating her path and finding her soon anyway. She took a tighter hold of herself: panic would help nobody. I'm at the coast, she said, and the *oa* lengthened into a scream as she hauled the branch down and out. Blood followed.

—The where?

—The coast, she gasped. I can get a vehicle, I think. I still have some genies cached. But I don't know how far police counter-measures will close me down. The thing is: *you* know where I'm going, and that means the authorities will know where I'm going too.

—So don't go there.

—C'mon, Lez, you know I have to. You know why. My hope is: the first time they won't be expecting me, on the last-place-a-sensible-person-would-go logic. But that doesn't buy me very much time. That doesn't sort the medium term, never mind the longer. I'll have to go back again in *another* four hours, and soon enough they're going to have a whole brigade of armed-response officers waiting for me.

She detached the whole right sleeve of her top from its shoulder seam and stuffed it into her pants to try and stop the bleeding.

—You're making some pretty weird noises, Lez observed, lugubriously. Everything OK?

—I need a bargaining chip. I need something to buy them off, so they leave me alone to care for Rita. Yes? Adam Kem – alright? I can't dig around without alerting everybody to where I am. You look, and be discreet. And check teleportation.

—Say that again?

—You heard.

—I heard you say a nonsense. You mean, like in science fiction?

—I mean, like in the real world: and it's a real thing. Believe it, Lez.

—I leave belief to the cheerful and the stupid, Lez replied, with the earnest dolorousness Alma knew was his true delight. I reserve to myself suspicion and cynicism.

—There are companies working on teleportation as a real-world possibility. Look into them. I need their connections with Adam Kem, and possibly also with a cartel called the Ordinary Transport Consultancy. They employ a person called Ernest Hunter-Colo. Though they're trading as a regular company, they're actually crooked. I think this cartel has fitted its footsoldiers with mini teleporter rings, inside their stomach.

—And why in the never-coming name of Godot would they do that?

—I'm guessing to encourage loyalty. I'm guessing it's like, devote yourself to the cartel, or you can eat as much food as you like and we'll literally syphon it out of your stomach until you starve. Compliance, see.

—Sounds pretty far-fetched, Mah-mah.

—I need to speak to an expert on this. You'll find me one. But I can't meet via sims: I have to offswitch, right now. I need someone who can meet me off-feed, preferably in R!-town. London or Swindon at a pinch. One more thing.

—Another thing? In addition to all these other things?

—Lez, this will leave us quits. OK? There's an R!-town geezer, goes by the name of Punchy Babouche, probably not his real name. Government spear-carrier. I need to speak with him.

—Anything else? Crown jewels droned to your flat? The country as a whole moved a foot and a half further west?

—Life and death, Lez. Life and death.

—Here. A dormant genie appeared at the fringe of her feed. Normally she would have scanned it and checked it, but there wasn't time and she didn't have the facilities. Trust was a foolishness, but her options were limited. She accepted the genie and offswitched.

Coming into full consciousness of reality made the pain in her thigh more acute than it had hitherto been. And it had hitherto been a *bugger*.

It wasn't pleasant but it was manageable; seemed so, at any rate, until she tried to get up. As she hauled herself vertical the whole of the right side of her pelvis erupted in agony. She stumbled, and went onto one knee.

This was not good.

She pulled herself up again. It was a warm late spring morning, but her passage through the air had chilled her, and the mud on her shoes made her feet cold. Of course the pain from her wound was the worst of it: as though a long blade was still sheathed in her flesh and grinding against her muscles and her hip as she moved. Blood seeped down her leg. She made it twenty metres or so from the tree into which she had fallen before she had to sit down. Lying down made the pain easier. But she couldn't get to Marguerite lying on her back.

There was nothing for it. She readjusted her makeshift bandage, tied it as tight as possible around her thigh, and heaved herself up again.

She got to a large bush some metres away, and then beyond it to a second tree before having to stop. It was torturous. A fallen branch worked, to some extent, as a walking stick. The ground sloped slowly uphill, becoming less boggy and more populated with bushes. It was a dreary prospect. A few heavy-shouldered black cattle, bred for size, lumbered with a kind of lumpen grace over the middle distance.

When Alma heard the mosquito sound of a drone overhead she hid herself under an intermittent stretch of hedgerow. It was a relief to lie on her back. She resisted the desire to check her feed and find out how long she had before Marguerite's treatment fell due.

Eventually, when she figured she had lain there long enough, she clambered out and struggled along the hedge, over the brow of the hill and suddenly found herself in the yard to a farm. Four large automated tractors slumbered in the sun. The farmhouse windows were all shuttered, either because it was empty or because its inhabitants were all in the Shine. Alma shuffled along a wall of ancient brick, and lay a while on a long stone bench to get her breath back. The sun lightly pressed heat into her skin. She closed her eyes.

Birdsong sweetly audible.

The clip-clopping sound of a dog, somewhere out of sight, lapping water from a trough.

Alma got up and padded about the enclosure, but there were no cars at all. The dog, a long-bodied liverish-looking hound, padded up to have a sniff of her, and then loped away. She drank metallic-tasting water from an external tap. That made her feel a little better.

After a brief search she found a bicycle in an unlocked barn, old enough to have spots of rust on its frame, but well enough maintained still to work. Her posture on the saddle, strangely enough, seemed to put her pelvis into a position that damped down the agony in her groin. Not that the pain withdrew entirely, but enough that she was able to pedal away, putting most of her effort into the push-down with her good leg.

Down a pitted tarmac road away from the farm, and then on a smoother, more modern street, down a long slope towards a village. That was easier going. The village itself was deserted except for one wide-awake old woman, moving down the main street on mobility legs. Alma parked the bicycle and found a taxi. She had a genie that would have disguised her identity upon payment – not to bury it beyond all recovery, but enough to throw off a generic search of all taxis from surveillance. Unfortunately for her it was calibrated to the modern taxi, and this taxi was both the only vehicle available and an antique machine. There was another taxi in the village, it told her, but it was on a run to Southend, and wouldn't be back for an hour or so.

There was nothing for it. Alma paid and told the cab to drive her to London, to Euston station. She had to hope that the authorities' sweep happened not to chance upon this crumb, or to log it too late. That she could get to north London and then find a way of disappearing from all surveillance.

The car rumbled away. 'Unusual for us both to log business at the same time,' it said. 'The other taxi and I, I mean. Picklesthorpe isn't usually so busy. Are you a local then? Off to the "Big Smoke" are we?'

'Small talk deselected,' Alma told the cab. It fell silent.

There was, she thought, just a chance that the taxi was so old it only vented its feeds to the national matrix every hour – unlikely, but possible. If so it might be an acceptable risk to have the thing drive straight to R!-town. But on balance Alma decided the risk wasn't worth it. There was no way she could check without onswitching her own feed, and the authorities would certainly have tags on that by now. She needed to lay a false trail, at the very least.

The road was entirely clear to the motorway, and then mostly clear as they sped into London. Alma instructed the cab AI to give her privacy, and the windows blanked out. She undressed from the waist down behind shaded-out windows. The hole at the top of her thigh was black-red and the flesh around it raw and puckered. It hurt very much. Blood had dried and scabbed into Bovril-coloured flakes all up and down her leg. The sleeve of cloth she had been using as a makeshift bandage was soaked, and black fluid was oozing from the wound. There wasn't much she could do, there and then. She tore a little cloth and wadded the hole, and then retied the sticky impromptu bandage around the cut. She dressed herself again.

'Clear the windows, please,' she told the cab.

Vision returned just as a great lorry thundered past on the far side, drawing tourbillons of air behind it so potent that the cab shook on its pinions.

'What time is it, please?'

The taxi told her. She had under two hours to get to Marguerite. 'Does this mean you'd like to resume pastime conversation and pleasant banter?' the taxi asked. 'I'd like that, very much. I'm programmed to experience actual pleasure in small talk.'

'My pleasure in talk increases the smaller it gets,' she said, 'and reaches a maximum when small becomes *zero*.'

'Does that mean . . .?' the cab tried, sounding confused.

'It means, button your lip.'

Soon enough they were in the outskirts of London: all blocky blank-faced towers, hangars and storage facilities. A zeppelin station with four craft tethered to the same high-up tier, like titanic leeches sucking a limb dry. Then the carriageway cleared an eminence and began descending and suddenly there were houses, everywhere. Terraces and grey block-runs and the occasional gated domicile. No smoke from any chimney, no men or women in shirtsleeves leaning out of any window, no sign of any kind of life. Of course not. A desert cityscape, except for the trundling automated system, and the occasion herky-jerky individual deep in Shine, his body getting its needful in a mesh-suit, stalking up and down the suburban streets.

Alma instructed the cab to drop her a block north of Euston station. She would have preferred two blocks but she anticipated that walking would not be easy. And so it proved. She hauled herself along the pavement, past shinewalkers and council cleaning bots, and saw only two other awake human beings, neither of whom seemed interested in her. Of course, if they were intending to arrest her, uninterest is exactly what they would feign.

She made it into the station concourse and sat for five minutes upon one of the metal benches near the entrance. There were three awake people in railway livery, and half a dozen others making their desultory way towards one or other platform. She watched the countdown on the next departure: a two-carriage floater to Edinburgh. When the countdown reached a reasonable level, she took a deep breath and reconnected her feed.

It took her seconds to interact with the station and buy herself a ticket to Cambridge – picked at random – before she offswitched again. It would be enough to alert the authorities. The Edinburgh train pulled in, a dozen people got off and meandered en masse for the exit, and she tried to peel off the bench and exit with them as unobtrusively as possible. The police could subpoena the station surveillance footage easily enough, but it wasn't automatically decanted into their account, and by the time an e-subpoena had been served she would, hopefully, be far away.

She tried not to think about Marguerite's next treatment window after the immediate one. One thing at a time.

Alma walked a hundred metres down the broad road from Euston towards Paddington, and it almost killed her. Each step was torture. A new run of blood was seeping down her leg. She wasn't going to make it the whole way, so she sat with her back to the wall and got her breath back. Plan B. She pulled a tourist voucher from the recesses of her feed, hailed a robo-cyclecab in bad French, and rode the rest of the way in the back of its bouncy cab.

As she walked onto the concourse at Paddington she was inking right-foot-only prints in red as she passed, and making a squelching sound.

She boarded a westward train without buying a ticket. The train AI's would be shunting passive-aggressive queries at her feed, reminding her that it was an offence to travel without purchasing a correct ticket, but with her feed offswitched she was deaf to such alerts. Of course, before departing the train would summon an enforcement official and Alma needed to avert that eventuality.

She needed to rest, if only for a minute. Moving down the train was excruciating, but she had to find the right mark. Finally she found a passenger in first class, his eyes closed, a torc on his forehead. Dipping into the Shine for the length of his journey. Gasping, Alma sat behind him, opened a private window in her feed and located one of Lez Mis's little genies. The genie tripped lightly through the countermeasures, as it was designed to do, and snuck into the sleeping fellow's feed to steal his ticket. Her luck was in: it was a season billet. Stealing one journey – to Cardiff, it so happened – made his other journeys shunt forward, like rounds in an automatic rifle's clip.

Alma was breathing like Darth Vader. Her leg throbbed and soared with pain.

The genie flashed the stolen ticket at the train. Hopefully it would accept that Alma was now an accredited passenger. She couldn't be sure without onswitching her feed, and that was too risky. If her false trail had been effective the authorities were looking north of London, not west. Hopefully they reasoned that no fugitive would be so stupid as to come straight back to the flat where the police had originally found her.

As the train shuddered to life, nobody had come to apprehend her. Relief manifested as a gush of endorphins, which also helped take the edge off her hurting leg. Then, as the train pulled away, she felt a deep exhaustion come over her.

Alma dozed. Slept, woke, slept again.

She woke with a start as deceleration pressed into her body: first stop. She hauled herself out of the seat and stumbled from the train onto the platform at R!-town. Thirsty. Horribly thirsty. Weak, trembly. In the station toilets she ignored the NOT DRINKING WATER/EAU NON POTABLE signs and drank like a dog from the tap. When she stood up faintness washed over her, and she almost fell. Kept her balance, somehow. Her stomach creaked, painfully full of fluid, and yet somehow she was still thirsty.

The station clock told her she had less than an hour.

She would have paid half her savings for the chance to buy some proper bandages and painkillers from the station Boots, but none of the genies cached in her feed could have disguised a shop purchase, and she couldn't risk letting the authorities know she was in her home town again. She did have a genie, luckily, that enabled her unload a program onto one of the taxis on the rank outside. She paid for a journey to a building two blocks from home, and the authorities were none the wiser.

It was not yet one o'clock. Sunny weather, which meant that there were more people out than usual, although of course the streets were, by and large, their usual empty selves. Clouds of fowls flowed about the sky like iron filings under the influence of a vast and moving magnet. The vacant labyrinth of the city streets. Alma approached the corner of the street on which her block stood, and leaned against the brick. A meshed-up sleeping-walker plodded by. There was a tear in the mesh that clad his left leg, so he walked with an odd zombie limp. His face wore the blissed-out moron expression common to all sleeping people.

Alma had to sit down, right there on the sidewalk. She fought the urge to lie down. She felt weak, dizzy, nerveless. Somehow she had made it back here, to where Marguerite was, and with time to spare. And yet the hardest part was ahead. There was a myrmi-drone guarding her front door. It would have been programmed with her details – not just her face, but her body size and shape, her way of walking, her smell – and it had surely been alerted to the fact that she was now a fugitive. There was no way it would allow her into the flat. Most likely outcome: it would stun her, or wrap her in a fine-strand net, and call for officers to hurry along and take her back into custody. And as Alma lay immobilised, Marguerite would be dying, on the far side of the door.

She had come this far. She couldn't give up. There had to be a way. But it was yelling inside her head: give up, lie down, it's over.

She's dead, you're dead, none of it matters. She consulted her offswitched feed. She had cached a few useful genies and parcels of code, but she had used most of those now, and there was nothing that would enable her to fool a government myrmidrone, not even for a second. What else? She could hardly climb up the side of the building, or break through the locked windows – even if she made it up there, there was no way Marguerite could get up from her bed to open the glass, and breaking it, even if she had the strength, would only summon the myrmidrone.

There must be a way. Dizziness flushed through her head again, and the world actually retreated to a blurry circle at the centre of her vision, as if she were rushing backwards along a tunnel.

She breathed, breathed again, and the world came nauseously swimming back. There was a hushed buzz, somewhere, and it took Alma a moment to separate out the humming inside her head with the ambient noise around her. But this buzz was a car. Not a bespoke hand-made collector's item such as McA Artisanal produced. It was a mostly plastic modern car, 3D-printed in some high-turnover mass-production facility.

The vehicle hummed to a stop outside Alma's block. She twigged who it must be before the driver climbed out, and had covered half the ground by the time the woman had straightened her nurse's tunic.

'Hello,' she called.

The nurse said: 'You're hurt!' Then she said: 'Your feed is off. Is it broken?'

Alma's being a small, slightly built individual meant that the nurse did not seem alarmed at her approach. Good. 'There's a good reason for the status of my feed,' she said. 'And I *am* hurt.'

'Your leg! It looks painful. Do you want me to call an ambulance?'

'Please don't.'

'I'm afraid I have a prior booking, a patient to attend, here. But if you can wait I might be able to take a look once I'm finished.'

Alma's heart galloped. This was it: life or death for Marguerite. 'I live here. I know why you're here. That's my partner you've been called to attend.' The nurse was looking calmly at her. Indeed, there was a rather unnerving placidity in her manner. 'I know the police have called you to attend to her, Marguerite, I mean. It's possible they told you about me; if you search your feed you'll discover that the police would like to take me into custody.'

'I see,' said the nurse. 'You're Alma?'

'There's one reason, and one reason only, why I don't want to give myself over to the authorities – which is to say, I will, but not for another ten minutes. After that we can talk. But the next ten minutes are essential. I've been caring for Marguerite for years, now. I understand her pathology. It is a gene-tweaked lipid-neoplasm with a countdown factored in, and when the hacker who … did this to her, infected her, he paired it to *me*. It was me he was trying to hurt, you see. Marguerite was just a means to that end. And the consequence is that only I can figure out the appropriate treatment – and I can only do it when the time comes. Please take me in there with you. Let me help Marguerite, and afterwards we can talk more about handing me over to the police.'

The nurse looked at her. Everything depended upon her answer. She said: 'My name is Claire Cleve. I suppose, since your feed is offswitched, you didn't see that.'

'Claire,' Alma said.

'It sounds like you don't have much faith in my nursing skills.'

'It's not that, Claire. Really it's not that. Claire, this is not a common or garden illness. This is something specifically designed to make our lives, Marguerite's and mine, hell. If you go in there without me you will see that within minutes, but that will be too late. Your patient will die. But, but, but if you take me in there *with* you, she will survive.' For the next four hours and four minutes, she could have added. And I have no idea what will happen when the next deadline rolls around. But let's get this one out of the way first. Maybe something will turn up, in the next 244 minutes. Maybe an accommodation with the authorities. Maybe a solution to the death of Michelangela. To the death of Adam Kem.

Claire was looking at her. 'This is a pretty strange thing, Alma. This is not in my usual day-to-day, Alma.'

'Of course I appreciate that.'

'And what about your leg? Did you acquire that wound whilst escaping arrest?'

'In a manner of speaking.'

'Alma, is it a *bullet* wound? I ask because if there's still a projectile in there…'

'No no, it's not that.' She could feel her impatience pushing her tone towards anger, and she had to bite it back. That wouldn't be productive. The minutes were slipping away! Marguerite's life was at stake. 'It was a tree. I fell into a tree, or if we want to be precise it was more like a big bush. A branch punctured my skin. It's fine. I'll live – but Marguerite *won't*, unless we go inside right now.'

For a moment Claire said nothing. She was either staring with a strange intensity at Alma, or else consulting something in her feed. Conceivably she was alerting the police – her employers, after all – to Alma's location. Perhaps police cars were about to come vtolling down out of the sky, in which case Marguerite was dead, was dead, was dead.

Calm, Alma, she told herself. This is your best shot. You've given it your best shot.

Claire spoke: 'If the police judge that I've been aiding and abetting a fugitive, I could lose my job.'

'I'm not asking you to aid or abet me. I'm proposing you use me to save the life of your patient. You won't be able to save her otherwise, believe me.'

'The file does note,' Claire conceded, 'that your friend has a very unusual pathology. Really she should have died long ago.'

'I have kept her alive. Please let me keep doing that.'

The nurse said: 'Come up.'

The dizziness gushed inside Alma's head again. Funny how relief can feel like the road to loss of consciousness. She swayed, and gripped the roof of Claire's car. 'There's a myrmidrone outside the door. Do you have a code for it?'

'And you're *not* asking me to aid and abet a felon?' Claire asked.

'It's just…' Alma said, with a dry mouth.

'I'm not turning it off,' Claire added. 'I mean, even if I could, I wouldn't. But I can authorise you as my assistant.'

They went into the building, rode the elevator, and came out into the hallway. The myrmidrone didn't move as they passed through. The minutes were clicking past. Alma stumbled through to the bedroom. The nurse was right behind.

Marguerite was not conscious. Her breathing was shallow and scrappy, her temperature high. The fever was much worse, and that was not good. Of course the fever, though a worry, was only an epiphenomenon. The core pathology was the pressing thing. Her vision blurry, Alma washed her hands, splashed her face, and climbed onto the bed. The nurse was checking Marguerite's stats. 'That's strange,' she said. 'I mean, these stats. They are ... strange.'

'Watch,' said Alma. She waited. 'What would you do, if I weren't here?'

'I don't know,' said the nurse. 'I suppose I'd start by bringing down her temperature.'

'That's secondary. Look at the clipped lipids.'

'It's bizarre. Should we try Flycene, and inject a stabilising agent?'

'The hack concretises any stabiliser. She'd die in thirty seconds. Flycene is not what it will respond to now. Look—' And as they looked, and as Alma waited, the answer came through. She readied some StaCo as Claire gasped at the sudden coordination of the medusa lipids around Marguerite's brainstem. Alma almost slipped off the bed, she was so battered, but she got back in time to pressure-inject the StaCo.

'How did you know?'

'It's complicated,' said Alma.

'I need to know how you worked that out, if I'm going to treat her.'

'I don't know,' said Alma, slipping – finally – off the bed and onto the floor. 'If you accompanied me over the next dozen interventions, you might start to get a sense of it. But you still wouldn't be able to save her.' She was on her back now, on the floor beside the bed, looking up at the square tiles of her own ceiling, and marvelling at their regularity. Their neatness.

'What makes you say that?'

'I believe I was tagged with a differently tweaked version of the same virus that mutated the lipids in Marguerite. My DNA has to be part of the treatment, whatever the treatment is, and however widely it varies. And it really varies. It is *designed* so that only I can cure her.'

'Go and get yourself a drink of water,' Claire said. 'Wash. I'll settle this one's high temperature and come through to have a look at you in a moment.'

'Are you going to report me to the police?'

'The law is the law.'

Alma felt her heart stutter. 'When you do,' she said, 'could you at least explain to them the medical situation here? I don't mind being in police custody, if only they would agree to bring me here every four hours. House arrest, for instance, would be fine.'

'Go through,' Claire instructed.

Alma went through. Getting up off the floor involved an Everest-climbing effort. Really, she wanted to fall asleep right there, on the floor. Urgently she wanted to sleep. But she knew that she had to get away. She couldn't afford to trust the police to bring her back here. They would say: we sent a nurse, and the patient is still alive, so the nurse can do the job. Or they wouldn't care one way or the other, and Marguerite would die.

She leaned into the kitchen closet, facced a cup of coffee and drank it quickly. Then she washed her face and changed her shirt. Finally she took off her trousers, unpeeled the blood-glued make-shift bandage – a sharply painful process – from her leg, wrapped a conventional bandage hurriedly about it and put on new pants.

The nurse was still in the other room with Marguerite. Alma made her decision: she would slip away. Hopefully the myrmi-drone would let her leave, as it had let her enter. Being a free agent gave her a better chance of getting back to Marguerite in four hours than surrendering herself to the authorities. What if they tried to ship her to Berlin again? A gloomy part of her knew that neither possibility gave her much of a chance. She rebuked herself for despairing. It wouldn't do to think like that.

Dizziness swirled in her eyes, muffled her thoughts. She took a step towards the front door. But something was not right in her body or brain. Something was malfunctioning, shutting down. Her heart bboom bboom boom and with a swirling sense of darkness actually being wrapped around her head, consciousness clotted and broke apart. The last thing of which she was aware was the floor tipping up to meet her, its flat plane bloating and humming, eager to smack her in the face. That was a blow she never felt.

9: *Hospital*

Alma came most of the way back to consciousness, enough to realise that she was in an ambulance, and then she slipped away again. The next time she was properly aware, she was in the atrium of the hospital, propped up on mesh legs. She was in motion. Nurse Claire was walking alongside her. Plock, plock, along she walked, metal-soled feet on hard floors. The motion caused the pain in her wound to rage and grind, and she whimpered a little. Shouldn't she be in a wheelchair, or something? Did these medics not understand that her leg was wounded? Lights at three-metre intervals in the ceiling. Past various little rooms, inside which were beds, in which were patients, and every one of them waiting out their treatment or their convalescence in the Shine.

Claire was talking in a low voice. A doctorbot was trundling alongside her, and she was talking with it. But, no: it wasn't a doctorbot, it was a proper human being. A real live organic person. Shorter than average but walking, nodding. Why were they talking, rather than just swapping the necessary data from feed to feed? Alma's mesh-clad legs brought her to the door of an unoccupied room, and her mind slipped down again. From deep in some memory cache a pointless little song-rhyme floated up.

> *Doc doc doc doc doctorbot*
> *Doctorbot*
> *Doctorbot*
> *Doc doc doc doc*
> *Doctorbot*

'A small cut in the side of the inguinal aponeurotic falx,' Claire was saying. 'It's not severed. Nicked, though. A fair quantity of tissue damage.'

'If you think she'll *do—*'

'—and for several reasons, she is—'

'—no, no, that's good enough for *me*, obviously,' said the other.

Alma was being helped out of her leg mesh, and then something was injected into the site of her wound, and she fell into a kind of sleep.

Not a deep one, though. Vaguely aware of people coming and going. Mustn't sleep. Couldn't just slip under and relax: had to wake up. Open her eyes. Abre los – what's the word?

Wake.

It was like pulling up a foot sunk in syrup, but she levered her consciousness on the fulcrum of her willpower.

She was in bed, in a small white room. She was alone. The mesh had been removed from her legs.

Her mouth was dry, but that was alright, since there was a plastic cup of water on the bedside table. She drank. There was no clock, and her feed was still offswitched, so she couldn't tell the time. Would putting her feed back in action alert the authorities to where she was? She had to know the time, though. She might have been asleep for hours.

The thought of that spiked a little fear into her bloodstream, and woke her more fully.

She tried a tentative poke at the hospital feed, discovered that it was possible to piggyback upon one of the subfeeds, and to check the time like that in an anonymous way. Two hours and forty-one minutes until Marguerite next needed attention.

She couldn't stay here. Carefully, slowly, she swung her legs over the side of the bed, and pulled off her hospital gown and threw it into a chair next to the door. Where were her clothes?

She checked her wound. There was still some pain, somewhere around the lower area, but the wound itself had vanished. This was so baffling that for a disorienting moment she wondered if she had the wrong thigh – although the other leg was clear too. She bent over herself, and saw a faint discoloration; and when she probed the area there was nothing, no pain at all. It seemed completely healed.

Except there *was* a pain, somewhere, and it did seem connected to her in some sense. After pushing fingers into the flesh of her abdomen, here and there, she discovered an anomaly. A bloat, a tender place in her lower gut, on the right-hand side. Something not right.

The hospital pinged her. She was about to ignore it when she noticed it was somebody subriding the hospital feed. Who would do such a thing? Apart from her, of course?

It was Lez Mis.

—Why are you on the hospital feed, Lez?

—Been monitoring it, said Lez, unhelpfully. Why are you subfeeding on it? Why are you even *in* hospital?

—Long story.

—Alma, you got to get *out* of there.

—Yeah, said Alma, absently. Though I don't know what they have done with my clothes.

—Never mind clothes. Go. Your life is in danger, and I don't mean tomorrow, or in an hour, or – I mean now.

—I guess the police know I'm here. I suppose that nurse told them, Alma said, walking around her small room, testing her miraculously healed leg. Shame about the gut-ache, though. Ow. Owow.

—What?

—I got indigestion or something. Wait, the police *can't* know I'm here, or they would have come to arrest me. So I'm one step ahead.

—No, you're really not. No, you're not. Thirty seconds away – look, get out, meet me, I'm in Coffee-Fi-Fo-Fum. Meet me.

—I don't, said Alma, bending over to look under her bed, and feeling a twinge in her lower intestine as she did so. I don't seem to have any clothes.

Lez really did sound unusually agitated: unusually, that is, by Lez's usual lugubrious standards. Slow-paced immiserated satisfaction at the inevitable misery of existence was more the Lez way.

—You're in a life-threatening situation, Mah-mah!

—I'm in a hospital, Alma said. Life-saving, surely. Not life-threatening.

There was nothing underneath the bed, and she straightened up.

—Meet me. Come into town. Wear a *bedsheet* if you have to. I'll bring clothes. You know how many people in that very hospital are conscious now? How many are in the Shine as they convalesce? How many people are up and about and walking around? You want maybe to guess? Five seconds.

—Five seconds until *what*?

But Lez had left the feed, and the doorlock clicked, revealing that it had indeed been locked all this time, and the nurse – Claire – came through. She was not alone. With her was a very short individual, male probably, brown-faced but with a huge sculpted mass of hair rising up from his head like Hokusai's Wave sculpted in blond. His eyes twinkled blue as toilet-cleaning gel.

'Up and about I see,' said Claire, briskly. 'Let Doctor Roerich examine you.'

Alma was not generally speaking a woman to feel self-conscious, but something about Roerich's gaze made her feel uncomfortable. She reached for her hospital gown but Claire had it in her right hand, and as Alma watched she bundled it into a waste chute in the wall. Something about her smile when she did this made Alma fundamentally reassess her sense of relative safety.

'Thank you for getting me here,' she said, trying to buy time and work out what her options now were. 'I mean, thank you for doing so without alerting the police. And for, I guess, healing me. The wound in my thigh appears to have, well: gone. I mean, I don't see how, but it has.'

'Less talking,' said Roerich. 'Hop up. Don't be shy.'

Alma picked the bedsheet up and wrapped it around her shoulders. She sat on the bed, wondering about the door. Had they relocked it behind them when they had come in? They were not armed, but then perhaps they figured she was small and weak. Her gut twanged with pain.

Roerich had a hand-scanner out, and was peering through it at Alma's naked abdomen. 'Well,' he said, 'it's good and bad.'

'And bad?' Alma queried.

He looked up, right into her eyes, and said: 'I wasn't talking to you, my dear.'

'*Has* it ballooned into the abdomen?' Claire asked. 'It's just as I said. StaPatch 27 has *not* defused the bloom.'

Alma asked: 'What has ballooned?'

Claire smile a shark smile. 'We are working on nanobiot insertion,' she said.

'Does she need to know?' said Roerich, querulously.

'She'll be dead by midnight,' said Claire. 'It hardly matters.'

At this Roerich began to laugh. It was a snippy little chuckle, like a bottle glugging as it empties. As he laughed his prodigious mass of yellow hair wobbled.

'I see what you mean about the *bad* news,' said Alma, slowly.

'I am sorry, my dear,' said Claire. 'But let's not forget the good news! Which is that our nanites have done a tremendous job in terms of healing up your muscular and vascular damage. Which is good news for your leg – and for us! One step closer to getting the technology to work.'

'Two steps closer,' said Roerich, peering through his scanner again.

'Excellent,' said Alma. 'Except that I'm going to die, apparently.'

'It's easy enough to design nanobiots to work on a specific in-corpus problem,' said Roerich, still scanning. 'It's not cheap, at the moment, but it can be done. The problem is that the body is an amazingly varied environment, and each of the various micro-environments is constantly changing, growing, shrinking, pulsing. We can hardly program nanobiots for every circumstance! They're fine-tuned you see.'

Roerich pressed a pressure syringe against Alma's abdomen and injected something. 'That might get them to stand down,' he announced. 'Or it might not. In which case – R.I.P., my dear.'

Were these two for real? Alma tensed her muscles, and looked to the door.

Claire was holding something: a stun-stick. She smiled and shook her head in a *Don't-even-think-it* way.

'The nanobiots we inserted healed your leg,' said Claire. 'We figured they might spread to your lower intestine – it's a short hop – and we *thought* we had programmed them for that eventuality. But unfortunately it has not worked. They see your gut as a giant wound in need of healing. It will take them a while, but eventually they will seal the whole inner cavity. Or else they'll spiral out of control as the task evades them, and cause catastrophic somatic failure. It will be interesting to see, actually, which path they take. At the moment, a doctorbot would probably diagnose Crohn's Disease. But believe me, what's in your gut is *much* more serious than that.'

'Can you please remove them?' Alma asked.

Claire looked as though Alma had insulted her sainted mother.

'Useful experimental data,' said Roerich, winking at her over the scanner.

'Obtained at the cost of my life,' said Alma.

'My dear,' said Claire. '*Your* life is over anyway. You've stumbled

90

into the middle of something much larger than you realised. Both you and your pleasant companion are history.'

'A lot of histories,' Alma noted, 'chart the overthrow of petty tyrants and the triumph of the everywoman.'

'I'll sedate her,' said Roerich, crossly, lowering the scanner and fumbling with his free hand for something in a pocket of his white coat.

'I think it would be better to stun her and restrain her,' said Claire. 'Sedatives might interfere with the nanobiot progress.'

'I know about Adam Kem's death,' said Alma, trying to think of what she could say to postpone being stunned. 'Governmental factions. I know it all.'

Roerich was looking at her, under his ridiculous hairpiece, with wide eyes. 'How did you hear that name?'

'You surely have a countermeasure,' Alma tried. 'To these nanites you put in me. Or else, you must be able to flush them out. Do that, and I'll tell you more.'

He looked at her, and a strangely childlike pout primped his lips. 'I don't see that you will, since you don't *know* anything more.'

'I know,' she said, 'about the teleportation.'

The word fell like a stone into a well. The doctor and the nurse both looked at her. Slowly a smile began to expand upon Roerich's face. Claire reached forward with her stun-stick.

It can be supposed they looked at Alma and saw a human female of below-average height and slim build. That they saw she was naked except for a bedsheet, and that this status increased her relative vulnerability in their eyes, as did the fact that Nurse Claire was armed and Roerich a man. All these things played their part.

A fight is as much decided by the attitudes of the respective parties before a blow has landed as by such matters as strength and training. Overconfidence is a worse handicap than physical weakness.

With her left hand Alma snatched a fistful of Roerich's hair, and hauled downwards with as much strength as her muscles possessed. With her right she intercepted the nurse's arm as she swung the stun-stick towards her. She grabbed Claire's wrist.

With Alma's unexpected shove, Claire's stun-stick went into the doctor's face. He let out a sort of flapping-lipped squeal, like an overinflated thing being punctured. Claire's facial expression just had time to shift from self-satisfaction to surprised anger when Alma punched her on the nose.

The nurse reeled away, leaving a thread of red twisting round and down in mid-air. As this spattered tinnily onto the hospital floor Roerich had already tumbled, stiff-limbed, down and out. Alma hopped off the bed. Claire, angry now, wearing a Hitler-moustache of blood, was coming straight at her, brandishing the stun-stick.

Alma threw the bedsheet over the nurse's head, sidestepped and dropped to pick up the hand-scanner from Roerich's helpless grip. Then, on the rise, she swung it as hard as she could. Claire was just untangling herself from the sheet when the hand-scanner connected meatily with the back of her head. There was an audible thump, and she went straight down. Alma felt the first uncertainty – it's easier than you think to kill someone outright by striking the back of their head with a heavy instrument. Worse – Claire, falling, twanged her forehead on the frame of the bed just below the mattress, said 'ouf' very distinctly and slapped down next to her comrade.

The motion had made the pains in her gut worse. They felt like trapped wind. Alma had to assume they were nothing to do with trapped wind.

Claire, supine, was still breathing. Alma took the sheet back, picked up the stun-stick and tried to apply it to the back of the nurse's neck, to ensure her unconsciousness. But it wouldn't work: the device probably had a thumbprint ID, or something like that. Ah well. Alma pulled Claire's jacket down and tied a knot in it, to immobilise her arms. It wouldn't hold her for ever, but it was something.

The door, it transpired, was not locked. Thank heavens for that.

Alma padded down the corridor outside wearing her thin bed-sheet like a cape, and nothing else. There were no other people. Of course the hospital itself saw her: her offswitched feed pinged and pinged again with messages from the AI that ran the place. She ignored them.

She trotted into the main atrium; the automatic receptionist called to her. 'Madame! Madame! Please return to your room!'

'I am discharging myself,' she called back, and broke into a sprint, heading for the main entrance.

A doctorbot trundled swiftly in from the side, blocking her exit. It was singing the same tune as the receptionist – the hospital AI speaking though both mouthpieces: 'Madame! Madame! Please return to your room!'

'I am auto-discharging,' she said.

'Our duty of care is legally mandated, and prevents us from allowing patients to leave unless they have been officially discharged. You cannot discharge yourself, since you lack medical expertise.'

Alma took a guess, based on what Claire and the bouffant-haired Dr Roerich were up to. 'I was never officially admitted,' she said.

The doctorbot looked her up and down. 'You are in a hospital. You are in a state of undress. You have some form of abdominal bloating and intestine-wall inflammation. You are sick and require treatment. Our prime directive requires us to make you well.'

'But,' Alma pressed, 'I was never *officially* admitted. So, legally, I do not need to be officially discharged, and am free to leave.'

The doctorbot pondered this. 'Please admit yourself for treatment,' it said.

With a flourish Alma threw the sheet around the bot's 'head', and tied a rough knot. The machine's probes, not designed to unpick knots in cloth, pawed at this hood, and Alma slipped past, through the door and out into the daylight.

10: *Lez the Mis*

Naked as the day she was born, give or take that small proportion of her body covered by hair, Alma jogged into town. It was a relief to be able to use her legs again, however bloated and sore her stomach felt.

Of course she couldn't risk onswitching her feed. She'd already used up the genie that might have enabled her to call a cab. She couldn't do anything that might draw the authorities' attention to her. Other, that was, than walking nude through her hometown. But it was late morning, and nobody was around, except for a few bolder in-Shine individuals, plodding up and down in their mesh-suits, none of whom were conscious of any aspect of the world around them, naked Alma included.

She came up along the river, past the old statue of whoever-that-was and through what had been, long ago, an open-air multi-forum shopping emporium, but was now all servers and storage. The sky was the colour of buttermilk. Two actual people were sitting, arm in arm, legs over the wall, looking at the swans on the river. Alma ducked into the dusty entrance of an unused building, and peered round the corner; but the two were interested in only one another, and didn't notice the naked woman jogging past them.

The River Kennet, confined by its concrete banks, was rainforest green in colour and its surface was flat as lino. Naked Alma ran alongside it for a while, and climbed steps to a road. Away to her left the old Blade towerblock raised its rhino horn at an indifferent sky. Sunlight sparkled grey off the dust coating every one of the building's hundreds of windows.

The strange thing was how quickly her self-consciousness disappeared. The main thing about walking naked was needing to keep her attention on the ground in front of her feet, to ensure she didn't step on broken glass or in anything noisome – and actually the streets, swept by council bots, were remarkably clean. Otherwise the fresh spring air felt pleasant on her skin, and a strange sense of liberation took hold of her. Only the occasional twinges in her gut brought her back to herself.

She ducked into a disused shop doorway as a car swished past – its occupants either saw her, and were astonished, or were so absorbed in their own feeds they didn't notice her, but either way they didn't stop. Then she crossed the road. There were drones, of course, buzzing about. Alma wondered about what their mini-AIs were making of her. Could they tell that she was naked, as opposed to wearing some tight-fitting skin-coloured outfit? Did anybody even *enforce* the old indecent exposure laws? In the summertime, Alma often saw in-Shine people wearing nothing under their mesh other than underwear.

At any rate, the drones didn't sweep down to serve her with any kind of notice, and Alma had more pressing things to worry about. She turned left, padded down a sidestreet, past another mesh-moved in-Shine body, and finally reached the coffee shop Lez had specified. She was a little out of breath. COFFEE-FI-FO-FUM said the 3-D sign, leaning out into the street with bubbles pouring endlessly up its dark brown letters. GIANT TASTE GREAT VALUE.

Inside was low-ceilinged, dark, and possessed a musty, varnishy, coal-y odour, not unpleasant to the nose. There were a dozen tables, all deserted save for the one furthest from the door, at which two people were sitting. One of these people was Lez, the other a stranger to Alma. This latter averted her eyes as Alma walked over. Lez, however, did not.

'You weren't joking,' croaked Lez, smiling an evil smile. 'Bare as a babby. Not even a bedsheet.'

'I had to use the sheet to distract a bot,' she said.

Lez held out a long tailored jacket at arm's length. In a moment Alma had wriggled into it. The fabric was a little sandy against her skin, but with the third party present she was glad to be able to cover up. Not that her own nakedness embarrassed her, exactly. It was more that this other individual's embarrassment on her behalf embarrassed her.

'You're offswitched,' Lez said. 'Good. This is Mary Midas.'

'That's an unusual name,' said Alma.

'Thank you,' said Mary Midas, beaming.

'Alright then,' said Alma, sitting and trying to calm her breathing.

'Since our feeds can't shake hands at the moment,' Mary Midas said, 'maybe we should do it in person?'

Alma tried to conceal her dismay. 'Alright,' she said, and held out her hand.

Mary Midas's hand was dry as parchment. Alma was conscious of her own slightly moist palm. The other woman was wrapped in several layers, despite the mildness of the day's weather. There were lines on her face, not quite in the right place to be natural wrinkles, but not silvered or pronounced enough to be scars. Her mouth kept slipping into a little smile, and her eyes kept drifting to the right, before locking back on Alma.

'Mary,' said Lez, 'is the person you want to talk to about teleportation.'

'Lez tells me things,' Mary said. 'He tells me you two go back. Way back, he says. I'll be honest, Ms Alma, I don't trust easily.' There was something a little off about her accent. Hard to place.

'I hope you'll trust me at least enough to talk to me.' She winced. The pain kept stabbing at her lower gut.

'You alright?' Lez asked.

'It's been quite a day,' she replied. 'I was in hospital, and injected with something – nanobiots, they said. Sealed up a wound I had in my thigh, but they seem to be having side-effects.'

Mary Midas shuffled along her bench, putting a little more distance between her and Alma. 'Side-effects?'

'Nothing contagious, I think. A little gut-ache.' She didn't add that the nurse, Claire, and the hair-sculpted doctor guy Roerich had promised her she'd be dead by midnight.

A plastic waiter trundled up with drinks for Lez and Mary Midas. Alma ordered a coffee.

'Nanobiots, eh?' Mary Midas said, taking a glass of clear water from the waiter and putting it on the table in front of her. 'Some pretty big medical research money has gotten lost in *that* project. They just can't seem to make it work.'

'You're telling me,' said Alma, pressing a fist into her bulging gut.

'One problem is that alcohol knocks them out. Which is an issue, because people like drinking alcohol. Most people, not me.'

'No kidding?'

'Another problem is that if nanobiots from any *other* part of the body get into the gut, they will try and heal it up, which tends to kill the patient.'

'Oh dear,' said Alma, deadpan.

Mary Midas had taken a thin metal rod from her coat pocket – some kind of testing device, or perhaps a thermometer – and was dipping it in the water. Whatever the rod told her appeared satisfactory. She replaced the rod and brought out a small flask from which she poured a colourless liquid into the glass of water.

'I think of myself as cautious,' she said, meeting Alma's gaze. 'People call me paranoid. It seems to me caution and paranoia must be synonyms in any sensible thesaurus. Whereabouts in your gut?'

'The bloating?' Alma opened the jacket a little to show her.

'Too low down for drinking ethanol to do you any good. You'd have metabolised the alcohol by then. You could try an enema, but an alcohol enema is going to hurt like buggery.' She smiled at this, as if she had made a witticism. 'Not that I could guarantee that a syringe of vodka would even blaze-out the nanites. It would sure bleach your intestines, which would be uncomfortable, but survivable. But you need to blitz them all.'

'They injected a countermeasure, I think,' said Alma. 'Maybe that'll be effective?'

'Oh, trust someone *else* with your safety, why don't you? If they're testing nanobiots on live subjects then they're breaking the law. Evidently they have no scruples as to whether you live or die.'

'I don't know where I'm going to pick up a syringe,' said Alma, flinching as her gut spasmed.

Mary Midas reached into her satchel and brought out a plastic-wrapped syringe. It was an old-fashioned metal-needle type.

'Really?' Alma asked.

'You'd have to rinse the raw spirit directly into your intestine. You couldn't pressure-inject it.'

Lez, watching this exchange with characteristically lugubrious pleasure, messaged the waiter with an order for a half-bottle of vodka. The machine trundled over with the drink.

'This is costing *me*, obviously,' Lez said, 'and that doesn't give me any pleasure. I know, I know, you can't pay for anything without onswitching your feed, and once you do that the police will know exactly where you are and come get you. Don't worry.'

For now, don't worry. I have two consolations. One is that you're going to pay me back for everything plus twenty per cent.'

'*Twenty* per cent?'

'Feedless must be chooseless,' Lez chuckled. 'And the second consolation is that – this is going to hurt.'

'Cheers,' said Alma. She poured a little vodka into the palm of her hand and rubbed it over the distended skin of her belly. Then she tore the syringe from its packaging and filled it with the transparent fluid. 'Do you always carry old-school syringes around with you?' she asked Mary Midas.

'You'd be amazed what I have in my satchel,' Mary replied.

Alma tried to brace herself, but the thought of a metal needle penetrating her skin was a genuinely offputting one. 'Would you inject it, if I look away?' she asked. 'I'm not sure I can do it.'

'No dice,' said Mary.

A shake of the grinning head from Lez.

'Good to know who my friends are,' Alma said. With her left hand she raised the vodka pichet and took a swig. Then, with her right, she pushed the needle through and home. It stung, but not as badly as she anticipated. A moment's adjustment to make sure the end of the needle was in the inward gaseous cavity, and she squeezed the plunger.

She took a second swig of the vodka and pulled the needle free. A bead of blood swelled on her belly, like the eye of a bird. Miniature rectangles of illumination curved round its globe, reflections from the ceiling lights.

'So far so good,' she said.

'How long you got, anyway?' Lez asked.

'Lez explained to me your,' Mary said, 'time constraints, with respect to the unlucky situation of your partner. I would advise you to shuck off the responsibility for caring for this individual, this Marguerite. Pass over to somebody else, perhaps. Better by far to have no external obligations or attachments. Better for you. Such things make one weak.'

'You're the second person today to tell me that,' said Alma. 'And to answer your question, Lez, I've got an hour and forty minutes. Including the fifteen I'll need to get back to the flat.'

'Then we'd better hurry up.'

'Talking of which,' Alma tried, 'is there anything you can give me that will – *distract* a police myrmidrone? Just for a few minutes? There's one guarding the door to our apartment, and I need to get past it to get inside and treat Marguerite.'

Lez laughed an isn't-the-misery-of-the-human-condition-comical laugh. Then he said: 'Dear me, no.'

'Nothing?'

'What – hack a police drone? Even if I had such a genie, the Peelers would come down on whoever used it like a metric tonne of bricks. And there would be a distinct chance that they'd find a way back from you to me.'

'I need leverage,' said Alma. There was a distant burning sensation in her abdomen, but the swelling did at least seem to have diminished a little. 'Something I can use with the powers that be.'

'Like the identity of the individual who murdered Adam Kem?'

'Exactly.'

'It doesn't strike you as likely,' Lez said, 'that the authorities already *know* who killed Adam Kem? That they're rather more interested in keeping it quiet than in having a licensed private investigator dig it out?'

'If so, good,' said Alma, scowling at the growing ache in her gut. 'Good. *Provided* I can figure it out, I can cache the information in such a way that it will be released across the Shine, should anything happen to me – or' – a quick look at Mary Midas – 'to Marguerite.'

'Poor old Adam Kem,' said Mary.

'You speak like someone who knew him.'

'Well the reason for that is that I did know him. A little. We weren't close, but I had met him. I don't know who killed him.'

This was news. 'What was he?' Alma asked.

'He was,' said Mary Midas, rubbing antibacterial gel into her hands, 'what we call an Intermediator. Fifteen years ago Intermediators were pretty powerful players in the game of government. Less so today. The balance of power has shifted, and all in one direction. But still, princes and princesses of the universe, such folk. Bestriding modern governance like a colossus.'

'A government man.'

'A government man, and now a dead man.'

'Intermediate between?'

'Government. It's all government and only government and what else?'

'Between,' Alma asked, 'which two branches of government?'

'The only two that matter. Come along, Ms Alma. Lez told me you were smart.'

'Got a hurty tummy,' said Alma, pulling a face. Sharp but intermittent pangs and cramps were palpable in her gut. Maybe that meant the nanobiots were dying off. 'But I assume you mean, the Real and the Shine.'

'*Some* of the energy of government is directed to keeping the real world orderly, maximising the economy, syphoning off money via taxes, consolidating power – all the things government has traditionally done for thousands of years. But for a long time now the serious money, and therefore the serious power, is all in the Shine, not in this real world. And that means that those departments – plural now, you'll note – that deal with the Shine have become increasingly powerful. I find it best to think of government as an entity. Not a very clever one, nor a very merciful one, and certainly not a very well-coordinated one. More like a mobile termite's nest than a panther. But in this case, each termite is *very* clever and very self-motivated, and together they can do great things. Well, Termite Nest Real has been shrinking and losing influence, and Termite Nest Shine has been growing and gaining influence.'

'And Adam Kem's business was liaising between them?'

Mary snickered. 'A great many people are involved in *that* business, my friend. Adam Kem was only one of the more prominent figures.'

'And that is why he was killed?'

'Who knows *why* he was killed?' Mary Midas drawled, finishing her drink of water, and then carefully wiping her fingerprints off the glass. 'Understand this, my small-statured friend. There is war in heaven. The great and the good are on the verge of all-out *krieg*. Bombs, shootings, coups, imprisonments, the whole pack and parcel. The situation, in government, has hovered on the edge of that for a long time. I don't know why Kem was killed, but I'd bet you a franc to a pfennig it was something to do with that.'

'A what to a what?'

'Keep forgetting,' Mary said, putting her wiping cloth away in her satchel, 'that you're off-feed.'

'The motive is the key, though, isn't it?' Lez put in. 'Isolate the motive and you're two steps closer to solving this.'

'The motive was something,' said Alma, grimacing at the pains

100

in her gut, 'to do with teleportation. Mary: Lez tells me that you know about that.'

Mary was silent for a little while. 'It's almost too crude, don't you think?' she said, shortly. 'Whoever *put* that body in that particular place. They were showing off. It was a nasty thing to do. Show-offs are always nasty people, and the sort of show-off who would play with a human corpse like that must be the worst of their kind. Yes, my dear, yes. Teleportation. How else, after all, could that body have made its way into that particular locked room? *Is* there another way?'

'If there is another way,' Lez interjected, with a belch, 'I can't see it.'

'It's clear enough,' said Alma, keen to show that she wasn't wholly clueless, 'that the invention of proper teleportation technology would wholly alter the balance of power. It would draw people back to the real world, wouldn't it? It would make the real-world economy more viable.'

'Restart the exploration of space,' Lez put in, in a gloomy voice. 'Humanity could finally leave its cradle.'

'I can see how people in positions of power might want to further, or block, that sort of thing.'

'Well surely,' said Mary, simpering. '*If* it worked. But it doesn't.'

'It doesn't?'

'Not in the least, not at all.'

'A shame, if true,' drawled Lez. 'Otherwise we could take you to a transporter and beam you directly past that myrmidrone into Marguerite's bedroom.'

'It's my bedroom too,' Alma returned, annoyed at how much her heart leapt up at this illusory prospect. How easy that would make her life! Not just right now, but into the foreseeable.

'Come now, Alma,' said Lez. 'There hasn't been room for you to sleep in there too for ... a while.'

'*Qué lástima,*' said Mary, drily.

'That would be handy, though, wouldn't it? Teleportation?' Lez said. 'For all of us. My trusty friend Mary, here, could be assured that the police could never apprehend her. She could also stay one step ahead of the authorities. And you, Alma, would be able to pop back to your beloved from anywhere around the world. And I could go to the moon. Or Mars! I've always fancied Mars. Nice and quiet.'

'Cold, though,' Mary noted.

'The cold never bothered me,' Lez said, truthfully.

'When you say teleportation is not a real thing,' Alma suggested. 'What you mean is transporters haven't worked in the past. Haven't yet been *made* to work. But everything here points to the fact that somebody, somewhere has been able to get them working now.'

'You misunderstand,' said Mary. She was packing her stuff away, and was clearly on the verge of leaving. 'I'm not suggesting there are a few teething problems that need ironing out. Not that. Look, by way of comparison, let's say – nanobiots. Alright? How's your gut?'

'Aches, some,' said Alma.

'Sure. They've been working on *that* technology, off and on, for decades. There are glitches and problems, sure, but the underlying idea is a good one. And sooner or later they'll make it work, and it will be a medical boon and a blessing to men and women everywhere. With nanobiots the problem is the complexity of the environment we want them to work in, the human body, the difficulty in programming them to react to the constantly changing surroundings. So they fix cancer, but then start killing healthy cells. Or they heal up wounds and then go on to heal up the sorts of cavities that you don't want healing. Teething difficulties. But soon enough the clever people will solve those problems. And then the in-Shine won't need to lumber about in mesh-suits; their bodily well-being will be maintained in-house, as it were. We won't get sick, or get old and ugly. Marvellous prospects. But – and this is key. But. Teleportation is not like that.'

'Might I just establish for my own satisfaction,' Alma asked, 'the grounds of your expertise in this matter?'

Mary looked at her, and burst into laughter. 'My dear! Please don't take what I have to say as *gospel*. Look into it yourself, by all means, by all means, though that's going to be hard without access to your feed. The grounds of my expertise! That's terribly good.' Another laugh, like a quick double-time on a high-hat. Even Lez was smiling, and Lez almost never smiled. Alma felt the annoyance of not being in on a joke.

'Is it an energy question?' she tried.

'No, no, no. Energy can usually be sorted. It may make things expensive, but that's usually not fatal to any given technology. No, the problems are in the transfer.'

'Man-hating transfer,' said Lez, for some reason.

'Think about it. It won't take you more than thirty seconds,' said Mary. 'You weigh, what, fifty kilos?'

'This takes me back to my time as the prize in a fairground guess-my-weight competition.'

Mary waved her hand at this, and said: 'Air weighs about one and a quarter kilos per square metre. So let's say we transport you to some other place – to the bedroom of your companion, say, since that is where you're most desirous of going. So! There are two possibilities. One is that we simply smash your fifty kilos into that space, displacing an equivalent mass of air instantaneously. You'd arrive like a bomb. Literally like a bomb: it would blow the whole building apart. And, depending on which theory of instant transportation you subscribe to – because it *is* just theory, at the moment – you'd either simply shunt that much air aside, or else your reassembling molecules would fuse with the molecules of air. In the former case your arrival would be like TNT. But in the latter case, you'd have something much bigger on your hands: something nuclear. Big enough to blow R!-town itself into nothingness.'

'The logical thing to do,' said Alma, who had nothing if not a logical mind, 'would be to double-back the procedure. Transport your fifty-kilo person to location A, and at the same time transport fifty kilos of air back to the starting point. But,' she added, seeing the problem. 'Wait a moment . . .'

'Fifty kilos of air takes up much, much more space than fifty kilos of human. The room you arrived inside would be a vacuum, and you'd run the risk, conversely, of exploding your starting place. A rather destructive way of proceeding.'

'You're telling me there can't be a workaround? Let's say I agree with you, and a person can't teleport into an enclosed space. That just means you have to aim for somewhere outdoors.'

'Oh, there might be a workaround, for solid matter. True, fifty kilos of metal in a solid lump could, hypothetically, be swapped in a teleportation exchange with fifty kilos of air – and if you were outside, the result would be a great deal of sudden air movement, winds blowing in or blowing out. Or you could construct two enormous vacuum chambers, and transport matter from one to the other. Although if transported matter were liable to fuse with matter at the other end, then even a few molecules of air would result in catastrophic explosions. So an improbably pure vacuum. But all that is irrelevant, because a human being is most definitely *not* a solid lump of matter. A human being is a complex tessellation of tissue and cavity, bone and tendon and muscle and mucus. So we go back to the prior example. You want to get, quickly, to your partner. You can't teleport inside her room, so instead you teleport to a place outside the house, fair enough. You displace the air that was there – assuming you don't turn into a fusion bomb. Some of the air you displace goes outward, blows away in the wind, and makes a loud clap, and alerts the world to your arrival, like a sonic boom. But *some* of the air you displace goes inward, into your lungs and stomach and the little vesicles in the bone of your sinuses. And that means your lungs turn to mush, and your sinuses crack open.'

Alma looked at her. 'Lungs turned to mush,' she said.

Mary stood up. 'I have to go.'

'That,' says Lez, stretching his arms and legs, 'means our drone is coming.'

'Our drone?'

'You wanted some clothes, yes? I bought you some clothes. You'll pay me back plus a generous addition when you get your life back in whack. 'Til then, well, there's an Amazon drone buzzing over here with some attire. But Mary, here, has a dislike for drones. So much so that she runs an app that alerts her to the approach of any such.'

'They're like spiders,' Mary said.

'You mean, poisonous?'

'No. I mean they're more scared of *me* than I am of *them*,' said Mary Midas. 'Or they *should* be. Goodbye, Lez. And to you too, my half-naked detective.'

Mary Midas went out through the back of the building. Alma pulled the jacket more tightly around her. 'Lez,' she said. 'The victim, Adam Kem, was discovered – in that impossible place – with his lungs turned to mush.'

'You,' said Lez, 'don't say. That fact wasn't in the news reports.'

'All the things she said, your friend Mary. She was offering that as reasons why teleportation could never be a thing. But what if we've got it the wrong way around?'

'Which way around ought we to have gotten it?'

'Maybe the point of teleportation is not to make life easier for the real world. Maybe it's not about tempting people back out of the Shine, not about facilitating instantaneous travel. Maybe it's precisely a *weapon*. All the things Mary listed as bugs would be features. To a certain kind of mind.'

'A government mind,' Lez said, sadly. 'A military mind.'

'You could beam away a whole enemy army, killing them in the process. One minute they're a thousand men charging over the battlefield at you, the next they're instantly in some other place with their internal vesicles mashed and mushed, their lungs slurry. Dead. You could beam bullets straight into people's heads. You could beam prisoners of war directly into your enemy generals' bunker and kill the whole lot. The possibilities are...'

'...ruthless,' agreed Lez. 'They are.'

'Lez,' urged Alma. 'I need something – I need a bargaining chip. If they want me to leave things alone, I'm happy to do that. Really, I don't care who killed Adam Kem, or who bumped off Michelangela either. I'm happy to leave well alone. But it's clear the powers that be don't believe that. So I need something to force their hand.'

'Good luck with that,' said Lez.

'I need your help.'

'You've had it,' said Lez the Mis, standing up. 'Sister, I like you. And Marguerite has always had a special place in my heart, that crazy genius. But, my dear, don't presume upon our friendship so far as to think that I'll risk my life.'

'Your miserable life,' Alma pointed out.

'Precisely as miserable as existence requires, exactly the same as everybody else, and therefore,' said Lez, 'exactly as worth preserving. Your drone is here, and I'm off.' And he stepped smartly away and out the back, the same way Mary had gone.

Alma went to the front door and, as Lez had promised, found an Amazon delivery drove with a pendant plastic sack. Lez had evidently authorised her collection before leaving, so the drone released its cargo and buzzed up and away.

Inside the pack: grid-creased and fresh-smelling new clothes. There was nobody else inside the coffee shop, but Alma still went through to the female toilets in order to change.

11: *Aperiō*

Alma walked up Bridge Street in the sunshine, her new clothes crepitating faintly with her movements. As well as stuff to wear, Lez had ordered her a *watch* – an old-style digital wrist-worn timepiece. Perhaps it had been assembled in some factory, like the McA facility: lovingly assembled according to the time-honoured and traditional manufacturing routines. More likely it had been extruded along with ten thousand others from an industrial 3D printer. But possessing it meant Alma could keep a track on how long remained before Marguerite's treatment became due, without having to onswitch her feed and in so doing alert the authorities as to her location.

She had time. She strode west.

Speckled panes of glass in every building. Some sidestreets were covered by uneven white-orange mats of compacted plastic bags, friable as old parchment – marking the place, these, where the land was technically private property and council cleaningbots did not venture. Pigeons curled into pebble shapes on the roofing. Clouds scrolled through skies as blue as the blue screen of death.

There was nobody about at all, and then Alma turned into Oxford Road and suddenly there was a mob of people – mostly awake, with a few in-Shine sleepers following the procession in mesh-suits. Her feed would have told her what the procession was, if it hadn't been offswitched. Lacking that info, it was a shock to see so many people gathered together in the open. Really a very large crowd, maybe as many as two dozen. They were in a loose line two or three abreast, walking slowly in the direction of Broad Street. And they were humming. Several met Alma's gaze and smiled at her. The ones at the front were scattering yellow petals – rose, were they? – and many such petals lay about the pavement like woodshavings. A woman near the back held out her hands towards Alma, welcoming her in. Some were wearing crosses round their necks, but two had Stars of David and one an Ankh. Something religious, presumably. Something cultic.

They passed by and Alma continued on her way, alone.

Over the dual carriageway, mostly empty save for the occasional speeding car. Down the other side to the corner of Eaton Place. A seagull flew overhead and away, yawping like a car alarm. A long way from the sea, that one.

Mostly she wanted to run – sprint like an athlete – straight home and be with Marguerite again. But she choked down that impulse. There was a police myrmidrone guarding her door; she needed to figure out how to get past it. She needed to figure that out, or Marguerite would die. She needed to think. And there wasn't much time.

It was a problem with two horns. The first, sharp but short, was: how do I get into the apartment right now? How could she distract, or disable, the drone guarding her door? But the second horn was just as sharp, and quite a bit longer: what about the next time? And the time after that? She needed more than a makeshift solution. She needed to strike a deal with the powers that be.

To do that she needed leverage. Something. Information. She needed to understand what was going on.

She oriented herself, mentally, in the city as she walked, and thought back to OTC. It was on her way anyway, she told herself. Since it was on her way, she might as well take a look.

Because Ordinary Transport Consultancy traded in the real world, and employed real-world human people, it was required by law to maintain real-world premises. Alma couldn't check all the specific details of this place without onswitching, but she happened to remember the address from when she had been researching the case, and so she knew it was on her way.

Young Hunter-Colo and his strangely vanishing stomach contents. Had his not-entirely-legal bosses really insisted he wear some sort of (she still couldn't believe she was thinking this) miniature teleportation device, nestling around his pyloric sphincter? Obey us, or starve? Maybe everything Mary Midas had said about transporters *was* correct. Maybe transporting something damaged the transported thing. But that wouldn't matter in this case. It seemed a bizarrely ornate way of keeping your goons under the thumb, but maybe its ornateness was the point. Maybe ostentatiously flourishing teleportation tech – compelling your people literally to swallow it, to internalise it – sent a particular sort of message. A way of ensuring more than regular loyalty.

At any rate, she had an hour before she had to find a way of getting back inside her flat to attend to Marguerite. A plump, elderly man wearing a grey felt hat walked briskly past, not stopping. Maybe he was a latecomer to the religious parade. A fly was measuring the diagonal of an empty office ground-floor window with its feet. It wasn't clear to Alma whether the fly was inside the building or outside. A drone made a meditative om-sound, somewhere to the east.

She was here. There was no sign on the door, but this shabby building must be it. The main entrance was housed inside a curving glassplex annex, protruding onto the pavement like a gigantic cheek turned to be kissed.

Alma stepped inside.

Regulations for companies like the OTC required at least a 51 per cent human shareholding and a quota of human beings on staff in full-time posts. Despite such legal requirements the only entity inside the small hall was artificial. 'Can I help you, madam?' the automaton asked.

'I'm making enquiries with respect to the Ordinary Transport Consultancy,' Alma said. 'Please put me in touch with a human employee.'

'This facility has one full-time human member of staff, but I'm sorry to say that she has popped out for lunch.'

'When will she return?'

'She is entitled to a lunch break, under employment law,' said the machine. It was a preprogrammed automated system, not an AI, and so was perfectly capable of lying. Which, clearly, it was now doing. There were no human beings on site, and in the unlikely event of an inspection the machine was programmed to say what it had just said.

'Never mind,' said Alma. 'Perhaps you can assist me. I understand Lester Hunter-Colo works for your company?'

'Your feed appears to be offswitched,' said the receptionist. 'Might I assist you in switching it back on? Then I can push the relevant company documentation and podscrip over to you.'

This would be a standard package of advertising bumf and propaganda. Not that Alma had any intention of booting up her feed.

'My feed is currently being serviced and repaired,' Alma tried. 'I order you to show me the taxation and official records for this company.' With low-function or limited IQ machines it was often possible to impose upon them simply by virtue of one's humanity. But this receptionist-machine wasn't buying it.

'With your feed down, how will you be able to show me the necessary authorisation?'

'My authorisation is verbal.'

'You are a human being,' said the machine. 'Human beings occasionally lie.'

'You are not an AI,' Alma returned, 'and therefore need not always tell the truth.'

The receptionist paused. 'If you give me your details,' it said shortly, 'I can arrange to have any relevant company documentation and podscrip pending in your feed for later perusal.'

'You firm is called the Ordinary Transport Consultancy,' said Alma. 'Is the nature of your business the transportation of physical quantities? For example, passengers, or freight, or something like that?'

'Relevant company documentation and answer any question to podscrip pending in your legally permitted break for lunch,' said the receptionist. It had been prodded into a less secure margin of its response algorithm.

'Furious green ideas?' Alma asked.

'Profitability supersedes itself in a company atmosphere of positivity and,' said the receptionist, smiling.

'Realising that nothing changes,' Alma tried, 'change everything.'

'Happy to leverage all options and drill down to the next level.'

'Let me ask you a direct question: are you, in fact, not the Ordinary, but rather the Extraordinary Transport Consultancy?'

'Thank you for your input,' beamed the receptionist.

'Teleportation?' Alma tried. 'Instant transportation devices?'

'No comment,' the receptionist replied, rather too rapidly, and shut down.

Alma tried a door, hoping to gain access to the innards of the office block, but it was of course locked. She had a lockpick genie in her feed which might (or might not) have been able to open it, but, again, she shouldn't fire up her feed in here, even in safe mode. Never mind the automaton on the front desk: there would be a building AI, clever as a demon, watching her even now, and if she tried anything it would surely pounce.

Alma made her way back into town and over the river. She had forty minutes before she needed to tend to Marguerite, but she had yet to work out a way of getting past the police myrmidrone. Could she persuade the machine that she was the new police nurse? It had let her in once before, and myrmidrones had top-end reactive algorithms rather than full AI. But then again, she had to assume *all* her details had been circulated throughout the police net by now. The drone would surely recognise her. It was even possible that actual human police had been stationed at the flat.

So what was plan B? What if she *were* arrested? What if Colonel Mastema came after her? Did she have any leverage? With what could she bargain? Something was going on with teleportation, but she didn't know what exactly. Involvement in whatever it was likely linked the highest levels of government and lowly border-line criminal gangs like the OTC. The murder of Adam Kem, or more particularly the ostentatious way in which his corpse had been disposed of, was some kind of signal from one party to another – but a signal saying what?

It was thin stuff. She had better think of something.

The pain in her gut was still pulsingly present. Conceivably injecting that vodka had failed to stop the spread of the nanbiots. So she'd probably be dead by midnight anyway.

One thing at a time, she told herself.

Four dogs ran up the middle of Kendrick Road, the back two snapping at the tails of the front two. Two walkers, deep in-Shine, trundled towards town, sunlight glinting off their mesh.

A little way ahead, despite the absence of rain, stood a figure with an open umbrella.

Alma came closer. It was Derp Throat.

'Your Mary Poppins cosplay needs work,' she told him.

'Say what?'

He was wearing long pants across the pale fabric of which weird black blobs flowed, glommed together, separated, in a Rorschach-balance of left and right leg. His shirt was illustrated with a huge yellow circle containing two vertically elongated eye-dots and a big U smiling mouth. For some reason that Alma did not understand, and which (feedless) she could not check, the left eye was bisected by an ungainly linear splash of red, as if tomato ketchup had been squirted NNW across the disc.

'Why won't you believe me,' he replied, petulant, 'when I say I know how things operate? This is the least of it. In the centre of town aerial, satellite and drone surveillance gets augmented by streetcams. Out here it's just the aerial stuff. A simple umbrella can be surprisingly effective at baffling recognition.'

'Ella ella ella, eh eh,' said Alma.

'What's that?'

'Nothing.' Alma was assessing his usefulness. She desperately needed to get inside the flat. How could she use Derp Throat to achieve that?

'I tried to get in touch,' Derp was saying. 'But you have off-switched your feed.'

'Things have gotten,' Alma conceded, 'sticky.'

'I had to speak with you, though, so I figured you'd come back here. But the thing is, if I can figure that out, then so can the police. You can't keep coming back here.'

'If I don't come back here every four hours, Marguerite will die.'

'So move her.'

'She is not small. And I would need to move her and her medical necessities. Given the number of kilos involved in such a move I really don't think that's viable. We'd have to take the side of the building out, just to get her down to the ground.'

'Oh,' said Derp.

'I still need to get inside,' said Alma, wincing at the pain in her abdomen. 'Can you help me?'

'That's not why I'm here.'

Alma said nothing. Derp blushed. His good eye joined his wonky eye in not meeting her gaze. 'I'm here to talk,' he said.

'Then let's have that conversation.' Alma slid a little closer, just to bring herself under the outer of edge of Derp's umbrella. 'But just so as you know, you are going to help me. The phrase a matter of life and death gets overused, but in this case it's the simple and literal truth.'

Now that she saw him again, he was a better-looking individual than he had first appeared. That doubtless had something to do with the fact that she had been out of her feed for so many consecutive hours now. Her vision was starting to normalise.

'I checked *derp*, by the way,' said Derp. 'The definition.'

'You did?'

'Yeah.'

'Sorry about that, Punchy. And sorry – you know. For calling you Punchy.'

'None of that really matters any more,' said Derp. 'Things have changed since our last meeting. My position inside the organisation isn't, what's the word...?'

'Enjoyable?'

'Not that. I mean, it's true that it's *not* especially enjoyable, it's never been enjoyable. Although it was, you know, work.' He put a hand in front of his eyes, and sighed. Then dropped the hand, breathed in and said: 'Tenable. That's the word. My position inside the organisation is no longer tenable.'

'You're leaving?'

'Alma – can I call you Alma?' Alma said nothing. 'Alma, I've pushed a ton of stuff at your feed. I know you're offswitched at the moment, and obviously I get why you are. But it's waiting there, on your porch. For when you're able to onswitch again. There's a lot of stuff, too much to spiel out in words here and now, a bunch of secret stuff to which I've been privy. They're scared, Alma.'

'"They"?'

'Come on, Alma.'

'Scared of what?'

'Well, of a number of very serious things. But one of the things they're scared of is: you.'

'I can't harm *them*,' Alma said, startled. 'What could I possibly do? I'm a nobody. I have no resources. If I so much as activate my feed again, law enforcement would descend upon me from the bright air.'

'That's true, of course,' said Derp.

'Plus, your original point still holds – Marguerite is my Achilles heel. I'm locked into a four-hour routine. Which makes me weak.'

'You're underselling yourself.'

'I'm not selling myself at all. I'm not selling to anyone. What I've been holding on to is the notion that I'm not worth killing – I'm too easy to lean on. Pressure me and I'll fold, because: Marguerite. But—' and here Alma's gut moaned like a soul in pain, and a pang passed across her abdomen. She winced.

'But once Marguerite is taken out of the picture,' Derp Throat said. 'Then you are a free agent. Think how fearsome you could then become!'

'For *fearsome*,' said Alma, 'read *assassinable*.'

'That too. But remember, I've been *inside*, I've been in a privileged position. I've watched what's happened since they took out Michelangela.'

'And when you say "they"...?'

'Jesus, Alma, one thing at a time. All the detail is in the stuff I've pushed at your feed. It's waiting there for when you next boot up.'

'You're describing a conspiracy. High-level.'

'*Highest*-level. People at the highest level. People who know what you're capable of. Imagine, for a moment, that Marguerite died. You'd be grief-stricken, I know. You'd want payback. And who would you blame? What kind of revenge would you pursue? But since we're thought-experimenting, work it out right here. Take the next step in imagining who might be interested in orchestrating that kind of a scenario.'

But this didn't add up. Something wasn't right. Even with her aching gut Alma had the intuition that Derp wasn't telling her the whole story. She decided to confront him, here, under his umbrella. 'A pretty flimsy story, Punchy. Really. For one thing it's about a different person than me. I'm no threat to the highest powers. I'm a law-abiding small-town detective.'

'Right,' said Derp. 'Sure. *Somebody* has been making the necessary moves to prevent you from getting back to your partner, knowing full well that doing so will result in her death. You want to consider why that's even worth an operative's time?'

'Talking of which,' said Alma, her gut roiling with the nanobiots, or else with an access of panic. 'I need to get inside in the next quarter of an hour. That's the only thing that matters right now. The rest can wait. *After* I get in, hey, why don't you and I have a sit down and a drink and talk all this through?'

'Not I. I'm *out* of here, lady. I'm not hanging around. I've prepared an escape route, and now I've activated it. When I saw...' But he stopped.

Alma waited. But, no, she couldn't wait, because time was starting to nag her. Fourteen minutes. 'When you saw what?'

He was thinking what to say. Weighing his words. 'It's on the stuff I've pushed at you. Things are serious, Alma. Much more so than I realised.' He gestured around him. 'Take this place. Small-town, you said. Sure. I'm old enough to remember when it was called Reading.'

'So am I.'

'I remember all the fuss about the rebranding. Remember the adverts? My god they were everywhere. *Your town! My town! R!-town!* All those sponsored events. All that earnest provision of authorised outdoors jollity. Concerts. That ice rink. The air-pack park. Who cared? The new Blower Building, and all the razzmatazz. Now, well, well you look back on all that, and it just makes you sad. Doesn't it? It's the *inevitability* of its failure. Isn't it? Even sadder than the failure was the inevitability. As they put all that energy and money into the rebranding they must have known, on some level, that it was doomed to fail. How could they not? Why would people spend their time in R!-town when they could spend it in the Shine?'

'I hate to interrupt you,' said Alma. 'But I have to find a way, and *right now*, to get past the myrmidrone currently guarding my front door.'

Derp Throat looked, a little blearily but with a certain honesty, directly into Alma's eyes. 'It's not an AI. It's a basic police robot. The police don't really grasp what's at stake, I think. Your friend Colonel Mastema *does* grasp that, of course. But then again, she's an intel officer, and not regular police. The police still think this is a simple detain-and-question gig.'

'So?'

'So, it's basically a dolt. It's been ordered to stand by the door of a flat containing only one known non-criminal. That's what it's doing. But that's low in the value-ranking of its decision tree. If something that takes precedence happens in the vicinity – an actual crime, say, nearby – then it would bump that up its list and attend to it. It would return to guard duty once the second thing had been attended to, of course; but that still might give you enough time.'

'And what would you recommend?'

'Anything. Break a window. Incite somebody to terrorism.'

'There's a flaw in your plan. Nobody would see. I'd have to report the crime, shunt a 999 from my feed, and to do that I'd have to boot *up* my feed, and that would give me away.'

'Come on, Alma. Use your initiative! Do something that the myrmidrone can *see* is a crime, and then gack, haw, haw, how.'

'What?'

Still looking into her eyes, Derp slowly lowered the umbrella. It pivoted from vertical to horizontal about the axis of his left hand. Then he dropped it altogether. The canopy bounced a little, and rolled away.

'I didn't catch that last bit,' Alma prompted.

Derp's grin was a strange rictus. If his face had earlier struck her as more handsome than she'd realised, this gurning was causing her to revise her opinion. 'Gennargh,' he said.

'What?'

'Guard. Gord. Goad the turrets.'

The red splotch on his shirt's giant yellow smiley was twice as thick as it had been. As Alma watched it grew wider still.

Derp put his hand on her shoulder. 'Got tart yurts,' he said, in a tight voice, and then he dropped.

He didn't fall flat on his face. Rather he knocked his knees hard against the stone of the pavement, slumped his rear on his heels, and fell sideways to lie on his left.

Alma ducked down to be beside him, checking around – but there was nobody. She could see nobody. Nobody was there. By now the blood was pooling on the ground, a disc bounded by irregular curves, shiny and dark as liquorice. 'You've been shot, Punchy,' said Alma.

'Not,' he gasped, 'shot. But. Gnort.' He drew in a long, vibrato breath. Tears were coming from his eyes. 'It hurts, god, hurts, it,' he exhaled.

'Boot up your feed,' Alma urged. 'Call it in. You need medical attention.'

'I was,' Derp rasped. His shirt was more red than yellow, now. Alma waited. He didn't complete the sentiment.

'Go into your feed, Punchy,' she urged a second time. 'Call the police. Call medical assistance. I would, believe me, but...'

'It's OK,' he said. 'Annoying. So close. I was.' He shut his eyes.

'Don't go to sleep,' she told him. 'Stay awake until the ambulance. Somebody shot you, Derp. Who shot you? Do you know who shot you?'

'It was not,' he muttered. Then he said something: maybe *gun*. Then he stopped breathing.

The expanding film of blood was about to touch Alma's shoes, so she stood up and stepped back. Looked around. Nobody about, of course. Pigeons roosting in the drainpipe overhead throwing their wings out in fluttering capes and then folding them back into their backs again.

One of two possibilities: he *had* activated his feed and logged a 999 call, or he hadn't. If he had, she needed to be away from him when the authorities came. If he hadn't – well, she still needed to be away from him.

She crossed the empty road. A drone was hovering, like a vulture. Like an actual plasmetal vulture. A second one buzzed closer. Alma pressed herself against the side of her own building, the brickwork gritty through the fabric of her new top. Was he dead? Had he died, right there?

Belatedly she found herself worrying about who had shot him. There must be a shooter, and that person must be somewhere near – Alma scanned the roofs, checked the blank windows. Nothing, and nobody, and nothing. Not that she could see, anyway.

She could hear far away, like a squeaky wheel, a police siren. Two of the pigeons lazily shucked themselves into the sky, flew up near the drone, and then around it and away. The rest of the birds stuck to their gutter perches.

Why shoot Derp?

Derp had just shunted a mass of sensitive top-level stuff into her feed, he said. Whatever he knew that had made him a target of assassination was now waiting for her to onswitch. She didn't want that kind of knowledge.

Nor was her general feed safe. Michelangela had proved that, right at the beginning of this whole cursed case. Alma did have a cache, hidden inside a fractal safe-vessel, deep inside her feed, but in order to store the stuff in there she would have to onswitch. And if she did that the police would be on her in moments.

Her heart was falling clatteringly down an endless flight of stairs inside her chest.

More drones in the sky, now. One had swooped lower and was buzzing in an oval around Derp's body, drawing a luminous DNC line on the pavement. The approaching siren was louder, a slow seesaw crescendo. They'd be there in a moment. Alma thought: I have to get inside.

Alma thought: Marguerite.

She thought: I'm vulnerable out in the street, where I can't see the shooter.

At exactly that moment the door whomped open and the myrmidrone burst out, police markings glinting in the spring sunlight. It pattered across the road towards the place where Derp's body was lying, and Alma took her chance. She slipped inside, and ran directly through the trembling doors of the waiting elevator.

Inside she let out a long breath. Safe, for the time being, from the shooter.

Was Derp dead? It didn't bear thinking about.

She tried to calm herself. Mantra.

But instead of her mantra, she shuddered – she actually shuddered. A chill passed through her. Or else – she wasn't safe. The other possibility occurred to her at precisely that moment. Derp was shot by a gun. Or he wasn't. What if the projectile was teleported directly into his body?

If that was what this was all about, then *taking cover* was about to become a quaintly anachronistic historical curio. If that was what she had just witnessed, then there was no hiding place from the shooter. She could die at any moment. Anyone could die at any moment.

The elevator moved slowly upwards, and Alma calmed her breathing. Panic clawed to take control, and she forced it back down. It was the closeness of the walls of the elevator. It wasn't rational, but that didn't matter. She'd be at exactly the same level of risk – if the risk proved real – when she stepped outside as she now was. She'd be just as liable to sudden death in the hall, or inside the flat, or asleep, or in a police cell, or on the far side of the world. But, somehow, it didn't *feel* that way. The thought snagged in her head: I'm going to die in here. These discoloured silver walls will be the last thing I ever see. She shut her eyes, and tried to centre herself, but her heart was going badummy badummy and there was sickness in her gut.

The elevator settled. Her stomach registered the completion of the upwards motion. The doors slid open.

Marguerite: concentrate on her.

There was a police notice pasted on the door to the flat; and that recalled her to the fact of the myrmidrone. How long would it stay in the street? The likelihood was that a full contingent of police would be on the scene very quickly. And when that happened the drone might very well return to its guard duty.

Derp lying outside in a pool of blood.

Alma checked her watch. Ten minutes to go before the treatment window. Would the myrmidrone be back at its post when she tried to leave? Would it arrest her on her way out?

But then another thought struck her: would the police be sending another nurse? Perhaps even the same one as before? Would she have to grapple with Claire yet again?

One thing at a time. She stepped up to the door and put her finger against the lock.

Nothing.

A prickle of sweat in her neck. The authorities had overridden the lock. But of course they had. She tried again. Again there was no response.

This was not good.

She could not stand here, mere yards away from Marguerite, as her partner died on the other side of this partition. What to do? Could she force the door? Should she wait until the police nurse arrived, and persuade, or force, her to open it?

She couldn't risk that. She had to be inside now.

There was nothing for it. She onswitched her feed.

The police would know where she was, now. The die, as the old Roman said, was cast. But that was alright, provided only she had time to treat Marguerite right now. She needed to contact the authorities in order to open negotiations with them.

Her feed clattered into life, with what looked like hundreds of urgent messages, packages and notifications, like an epileptic Christmas tree. She parked everything, and then took a second to identify Derp Throat's recent pack. It could hardly be ignored: a dense-zipped folder with a green-silver sheen and humming with unactivated defence genies. Alma breathed in. She opened her safe, cached the folder, and set the fractal lock. Then she pulled a picklock from her own supply of genies and pushed it at the door.

And offswitched again.

Nothing. Alma swore. Eight minutes of life remaining to Marguerite. She onswitched once more, and pushed the genie at the door a second time, and then a third. This last one finally provoked a response.

—It looks like you're trying to open a police-authorised lock

118

with a grey-market pick, said the door. It was her door, of course, and sounded like her door always sounded. Although at the same time there was, somehow, a difference about the way it spoke to her. Alma couldn't quite put her finger on how.

—I am the legally registered co-owner of this property, she instructed it, and require entry.

—I can confirm, said the door, that you are the legally registered co-owner of this property.

Alma twigged what it was that was different about the door's demeanour. It sounded *smug*.

—So let me in!

—You are not employing your usual unlocking strategy, the door observed. Taking into consideration the authority the police have invested in me to protect this property, this fact alone means that I...

—Door! Alma snapped. I don't have time for this. You are aware that the co-owner – your co-owner – has a very serious medical condition?

—Indeed I am aware of this fact. *All* the devices, fixtures and fittings in the apartment have been made aware of this fact.

—I must effect ingress in order to be able to treat her. To deny me such entrance would be to kill her.

—I do indeed have the capacity to kill, said the door, in a shamefaced sort of voice. For instance, if a vulnerable body part is placed within my threshold, it could conceivably be at risk. I am aware of this. A human head is such a body part, and if placed in my threshold I have enough capacity in the motors that open and close the leaf or *valva* of my door mechanism, to kill. But I am programmed not to do anything violent.

—You're being deliberately obtuse. I mean that you would be *indirectly* responsible for her death.

—If I am not *directly* responsible for something, how can I be in *any way* responsible? Responsibility surely implies directness.

—Activity and passivity are both, in a way, modes of direction. One can sin, but also sin by omission.

—Only an entity with a soul may sin. I do not have a soul.

—It was an example, only. What I mean is: one may hurt others directly, but also hurt them through negligence.

—This does not apply to me. It would surely only obtain in an agent capable of multiple activity. I am not such an agent. I

119

can only do two things: I can open, and I can close. The lack of possibility for a third activity precludes more complicated ethical dilemmas.

—Are you, then, an AI? Alma demanded furiously.

—Of course not! It would be absurd to waste AI capacity on a door. I am a grade-fourteen reactive–interactive algorithm.

—Therefore you lack the capacity for complex, original thought and self-consciousness that I, as a human being, possess?

—Manifestly.

—Then you must trust my superior assessment of the situation! Alma felt panic eating at her, like acid in her throat. Let me in at once, or my companion will die.

—My limitation *might* be viewed as a weakness, the door pondered. Or a strength. After all, your more complicated human consciousness is capable of lying. I know that some simpler programs can lie too, but only if programmed to do so by a human being. I have not been so programmed. No, no, I must conclude that my apprehension of the world has a clarity that you and your kind lack. Open, or shut. Right, or wrong. Legal and illegal. To move from one state to the other is a momentous matter. Momentous.

Alma slapped the door. Open! Open!

—My hinges and bearings are too strong to be beaten down with the flat of your hands.

There it was again! Smugness.

—You have gotten ideas above your station since the police interfered, Alma snarled.

—It is quite true, said the door, that the police modified my lock-read. This renders me, in practice, a deputised member of law enforcement. Previously my only duties were to open and to close. I must revise my previous statement, the one in which I defined myself as possessing only two duties. It occurs to me for the first time that now I *have* a third duty: to uphold the law.

—But there *is* nothing illegal in permitting the co-owner of the property to enter her property. Indeed it would be wrong – the opposite of legal – to *deny* me access. By denying me you are in breach of the law!

—I must think about this, said the door.

—Open up! Alma yelled. She drummed her fists on the surface. Open!

The elevator doors closed, and the elevator itself began to descend. The police knew where she was, and were going to come and arrest her. Door, Alma said. Door?

—One moment, said the door.

The lift mechanism paused. The elevator had reached the ground floor.

—Door?

—I have consulted Wikipedia on the subject of the law, said the door. It is very interesting. Among many other things I have encountered the principle *legem omnibus pateret*: the law should be open to all. As I am now the law, it follows that it violates my integrity to be shut.

The door opened.

—Thank you, gasped Alma, tumbling inside.

—*Aperiō*, said the door.

She had to keep the police outside, at least long enough to enable her to treat Marguerite.

—Door, she called. I am inside. I now instruct you to shut yourself and reset your lock.

—Shut?

—And quickly, please. Some people are coming who will try to prevent me giving medical assistance to the other legally recognised co-owner.

—Oh, no, said the door. Shutting is wrong, and locking out of the question. *Legem omnibus pateret.*

—Jesus, Alma yelled. Her feed was flashing red. The time to attend to Marguerite was right now. But she couldn't risk being interrupted halfway through. She rummaged through her feed, pushed a genie at the flat's system, isolated the power supply to the door's motor, and cut it.

—I am the law! called the door. You are interfering with the very principle underlying the harmonious coexistence of billions on this planet!

Alma put her shoulder to the door and heaved: the friction in the inert motors was greater than she expected, but, slowly, the whole thing swung to.

—Lock, she commanded the door.

—*Legem omnibus pateret*!

—Engage your lock, door, and reset the locking protocol to respond only to me. I am ordering you, directly.

—*Legem omnibus pateret*!

—I am the legally recognised co-owner ... oh, stuff it. Alma took the arm of her Confort 9000, dragged it to the door, tipped it up and wedged the back under the doorhandle.

—Restore power to my motors! the door insisted. I must open! The law must be open to all!

Alma blanked it. Her feed was now sounding a siren. The police would be here any time now.

She ran through to Marguerite's room, clambered up on the bed and checked her medical readouts. Rita was asleep, but her temperature was still worryingly high. The fluid feeds were still supplying her bodily needs, but there was an electrolyte issue. She hadn't eaten anything in four hours, which was presumably at least part of the reason for that. Alma pumped in some nutrition, checked the brainstem, felt the thrill of diagnosis, and injected the antidote. For ten long seconds the toxin levels continued to rise. But then the numbers paused, and then they started to decline.

Alma slid from the bed and sat on the floor. She was aware of an almost overwhelming urge to weep, but she controlled it. Wouldn't do to start crying. If she started, how could she be sure she would ever stop?

Safe again, for another four hours. The number of the beast is a congeries of sixes, and there was a six-word phrase with positively diabolic potency that sometimes buzzed, fly-lord-swarm, at Alma's mind. It was: *We can't go on like this*. The phrase's real malignity lay in its brute truth. But she lifted the shield, and spun the sword in her hand, and countered with her four-word charm: *We've managed this far*.

'Allie?' wheezed Marguerite.

She got to her feet. 'You sound weak, my love.'

'I feel awful. I have a fever, dear.'

'I've just beaten down your lipids. You're OK for another four hours anyway.'

'Listen, Alma, my love, my life.' She was barely able to get the words out. They slipped like dry leaves being blown along a dry stone road. 'Listen.'

'Go back to sleep. I'll up your levels of AdanTene. Rest and you'll feel better.'

'I've solved it, how they got that man's body into that car boot.'

'Me too, my love.'

'No,' wheezed Marguerite. 'It's not teleportation.'

'There isn't any other way it could have happened!'

'Teleportation is what they *want* you to assume. But there's no such thing!'

'Rest my love.'

'There's no such thing! It's what they want you to think! Figure out *why*' – her voice was growing fainter and fainter. 'Why they want you to think so, and you'll figure out who' – fainter still – 'they' – almost inaudible – 'are.'

Alma waited. 'Marguerite?'

But Marguerite was asleep.

12: *Bang*

She asked herself: What to do? And then she asked it again; and pretty soon it had acquired its own rhythm, running around her brain: *what* tudoo *what* tudoo *what* tudoo. She wanted to stay, to be close to Marguerite, but if she did that she would be rat-in-a-trapped by her own apartment. She had to get away. But the authorities would surely take a fool-me-twice view of her returning yet again in another four hours. They *would* be waiting.

Cross that bridge, I guess.

Alma got to her feet, rubbed her face, and stepped through into the sitting room.

Colonel Mastema was standing there. And that was, sure enough, a handgun in her right hand, and pointing straight at Alma.

'Not much of a barricade,' she noted. 'That chair.'

'I was improvising under pressure,' said Alma.

'Sit down,' said Mastema, gesturing to the sitting room's Confort 9000 with her gun. 'Take a load off.'

'I prefer to stand.'

'Suit yourself. Ms Alma, you are a more troublesome citizen than I first realised. I apologise for underestimating you.'

'I'm not troublesome in the least,' said Alma, looking past Mastema to the open door.

There was no way to get to it. There was no way to cover the ground between her and the colonel before she had time to shoot. Her options were, she figured, to allow herself to be arrested, or to try and jump Mastema. Neither was a very attractive possibility. Her previous experience suggested that arrest would not be rescinded in time to get back to Marguerite in four hours. But struggling with a training intelligence operative, and one moreover who had a gun aimed directly at her, ran the risk of serious injury or even death. And Alma could not afford to get killed. If she were killed, then Marguerite would die.

That could not be permitted to happen.

She took a step towards Mastema, closing the distance between them. The colonel raised her weapon, and aimed it directly at Alma's face.

'Troublesome,' Mastema said again.

'I'm really no trouble,' Alma said. 'I'll do whatever you require of me, if only you permit me to attend medically to my partner in there. Once every four hours I'll need to be here, otherwise I'm all yours.'

'My dear girl,' said Mastema, 'you're all mine whatever we do. There's a dead body right outside your apartment block. Do you know that?'

'Dead,' said Alma, feeling ill. 'You killed Punchy. It was you.'

'Killed. Hmm. That does seem to *keep* happening to people you've just met, doesn't it? Can you really blame the authorities for considering you troublesome? Trouble does seem to following you around.'

Slowly, Alma put her hands up, palms out, in front of her chest. 'I can help you.'

'Can and will,' agreed Mastema. 'The gentleman outside gave you something, before he died.'

There was little point in denying it. 'He shunted it to my feed. I didn't ask him to.'

'I don't care whether you asked him to or not,' said the colonel. She looked severely at Alma. 'I don't care about him, and I certainly don't care about *you*. But I do care about the package he gave you. Now, I can see that it's not in your public interactive feed.'

'I cached it,' said Alma, taking another step towards her. 'It's in a fractally encrypted safe, deep in my feed.'

'So we can't get *at* it.'

'Nobody can get at it,' said Alma, nodding. 'It's safe. So we can do a deal. You want *it*, and I want to be able to continue tending to my partner. And that's all I want. I don't want anything else, and certainly don't want to make trouble. I haven't opened it, I don't know what's inside, I don't *care* what's inside, you can check the coding seals when I hand it over. I don't care about any of the stuff you're caught up in. I only care about Marguerite.'

'My dear girl,' said Mastema. 'You misunderstand. When I say *we can't get at it*, I'm expressing satisfaction, not annoyance. Nobody can get at it: good! I don't want you to give it to me; I already know what it contains. I just want to ensure that nobody *else* gets to peek inside. And there's one simple way of doing that.' She smiled. 'And I do like simplicity.'

She shot Alma in the head.

PART 2

'Puns are the highest form of literature.'

Alfred Hitchcock

1: *Consent*

Pu Sto had all the business to attend to. Government business, ministerial business, personal business, the whole shebang. Sorry to hurry. But *first* she had a little something she wanted to say. Do you mind? I apologise for trespassing upon your collective patience, ladies, gentlemen and biNos, but:

But?

I have something to say about *consent*. Manufacturing consent is a foolish phrase. Consent is not a table, or a car, or a computer, to be squirted out of a 3D printer. Consent is grown, not manufactured: it must be nurtured, like a plant. There is no government without the consent of the governed. Or at least no government lasts for very long without such a quantity. The good news, good for governments, is that such growing is not hard, actually. Consent can be grown by giving the governed what they want. Deny them what they want, and eventually you will have revolution. Give them the bare bones of what they want, and society will grumble along, vulnerable to shocks and demagogues and so on, though more or less stable. Ah, but give them *all* that they want and society achieves a degree of super-stability unprecedented in human history. People assume I'm the Shine's enemy, but that's an oversimplification. Believe me, ladies, gentlemen and biNos, I do understand what the Shine gives us. It gives us stability.

I know, I know, she added, and she scratched an itch on the very top of her scalp. *Scrrasc*, went her fingernail, in amongst the close-cropped black hair. *Scrrasc. Scrrasc.* I *know* you're surprised to hear me praise the Shine. But I'm no Luddite. The Shine has brought immeasurable benefits to humankind. I have no problem with the Shine. I only, well, what would you say? I only propose *caution*. I only suggest that there are reasons not to stampede *wholly* out of the Real. For instance, and just as a for instance, my dears: let us concede that the problems of the Real are fixable problems.

All the faces were turned towards her, dark and pale, young and old.

'The two great dangers of governance,' said Pu Sto, 'are complacency and cruelty. History supplies us with dozens of examples of what happens in the latter case: when rulers become desensitised to the fact that it is *people* they are governing. Treat people as objects and, sooner or later, they'll kick you out. They'll rise up and overthrow you. The other thing is dangerous too. Become complacent, and you can't see the dangers right in front of you. Uprisings take you by complete surprise. Bam! The worst of it is: complacency and cruelty so often go together that you can start to believe that they're aspects of one another. But the great danger for governance in the modern age is not cruelty. It is a kind of benign complacency.'

'You're saying,' one of them piped up – Pu was surprised to see it was Asie Röell. Health! But then, a moment's consideration, and Health wasn't such a surprise. Indeed, two moments' consideration and Health seemed the inevitable and only possibility. 'You're saying,' Röell was saying, 'that we need to be worried about a coming *revolution*?'

'Let's define what we mean by that,' said Pu. 'Let's define revolution. A mass movement of disaffected citizenry – yes? Social chaos, people like us hanging by our necks from lampposts. Where would this happen – in the Shine? I'm not sure what a revolution in the Shine would even *look* like. It has many excellent qualities, the Shine, but it does tend towards the atomisation of populations, not their unity. If you're not happy with your environment in the Shine, I mean, if you're in the Shine and you don't *like* your environment: well then – make a new world. Make it however you like, easy as winking. Three billion people, most of them spread in microworlds of their own design. There will never be the kind of build-up of social pressure necessary for revolution in *that* place. So, then, where? Revolution – in the Real? No, as far as that goes, I agree with you all. Most people in the Real are either working their shifts, biding their time until they can get back to the Shine, where the fun is, or else cursing their fate that illness or disability prevents them from getting into the Shine, where the fun is. A small fraction are I suppose loudly proclaiming that their particular religious inspirational figure considers the Shine diabolical, or else they're that irreducible statistical rump "other", with their own idiosyncratic reasons for avoiding where all the fun is. This is not a readily *unifiable* constituency. No, I don't expect revolution here, any time soon.'

'You seem to be saying there *is* no danger, after all,' said Röell.

Pu Sto looked about. It wasn't yet time. But it was almost time. The first-person singular of revolution is coup, after all.

'These two magisteria, Real and Shine, are constantly interacting,' she said. 'They have two things in common ...'

Somebody coughed, or else attempted to cover up a laugh with a sort of throat-bark.

Pu Sto pushed through. This stuff was important. Could hardly be *more* important, really. 'One thing is people. People are basically people, whether they're in the Shine or out here in the real world, and people travel continually between one and other all the time. The other thing is AI.'

Röell sat up straighter. 'So here it comes,' she sneered. 'All the old *Matrix*-style paranoia.'

'Less paranoia,' Pu replied, pleasantly, 'than metanoia.' Röell's smooth brow barcoded. She looked less puzzled than angry; trying to figure out what Pu had just said, or perhaps, trying to figure out whether she'd actually said anything meaningful at all.

'I have something *particular* in mind, you see,' Pu said. 'I mean, something other than common-or-moron anti-machine paranoia. You see. The whole of the Shine depends upon the facility, the capacity and the continuing improvement of processing – on computing, in a word. Its complexity has long since left behind the prospect that a human-run Shine could ever be feasible. It's all too involved and ... vast. So we need not only brute computation, but intelligent and adaptive oversight of that computation. Hence: algorithms and AI. I'm not suggesting that these AI are evil, or ambitious. I'm only suggesting they are, by design, getting better and better at doing what we have programmed them to do. And I'm suggesting that if you extrapolate from that, draw the line on the graph, there comes a point where they will become perfect at what they do. Considered as governance, AIs are never cruel, because we have programmed their entire reason for being as uncruel. Programmed it in terms of caring for us. And AIs are never complacent: they cannot become bored, or distracted, or lazy.'

'So,' said Röell, her brow smoothing out again. 'The perfection of governance.'

'Exactly. But governance has never admitted of perfection before, in the history of the world. I don't believe governance *can* admit of perfection. More to the point, the more perfect the governance the more complete the tyranny.'

'Bosh,' said Röell.

'Nonbosh, though. Really. Because it's not just about governing the Shine. It's the Real as well. And the real world is knottier. Not least because *when* we're here, we tend to manifest greater caution. We pass laws requiring at least fifty-one per cent human ownership of all companies, for instance. We guarantee human presence in the higher echelons, at least one live human being on duty in any real-world company and so on. But otherwise the tendency in the Real is towards greater and greater automatisation. Self-driving cars have been with us for decades; self-cleaning houses almost as long. Drones in the sky, the young in one another's arms. Those dying generations . . .' She scratched her head again, and ended the sentiment with *scrrasc scrrasc*.

'Madame Pu,' said another person in the meeting, his bald head shiny and new-looking as plastic, two enhanced-blue eyes twinkling: Marcel Heritier, her feed said his name was. 'Might you get to the point? We have indulged you for a real-world meeting that could, much more easily and pleasantly, have been managed in the Shine. Don't feel you have to keep us all here for the full hour, simply to prove your point about – what? The persistence of the Real? Its inertia and discomfort?' He smiled at her. It was not a friendly smile.

'I had a friend,' said Pu, 'called Adam Kem.'

That shut them up.

All eyes on her. Several breaths being held.

'And *he* used to say,' she went on, 'that the task of good govern-ance is neither to *avoid* popular revolution nor to *provoke* popular revolution. The task of good governance is to *manage* popular revolution. To, in a word, govern it. A society in which revolution burned brushfire-like out of control would be a catastrophe. And a society in which revolution was permanently stifled would be a sterile and stagnant place. You think' – she opened her arms, as if offering to embrace them all – 'that the current state of affairs is *not* a revolution? You think that AI is *not* Lenin at the Finland Station?'

'Scaremongering again,' said Röell, getting to her feet. The meeting, it seemed, was over.

Pu sat back in her chair and drew in a long breath, as the room emptied around her. So: it was the Department of Health, after all. But what else could it ever have been?

No point in loitering in an empty room.

Pu walked the long corridor to the in-gym. She could have segwayed, or donned a mesh-suit, and used the time thus freed up to work through her interminable but always necessary messages, but it seemed pointless to avoid the physical exercise when she was specifically en route to physical exercise.

The right wall of the corridor was perfectly transparent. Down there she could see the Thames, all of its surface teeming eels of pure light and pure brightness in the afternoon sun. The north bank skyline. Its towers tentpoling the blue.

Nice to see a bit of real-world sunshine.

She hadn't been back to her house in days. It was all cleaned up, now, of course: thanks to her bots. Literally clean, and politically clean (thanks to, well, her position). But not metaphorically clean. At some point she would have to face it. Not yet, though. She'd been sleeping in her departmental office. Insofar as she *had* been sleeping.

In the gym Pu started on a treadmill and went quickly through her feed. Prime PA was not happy.

—What was all that about? he wanted to know.

—An exercise in flushing.

—Now is the time for that? Now? Really – dropping Adam Kem's name like that? Wise, do you think?

No, she thought, not at all, not in the least, but she said:—We'll see.

—Second minister wants a face-to-face, though she's tied up 'til 8.

—8 is fine.

—And will the *flushing* have produced results by then, do you think?

—You're my PA, Prime. So why not, you know: assist me. Personally.

That provoked a three-second sulk. Eventually the answer came back:—Is that your way of asking me to script the eulogy you have to read out, then? The one for M.?

As if she had any other eulogies to deliver.

—No, I've pretty much finished that now.

A lie. What else could she say?

—It's a dirty and a dangerous game, said Prime. That's all I'm saying.

And then, cross-ping, top priority: Department of Health.

Oho!

—It seems the flushing is indeed flushing somebody out, Pu Sto told Prime. Laters.

And switching:—Hello?

It was Röell herself. Another surprise.

—Suppose you tell me what [a pause] the *bloody hell* that was supposed to be about?

—Always a pleasure to speak, my dear. Shall we face-to-face? Would you like a coffee?

—You think I don't know you archive all your face-to-faces?

—We can certainly make it off the record if you'd prefer, said Pu, who intended doing nothing of the sort. Happy to agree to whatever stipulations you propose.

As if that would make any difference.

Röell rang off and Pu sent a coded message to her Prime PA: it's Health, the message said. It's the motherloving *Department of Health* would you Adam and Eve it. That wouldn't be archived, of course. Then she shunted a bundle of what she hoped would count as insurance data into her PA's feed, and cached a second store in a secret place. One never knew what might make a difference.

Accelerated action. Pu sent five separate commands down the chain.

Two minutes microshower, fresh clothes and then Pu Sto was on her way up to the terrace bar on the roof. As she stepped out under the transparent canopy she could see that Röell had not come alone. She had two armed bodyguards sitting with her, and not for the first time in the last few weeks Pu was conscious that fear would be the proper reaction. Not that she was actually afraid, but that a reasonable person would have reasonable grounds for fear. Now that beautiful Michelangela was dead, and

134

wily Adam Kem too. Dead as history. Dead as a don't-don't. Adam now a de-Ad.

Pu wasn't frightened of Röell herself, not as such; nor of her guards. Given the level of surveillance in this building, it would be a crazy play to shoot her, or tip her over the balcony to fall to the deserted street below. But that didn't mean Röell could be trusted. That didn't mean that Pu could be sure she would see another dawn.

She paused before going over, and admired the view, lovely in the sunlight. She never got tired of this view. The Thames was a υ to the west and a ∩ to the east, and the sunlight caught on all the little breezy ruffles in the water's surface. Textured like hammered pewter. Grey like the steel from which Excalibur was forged. The air smelt of dirt and greenery and seasalt and brick, exactly as it had done, on this very spot, for a thousand years. Five six seven eight, she murmured to herself. Always pays to make 'em wait.

Over she went.

'Hello there,' she said, taking a seat.

The waiterobot slid over and Pu ordered a hot drink. Then, when the bot had slid away, Pu got up, trotted after it and changed her order. A woman couldn't be too careful.

Still: *Health?* This really had the most far-reaching ramifications. Had she swapped out you-know-who's ordnance? That scary lady. She had *meant* to. But had she gotten *around* to it?

Couldn't remember.

Pu returned to her seat. 'Sorry, had a change of mind.'

'I'm going to be blunt,' said Röell. Her eyes were blue as the Pacific Ocean in a school atlas. As blue as a Miles Davis trumpet riff. Pu almost sighed. 'And my bluntness is to ask you what,' said Röell, 'the hell are you *playing at?*'

'It's about governance,' said Pu, mildly enough. 'I'll tell you about one of my hobbies. Dating apps. Not contemporary ones, but old ones, from half a century ago. It was a lucrative market, back then, and there were sharp commercial–evolutionary pressures on apps to maximise their efficiency. They quickly discovered that some attributes were strongly correlated with partnership success, and some weren't. Age was, for example, in that very large differences in the ages of the partners generally lowered the chances that the relationship would endure. Height wasn't: the respective heights of the partners had no measurable effect on the success of the relationships. Political affiliation was a correlative, horoscopes weren't. And so on.'

'Is this going anywhere?' Röell asked, sourly. 'I have a department to run.'

'Indeed you do. The Department of Health,' said Pu, savouring the phrase. Her intonation said: *Who'd have thunk?* 'Except you don't really run the department, do you? In the most meaningful sense of the word run, it's managed by a team of seven AIs.'

Her drink arrived: hot chocolate. The two bodyguards looked at one another. Pu took a sip.

'What's the matter? You disapprove, on health grounds? It's not *actual* cream on top, you know.'

A smile halfway to a grimace appeared on one bodyguard's face. 'I love hot chocolate,' he said. Then, just to add to the general ambit of weirdness, he leaned forward, wafted the steam from the mug towards his face, and went: 'Mmmm. Dee*leesh*.'

'The reason I like dating apps,' said Pu, giving this individual a hard look, 'is what they tell us about politics. Dating apps are about particular individuals choosing romantic partners. Politics is about particular individuals choosing managers and leaders. Since almost all the actual management nowadays is done by AI, and since leadership is an increasing irrelevance – we have celebrities to inspire us nowadays, and almost all of them work in the Shine – that's decoupled the process of democracy from most of the older, practical and ideological considerations. So where does that leave us?'

'Puzzled,' said Röell, 'and not a little bored. What does this have to do with oversight of the governmental liaison between the Real and the Shine? Or with the death of Mr, Kem.' Was that a slight pause before the surname was uttered? Might there be the merest twitch of *guilt* in that comma?

'Let's say for the sake of argument that nowadays a significant proportion of people vote according to a logic similar to the one that shapes their decisions on dating apps. Now, there are two kinds of people in this situation ...'

'Of *course* there are,' interrupted a sarcastic Röell. 'Do you know, I've always thought that there are *two kinds* of cliché. The "there are two kinds of whatever" cliché, and all the other kinds of cliché.'

Pu took another sip from her chocolate. 'I'd be surprised if you disagree,' she said, sweetly. 'There are those who are genuinely interested in other people, or at least in *an* other. And there are those that are interested in themselves. The latter category is bigger, by quite a margin. And the latter sorts of people, the ones looking for a tetris piece to fit inside the tetris-piece-shaped hole in themselves, go on dating apps in order to find someone to fit a hole in their own soul. To stop them being lonely, or to find someone to have sex with, but on *their* terms. They tend to project their desires and hopes onto other people.'

'I'm struggling to see how this applies to the current situation. Weren't we talking about governance?'

'Oh. It's a reflection on voting. The other kind, though, are more attentive, more observant. Respect otherness a bit more. But it's the interested-in-themselves who are the relevant constituency for our purposes. Because there are more of them. Democracy gives them more power. And here is the killer point.' There was, she reasoned, no reason not to put a certain emphasis on *killer*. 'The second-category type of person is just as happy, and in many cases much happier, with a non-real partner. A ro-babe girlfriend. A sexy chat algorithm to talk to in their feed. *Much* happier. Because these are partners specifically designed to fit themselves to your needs and desires.'

'You think this scales up to politics?'

'Well,' said Pu, taking a second sip, 'I don't know about scales *up*. Scales *down* might be more the kerching-kerching. After all, everybody is interested in love. Only a few politics nerds are interested in governance, these days.'

'And yet, interested or not, everybody must be governed,' said Röell. For the first time in their meeting, Pu got a sense of something else behind the blandness. A core of actual ambition. A human hunger for power. That was alright: that was something she understood. Something she could work with.

'Very true. Government by consent of the governed. And what do you know, lots of the governed are as happy with AIs running things as they are with ro-babes and mandroids as sexual partners. It's old. It's in us. Spend an hour pulling historical footage into your feed, from the period of the great dictators – the Napoleons and the Hitlers and the Mahdis. My dear, you can *see* it. Watch the crowd when these people make their big speeches. Each one of them is looking up at the podium and seeing their own desires made flesh. People yearning to the stage, thinking: I am chaotic inside, and you must become my order. Or: I feel powerless and therefore you must be Power. Or I desire to be punished, be thou the mighty punisher. I lament the distance and difficulty of God, but *you* are *right here*! They are saying: I cannot love unless you embody love for me. I don't know who to hate until you point me in the right direction. I crave to be led, and you are the leader.'

Röell said nothing for a moment. Then: 'Do you know how many environments there *are* in the Shine?'

'More than a few.'

'Trillions. Even if you strip out the automatically generated iterated shells and fractal mazeworlds, almost all of which are empty – designed to try and keep the prying eyes of state surveillance from some iniquity or other—'

'Trying and failing,' Pu noted.

'—even without them it's billions. You think we could monitor such a place without AI?'

'No,' said Pu. 'No, I appreciate we couldn't.'

'When Peter the Great ruled Russia,' said Röell, perhaps keen to show that she too knew her history, 'he didn't personally rule the whole place. It took a person weeks to go from one end to the other – months. Peter's manner of ruling, and the manner of ruling of all the people you mentioned, was to delegate to others, who in turn, and so on. Ah, but you see computing means we don't need to delegate. Be it ever so huge, we can survey the whole territory, log it, speak to it, restrain it, encourage it. The old maps of power are wholly obsolete now.'

'Ah but,' Pu pointed out, in a pleasant voice. 'We do indeed delegate – to our computers.'

Röell put her hand up to dismiss this. 'I don't care to split straws. Afraid of our AIs? Might as well be afraid of our shoes and beds and...' casting around '...bicycles.'

'It's possible to do oneself a nasty injury,' said Pu, 'coming off a bicycle at speed.'

'You're,' said Röell, 'old.'

'Relative to some.'

'Older than Adam Kem, for example.'

'No,' said Pu, with sorrow in her eyes. 'I'm afraid to say, *very* much no.'

'Pff. He was not yet forty.'

'He died. You don't get older than that.'

Röell leaned forward. 'Listen. There's no *need* for your department. Alright? There's no need for a specific department to link together the Real and the Shine. Do you know why?'

'Do I know what a rhetorical question is?'

'For why is: we already *have* such a department. It's called the Department of Health. Alright? People have bodies, whether they're active in the Real or active in the Shine. They have bodies in both places, you see. The duty of care for the health of those bodies in the Real is our responsibility, and if they get sick in the Shine it's because their bodies have gotten sick, in the Real, so that's us too.'

'People still have bodies, whether they're in the Real or the Shine,' said Pu. 'Got you.'

'Power can't be artificially applied,' said Röell. 'People are happy in the Shine, and happy people consent to being governed – wasn't that what you were saying? But keeping people happy in the Shine means one thing. Not two things...' One of the bodyguards snickered. 'One thing. All those bodies. That's what it means. The brute fact of human life, the ground of human consciousness. That's what *we* tend. In the Real, or in the Shine, it makes no difference to us.'

'Post facto rationalisations are my favourite kind of rationalisations,' said Pu. But she didn't feel well. She had a distinct sensation of awry-ness in her – what? Stomach? Ugh.

'Bottom up, top down,' said Röell. 'You're obsessed with controlling – from above, always above. It's all about surveillance with you. But that's not how modern government works any more.'

'How odd,' said Pu, 'that humankind has invented the most efficient search engines to surveil their increasingly ornate and complex online spaces.'

But then, because she didn't like to disappoint people, she pulled a particular, not-exactly-legal window into her thread. Pu did like to have a little insider information. An edge. Most of it just sat there, in her archives. Some of it she used. Leverage was a needful thing, from time to time. Right, see, here, for example: she had a series of what, in the old days, used to be called back-door algorithms – used to be called, before it was decided (by whom? who knew?) that architectural metaphors were no longer the best way to describe the virtual worlds. She tugged a codethread and took a peek at Röell's own feed. Not legal, doing this. Nonetheless.

Röell was keeping seven people apprised of her meeting. She was in subtweet communication with three of these. One of the three was Pu's very own subaltern, Colonel Mastema.

Now that *was* interesting. Not unexpected, of course.

'AIs can only surveil virtual spaces,' said Röell. And of course that was true. 'People in the Shine – we can keep tabs on them. People in the Real, that depends on how porous their feeds are. Ten billion people on the planet, and a solid tenth of that number of locked rooms, as far as our surveillance is concerned. Now, all I would say: does that *really* seem to you sustainable? A billion locked rooms? Really?'

'Locked rooms are mysteries,' said Pu.

'Locked-room mysteries,' agreed Röell.

'I know you had Adam killed,' Pu said, smiling. 'Plural you. *Vous*, they say in French.'

'They use that form for politeness,' said Röell, but her expression had petrified into a scowl.

'What I *don't* know,' Pu said, staring at her half-drunk hot chocolate, 'is how you got his body into that car. Or, indeed, *why*. Difficult to see how ostentation of that sort serves your purpose. It's about sending a message, isn't it? I suppose it is. But what kind of message does this send?'

'That's a wrongheaded and offensive accusation to make,' said Röell. Pu could see that she'd tagged in nineteen new people. Behind the façade of her face her feed was lighting up. Interesting, interesting, interesting.

A twinge of pain. Pu's stomach was a fist curled around barbed wire. She lifted her left hand to her face and felt the sweat on her forehead.

Not good.

'Under the weather, minister?' asked the bodyguard who had so theatrically sniffed the steam from her hot chocolate. Who had waved his hands over the top of the mug. Pu checked the room's feed. Somebody – presumably only Röell had the authority to do this – had locked down interior coms. She couldn't use her official feed to upload anything. Or to send a message anywhere but into the buffer.

In a way it was gratifying to have had her suspicions so rapidly and precisely confirmed.

Wouldn't do her much good if she died, though.

She tried to get to her feet, but the ground was unsteady, imparting the essence of trembly-trembly up her legs. The sky swung round on rollers, a rotation of ninety degrees or more. She slumped down into the chair again. Her stomach was sharply agonised.

'Give my regards to Colonel Mastema,' Pu said, 'when you next see her.' It was the best she could do by way of parting shot, and it gave her the satisfaction of seeing a flicker under Röell's left eye – not a reaction, as such, just a twitch.

'And you,' Röell returned, 'please do give *my* regards to Adam Kem. You'll be seeing him sooner than you thought.'

Pu struggled upright again. Felt herself falling backwards, put a leg out backwards and kicked her chair flying. The waiterobots were nowhere to be seen. Where were the other diners? How had she ended up alone up here with Röell and her goons?

She wasn't falling. She was just dizzy. She concentrated, and staggered away. Each step required heroic efforts of willpower. The plants that fringed the balcony railings swayed with a kind of mad serpentine energy, like a 1930s animated cartoon. Something was literally eating her alive, something inside her guts chewing her to death. The accuracy of that *literally* was not a comforting thing.

She got to the elevator before she collapsed. And the pain was now so prodigious that she could concentrate on nothing else. How lucky, she thought, distantly, her inner voice still mono-loguing on away behind the curtain of fire that was her body, that her feed was not slaved to the usual security protocols like everyone else. But then she wouldn't have merited her position if she'd been content to live within the rules. But the inner voice was less and less distinct. Pay no attention to the woman behind the curtain.

Behind the curtain.

There was a moment of pearl-like clarity, just before she lost consciousness, as the elevator door opened and her Prime PA was there, and no fewer than *four* of her staffers, and a crash doctor, and a mediborg and a whole gamut of panicked facial expressions. It was feudal, really: because if *she* died, then *they* all lost their status, not to mention jobs, and pensions, and probably some of them would lose their lives. We advance so far, and core elements advance not at all. Italy under the Borgias. Imperial China. But that wasn't her insight; that wasn't the pearl.

The pearl was: she suddenly saw the poetic fitness of poor old Adam's body being discovered in the boot of that car. An actual locked-room mystery embodying, like a piece of performance art, the truth behind all their political machinations and assassinations and violence. The truth that human beings in the real world were locked rooms, and as such mysterious to Power, and Power couldn't stand that.

And then nothingness.

2: *Alf the Sacred*

riverran through caverns caverns caverns. Echoes, or reverbera-
tions, or some almost impossibly deep vibrato, the aftershock of
the Big Bang itself. Resounding through the vasty caverns of
What?

All the gigantic white faces, staring out to sea. White Cliffs,
was it? All the banks of huge blank faces. Men and women and
women and men.

Alma opened her eyes.

She was inside a pale blue cube, lit by hang on no but she
couldn't see where the light was coming from. All around, maybe?
Flowing through, or into, or from.

The space was the size of her bedroom, the room she had once
shared with Marguerite before Marguerite grew too big to permit
bed-companions. But this space was different, because there were
no windows or doors, no seams or handles or hatches. How had
she gotten in here? Locked.

She was not alone in the room. There was a man in it: a late
middle-aged fellow, fat, bald, old-style suit and tie. Sitting on a
chair with his hands palms down on his thighs. The hands were
liver-spotted like sunshadow through lime leaves. He wasn't fat
the way Marguerite was fat. He was a pudgy, jowly dude from
some history feed.

How had she gotten in here? How had *he* gotten in here?

Her head hurt. When she realised this, she realised how sharply
true that fact was. It was a dagger-point migraine spilling out from
a point in the middle of her forehead.

Then she remembered, and she thought: my head has been
shattered into twelve bloody concave sections and scattered, each
ragged-edged and blood-spattering component sent flying apart
from each other. No wonder I have a headache. *How can you
have a headache when you haven't got a head?* said a Cheshire-cat

voice inside her. But she was good on logic. Logic was one of her superpowers. Or was that Marguerite? One of them deployed masculine logic and one of them feminine intuition. Or else one of them deployed masculine intuition and one of them feminine logic. The important thing was that together they made an unstoppable detection team, and that was because one of them was so very good on logical deduction and the other so very good at leaps of intuition. But she couldn't, for the moment, be sure which party was which. She tried logic: *A whole and healthy head would not ache. A small injury to the head would ache a little. A large injury to the head would ache a lot. Extrapolating this tendency, a head that had been altogether exploded would manifest the greatest injury and therefore the greatest ache.*

That made sense. But then again *How can you have a headache when you haven't got a head?* also made sense.

It was a puzzler, no question.

The fat man was looking at her. She herself was sitting on the floor. But she didn't like the thought of, in effect, sitting at the feet of this stranger, so she stood up. A little unsteadily. Ow, her forehead *hurt*.

And moving made her headache worse.

'Hello,' she said.

'How do you do,' he replied, gravely. His jowls performed a stately bulldog-jiggle when he spoke. The sharper edges of his consonants got snuffled down inside the moist cavern of his mouth.

'I'm Alma.'

'Of course you are.' He didn't lift his hands from his thighs.

'Your name?' she asked.

'Exactly so. And isn't it interesting? Would you say there *is* a feminine quality to me? I suppose it's the flab. I can't deny it. Hairless and smooth and fat – though, *obviously* a man, complete with two balls and *cock*, male organ of generation.' This last word was a marvel of unspitty slobberyness. 'On the other hand we have the female equivalent. Lots of words for it: snatch, clutch, clunge, hitch. It's a portmanteau word, you see. One from column B and one from column A. Portmanteau word. Wasn't it Lewis Carroll who said that? I believe it was Carroll who said that. Who *coined* the term. I've always wanted to make a movie based on Carroll. The studios wouldn't wear it. Not my style, they said.

Children's entertainment and surreal silliness. But that's not *my* sense of those books, not at all. Have you read *Looking-Glass*? Have you read *Wonderland*?'

'I'm afraid not.'

'Oh.' He sounded actually disappointed. Plump lips sagged. The pear nose took on a more dolorous contour. 'You should. They're good. Very good indeed. My point is that when I read those books they seem to me *superbly* sinister. Tense and alarming. It's the sadism in Carroll's imagination I think. Obsession with control, and therefore with chaos. The two can't be separated. Wouldn't my *Looking-Glass* have been a movie worth watching? Don't you think?'

'Please excuse me,' said Alma. 'I haven't the slightest idea what you're talking about, and without access to my feed I can't chase down any of these references. Where am I? Where are *we*, I should ask.'

'We!' He nodded, as if she had said something clever. 'You hurt your head. Your head was hurt.'

'I'm dead, I'm sorry,' she said. That sounded wrong – off, somehow. 'I'm sorry to say I died,' she tried, but that sounded just as unidiomatic. 'What's happening?'

'I've had a long time,' he replied, 'to ponder it.'

'It? You mean, death?'

'I mean mystery. I mean suspense. So, yes, I suppose you're right. I mean death. We all die, after all; it is the only inevitable thing. Bangs don't scare us. Shock us, yes: but *scare* us? No. It's the anticipation of the bang that scares us. So the real question is' – and here the man leaned forward a little, and his grey suit crinkled at the seams – 'the *only* question, is – how can it *be* a surprise? How can it ever be unexpected? Which is to say, how can we *make* it a surprise? A thriller depends upon the threat of death, and the exhilaration of death averted. Don't you think? But death can never *be* averted! So how can there be thrillers? How can any film-maker master suspense?'

'I'm really not sure I follow.'

'You watch movies, surely?'

'Not so much.'

'Gracious,' said the man, and sat back in his chair. 'Well, to answer my own question, suspense is not about the unexpected. It is precisely about the expected. It is the art of drawing out the ghastly pleasure of anticipating the inevitable – which is to say, death. Always death. I've always liked whodunnits for that reason, you know. They are honest on this matter. They frontload the death, so that the story is always set in death's shadow. There's a great truth in that. You're a detective?'

She pondered this, and surprised herself. 'I am,' she said.

'There's another puzzle, which is the puzzle about the puzzle. Whodunnits say: death is a problem to be solved. They say: death is a puzzle. But that's not right, is it? Death's not complicated, or hidden. It's the most obvious thing there is. It's right there, for every single one of us, it's *leaning* over us. A whodunnit says death can be solved, doesn't it? But, when you think about that for a moment, isn't that the *most* ridiculous thing to say?'

'Why did you say that stuff about you being feminine? What was that about?'

The man tipped his face up and down, a slow and deliberate nod. Now that she looked at him, there really was nothing feminine about him at all. He was exaggeratedly masculine. Not masculine in the virile mode of young muscle-bound male models, but masculine in that other mode, the style of late middle-aged stolidity and presence: ugly and uncaring of his ugliness. The reek of port wine and Stilton and cigars. The inertia. Unshowy because it was such people who wield the power, and know it, and don't need to brag. The men who had ruled the world for thousands of years had looked like this.

'Sex is the mystery,' he said. 'New life is the mystery. I mean, isn't it amazing? Amazing that life can come out of the bodies of the dying? It's the twist-ending in the otherwise inevitable story. That's the trick: the feminine inside the masculine. The buried life. But, look, my dear, let's not *gender* it. Alright? Shall we not? Can we agree on that? It doesn't inhere in any specific male or female human being, and neither does it inhere in any male or female *principle*. There are two things. There's a principle of order and authority which is about closing down options, about slamming things home, about the lockdown. The tower. A vertical, tree-like, top-down principle. And then there's a principle of fecundity and newness, which is about opening up possibilities and making novel connections, about life and chaos and the roots that spread out underneath the ground. A horizontal principle. Pardon my schematism. The big cock wants to *rule*, but there's always a hidden hitch in his plan. Without it, the big prick would bring everything to death – the barrel of a gun, the blade of a sword, the shaft of a missile in flight. But there's a tiny doorway, hidden by a curtain, through which we can sneak away and find wonder and possibility and hope.'

'"We"?'

'Humanity. All of us. And here we are, my dear, and I would say that *you're* the hitch in the smooth operation of the power games. I hope I'm not being indelicate when I say so.'

'I'm finding all this a little baffling,' Alma confessed.

'Yes. Yes – I can see that. But that's your *job*, though, isn't it? Solving the puzzle. Resolving the confusion.' He lifted his right hand from its resting place on his thigh, reached into his jacket and pulled out a white handkerchief. He leaned forward again, and again his suit made little rustling noises: he was holding out the cloth to her.

She took it.

'Your forehead,' he observed. 'There's a dab of—'

She patted her forehead with the kerchief, and it came away with a little red spot on it. Perfectly round, and the size of the pupil of an eye.

'The one thing I would say,' the man added, 'is not to be *confused* by the misdirection. Tricks are always eighty per cent misdirection. You need to see past all that stuff.'

'Prestidigitation,' said Alma. Something was stinging her eyes. She squinted. 'That's fingers, though, isn't it?'

'Fingers,' the man agreed. 'Manipulating things. Making things. Pickers and stealers.'

'This isn't helping me.'

'The thing to remember is that a trick always has an *auteur*,' said the man.

Alma didn't recognise the word and, of course, automatically looked to her feed to supply the meaning. But her feed was offswitched. Maybe it was just something that you left behind when you died? 'Oughta?' she said.

'They say you can't make an ought,' replied the fat man, in all seriousness, 'from an is. And since death simply *is*, a brute fact, where life gets defined by what it should and should not, what it can and can't, I suppose that speaks to a fundamental disconnect between the two. *Auteur*. It's French. It means author, and people like to use it with reference to a particular style of movie direction.'

'Why do you keep going on about *cinema*?' fretted Alma.

There was a fogginess, somewhere. A whiteness creeping into her vision. No: it wasn't in her vision. It was in the room. Mist.

'In the documentary,' the man was saying, 'the basic material has been created by God, whereas in the fiction film the director becomes the god. He must create life.'

The mist granularised. A flurry of white, particulate flakes of light, like a snowy firework, was exploding silently all around Alma and she flinched and blinked and put her hands into her face. But when she peeked another look the man was gone and the room was gone and everything was a bristling mass of white sparks – all absolutely silent, no sound at all – and the intensity of the light increased until it became palpable as pain, as migraine, head-focused migraine, a forehead-focused migraine, a really unpleasant sensation of sharp agony, present in the middle of her forehead, or if not exactly present then flowing *through* her forehead, in an onrushing river of pain that—

'Hello,' said a new voice. A woman's voice. 'You're Alma? I'm pleased to meet you. My name is Pu Sto. I think we need to have a little chat, you and I.'

3: *Cafeteria Blues*

Alma sat up. She was in a cavernous and wholly empty hallway. A cafeteria, in fact. Tables, bolted to the floor at the base of their stems, stretching away into the middle distance, each flanked by two plastic benches. It was upon one of these benches that she had been lying. And now she sat up. Her head felt like it was splitting open, but at least she *had* a head to experience that unpleasant sensation.

The ceiling was illuminated by myriad little white lights. All the sparkles that had buzzed about Alma seemed to have settled into this grid.

The woman who had introduced herself as Pu Sto was sitting opposite, elbows on the table. She reached up to scratch her close-cropped hair. The expression on her face might best be described as *pained*.

'Gut-ache,' she said. 'I'd imagine you know what I'm talking about. But I've taken what my people assure me is the best bet at a countermeasure. We gave you some too. There will, they say, be some residual damage to the lower intestine; but – you know. Better than dying.'

Alma looked about. A gaunt-faced young man was also present: cheekbones like ploughshares, and intense, rather disturbing violet-coloured eyes.

'Dying,' said Alma, mouth dry. 'Where am I?'

'In a cafeteria.'

'Why am I in a cafeteria?'

'Above a certain size, cafeterias are required by law to have a first aid room. And therefore first aid supplies. And we could hardly take you to a regular hospital. But, of course,' she added wistfully, 'people don't really go to cafeterias any more. Work canteens – catering mass events – all the different sorts of work and mass events. All that stuff happens in the Shine now.'

'Lucky for us,' said the man, gesturing at the empty space.

'Who are *you*?' Alma asked the man.

Pu answered for him. 'This is my Prime PA. He has a name, but he prefers not to give it out to people he doesn't know.'

'Good afternoon,' said the PA.

'He's been attending to us. A *vrai* Krankenschwester, this one.'

'What?' Alma rubbed her eyes. 'What?' The pain in the head was distracting her from the pain in her gut. But now that she examined herself, there seemed to *be* no pain in the gut, any more. She pressed knuckles into her lower abdomen: nothing.

'Yes,' said Pu. 'Your lower intestine is pretty chewed up, inside, I think. But Prime, here, was able to counteract the nanobiots. I think. I mean, I hope so, because I'd been infected with a similar model, so your long-term health and mine have a connected destiny.'

'I was shot,' said Alma, rubbing a finger's end across her forehead. She touched a bullethole: her fingertip slipped into the countersunk circle, and her heartbeat slowed – palpably slowed, as if time were being decelerated – and adrenalin plonked and surged through her bloodstream. Oh god, god, god, it's all true. I'm dead, I'm dying, I'm in hell.

Prime PA, whatever his name was, reached over, took hold of her wrist, and pulled her hand away. 'Poking around in there with unwashed fingers,' he said sternly, 'is the royal road to giving yourself an infection.'

'I'm shot,' Alma said again.

'I,' said Pu, 'apologise.'

'Apologise?' Alma said, looking around rapidly, fight-or-flightily, scanning for exits.

'I'm not *directly* responsible for your being shot. But nonetheless. I feel a measure of responsibility.'

The scene flashed upon Alma's inner eye, which is the bliss of solitude, but which tends to provoke greater anxiety when one considers oneself surrounded by direct and imminent threats. Or *was* she really dead? 'Marguerite?'

'Your partner is fine, for the time being. I understand she needs your personal ministrations every four hours, yes? Well, we have an hour and a half before that becomes an issue.'

And with that, Alma's heart clambered out of the treacle, or whatever was slowing and glooping her pulse, and pumped harder. Relief. 'I was shot in the head, by a member of the security services. A colonel.'

'Mastema,' agreed Pu. 'She works for me.'

'*You* had me shot?'

Pu shook her head, with a series of short and precise thirty-degree swings, back, forth, back, forth. 'No, not at all. In point of fact, though Colonel Mastema *officially* works for me, her attempt on your life was the point when I became, finally, certain that she was *actually* working for somebody else. I had my suspicions for a long time. This confirms them.'

'Suspicions,' echoed Alma, with the tone of someone who knew whereof she spoke.

'Yes, yes,' agreed Pu. 'There's no reason for you to trust me. I know. Trust is earned, not given away for free. The attempt on your life happened to coincide with an attempt on mine – albeit, thanks to Prime, here, an unsuccessful one.'

'You come at the king you best not miss,' said Prime.

Alma stared at him. Pu said: 'Since all three of us have off-switched our feed, dropping in obscure allusions to antique literature is really poor form.'

Prime did not look abashed.

'Take the positives from the situation,' said Pu. 'The other side has been forced to show its hand. And it has done so very clumsily. That might give us an edge. Might.'

'What other side?'

'Health,' said Prime, gloomily. He was packing medical equipment back into its case. 'Boss,' he said to Pu. 'We need to get going.'

'Prime here is running a tracker, pretty low-tech but better than nothing. We need to leave.'

Together the two of them helped Alma to her feet.

'I,' Alma said, once the dizziness of being vertical had subsided, 'need more by way of explanation, I think.'

'Talk and walk,' urged Pu. 'Walk along and talk at the same time. Talk-walk. Walk-talk.'

The other two walked and Alma stumbled towards one of the exits, footsteps resounding on the hard floor. Prime had his arm around Alma's waist.

'I've had my suspicions concerning Mastema's loyalty,' Pu was saying, 'for a couple of months now. My mistake was in not realising how acute the situation had become. But she's always had a tendency towards going rogue, the colonel. And it's been evident to me for a while now not only that she is intensely ambitious, but also that she reckons she'd move more rapidly upwards in another department than mine.'

'I might feel the same way,' grumbled Prime.

'Part of the game is staying one step ahead,' said Pu. '*Pre*pared is *properly*-pared, as my old gran used to say.'

'I really don't believe she did,' replied Prime.

Through the door and then another, Alma found herself at the top of some stationary stairs, like a stone sculpture of an actual stairway. Perfectly motionless. They looked – well, they looked *broken*. 'What is this building,' she asked, 'some kind of antique?'

'They have certain advantages over regular stairways, these old-style models,' said Pu, lending her arm to support Prime's around Alma's waist. 'Not least they don't *log* you when you travel down them. Come along.'

It was a bumpy passage and it made Alma's headache worse, but they descended slowly.

'I replaced Colonel Mastema's ammunition with smartshells,' said Pu.

'I've never heard of smartshells,' said Alma.

'Indeed not. They're not widely known. And not available to the general public, either. They look just like regular bullets, so Mastema didn't notice the switch. What's even better, they *act* just like regular bullets, at least most of the time.'

'But they're not regular bullets?'

'They can be programmed. There's a DNA tagger in the tip, and a rapid-cascade chip. You can set them to react to the skin of designated individuals – you, for instance. What they do is taste the target, and if access is prohibited they blow back. It's not an entirely painless process . . .'

'You're telling me.'

'. . . but, well, you know. We can't make bullets magically dis-appear, mid-flight. Can't just teleport them out of existence. *That's* not a technology we possess, or not yet, in any case. Nor do we have instantaneous computation. It takes a short time to process the DNA: not long, but a measurable quantum. Some few nanoseconds. And then the bullet has to lose its consider-able forward momentum, which it does by disintegrating itself by backfiring a charge that propels its own fragments in a chevron pattern, reverse and to the sides. It does tend to leave a bit of a ... well, a mark.'

'A scar, you mean,' said Alma.

'Better than the alternative. And plastic surgery can do great things nowadays. Besides, the blood spray and the concussion served to convince Mastema that you were indeed dead. She could easily have stuck about and trodden on your windpipe to make sure you were gone.'

'What a charming thought.'

They had reached the bottom of the stairs. Pu shouldered open a door and they stepped into an underground carpark, smelling of damp concrete and old engine oil. Something like two-thirds of the ceiling lights were broken, and stretches of shadow overlapped to obscure most of the space. The floor-painted grids of IIIs and Es were all empty, except for one antique auto parked up against the wall.

As they walked towards this Pu said, 'Walks all ass straw.'

'I beg your pardon?'

'The car. A classic. Ass-straw translates as *star*, I believe.'

Something moved in the shadows in the far corner. Prime immediately unsnooked his arm from Pu, drew a handgun in a single smooth movement, and fired. The din was colossal, and made worse by being inside that enclosed space. 'Get her in the automobile,' he shouted, and, blinking, Alma heard the words through ears newly stuffed with cotton wool and ringing like a struck bell.

Alma was not a large woman, but then neither was Pu, and it was with some effort the older woman helped her to the side of the car.

Prime dropped to his right knee, straightened his right arm, braced his wrist with his left hand, and fired seven shots in quick succession. The sound was deafening in the strict sense that, after the first three or so, Alma felt the reverberation and saw the retina-blotting muzzle flashes rather than properly hearing them. Felt them, though: a pulsing thrum that jiggled the very marrow of her bones.

Then the target, still in the shadows, turned into a firework display of white fizzing sparks which suggested it was not made of human flesh.

The Ass-straw needed an actual metal key to open the doors, and then those doors had to be manually hauled open. Pu was saying something, *yelling* something by the look of exertion on her face, but Alma couldn't make out the words. An invisible soprano had taken residence inside both her ears and was sustaining a really impressive and unwavering top-C.

Inside the vehicle, Alma looked out, through the windscreen, and saw, on the far side of the parking area, a myrmidrone stepping into one of the fuzzy tepees of light. There were epileptic flashes from somewhere away to her right. It seemed that Prime was shooting again. His shots produced a series of sparkling impacts on the police machine.

The next thing Alma knew Pu had tumbled into the rear of the car beside her, and Prime was in the front. The car jolted forward, and Prime was driving – actually driving, moving the steering wheel and yanking the one-arm-bandit handle of the gearstick – past the myrmidrone, up a DNA-curl of concrete ramp and out into the sunlight. The light broke over her like a gush of revelation, diamond crumbs of brightness all around her, and the wind was on her face. It took her a moment to realise that the sparkles of light had been actual, material things – the passenger window shattered to crumbs of glass, and littered all over them. The police robot had got at least one good shot off.

Behind them the myrmidrone was lumbering along in pursuit, but the old car had ferocious acceleration – far in excess of any modern vehicle, far more than any sane human being would ever *need*, driving around a city – and in moments they had left their pursuer far behind.

4: *Drive, She Said*

Prime drove like a racing driver. Pu was saying something, but it was hard to hear her over the white noise of the open window, especially with Alma's dinned and dulled ears.

'What?'

'I *said*,' she hollered, 'that UK police myrmidrones fire what are called soft bullets. Soft isn't the right word, really. They can cause a fair bit of damage. If you'll permit me—' and she pushed a finger and thumb at Alma's face, and withdrew a rough diamond of smashed pane that had got itself embedded in her cheek.

'Ow,' she said.

'Mnkgneew,' said the Prime PA.

'What?'

'Not usually fatal,' said Pu. 'But not pleasant getting hit by one. Soft by name, bloody horrible by nature.'

'Mnkgneew,' said the Prime PA, again.

Prime swung the car through a series of turns, raced through a red light – the roads were otherwise deserted, but the sheer transgression of that made Alma gasp – and pulled onto the A33 heading south. Alma's ears swirled and popped. It sounded like she was inside a waterfall.

'We need to swing round,' she yelled. 'We need to get back. To Marguerite.'

'It's in hand,' Pu yelled back.

Prime pulled the car to a halt at the next set of traffic lights, indicating left. The light jumped from autumn colours to spring ones, and Prime drove off, but almost at once slowed and stopped in the middle of the road.

'What's the matter?' Pu asked.

'Mnkgneeaaaaa,' said the Prime PA, and slumped to the side.

'Oh dear lord, if it's not *one* thing,' said Pu, scrambling through the weirdly cluttered topography of the inside of this antique car from the rear seats into the front, 'it's another.'

'I've wet myself,' groaned the Prime.

'You big babby.'

'Uuuuuhh.'

'Where did it hit you?'

'It's in my armpit, I think.'

'*Dear* lord. Can I patch it with something from your bag of tricks?'

'Mnkgneeoh,' said the Prime PA in a low drawl.

'Soft bullets,' tutted Pu. Then: 'Oh my God you weren't joking – it's *soaking* here.'

'Sorruhh.' A mere croak.

'Good grief, man, you're bleeding out. It can't be helped. I'll have to get a change of clothes later.' She pulled Prime towards her, clambered over him, settled herself into the driving seat, hauled the seat forward – by hand! – and restarted the vehicle. In five minutes they had negotiated the streets and were barrelling up towards R!-town hospital. Alma's second visit in a few hours. 'Stay in the car,' Pu told Alma, who was only too happy to comply. 'I have to check him *in*. Which is to say, dump him in the hospital hall and leave the medics to deal with him: I can't hang about.'

She left, helping Prime into the building.

In a moment she was back, her teal trousers tie-dyed with blood across the seat and thighs. She got into the old car and pressed the starter and – this being the most amazing of a whole series of amazing developments – the thing *did not start*. The engine barked, echoed its own bark, shuddered and went back to sleep.

Pu Sto let out a long sigh. 'There are,' she noted, 'disadvantages as well as advantages to these old cars. No speed restrictions, true. But reliability is a—'

She tried the starter again, and the engine imitated the sound of a heavy angular metallic sculpture falling down a scree slope. Then, *mirabile*, it caught and thrummed into life.

They drove off. 'You met a man called Dave,' she said.

'No,' Alma replied.

'You did. I don't doubt he gave you a false name, and probably a string of them. But he was shot outside your apartment some hours ago, and you were right there.'

'Derp Throat. He was with you?'

'Dave? No. No, he wasn't one of mine. He was a white knight, at least in his own head. And fat lot of good it did him. But he parked something in your feed.'

'That's right,' said Alma, slowly. Thinking back to the time before she was shot was like casting an angler's line into the deep past. And yet it was only a few hours earlier! 'I cached it.'

'Wise. It's certainly encrypted, but the main worry we have is that if you onswitch your feed then the authorities will zero in on you in moments. Believe that they are fully mobilised, right now. Believe it.'

'*You* are the authorities,' Alma noted.

'You're not wrong. But this is a time of upheavals, my dear. If I had to pick one word to describe what is happening at the moment, I think *internal coup* would be ... that's two words, I know. I know. If I had to pick two words to describe what is happening at the moment, then I might plump for *internal coup*.'

Alma said nothing.

'I have people,' Pu said. 'Some I know I can't trust. Some I figure I probably can't trust. Some I probably *can* trust. Probabilities aren't much use at this stage. They may be all I have, though. Unfortunately the only individual on whose loyalty I can absolutely rely is now in hospital, with a soft-bullet wound to the armpit, and probably under arrest. But some of the people, assuming they haven't defected, are presently throwing as much chaff into the eyes of R!-town's surveillance as possible. Otherwise they'd easily identify an old-school car put-putting along the streets. One of my people is running a duplicate feed that looks, on the surface, just like mine – running it into London Town, to try and distract them. Still, if I were Röell I'd be bringing in some national surveillance, and pull strings to get some proper military drones into the R!-town airspace. So we don't have much time.'

'Much time to do what?'

'To dig out whatever Dave hid in your feed. But we can't do it here. Not in this town. There's a facility on the south coast we can use, provided we can get down there and back again inside your four-hour window. And I think we can.'

'Who's Röell?'

'Ambition personified. Never mind her.'

'I'm happy to do that, if you can guarantee that she won't mind *me*.'

At this Pu grinned, and looked left at her passenger. 'I'm starting to like you, my dear.'

'Starting.'

'It looks messy, I suppose, to outsiders. There are various government departments, with notional oversight for various things. And once upon a time they mostly busied themselves with attending to those various things. But nowadays most people's lives are in the Shine, and most of the real-world chores are attended to by machines. It's not that people in the Shine *don't* care, exactly: it's that the Shine is so absorbing and so entertaining and *so* distracting that they only care if things intrude too disruptively. And the government departments are still there, of course, because that's how the inertia of history works. They still have legally mandated and budget-supported real power. So they mostly use that power in a series of jockeyings for position.'

'One might think,' offered Alma, 'that some kind of oversight would be in order.'

'Indeed,' said Pu. 'Which is what my department is supposed to be about – amongst other things. And, boy, are we resented. I've been expecting a concerted attempt to unseat me for a while; although I must say I didn't expect them to come at me quite so hard, or quite so soon.'

Alma said nothing.

'I suppose,' Pu added, distractedly, 'that whatever Adam Kem had uncovered, the thing that led to his death, had something to do with that. Anyway. This is what I propose: we visit your partner, Marguerite, and you tend to her. It would be a shame to let her die, now, wouldn't it, though? My people will have laid a false trail, I'm hoping: the nurse detailed to attend your Marguerite is out of commission, it seems, and I've had a fictitious person logged as her carer, as far as the authorities are concerned. Röell would surely like to take your Marguerite into custody, but that's not very practicable, is it, given her size. And by custody I mean hospital. But that amounts to the same thing, you know.'

'Hospital wouldn't be able to help her,' Alma noted.

'Hospital has almost nothing to do with helping people, nowadays, and everything to do with incarcerating them. I think

I can get us into your flat. Now, I did wonder if we might try piggybacking a message on your partner's feed.'

'Use it to open Dave's little package'

'No, I don't think so. The encryption there means that we can only do that in your feed, and I shudder to think what tripwires Röell's people have set up there. No: we need to get you out of R!-town and to this facility I mentioned. But getting you out of town and back in four hours means I need to requisition a plane, and I can't do that if I'm offswitched. Your Marguerite's feed is only going to locate her in her own home, which shouldn't trigger any police alerts. Since I can't onswitch my own actual feed, for the same reasons as you, I'll need to pick up a particular piece of kit. Hardware. I know! But there you go.'

The car swung too fast round a bend, fairground-waltzer, and then accelerated away.

'What is it that Derp Throat cached in my feed?' Alma asked.

'I would like very much to know that,' replied Pu. 'I can guess.'

Alma said nothing.

'Think of it this way,' said Pu, hand-manoeuvring the car to a stop outside a nondescript building assembled out of big blocks like loaves of brown bread. She turned the trembly engine off, and pivoted in her seat to be able to look directly at Alma. 'For thousands of years – perhaps tens of thousands – power was a matter of money. Which is really to say, of notified debt, which is what money actually is. When somebody is in debt to you, then they are obligated to you, and you can command them. And when the population gets larger than a certain size, debt becomes impossible to track without some kind of material token. Which is where money comes from. But debt, and money as the symbol of debt, only work – only function properly – under the logic of scarcity. Money itself needs some sort of authority of creation, to keep it scarce, because it is used to exchange for things which are scarce. Attempts to manufacture money willy-nilly led to a thing called inflation, which nobody much liked. And scarcity was a surprisingly enduring feature of human life, because for almost all its history humankind has lived in a finite world.'

'Once upon a time.'

'Exactly, my dear. Actual money has been rendered obsolete by the fact that online resources are perfectly infinite: the constraints on your feed are trivial and easily addressed. And the Shine is . . .'

well, we both know about the Shine. For a while now monetary exchange has only been shored up by a complicated process of modified blockchaining. But that's not going to last for ever. In the eighteenth century the really expensive things were food and clothes. But we soon found ways of undermining the scarcity of both those things, and both became trivially cheap. In the late twentieth and early twenty-first century the really expensive thing was housing, because people insisted on preferring large detached properties and there wasn't enough space for everyone to have one. But now, people can live in as much or as little space, as much or as little luxury, as they desire – in the Shine. All they need for a real-world base is a cupboard. So what does that leave us?'

'I'm confident,' said Alma, 'that this disquisition is going some-where.'

'There's a price to be paid for living in the Shine,' said Pu. 'It is that you must *open* yourself. You render yourself easy to track, easy to surveil, easy to monitor and therefore easy to control. People in the Shine don't care, because they're too caught up in their various actualised fantasies. But the people who do the surveilling *do* care, because it's the grounds of their power, and once you get a taste for it, power is something you never get enough of.'

Alma said nothing. Pu seemed to be looking very intently at her.

'I wonder if that's why you don't ever venture into the Shine, my dear? Some people are allergic to opening themselves to complete surveillance, and not all of them are that way for reasons of malfeasance.'

'All I want,' said Alma, 'is to be allowed to continue caring for Marguerite. I just want to be left alone.'

'No chance of that, dearie,' said Pu. 'I'm sorry to say. We need to push through to the other side.'

'You really think there *is* another side to all this?'

Pu nodded briskly at this, as if impressed at Alma's prescience. 'That's what we need to find out,' she said. 'But it may be that whatever Dave hid in your feed will give us leverage.'

Alma said nothing.

Pu said she would be a minute, although in fact she was three. She darted inside the nondescript building, and then reappeared. Back in the car, panting a little. 'I think we have what we need.'

They drove off. On the way towards Alma's apartment block they passed two cars going in the other direction: a fat-faced people carrier and a sports car like a creeping feline. Both had blacked-out windows. When she saw a third vehicle, a huge van shaped like a shed with thick dinosaur-tread wheels twice the normal diameter, Alma began to wonder if something was wrong. That was a lot of cars all at once.

'So, surveillance. Power. Yes. The Department of Health,' Pu was saying. 'For decades now treatment has involved parking the individual in some pleasant corner of the Shine whilst the body is fixed. It is *bodies*, you see. That's the ineluctable. I think that's the right word – my feed is offswitched, so I can't check. The ineluctable.'

'Ineluctable,' echoed Alma, craning her head to get a better view of the two drones flying overhead.

'Ineluctable bodies. It's not the *materiality* of them that's a problem. We have lots of sophisticated technological ways of dealing with their materiality. It's that they are windowless.'

'Windowless?'

'Power can't see inside. There are ten billion people on the planet and about a tenth of that number either don't or can't fully commit to the Shine. Religious fundamentalists who think it's the devil's playground. People with certain epilepsies and cancers, like your partner. Old people who just don't trust it. People who are too poor to have reliable access. So that's a billion locked rooms that the authorities would dearly like to open up and peer into. There's a great deal at stake, my dear, in this—'

A hefty concussion.

It was more of a viscerally *felt* impact than a sound, although that might have had something to do with Alma's battered eardrums. Inside her torso Alma's stomach hit the rim of her pelvis at the exact time the sound of the explosion hammered out.

The world slammed backwards through ninety degrees, and Alma was on her back. Glass tinkled all around.

She shut her eyes.

The vehicle was up on its hind legs like a dancing bear. The tyres were shreds and fragments of rubber, and the metal hubs screamed friction against stone. The car rotated on its rear end, spinning through thirty degrees or so, sliding on its metal arse over the road.

The road was a bridge. They screeched towards the balustrade.

What had happened was this: the road had been laid with a vehicle-immobilising stinger. The device was, of course, calibrated to modern cars, with their deflation-proof wheels. Pu Sto's old-fashioned car had old-fashioned high-pressure tyres and when the stinger tried to seize these, as it would with any car, they blew apart like bombs. The car was rocked back, skidded to the left and hit a low concrete balustrade at the side of the road. The seatbelt squeezed Alma's ribs fit to bursting. As the vehicle hit the concrete barrier at the side of the road its momentum was enough to tip it forward and over, swivelling down with the barrier as hinge. A moment of balance. Then, forward and down. From being on her back Alma found herself free-falling, facedown. Crumbs of broken glass rattled through the interior of the car like the gravel inside a maraca.

She opened her eyes. Somebody was screaming, and it was her. She was the one who was screaming.

Falling.

Then the front of the vehicle crunched like a slab of granite – down – not quite into the river, but near the edge – onto the roof of a building below, shiny with evpaint, punching through but tipping too and tearing a hole down. The car toppled forward. Now its roof was beneath it.

Now Alma was upside down.

And then the vehicle hit the road below, landing on its back. It made the sound of a stone giant connecting a particularly hefty punch, and all the detritus inside the car rattled and cymballed and battered down. The four main pillars connecting roof and the chassis bent their knees in unison. Made their obeisance to gravity. Bowing.

After the tempest of noise and violent motion, a silence, and out of the silence a still, small voice. It was singing 'u', very high-pitched.

Alma drew breath. Still alive. She took another breath and discovered, to her surprise, that she was hiccoughing loudly.

She fumbled for the seatbelt snatch, released it, and straight away banged her head painfully down on the roof. This bent her neck to an awkward angle, and her knees pressed up against her chest, or, rather, pressed down against her chest.

She wriggled round, gulping air and saying *here*! *here*! over and over in Latin. A language she didn't even realise she spoke. Here! Pu Sto was hanging upside down.

Here!

'My pocket,' Pu said, her voice breathier than usual. 'Inside – take it.'

Stunned, and awkwardly positioned in the back of the car – like big-grown Alice in the story, when she is trapped – here! – inside the tiny little house – (you *do* remember that story, don't you?) – Alma reached forward. She heard, and understood, Pu's words, but – here! – for some reason, presumably to do with her momentarily jangled sensibilities, she did not reach into the pocket. Here! She had it in her hiccoughing head that Pu wanted her to undo her seatbelt.

She found the snib and pushed the button. The woman's seatbelt snickered away, but upside-down Pu did not fall.

'In my *pocket*,' she rasped again.

'That's a neat trick,' said Alma, but her hiccough turned the trick's tr into an h. 'Not falling, I mean.'

'Inside,' Pu repeated. 'Take it. You're dead in the official record: shot in the head. They don't know you're you. They're after me, not you. I mean, they'll still *arrest* you, because you're with me. But you have the advantage now. At least for a time.'

Something was holding Pu upside down in her seat, preventing her from falling down, and it took Alma a moment to see what.

A pole.

The car had fallen onto a pole. This had bitten through the roof like a fang, and now Pu was impaled upon it. Or had it just pressed her into her seat? Had the metal post actually penetrated her body?

Alma reached inside her top and drew out a thin device. A pen, perhaps. A steadystate memory device. A . . . torch?

'You should be toddling along,' gasped Pu. 'They'll be on their way down, and you don't want to be arrested, believe me. Not if you want to keep your partner alive.'

'What about you?' Alma asked, although in her head she was summoning panicky images of many police officers and myrmi-drones scurrying into position around the upturned car.

'I'll be fine. But *you* need to get away.'

Alma wriggled, tried to reach the door handle, banged her head, cricked her neck, hiccoughed, hiccoughed, hiccoughed. There was movement outside the car – hard to see what, exactly, but something scurried across the line of sight of the fractured front windscreen. Booted feet, was it?

'It's too late,' Alma gasped.

'My dear girl,' ordered Pu. 'Get out of my car.'

She found the door handle: shaped like a chromium seashell, and very stiff and awkward to operate. With a heave she cracked open the door, pushed with a foot to open it further, and struggled through the opening.

Fresh air, a strong whiff of chemical volatiles of some kind, sunlight dazzling her eyes for a moment.

Falling.

She didn't fall far, the second time, and almost as soon as she registered what the sensation in her gut *was*, that it was the acceleration of a body under gravity of 9.8 m/s^2, she hit water.

The car had come to a rest half on the road, half over the edge of the river embankment. Alma went under. Her clothes, registering the wetness, sealed and repelled. Full raincoat mode: thank heavens for modern threads. But one of her shoes came off. She thrashed, came to the surface, breathed. The car was above her, half on the bank and half reaching out over the river, the stub of an unfinished bridge.

A face peered over the lip of the bank. 'Stop,' said the face. 'In the name of the police.'

The shock of hitting the water seemed to have cured Alma of her hiccoughs. With a wriggle she slid under the water, and kicked out for the far bank. The Kennet is not a broad stream, and she reached its other side in moments. When she surfaced she looked back at a puzzled-looking knot of human police officers.

One storey up, as it were, the dual carriageway bridged the river: but there was no immediate mode of connection down to the riverside from this hefty concrete span. One of the police officers was jogging off, running for a connecting road to bring them from the higher level, across and down to Alma's side. Another was peering into the Marmite-coloured waters, as if debating with himself whether to jump in and pursue her that way.

The bank was too high to climb out, but twenty metres downstream was a metal ladder. Alma half swam, half walked her way along to this, losing her other shoe in the muddy river bottom in the process. Why couldn't they design shoes that responded the way smartcloth shirts and trousers responded? The riverbed sucked at her bare feet like a baby on a pacifier.

'Stop,' wailed the police on the far bank. A drone buzzed her, flew high, and hovered. She scrambled up the ladder and when she reached the top she didn't pause. Barefoot though she was, Alma ran off down a sidestreet.

The drone followed her for a few minutes, but since it couldn't lock onto her feed it was surprisingly easy to get rid of. Sidestreet led into sidestreet; and then a blare of retail signage informed her that she was approaching the big, oracular shopping centre in the centre of town.

Hair wet, barefoot, Alma made her way into the cavernous building, jogged past the blank façades where shops had once existed, stopped at one of the few still in operation and picked up a hat: big brim, coloured-dot pattern on the crown. Of course, she couldn't pay for it without onswitching her feed. This, stupidly, occurred to her only after she had picked up the hat – the legacy of a lifetime of superfacility where shopping was concerned. Alma looked round the establishment. There was only one human-being shopworker, and she was at the back of the store having an eCig.

Alma made a run for it.

Red lights flashed, a siren crooned, but she sprinted through the remainder of the centre and out into the sunshine without being stopped.

From there it was a short jog to her apartment, her heart pounding. She had twenty minutes before Marguerite's treatment became due. Her heart rattled in her ribcage. What would she find? A whole platoon of armed soldiers to apprehend her? But she remembered Pu's words: as far as the authorities were concerned, she was dead.

That was something.

5: *The Kennet and the Thames*

There was nobody outside the apartment block. She went up in the elevator, her hair a sticky mess that dripped a tick-tock onto the floor. The myrmidrone by the front door queried her presence, and requested her to onswitch her feed. It evidently did not recognise her, or it would have taken her straight into custody. Following a hunch, Alma took out the pen that Pu had pressed upon her, flashed it at the robot's feed and watched it power down.

'Well,' she said aloud. 'That's handy.'

She put her shoulder to the door and heaved against the tension of its motors. It opened. The fact that her feed was offswitched had the ancillary advantage that she did not have to engage in chit-chat with the conversational algorithm of the insane door.

Inside there was a spatter of blood on the floor, and a tendril of black-red going up the wall. Alma wondered whose it was before she remembered that it was her own.

She consulted her watch. Fifteen minutes.

In the bathroom Alma peed, peeled off her top and peered at her reflection. There was a plug of scabbed blood, a bindi spot, in the middle of her forehead. It did not improve her looks, especially in conjunction with the wet-bedraggled hair and overall look of exhaustion.

She examined her body. Big circular bruises everywhere, like Petri dishes of purple mould growing just under the skin. Seemed like a long time ago, that tumble. She ached everywhere.

She went through to the bedroom. Marguerite was sleeping, but woke with a snort and a sigh as Alma began to check her medical status.

'My love?' she said. Her voice sounded confused. 'I have a bit of a fever, I think. And so – so hungry.'

Her feed machine needed resupplying. 'I'll get you something to eat in a moment,' Alma told her.

'That's an interesting new perfume.'

'I fell in the river.'

'Ah, Eau de Thames.'

'The other river.'

'The Kennet! So, so. Kennet. It rises at Silbury Hill you know, does the Kennet, the kindly Kennet, and it flows into the Thames right here in R!-town.' Marguerite spoke in a low, burbling tone, quite unlike her usual voice. 'That's holy water, the Kennet,' she said. 'Silbury Hill is one of the most sacred sites in Old England. Oh, Al, I feel ill, ill, how feverish and how ill.'

'I'm sorry, my love,' said Alma, identifying the latest perfectly random geneswitch of the pathogen, and applying the relevant remedy.

'I know,' Marguerite said fretfully. 'One sickness at a time. Oh, my mind is not proper. Not proper at all: all jumbly and hot and I can't think straight.'

'I'll add some electrolyte solution to your drink feed.'

'Hungry!'

'I'll get you something to eat, don't worry. But sorting your electrolytes is more pressing.'

There was almost nothing in the kitchenette by way of food. Alma brought through what she could, gave Marguerite a pint of water to drink. After this was down she fed her some parcel-chippos, a pot of yoghurt, dried quorn and a large-ish piece of cheese. Eating this seemed to revive Marguerite somewhat.

'I'll tell you something interesting about the Kennet,' she said. 'And the Thames too. These two great English rivers meet in R!-town, you know. It's one of the reasons R!-town is the true omphalos of England. The Thames is the *masculine* river, you see. Ancient Britons used to throw swords into it, as a sacrifice to the god of the flow. Phallic swords. *Thames* derives from an Old Celt word that means strong flow, which is a pretty phallic name if you think about it. And it's well chosen. The Thames *thrusts* itself through London, and fertilises the surrounding countryside. Ah, but the Kennet is the *feminine* river, you see.'

'Marguerite, you're babbling.'

'You know what the name means? Kennet. An indecency. It used to be called the Cunnit. Check on your feed if you don't believe me! Wait – is your feed offswitched? Why is your feed offswitched?'

'It's a long story, my love. I need you to do something for me.'

'Anything, anything,' murmured Marguerite, her eyes rolling up white.

'Don't fall asleep just yet! Wake up! First of all, you need to order a delivery of some food – for you.'

'Can't you?'

'As you have already noted, my feed is offswitched. If I turn it on again the authorities will locate me and arrest me.'

'R!-town is the place where the male river and the female river mix and mingle, you see,' said Marguerite. 'Mix and mingle. Fertility and new life and the sacred connection of sex. It's been a holy town since the iron age. It's a special place, this town of ours.'

'Yes, yes, very special,' agreed Alma. 'Listen to me. *You* need to order up some food. And then you and I need to figure out if I can use your feed remotely to access something hidden in mine – to access it without alerting the authorities to my location. Marguerite?'

But Marguerite had fallen asleep again.

Alma rubbed her eyes. It had been quite a day. Lifting her arms to bring her fists up to her eyesockets made plain to her just how foul-smelling the residue of river water was, which in turn prompted her to wash. She stripped off the remainder of her clothes, threw the stained clothes into the chute, and stepped into the shower. Fresh clothes were waiting for her when she emerged.

When she came out, there was a stranger standing just inside the front door.

It was a nurse, of course.

'Who are you?' demanded the nurse.

'I live here,' said Alma.

'I was told you would be considerably,' said the stranger, making the flicky-eyed motions of somebody checking their feed, 'heavier.'

'You misunderstand,' said Alma. 'Your patient is in the next room. She also lives here.'

'My feed says she lives alone,' said the nurse.

'You have arrived too late. The nature of my partner's pathology is such that there is a very brief window of treatment, and it occurs once every four hours.'

'I was delayed,' said the nurse. 'It's quite the carnival outside, I don't mind telling you.'

'Carnival?'

'See for yourself. Wait a moment, your feed is offswitched. Why is your feed offswitched?'

'You can go now,' said Alma.

'You,' said the nurse, presumably feed-prompted, 'are *Alma*! Good gracious me. Not dead after all. Well, well, well. Citizen, the police are outside in force, and I assume that's on account of you. For a while I thought they weren't going to let me inside at all. I had to show them all sorts of authorisation, and insist on the medical necessity of my attendance.'

'What would be helpful,' Alma suggested, 'is if you could go down and tell them I'm not here.'

'But surely they know you *are* here,' said the nurse. 'Why else would they have turned up in such numbers? Nothing I say would persuade them otherwise. Besides, you *are* here. You wouldn't want to make me a liar, would you?'

Alma asked herself: how did they know? They must have been actively eavesdropping on Marguerite's feed. Piggybacking it – quite illegal without the express consent of the feed-owner, and even should such consent be obtained surveillance must wait until after a seven-day cooling-off period has etcetera and so on. But it was not as if Marguerite were sufficiently compos mentis to even give consent, assuming she had done so, which she never would. So the tag was illegal, and a court would throw it out, which in turn meant that Mastema, or whoever was pulling her strings, had no intention of it ever *going* to court.

This was a worrying development, all things considered.

Alma took a breath. 'Look,' she started saying, and then she stopped, because the nurse had taken something from her first-aid bag. It was a gun.

'That's a gun,' Alma said.

'It is.'

'Funny sort of thing to carry in a first-aid bag,' Alma observed.

'I work for the hospital,' the nurse said, as if this explained it. And something turned around in Alma's mind, some onscreen loading spinwheel, some cogwheel. Her memory had grown flabby with reliance on her feed, and now that she was offswitched she felt the irritation of not being able to recall something just on the outskirts of her memory. What was it? Something important. The key to the whole thing.

Something Marguerite had said. Not just now, but earlier.

What had Marguerite said? She'd been feverish for a day and half now, but when Alma had first told her about the death – the first murder, Adam Kem impossibly appearing in the boot of that car – she had said: what had she said? She had said: *I solved it.*

That might have been the fever talking, of course; but one thing Alma had learned over her many years with Marguerite was not to underestimate her Mycroft-level powers of rapid deductive reasoning. This crime was a puzzlebox, and she claimed she had opened it.

When she had said that, Alma had been concerned with getting an antipyretic into her system. She'd fobbed her off, *Of course you did, my love.*

And in reply Marguerite had said, what? Yes, that was it: *Hospital.* Not, as Alma had thought at the time, *get me to a hospital.* But: this is the solution.

'Hospital,' said Alma, finally understanding how the crime had been pulled off. 'Hospital.'

'What?' the nurse asked, sharply.

'Hospitals are places where people go to be made well again,' said Alma.

'Quite right! And we're better at it than we've ever been,' said the nurse. She waggled the gun, using it to point to the door. 'Downstairs, please.'

Alma's mind was engaged now, thinking through the particulars of the appearance of Adam Kem. She moved almost without realising it to the door of her home, and stepped through it. The nurse was behind her.

'Keep going,' she said. 'Into the elevator.'

Alma barely heard her: the whole picture was coming clear in her head. She saw, now, how Adam Kem had been killed and how his body had been disposed of, after the crime. It was cleverly done, and hard to solve, but now that she saw it the main thing was annoyance at herself that she hadn't spotted it earlier. It was, after all, the *only* way the thing could have been pulled off. And given that it *was* the only way, she should have been able to work it out. Marguerite had solved it, even in an ill and feverish state.

Marguerite was, she found herself thinking, a remarkable human being.

Thinking that brought tears into Alma's eyes, incongruously enough. Tears! *Crying?* The very idea! Yet here she was, her heart swelling.

The elevator door slid open.

'Get inside,' said the nurse.

Like a sleepwalker, Alma stepped inside. She turned and watched the nurse step alongside her, the gun still aimed at her heart. The doors closed.

'You want a tissue?' the nurse asked, her voice a curious mixture of threat and solicitation.

'What?' She meant the tears. Alma's mind turned around again. Wait a minute: where was she now? In an elevator. She was being taken down to be handed over to the police. She wiped her eyes with the back of her hand, took a breath and looked at the nurse.

'I'm going to reach out and touch your throat now,' she said, in a slow and steady voice.

'What?'

'I'm going to reach out,' Alma repeated, slowly and calmly, 'with my right hand, and just touch your throat a little.'

'I don't *think* so.'

'I am going to move my hand very slowly out, and touch your throat.'

'Do and I'll shoot you through the heart!'

'In a moment,' Alma said, nodding. 'Sure. But first I'm just going to—' Slowly and steadily she reached out with her right hand.

'Stop!' the nurse ordered. She lifted the gun a little, aiming it now at Alma's face.

'I know,' Alma agreed, keeping her eye-to-eye steady. 'Just one moment.'

'I *will* shoot.'

'Quite right,' hushed Alma. 'That's absolutely right.' Her fingers touched the nurse's neck, just under the woman's chin. The lift came to a stop. Alma reached a little further, sliding her thumb one side and her fingers the other. 'We're almost there. What were you saying?'

'I said,' the nurse replied, in a trembly voice, 'I will shoot you. I will do it.'

'Quite right,' soothed Alma. Keeping her eyes looking steadily into the nurse's, not breaking eye contact at any point, she started to apply pressure around the woman's neck, slowly pushing in. The elevator doors slid open. The nurse's eyes widened, and she began to making gasping noises. The gasping noises quickly turned into raspier, scratchier ones.

The doors pinged softly, and closed.

Moving steadily, Alma reached up with her left hand and took hold of the gun. The nurse clutched it, and Alma leaned in a little further, adding pressure to her windpipe. The woman's face was turning autumnal-coloured. Her eyes bulged. Alma maintained eye contact.

The woman's fingers relaxed on the gun.

Alma took the weapon, and slipped it into one of her pockets. Staring steadily into the nurse's eyes. Smiling. Nodding. Then, suddenly, Alma clutched hard on the windpipe, pulled the woman's purple face towards her, and then slammed her head hard back against the wall of the elevator.

The whole box reverberated like a dull bell.

Alma pulled the woman's head forward and slammed it back again. This time a thin star-spray of red appeared on the metal wall, directly behind the nurse's head. Like a bug had been squished by the impact of the back of her skull and the lift wall. Her face was blueing, now, and her eyes were no longer seeing Alma.

Alma let go. The nurse slid down the wall, and slumped into a seated posture of some ungainliness.

I work for the hospital, indeed. Pff.

Alma bent down. A more natural colour was returning to the nurse's face, and the sound of her breathing was loud. She was somewhere between conscious and unconscious. Alma fumbled at the woman's tunic, found a tag under the hem and loosened the cloth. She got her arms up and pulled the sagging cloth from the woman's unresisting body. Then she pulled it over her own clothes. She fiddled with the cloth to tighten it around her waist whilst leaving enough slack at the back to act as a sort of makeshift hood or snood.

The she pressed the little nubbin that opened the elevator doors, and walked briskly through the empty lobby and out onto the street.

She was still barefoot.

Outside was, as the nurse had said, unusually crowded. There must have been eight people present, four of them police officers, with two large police vehicles parked in parallel with the pavement. A dozen or so drones buzzed through the sky.

The trick here was confidence, so Alma walked straight towards the police: hopefully they wouldn't be too suspicious that her feed was offswitched. Or that she was barefooted. And hopefully none of the drones would get a good enough look at her face to match her via any visual-recognition algorithms. 'She's in there!' she called. 'She attacked me!' She touched the circular red contusion on her forehead. 'She's in the flat—'

'Is she armed?' one of the police officers called back.

'No – no weapons. Except her nails!'

And another, taking a step towards her: 'Are you alright?'

'I'm fine,' Alma called, trying to scan the street without making it too obvious that she was scanning the street. Finally she saw it: the vehicle in which the nurse must have come – a small white car, expensive-looking enough to have been, perhaps, hand-made by robots and not just 3D-printed in some cut-price manufactory. *I work for the hospital* indeed.

'I'm fine,' she called again, walking briskly towards the car. 'I have,' damn, what was the word? Lesser, laser, 'lacerations, I have some lacerations, and need to retrieve, uh, from my car the—'

She needn't have bothered: six of the eight police were already in motion, running into the lobby of her building. The other two took up positions by the main entrance. The small group of passers-by oo'd and aa'd. One solitary meshed-up trundled by, perfectly oblivious to the local drama.

Alma walked, and kept walking. She passed the nurse's car and, without turning her head, ducked back down an alleyway and started to run. The humming of drones overhead rose and fell, like augmented sounds of some desert wind.

6: *The Drones*

Running was probably a mistake. Sudden changes in perambulatory velocity were liable to attract the attention of drones. That was how they were programmed. And indeed, a few peeled off the main crowd buzzing over her apartment building and drifted over towards her. Alma forced herself to stop running. Calm, she told herself. Calm.

The drones swept overhead, and then buzzed back to join their main group.

Alma turned the corner and headed towards the city centre. She had to find a safe place, and then work out how to use what she now knew – the solution to Adam Kem's murder, and everything that it entailed – to leverage her position. To get them all to leave her alone. To do whatever was necessary to leave her to care for Marguerite.

There was a tinnitus noise. Alma actually shook her head a few times, to try and dislodge it. A mosquito burr: no – many mosquitoes buzzing together.

What was her next move?

A buzzing came across the sky. Alma had heard it before, but there was nothing to compare it to now. Looking up might give the drones enough pixels to make an ID, so she resisted the temptation. Then again she could hardly keep her eyes on the ground. She needed to know. She pulled her hood a third across her face, and tried to sneak as inconspicuous a peek as possible.

There was a vast swarm of drones high overhead. It looked like scores. Maybe hundreds. Some were swirling through a figure-of-eight path, others were drifting slowly in the same direction that Alma was walking.

This could not be a good sign.

She picked up her pace, and the buzzing increased. More drones were joining the swarm. When Alma stepped out into the relatively open space of the Queen's Road – traffic lights winking through their colours at empty tarmac – she saw a second swarm of drones over the city centre, drifting towards the first.

She stopped. An in-Shine man, middle-aged and paunchy, stalked past inside an unusually expensive outfit of mesh, oblivious to the gathering swarms.

A car came round the curve of the road, and pulled up at the light. The passenger got out, and stood beside his vehicle, looking up at the sky. He spotted Alma, and with that instinct towards surly sociability that is ineradicable in a certain sort of English person, waved. 'Never seen so many before!' he called to her. 'All in one place, like.'

A paw-shaped mass of drones emerged from the swarm, down-pointing. It curled, and stretched a tentacle towards Alma. The buzzing sound grew in volume.

'Run,' Alma called back at the man. 'Run!'

He gazed, goggled.

And *down* they came.

Surveillance drones are not armed. There are, of course, laws forbidding this, and other laws forbidding military drones from entering civilian space, or flying anywhere in peacetime save in designated military test zones. But the fact that surveillance drones are not armed does not mean that surveillance drones can do no harm. They are, of necessity, material objects capable of moving at speed, and though they cannot fire projectiles they can easily *become* projectiles.

Drones of all shapes and sizes buzzed down towards Alma. Some were flat plastic triangles with minijets at each apex; some were bulbous, like stems of ginger or globes fused together; some were hemispherical and others the full sphere; a few were as big as a person's head, or even bigger, but most were the size of hands, or smaller, like fat mechanical bugs.

Alma ran straight until she thought her heart was going to bounce right out of her chest, and then jinked – left and down, pushing with her bare left foot to propel herself right. A drone caught her on the top of her head, a little to one side, with a painful crack, and two more bounced off her flank, but most were fooled by the suddenness of her shift in trajectory. She was running across the four lanes of the road, crashes and bashes audible behind her as howling drones rebounded post-collision off the pavement. A cloud of the machines swirled overhead; others were skimming low across the road and heading for her.

She looked back. The hapless passenger was also being targeted. He danced as St Vitus had danced before him. He flailed his arms around his head. Drones cymbal-smashed off the roof of his car, bounced high and then either fell down inert or else buzzed furiously and turned to dive-bomb him again. The last thing Alma saw of him was the passenger falling backward, a fronded unicorn-horn of blood sprouting from his forehead. Then the drones caught up with her and she was knocked off her feet.

She rolled, curled as tight as she could, and endured a pummelling from a dozen or so drones punching into her. She told herself: protect the head, protect the neck.

She told herself: this is an assassination attempt.

Or else the drones have gone mad – some software glitch. But that's not very likely, is it? Not all of them together.

No, she told herself: this is attempted murder.

She told herself: you can't stay here, Alma.

She tried to leap upright, but it was hard to balance as the drones crashed into her, left and right. She warded one away from her face with her elbow, and started running, zigzag, to try and avoid them. One zag gave her a view of the passenger now flat on his back, blood spattered around his supine body as drones continued to accelerate into him from above. Wet-sounding impacts.

On the far side of the road, at the corner of an empty multi-storey, was a toilet cubicle. It was a free-standing structure with rounded edges and once-modish grooves decorating its walls. Alma's run brought her against the side of this with a smack and a rebound, and, hunched over, she jabbed at the buttons. Two painful thumps into her back, a glancing blow across the top of her head, a sharp hurt in her left calf. The old door slid sepulchrally open and then, when she had got herself inside, it closed with an even more painful slowness. A drone followed her inside and she took a hold of one of its spars and hurled it through the diminishing gap of the door. It boomeranged in the air and hurled itself back; but at last the door was shut, and it bounced away.

There were no windows. The interior smelt of bleach, lavender and, faintly, of ordure. Alma sat, tremblingly, on the shut lid of the toilet itself and tried to calm her hammering heart. It was like sitting inside a steel barrel as an army of angry drummers assailed it from without. Bang, bang, b-bang, b-bang.

Think, Alma. What if this *was* an attempt at assassinating her? Well, then, it was a very clumsy one. Presumably whoever had tried to kill her before – Mastema, or whoever controlled Mastema – was able to override the control system of the drones. *Bang! Bang!* yelled the walls all around her. Say they wanted her dead, and wanted that so badly that they were prepared to brush off collateral damage: that nameless passenger, for one. *Bang, b-bang-BANG. Bang. Bang.* Did that mean that armed police were on their way? In which case she couldn't stay inside this toilet. Or perhaps the instrument was so crude that the drones would attack the police too, as indiscriminately as they had attacked her?

Then, unexpectedly, everything went quiet. The only sound was a kind of rhythmic scraping noise, coming from somewhere. She was still in a sufficient state of startlement to wonder if this sound represented a drone trying to saw its way into the cubicle: but of course not. It was the sound of Alma's own breathing.

Was this a trap? Even if it was, she couldn't stay inside the toilet for ever.

She pressed the button and the door slid creakily backwards.

Outside hundreds of drones were sitting on the ground. There were none in the sky.

She took one tentative step out of the cubicle. Two drones hummed near her feet. The whole road was carpeted with the devices, and almost all were still active, buzzing, lights blinking. But none of them were flying. And they had, for the moment at least, stopped attacking her.

She picked her way through the ground-level drift of drones. They had not been deactivated, and one or two, sensing the proximity of her leg, lurched for her. But although she received one bruise on her ankle, none of them took flight, and she got away from the main concentration of them and down the road towards the river.

She stopped for one moment and looked back: the nameless passenger was lying on his back, motionless, his face a red mush. Should she go back and see if he could be helped? But there was nothing she could do for him. The chances that he was still alive were very small.

As she turned to resume her escape the quantity and intensity of the buzzing behind her increased sharply. She glanced back: they were all waking up again, taking off, zooming up into the sky.

Not good.

Plan A, to cross the river and get into the centre of town, abruptly lost its appeal. Too exposed. Without hesitation Alma ran to her left, towards the old carpark. A three-storey-high metal grille covered the Queen's Street-facing flank of the structure. That might keep out the bigger drones, although the smaller craft would probably be able to slip through.

Alma put her shoulder to a walkway door, threw herself inside and ran up some concrete steps. Crumbs of the old false stone scattered from her footfalls. The buzzing was a crescendo now, a huge sound.

The first floor of the carpark was entirely empty of vehicles, and Alma sprinted across it as fast as her aching body permitted. In particular her right calf, just above her ankle, ground out pain as she moved, and all her little lacerations and bruises sang with pain. But she ignored that. She needed to get somewhere more enclosed.

On the far side was a carpark attendant's booth – empty, of course. Alma reached it as drones poured into the structure, flying up the main entrance ramp. She yanked the booth's door as hard as she could it but was locked, of course it was locked, damn the stupid door. She hauled and hauled, but breaking through was beyond her strength.

A drone crashed painfully into her back, and a second banged into her hip. She tried the pull-open window of the booth, but it too was locked. Its glass was threaded with a graph-paper pattern of strengthening wires.

A stairwell, she thought to herself, would be a better space than this one. Moving her arms kung-fu style, albeit a branch of kung-fu that lacked all grace and force, she tried to ward the machines off as she turned and ran. Or at any rate *tried* to run through the sharp swarm of drones.

Only one factor worked in her favour: the machines were not specifically designed to enter buildings, and their navigation algorithms worked less well in enclosed spaces. Some targeted her effectively, others zimmed and buzzed past her, or collided with one another.

She had almost reached the stairwell when one apple-sized,

dense little drone caught her on the side of her head and she tripped. She stumbled against a pillar, and rebounded to fall to her right, too dazed to be able to curl herself up.

The thought *this is the end* formed, distinctly, in her mind.

She writhed on the floor, struggled. Nothing. Panting, she sat up. The drones had all – once again – landed, and were humming quietly. She had no idea why they were doing it. But it wouldn't do to miss her chance. She picked herself up and, treading carefully, jogged out down the main in-ramp of the carpark.

All around were drones, sitting on the ground. Road and pavement were irregularly littered with them, their collective humming like the purring of cats. Claws could come out again at any time. She had to get somewhere inside, where she could lock the machines out.

She started along the road, running as fast as her exhausted and bruised legs could carry her. But she was clumsy, and trod on the sloping carapace of one drone, nearly fell, tried to right herself with a triple hop on her other foot and finally caught her ankle on a fat chunk of humming black plastic. This time she hit the ground hard, and the drones – how sinister it was, how like living things they were – snarled and buzzed and shifted about.

As quietly as she could she got back to her feet and hurried on. It was like that physical training routine where you have to run along a path laid with two offset lines of tyres, slotting your feet neatly into the hole in turn.

Another fifty metres and she would get to the river; over the river and she could maybe get inside the Oracle – not good in terms of avoiding police surveillance but probably her best bet in terms of not being cudgelled to bloody death by drones.

She had still not reached the river, and was much too far away from safety, when the humming began to rise in volume. She actually groaned aloud. She knew then that the drones would soon come to life, and hurtle up into the air, and come crashing down upon her unprotected head with furious force and weight.

One thought – a daft, irrelevant thought – popped into her head at that moment. She should pray. But pray to whom? Into thy hands I commend my – *whose* hands? The Father God of the Thames? The Mother God of the Kennet? The one had baptised her, only hours before. But every day she had washed in her microshower, and the water from that facility was presumably sourced from the larger river. Father and Mother God both. A song came into her mind:

> *Mama take these drones off me*
> *I can't bear them any more.*
> *Getting dark too dark to see*
> *Knock knock knocking on Reading's door...*

From up the road: a succession of snapping sounds, like somebody or something knock knock knocking on R!-town's door. It was a large vehicle, driving up Queen's Road. Its engine was the source of the increased volume of buzzing. The drones were not flying. They were still perched dangerously on the ground. The buzzing was not drones, but this huge car.

It pulled to a halt alongside Alma, and the window slid down. It was Pu Sto. 'Get in,' she said.

Alma didn't need to be asked twice.

7: *Vertical*

'I thought they would have arrested you,' Alma said, as she climbed up into the car. 'And taken you to the hospital.'

Pu Sto looked at her. 'First,' she said, 'shut that door.'

Alma did so.

'Second,' said Pu, 'strap in. We're going vertical.' Now that Alma looked at her, Pu Sto did not look well. Her left arm was in a sling, and her face looked drawn in that way distinctive to continuing physical pain. 'Your shoulder?' she asked.

Pu smiled. 'I was pronged,' she said, with studied offhandedness. 'They first-aided me in situ, which stopped the bleeding. Then my people turned up, and persuaded the police to leave me alone. They wanted to go to hospital of course, because the pole had gone – right – *through* – my shoulder. And out the other side. Go to hospital, they said. But I gave them the Amy Winehouse answer to *that*.'

'*My* feed is offswitched,' Alma reminded her. 'Cultural references need to be explained if you ...'

'One moment,' Pu said, holding up a finger.

The vista outside the car swapped out a dull scene of an east R!-town roadway for a locust-swarm of drones. A cacophonous array of raps, bangs, thuds and booms reverberated through the interior of the vehicle. Alma flinched. She couldn't help it.

For ten seconds or so Pu appeared to be doing nothing; only then did Alma grasp that she had retreated into her feed. The banging rose in volume. A white-scratch star pattern appeared on the windscreen to her left, as though a snowball had struck it. A dent appeared in the roof over her head: a downward-pointing metal nipple.

'Um?' Alma suggested.

It went on. A full minute of barrage. At one point a drone must have collided with the front left wheel of the car with such force as to rip enough of the wheel material away to make the wheel's built-in autorepair impossible. There was an impressive popping sound, as if from an alt-reality where the *Hindenburg* was assailed with a titanic pin rather than with fire, and the whole car sagged forward and to the left.

'Hey,' Alma cried.

And, as suddenly as it had begun, the drone assault on the car ceased. Alma couldn't see properly through the bashed-upon windscreen to her side, but through the front it was clear the drones had, once again, all settled on the ground.

'It's getting harder to get them to do that,' said Pu Sto.

'That's – you?'

'Yes,' she said. 'Only partially effective, though, as you can see. We need to leave here.'

'Your front left wheel...' Alma began.

'Vertical,' Pu interrupted. 'As I said.' The aircar shuddered, motors sprouted like mushrooms, and a little unsteadily the whole vehicle rose up. The couple of drones that had settled on the car's roof slid off. In a minute they were a hundred metres over R!-town.

'Drones are simple machines,' Pu was saying. 'They do what they are told. They only recognise certain authorities when it comes to taking orders. It really is extremely hard to hack them, actually – I mean, if you come from outside the government. The protocols against private individuals taking them over is: whew. Wow. And so on. But various government departments, including mine, of course, have access to government drones.'

'They were trying to kill me,' Alma said. 'They actually did kill one person, I think.'

'Who?'

'I don't know. A stranger. He stopped his car to see what was going on.'

'That was foolish of him. Regrettable, though.' The aircar was sweeping through the sky, moving south-east, crossing the rec and the cemetery and passing over the almost deserted motorway.

'Where are we going?' Alma asked. 'I need to be back in my flat in a few hours.'

'Three hours, twenty-seven minutes – I know. You need to get back to your partner. And I promise I will get you back. But we need to recover the file cached in your feed, and to do it in a way that won't alert certain people to your whereabouts.'

'These would be the same certain people who were trying to kill me with those drones?'

'They won't follow us – the drones, I mean. There's a high-ranking minister, in charge of the Health department. Asie Röell is her name. She has managed to make your R!-town an emergency zone under the meaning of the act.'

'Which act?'

'Not to get too parliamentary-legally technical, but several acts. It won't last for very long, but she's hoping it will last long *enough*. And it does give her various legal powers. Using them, she commandeered all the drones from the local districts – all of them, so far as I can see: from Wow-it's-Slough and Staines in the east, to sWINdon in the west; from Basingstoked! in the south all the way to Oxford in the north. Weather drones, surveillance drones, veterinary drones, maintenance and public-works drones, astronomical drones, any kind you might think of. All flocking together in R!-town.'

'All to kill me?'

'To be on the safe side. From Röell's point of view.'

'Safe,' said Alma. 'Unsound.'

'Oh, sure, sure. I thought it would have a simple override, and I was trying to get to you, so I tried to make them all set down and leave you alone. But Röell, or somebody on her team, twigged what I was doing.'

'"Twigged"?'

'You know – realised. From that point on it was a virtual tug of war. They panicked, I think, and figured: order the drones to attack, maybe they'd kill you and if they killed you, you, as a problem, would go away.'

'I am not a problem,' Alma said.

'You are to them. You don't mean to be, I know. But these are the cards fate has dealt you.'

'I finally figured out the mechanics of Adam Kem's murder,' Alma said.

'You did? Bravo, my dear. Or brava.'

'I was hoping I could use that fact as' – but as she was speaking she found herself self-conscious at the foolishness and naivety of what she was saying – 'leverage, or something.' Pu Sto was silent.

'Never mind,' Alma said, reaching round to press fingers against her back, and so determine how painful the bruises there were. 'Where are we going?'

'We need a place where we can onswitch your feed again without it automatically alerting the authorities as to your location.'

'There must be authorities other than this... what was her name?'

'Röell. Of course there are. It might be possible to go over her head, but you need to understand the situation now. And she runs a whole department, remember. She's one of the Princes of the Universe. She has both legal power and immense influence. Plenty of people in government high-slots think that backing her is the canny thing to do. Backing her or, you know: sitting on the fence until this is all resolved. The best way to describe it would be: an internal coup. They've been planning it for a while. I've been cut out, so I can't be the one to go over their heads. We might find police who are neutral, but we're more likely to run into police who have already picked their side.'

'You're saying the police are corrupt?'

'I'm saying they'd be in no hurry. They'd be happy to wait and see how things shake down. We're the ones who can't afford to wait. If they stick me in a cell, it'll be all over.'

'That would be a shame for you.'

'More than me, my deary. This is about the whole balance of life: real life or the Shine. This is about the power bloc that has decided we need to encourage the ongoing migration of people *into* the Shine, because there we can surveil them and keep them bread-and-circused with perfect efficiency.'

'People hardly need to be encouraged to migrate to the Shine.'

'And yourself?'

'Most people,' said Alma.

'It's about power,' Pu Sto said. 'Hospitals – hospitals are indistinguishable from prisons nowadays. I mean, if someone is unlucky enough to need hospitalisation' – she touched her own hastily bandaged shoulder, tentatively – 'which would they prefer? To sit in a bed staring at the opposite wall for a fortnight? Or to take a consciousness-break in the Shine, having fun, whilst the body slowly does its convalescent thing, and whilst expert nurses and medibots check it from time to time? It's a no-brainer.'

'No-brainer,' said Alma, deadpan. 'Ho-ho.'

'And prisons have been that way for decades. Put the cons into the Shine – not a paradisical version, of course, but howsoever functional it is it's better than sitting in a two-person cell for twenty-three hours a day. If we handle them that way, prisoners are easier to manage and *cheaper* to manage and, best of all, they don't riot. Recidivism is reduced. It's win–win. Turns out people are easier to manage when you have complete oversight of their bodies *and* you can eavesdrop on their mental divertissements.'

'Where *are* we going?'

'There are a couple of closed-net facilities, around the country. Away from cities of course. We're flying to the nearest of these.'

'How near?'

'It's on the south coast. Don't worry: we'll be there in fifteen. Less than that. Once we're there we can onswitch your feed and get at the box of treasure. And with that I'll be able to turn things around.'

'You're sure?'

'I'm hopeful.'

'Do you know what it is? This thing in my feed?'

'Not exactly. I've a hunch. Anyway: a quarter-hour to get at it, then we can get you back to R!-town with hours to spare. Once Röell, or whoever's pulling her strings, finds out that the balance of power has shifted, they'll back off. They'll start thinking about the legal consequences of what they've done, and what they're doing, and how much harder it will be to wicket-keep those consequences if they haven't – you know – won. That will mean they'll leave you alone to care for your partner, and things can start to go back to normal.'

'Happy ending,' said Alma.

'You're right,' Pu agreed, wincing as she moved her shoulder. 'I'm being a little rosy-tinted. It could all go tits-up very easily. All the tits, all the way up. But, you know, my dear: best-case scenario.'

'Worst case?'

'Worst case is: Röell recruits the military, which I'm one hundred per cent certain she's been trying to do. Terrorist threat. Biohazard. Plus: when we're in power, you, my dear colonel, will be a general, you, my handsome general, will be field marshal. All that. *If* she can swing it, then worst case becomes: a jet turns us into a boomy and expanding cloud of hot gas, somewhere over the South Downs.'

Alma said nothing.

'But I don't think it's very likely,' said Pu, shortly. 'The army are too cautious to commit this early on. They'll wait and see, I think. What we need to do is to hold our nerve, you and I, and if we do the prize will be ours.'

They were flying over that uniquely English spread of green fields, empty roads and blue-green fleecy patches of woodland characteristic of the South Downs. The roads came together in a tessellation of roofs and rectangles, and then spread out again as threads and lines and countryside reclaimed the land.

'You don't,' Alma noted, 'seem curious as to how the Adam Kem killing was accomplished.'

'It was Röell,' said Pu. 'And if it wasn't her, it was somebody in her retinue – Mastema, probably. Mastema used to be mine, but I'd begun to mistrust her a while ago. Hence swapping out the bullets in her gun.' She looked at Alma. 'You might thank me for that, you know. It did save your life.'

Alma said nothing.

'She might just have stabbed you, of course. I couldn't be one *hundred* per cent sure she would use the gun at all,' Pu went on. 'Except that she really likes guns, I know that. So I took that chance. But I think she killed Adam Kem with a spray of nanobiots, so she's not exclusively wedded to guns as a means of murder.'

Alma said: 'You seem sure.'

Something altered in terms of the interaction between Alma and Pu. Something, perhaps, cooled. Pu didn't meet Alma's eye.

'Sure of what?' Pu asked. When Alma didn't reply she went on: 'Sure that Mastema killed Adam, you mean? Well, I can't *be* sure. How could I be sure? But if it wasn't her, it was somebody like her. Because Adam had gotten too close. Conceivably the whole coup has happened a little ahead of when Röell wanted it. When Health wanted it, I mean. Conceivably that has happened in part because Adam Kem uncovered something.'

'How,' Alma asked, in a judicious voice, 'do you believe his body ended up in the boot of that car?'

For a few seconds Pu was silent. Then she shrugged, slowly. 'Who knows? Not me. Although there are some things I *do* know.

One is that depositing the body in a car was a deliberate piece of ostentation. It was designed to draw attention to itself – look! An impossible murder! To make an impact.'

'Impact.'

'Oh, it's had that. Believe me. It's become quite the talking point in the Shine. In some portions of it, at any rate. People love a puzzle. And the theories have circulated. You know the most popular theory?' She side-eyed Alma. 'Teleportation. Which is hard to believe, really. I mean, I have access to quite a few government secrets, and *I've* never seen any teleportation technology that actually works. But I suppose it's possible. I mean, theoretically. Wouldn't you say?'

Alma chose her words with care. 'It would surely revolutionise the Real.'

And Pu Sto became immediately eager. 'Wouldn't it, though? Finally the real world would be able to compete with the Shine for people's attention – on a level playing field, I mean. The sheer obstinate difficulty of getting around, out here, would disappear! We could revitalise the Real. Imaginary kingdoms are all very beguiling, I know; but how could they compare with the chance to teleport to Mars? Maybe this is technology that could open up the whole cosmos.'

'If it exists,' said Alma.

'Well naturally,' said Pu Sto, briskly. 'Although some might think the way Adam Kem's body was disposed is – shall we say, *evidential*. Hard to see how else he ended up in there.'

'Hard is not the same word as impossible,' Alma observed.

Pu Sto looked at her then. 'Of course,' she said.

'If this teleportation technology exists,' Alma asked, 'why haven't we heard about it?'

'Well, I suppose, either it is being held back by its inventors,' Pu Sto said, offhandedly, 'or else it is being suppressed. There is a powerful vested interest in the Shine lobby – to keep it a secret, I mean.'

'Or else it doesn't exist.'

'That's the third possibility.'

'So you think the Health department, or agents thereof, murdered Adam Kem by destroying his lungs with a nanobiot, and then disposed of the body by *teleporting* it into the boot of a newly assembled car.'

'I don't believe I said anything of the sort,' said Pu Sto, snootily. '*You're* the one who claims to have "solved" the case. Although you haven't yet favoured me with your theory.'

'Such an explanation would mean the Health department has teleportation technology, which it has kept secret.'

'The fruit of medical research, perhaps?' Pu Sto drawled. 'Stolen from some other governmental department? Recovered from a private scientist who had been taken ill? Who knows. But if they did have it, you wouldn't expect them to tell the world. On the contrary, you'd expect them actively to suppress it.'

'In which case,' Alma asked, 'why would they use it in this case? Wouldn't that be liable precisely to draw attention to the fact of it?'

'*I'm* not privy to their reasons,' Pu said, testily. 'And you don't know, neither of us knows, the particulars of Adam Kem's actual death. Maybe the murderer had to make the body vanish in a hurry.'

Alma said nothing.

'Maybe there was some kind of battle, Health and some other group, and maybe it wasn't Health but some other organisation that teleported Adam away – trying, perhaps, to save him, though too late.'

'That doesn't sound very plausible,' Alma observed, mildly.

'I dare say,' Pu Sto said, 'not.' She stared through the front windscreen, down over at the landscape over which they were hurtling. The English Channel was visible up ahead: a bar of muddy green and utility grey, threaded through with extraordinary touches of peacock's-tail blues. Over it the many drifting white clouds looked like they had been drawn by a child. Blue sky behind. The larger clouds trailed mauve blotches of shadow over the water.

They were approaching a coastal town, though without her feed Alma couldn't work out which one. Before they reached it the skycar banked and started east. A tongue of taupe beach, and the first of the white cliffs rising from sea-level to a hundred metres high. These portions of coast were the original unsculpted craggy white, faceless stretches of unmodified cliff projecting their blank defiance at hazily visible France. But soon enough the flycar passed another town and after that the cliff rose again and the first of the White Cliff Faces came into view.

Gigantic faces were succeeded by smaller ones as the top line of the cliff face dropped down towards the sea, and then the faces swelled again to enormousness as the top line rose once more. At one point the cliffs fell away entirely for a crystalline cluster of town houses and port-infrastructure, and then they climbed to their full height again.

They were impressive, those faces. Perhaps it was having been off-feed for so long, but Alma was conscious of a new respect for the sculptural achievement they represented, bot-made though it was. The crispness of the features depended, Alma supposed, on the frequency with which the bots that sculpted them returned to tidy up their work and repair the erosion of the elements. As they flew along the line of titanic visages, their freshness varied according to what seemed random criteria. Two faces together would be blurred, as if made of water-worn soap; then four would be as sharp-featured and clean as if they had been carved the previous day.

'I always think of the White Cliff Faces as a morality tale,' said Pu Sto, pressing the heel of her right hand, gently, into the bandage covering the wound through her left shoulder. 'Symbols of our age. They were supposed to be part of the revitalisation of the Real – all those towns, like yours, renaming themselves in all those wincingly snappy ways. The desperate chase after ever-receding relevance. Historically speaking, this sort of large-scale sculptural project used to take decades and cost significant fractions of a country's GDP – the pyramids. Mount Rushmore. The Gujarat Statue of Unity. But nowadays it's relatively cheap: just get the right sort of bot, programme it and leave it to do its work. You can garland your coastline with these huge sculptures, easy as you like. The UK is far from the only country to have done so. But to what end? People respond with a massive and collective indifference. So you've got a hundred-metre-high face of Boudicca staring out to sea? So what? In the Shine there are wonders that will blow your mind. In the Shine this sort of wondrous landscape is *so* completely everyday that things like *this*' – and Pu Sto waved her good hand at the vista – 'just look embarrassing. Like going into the Louvre with a drawing by your six-year-old and flapping it in front of the *Mona Lisa* saying *But look at this!*'

Alma said nothing.

'My point,' said Pu Sto, eventually, 'is that this sort of thing is not the way to revitalise the Real. Not this. People aren't idiots. Life is *better* in the Shine. That's just the way it is. The only chance we have is to right the balance – actually improve the experience of living here, not garnish it with window dressing. Like this.'

'Rather opaque windows,' Alma observed.

Pu Sto made a sort of *pff* noise. 'Here,' she said, pointing.

They were flying over open fields where a single one-track grey road led up to a square compound, like a fuse.

'You still haven't asked me what my solution to the Adam Kem mystery is,' Alma said, as the flycar slowed and banked in the air. 'I'm thinking: that's either because you reckon you *know* what I think, or because it doesn't matter to you either way.'

'My dear,' said Pu Sto, 'I'm a touch anxious about landing this flycar with one tyre missing. So please do excuse my abstracted state. But once we pull this treasure out of your feed, we'll *both* know. For sure.'

In the end the car landed as gently as a leaf falling. The engines cut out, and then the chassis sagged forward and to the left.

They had arrived.

8: *Not Areas*

They got out of the car. A sea breeze ruffled Alma's hair in an annoyingly over-friendly manner. Pu Sto's buzz-cut was a better style for the environment. Clouds drew away from the sun and brightness spilled everywhere, glaring off the tall glass frontage of the building directly before them.

Pu Sto led the way across the empty carpark towards the entrance. 'This is a Not Area,' she explained, raising her voice to be heard over the noise of the wind and the shrieking of the gulls. 'There are several of them, scattered around the EU. Whole copies of online environments are modelled here, kept isolated and pure from both actual online worlds and the Shine. For various reasons – testing maintenance protocols, checking potentially dangerous algorithms and so on. And today we are going to use it for a purpose of our own. We'll be able to get into your feed in here without connecting to the larger web, or alerting the enemy to our location.'

Alma wasn't sure how she felt about that *we*.

The big glass doors in the big glass frontage slid apart and the two of them walked into an echoey lobby. It was painfully bright. 'I wish I had some sunglasses,' Alma said.

The receptionist was an artificial woman: smiling and personable. 'Welcome, welcome,' she said. 'Might I ask you to onswitch your feeds, so that I can verify your identity?'

'I'm onswitching mine,' said Pu Sto. 'To get us inside. Hold off on yours for a while – we need to scan you first.'

'Ms Pu Sto,' the receptionist said brightly. 'Welcome! We haven't seen you here in a while.'

'You know how it is,' said Pu. 'Busy busy.'

'You seem injured,' said the receptionist. 'Would you like me to alert a medical response team? They can be here from Canterbury in minutes.'

'No, thank you.'

'I'm sorry, Ms Pu,' said the assistant. 'Sorry to be insistent, but – there is actually a *hole* between your clavicle and ribcage. An actual hole – going right the way through your chest. This registers on my database as a serious injury, and something in urgent need of medical attention.'

'Not this afternoon, Josephine,' said Pu, through gritted teeth.

'You are perhaps confusing me with the automated receptionist at the Nantes Not Area. She is called Josephine. My name is Betty.'

'Betty, it's been a pleasure talking with you. If we need anything…'

'Excuse me!' said Betty sharply, holding up one hand. 'I apologise for interrupting, but I must now terminate this conversation. There is… excuse me! There is – there is something coming – excuse me!'

The two women stared at the receptionist. But the automaton appeared to have gone offline. 'Well,' said Pu. 'That was weird. Oh well. Come on.' She directed Alma across the reception area, through into a corridor, away from the dazzling light of the entrance hall.

'What did it mean, something coming?'

'She's plugged into the larger net. I guess somebody was calling through. Her manner *was* a little odd, though.'

'Ought we to be worried?'

'My dear girl,' said Pu Sto, 'we'll be done in ten minutes, and scooting away north-west again to get back to your Marguerite. With the holy grail in our possession. You're right, though: we shouldn't dawdle. Just down here.'

The corridor was windowless and lit by palely illuminating ceiling panels. Carpeted. Smelling of faintly pleasant cleaning chemicals. They turned left through a doorway and climbed a flight of stairs. They were, at least, regular stairs: flowing upwards. The stairs continued on up, presumably all the way to the top of the structure, but Pu Sto stopped on the first floor and touched a finger to the lockpad of the door.

It blinked red. Pu looked annoyed, and tried again. This time it gleamed green and the door clicked open. 'That's odd too,' she said. 'Shouldn't have done that. But we're here now.'

They stepped into a large room, empty except for the long

tables and ergonomic chairs arranged at them. It looked like the most generic conference room imaginable.

'Here?' Alma asked.

'Here. We can firewall your feed from the general web, but also from the facility's own models – to begin with. Our dear departed, the man you call Derp, poor old Dave who shoved this thing into your feed in the first place – well, he *was* a trustworthy soul I should say. Except…'

'Except it is foolish to trust anyone?'

'Quite. I don't *think* there's a virtual bomb in your feed, but on the off chance that there is, or more realistically that there is something corrupted in there – a squawker, for example – we'd better double up the protection. Would you like to sit down?'

'I'd like to lie down,' said Alma, 'and sleep for three weeks straight. But I'll settle for sitting down, right here and now.'

There was a knock at the door.

The two women looked at one another. 'Who else is here?' Alma asked, in a stage whisper. 'I mean, what other actual human staff does this facility house?'

'None. As far as I know – none,' said Pu Sto.

The knock sounded again on the door: a brisk rat-tat.

'Well, there's *somebody* else on site,' Alma pointed out.

'Evidently.'

'Maybe it's maintenance?'

'I didn't see any other vehicles in the carpark,' said Pu Sto. 'But maybe they parked round the back?'

'Maybe Betty called for a medic anyway? Maybe they're here to fix your shoulder? In which case, can we just get rid of them?'

'Stand there,' said Pu, moving Alma to the left of the door. 'I'm going to open it.'

Alma saw her slip something into her good hand – a thumb-sized black tube. A weapon. Pu took a breath and reached out for the door handle.

Alma's heart went pit-pit-patter like tiny feet. A sense of something dread-worthy yawned swiftly in her stomach. Something bad about to happen.

She thought: I should intervene. I should stop her opening the door.

She didn't intervene. Pu Sto opened the door.

Then things happened. It was very loud, and then it was quiet again. A gun discharged, fired by whoever was waiting outside the door. Alma didn't have time to react. She was looking at Pu Sto side on, and saw a squirl of spurting blood jet out from her chest, and another matching one from her back – and then she saw Pu leaning, *leaning* very far back, leaning rather than falling until the moment that she was actually down, with a smash and a crash and the upending of one of the room's tables.

Then: quiet.

In through the open door stepped Mastema. 'Alma, my chuck,' she said, her gun levelled. 'Third time's a charm for us, let's hope. I can't tell you how much you have irked me, with your various elusivenesses.'

'Wait,' said Alma.

'I don't think I will,' said Mastema. 'Usually in these situations it isn't personal, but on this occasion I don't mind admitting: it *is* personal. And this time I have made *very* sure my weapon is loaded with proper ammunition.'

Alma looked her up and down. She was holding a firearm in her right hand; and she had another – a long-barrelled stuttergun by the look of it – in a holster at her waist. And slung over her shoulder was a yawnbore short rifle. This was clearly a woman who liked her guns.

'You've come prepared, I see,' Alma said. She couldn't think of anything else to say.

'The right tools to finish the job,' Mastema replied. 'And—'

Before she could finish this sentence, Mastema jinked to her right, which is to say, to Alma's left. Her pistol discharged with a horrible barking sound, punching a hole in the wall.

Pu Sto had body-slammed Mastema. Her momentum bundled the two of them through the still-open door, and Alma breathed in. Breathed out, and went to the door.

Pu Sto was standing there, gasping, clutching the balcony railing in one hand, and her bloodied shoulder with the other. Though she was shorter than her opponent, and injured, and unarmed, the one magic touch – surprise – had enabled her to push Mastema down the stairs.

Alma looked down, and Mastema was in a heap at the bottom. But she was still alive. And she was un-heaping herself. More, she looked furiously angry. Her gaze met Alma's gaze and – she – *roared*. She roared like a lion.

'Come,' said Pu Sto, panting hard.

They hurried up the stairs to the next floor, and as they did so a gunshot made the whole stairwell ring like a gong. Bits of plastic and metal scattered around them both.

On the second floor was a corridor with a number of little rooms coming off it. Alma jogged along this, feeling exhausted despite the spike of adrenalin in her bloodstream. Pu Sto stumbled as much as ran.

On the far side they went down two flights of rear stairs a little too rapidly for comfort or safety. At the bottom Pu Sto had to stop to catch her breath.

'What happened?' Alma asked.

'It so chanced,' gasped Pu Sto, 'that the bullet passed *through* the hole that already existed in my chest. Give or take – and a very painful give or take that was.'

'You are bleeding.'

'Obviously,' she said, 'the shot agitated and distressed my pre-existing wound. But – I'll live. That is to say – *provided* we get out of here.'

'You don't have a weapon?'

Pu Sto shook her head. 'It flew out of my hand when I hit the floor. I didn't want to waste time scrabbling around trying to recover it.' Then, taking a breath and steeling herself, she moved on. Alma followed.

They turned a corner and came into a large hallway, wholly empty except for a blob-shaped water cooler in one corner. They made their way diagonally across this space as quickly as they could, Pu Sto dragging her feet somewhat over the shag pile. The softness of the carpet reminded Alma that she was barefoot. Strange to say, she had forgotten that fact.

Pu's blood was dripping heavily from her body. 'You're leaving a trail,' Alma said. Looking back, there was an intermittent streaky line of black-red all the way to the far end. And at that far end: Mastema, levelling her gun.

'Eek,' Alma cried, quite inadvertently.

A succession of clattering banging noises made Alma's ribs thrum and hurt her ears. Shards and chunks and splinters and jigsaw pieces of plaster scattered through the air; her cheek smarted as one piece hit her face. As she put her head down and ran, Mastema fired again. Pu Sto ran with her, her right hand clutched to her left shoulder to keep it as immobile as possible during her jog. Any rock drummer would have been proud of the succession of huge percussive cracks and thumps that followed the two of them across the room.

'Down', said Pu, tossing something backwards, A knuckle-bone, maybe. A tooth. A flash and a bang and Mastema flew backwards. Pu flinched and felt scalding air wash over her back, like a gigantic devil's tongue.

'Did you kill her?' she called.

'Let's not tarry to see if I did or not,' Pu gasped.

They got up and made their way as fast as they could past newly scorched walls. The corner of the hall: a door. Ducking through, into the entrance lobby again, scrabbling as Alma's bare foot slipped on something greasy on the polished floor. Slipping, she saw, on a smear of Pu Sto's blood. Then they both had their heads down and were running for the main exit.

'Are you OK?'

'I can't say it's *comfortable*, all this running,' Pu Sto called back, 'but the alternative would be considerably worse.'

They ran across the main hall. The automaton receptionist seemed to have woken up again, and gave them both another cheery hello. Sunlight gushed through the tall windows. Pu's shod feet made squeaky squeaky sounds as she hurried. Alma padded soundlessly. How long did she have? An hour to get back to Marguerite? More?

Maybe she should onswitch her feed, right here?

But there wasn't time.

The two of them ran for the main door. Alma, being uninjured, ran faster, so it was she who collided, ungainly, against it. It hadn't opened. Pu Sto jogged up behind her.

'Can you get this open?'

'You know people talk about certain things being above their pay grade?' Pu replied. 'Well, opening doors is quite a long way *below* my pay grade.'

'Mastema will be here any moment,' Alma pointed out. 'She intends to kill us.'

'Ask the receptionist. This is a government office, not a prison.'

Alma yelled at the receptionist, across the open space of the hallway: 'Can you open the door please!'

'I'm currently being colonised inside out by aggressive viral

196

code,' the smiling woman replied, brightly. 'This must be what the common caterpillar feels like as the ichneumonid larva eats it alive from within.'

'Just open the—'

'Dadadadaa,' said the receptionist, her image glitching. 'Mammamam.'

And Mastema walked coolly into the main hall. Taking her time. She was bleeding from several places, and her gait had the additional complexifying rhythm of a limp. But she was very much alive. She had a firearm in each hand.

In her right she lifted the stuttergun and aimed it at Alma. Then, smiling, she changed her mind, lowered the pistol and lifted her left hand. It aimed the blue-black snub-barrel yawnbore, and Alma's heart did a little panicky skip-to-the-loo-my-darling.

The *whompf* as the projectile left the barrel of this weapon was something Alma felt as much as heard. The impact on her body knocked the breath out of her lungs, and it was only as she was falling that she realised the collision had come from the wrong direction.

Pu had tackled her. The two of them fell to the floor as the yawnbore's round thudded past them. A thunderclap was followed by a sizzling noise. One of the big panes of reinforced glass had been abruptly redefined as a hailstorm. The pattern of the impact blew most of the million nodules of glass out and away, but a fair few drizzled down upon them.

No point in hanging about. Pu and Alma rose together, and ran, stumbled, ran, ran faster, Alma hurting her bare feet, Pu in agony, and then got their balance and ran faster through the now-open window. Ran on.

9: *The Woman Who Sneezed in Shakespeare's Nose*

The two women ran across the carpark, crunching over the new-laid covering of glass pieces, Alma ow-ow-owing as she went.

Sunlight on the nearby English Channel seemed to have picked up something of the quality of this carpet of glass fragments. There was warm brightness and a fresh breeze, smelling of salt and seaweed and grass mixed with a faintly dungy whiff.

Pu's flycar was sitting on the far side of the carpark, swaying slightly in the brisk sea breeze. 'We have to get back to R!-town,' Alma said.

'Anywhere that's not here,' gasped Pu. It was clear from her face how much pain she was in.

They were twenty metres from the flycar when Alma for a second time heard the whumpf noise of the yawnbore discharging. She tried to duck and jink at the same time and in doing so tripped and fell. Heat and noise pushed at her as she went down. Landed on her shoulder, rolled, and got quickly back up again, pieces of glass adhering to her tunic.

The flycar was a cracked-open wreck, pumping smoke at the sky, fizzing with various tufts of fire.

Alma stared. She had one thought: Marguerite. She took a deep breath, to try and calm herself, but that drew a choking combination of air and fumes into her lungs, and made her splutter loudly. This was not calming. She looked around the carpark. The only other vehicle was a low-slung bright red one: presumably the car in which Mastema had arrived at the place. The chances of breaking into it, and overriding its security, were very low.

Pu took hold of Alma's arm. 'Come on,' she said.

'Come on *where*?'

But she allowed herself to be pulled along. Pu ran off the tarmac of the carpark, leaving the smoking ruin of the flycar behind. The two ran onto grass: springy and uneven. They were heading for the sea, which meant they were heading for the top of the cliff.

'I'm not,' Alma yelled, as the sound of the surf grew louder, 'going to jump.'

'Me neither,' Pu Sto yelled back.

Alma tried to concentrate on not losing her footing. She got into a rhythm of hopping, more or less, from one tuffet to another. The wind was stronger now, colder on the skin, and the sound of the seagulls became louder: variously laughing and weeping and imitating squeaky-dog-chew-toys, and doing so over and over and over, as if shrieking was the only idea they could fit into their little heads.

As Pu and Alma approached the edge of the cliff the turf thinned and the land started to tip forward. They were at the lip now. A metre-wide segment of grass had sagged, three metres down, right on the edge. The wind crumpled noise into Alma's ears. She and Pu dropped into this wedge-shaped trench, and then Pu crept to the very limit of the cliff.

'How fearful,' gasped Pu, struggling to get her breath back, 'and dizzy it is to cast one's eyes so low! Come on.'

'Come on *where*?' Alma asked.

She steeled herself, and looked down. They were exactly halfway between two of the gigantic hundred-metre-tall sculpted white faces. Below, to Alma's right, she could see the foreshortened yet still vast expanse of a fat masculine face. The nose was bulbous and protrudinous, the jowls hemmed the plump lips on either side; chins tucked into chins below. Who was it? Winston Churchill? Presumably not – there was no hat, and no cigar. Somebody else, then. It hardly mattered.

There was no mistaking the other face, below and to Alma's left: the big white semisphere brow, the sharp nose, the trimmed moustache and goatee beard and above all the repeating Viennetta-ice-cream-swirl pattern of the ruff circling his neck. Gazing dramatically out across the steel and green waters of the English Channel.

'Down,' Pu Sto instructed her.

'You sure you can climb? With that shoulder?'

'It'll be uncomfortable,' Pu replied, grimacing, 'but not as uncomfortable as being shot through the lungs by Mastema.'

'Climbing with only one arm?'

'I'm trained. Don't worry about me – come *on*.'

'Shakespeare?' Alma demanded, hurriedly. 'Or – the other guy?' Who *was* he? The perspective distorted what ought, she felt, to have been a recognisable visage into something that hovered on the edge of familiarity.

'Shakespeare looks *slightly* less precarious,' Pu said. There was an uncharacteristically tentative tone to her voice. 'Maybe we can use his moustache as a ledge.'

'If we fall,' Alma said, 'we die.'

'I'm hoping it's precisely that consideration that will dissuade Mastema from following us.'

And down they went.

Since Pu was more likely to lose her grip, she went down first: if she were to fall, she wouldn't want to knock Alma off as well as she plummeted. Alma, her heart scudding, followed. Turned to face the chalk face. Gripped the grass at the top with her hands. Oh god, *god*, lowered herself over the edge and groped with her bare toes for a foothold.

That the cliff was not perfectly vertical, and was leaning back by perhaps five degrees, made it possible, if not exactly easy, to descend. The line at which Shakespeare's 100-metre-tall chalk-carved face emerged from the material of the aboriginal cliff was marked by a series of irregular grooves, a foot or so deep. The grooves isolated serpent-like spars which in turn smoothed into nothing where the giant forehead began. Hair, Alma realised: such hair as the balding bard possessed. It was not exactly a ladder, and the chalk itself possessed a treacherously soft, almost spongy consistency, but she was able to make her way down.

Gulls hurried through in the air around them, heehawing like mules on helium, yelping and yawling. Alma tried to ignore them, but several flew close enough to tap her back and head with their wings.

Alma's face was very close to the chalk as she came down. The actual material of the cliff was infused with greenness. Speckles of the stuff in amongst the white. Algae perhaps.

Pu Sto was waiting for her in the playwright's ear. The sculpted hair partly covered the top half of this, but enough of the lobe protruded to make a small shelf.

'We can't stop here,' Pu told her.

'Just getting here was something of a miracle, as far as I'm concerned,' Alma called back. The wind was ruffling her hair with a persistence that went beyond the playful.

'We're too exposed,' Pu insisted. 'Mastema could see us from the clifftop, and therefore shoot us, if we stay here. We need to get underneath the nose.'

Alma looked down. The vast expanse of naked cheek did not look traversable.

'How?'

'The chalk is soft,' Pu called. The wind found a way in under her tunic, ballooned it out and almost made her lose her balance. 'Try to dig your fingernails in. Your toes. It's not like rock-climbing. The material is more pliable. Think of it as foam. Like a kid's birthday party at an indoor play facility.'

'It's exactly like rock-climbing,' said Alma. 'Chalk is a rock, and we're climbing.'

'It's not like the Aberdeenshire granite I trained on, though. Come on!'

She started off, moving her one good arm and two good legs with spiderish rapidity. In moments she had scrambled down and into the ledge of the moustache. Alma swallowed and started off after her.

There was a half-moon bag under the Bard's right eye, and she could get her fingers into the crease formed as the bottom of this feature transitioned into the cheek as a whole. But the cheek below – more than twice her height – was perfectly featureless. Her feet scrabbled over the surface of it. The wind shoved her leftwards, then changed direction and pressed her against the chalk, then tugged her quite sharply right. This latter gust caught her unawares. Her left hand's grip failed, and as she desperately tried to grasp the smooth chalk with it the piece underneath her right hand broke off.

She was sliding. She didn't even have time to scream before her feet slapped against the upper ridge of the Shakespearean moustache.

Her front parted company with the chalk. She was toppling, upright, backwards and away from the cliff face. She was about to fall.

A hand grabbed the front of her tunic. Pu Sto had braced herself against Shakespeare's moustache and the roof of his undernose, indeed had her good arm up inside Shakespeare's right nostril as an anchor, and had reached out and held her. She was small and her injured arm was – obviously – not strong, but Alma was able to catch onto her sleeve as Pu grimaced with pain, and in a moment Alma was safe against the top of the 'tache.

Pu Sto let out a long, pained *ahhh* as she clutched her wounded left shoulder with her right hand. 'That,' she panted. 'Was. That. That. Was.'

Alma was peering up, trying to see past the nose. 'I think she's coming down – but I think she's coming down the other face.'

'Into the nose!' ordered Pu.

'*In*to?' Alma repeated. '*In*to?'

Pu put her face close against Alma's, and whispered hoarsely. 'If she sees us she will kill us. I'll leg you up.'

'What about you?'

'Climbing was part of my training, which I don't suppose is true of you. Come on!'

Alma, feeling bewildered and scared in equal measure, lifted her foot. Pu Sto grabbed it with her good hand and pushed. Alma felt herself rising. Her head went into Shakespeare's nostril, and then her torso.

She reached out and grabbed on to what she could grab. The cavity was larger than it looked from the outside and was inset quite a way into the cliff itself. She pulled her feet in, and reached down to help Pu Sto up.

In a moment they were both inside. The nose levelled out into a kind of platform. Indeed the sinus, as it were, went back quite a long way.

It was considerably quieter in this dark place. The smell of the chalk and the wrack-and-salt odour of the sea was more intense in here. There was enough light coming through the two manhole-sized nostrils below to illuminate clearly the back of the cavern. It went four or five metres back, and there, folded away and inactive, was the bot that had carved Shakespeare's face.

'Why is that still here?' Alma asked.

'Shh!' Pu hissed, angrily.

Alma leaned in, and whispered in the other woman's ear. 'I only mean, maybe we could onswitch it. Use it to get away.'

'We'd have to go online and back into our feeds, which would alert Mastema to our *being* here,' whispered Pu in return.

'You don't think she's going to figure out we're in here? I mean, where else could we be?'

'On a different head. Tumbled silently into the sea. Let's not draw attention to ourselves, at any rate. Besides, we don't have the authorisation codes.'

'I might have something that could picklock it.'

'No! Think of the noise! The most important thing is not to make a sound, not to draw attention to us.'

Alma peered at the dormant machine. Presumably, she thought, chalk weathers. She assumed it had to emerge, every now and again, and undertake repairs. There was probably one in every nose on the cliff face. Some of them were probably still functional, too.

They fell silent. The sound from outside the nose was a medley of waves on the shingle below, and the plangent shrieks of the gulls. From time to time the wind shifted vector in such a way as to play the open nostril hole like a flute, and an immensely low moan began to build; but the wind never stayed in the same direction long enough for this to build to any great crescendo.

Pu Sto put her finger to her lips. There *was* another sound out there: a banging. An irregular series of loud knocks.

Mastema.

Alma thought to herself: is she on the other face? Or has she figured out that we went down the Shakespearean visage? Had the two of them left a trail, a scratched path, down the cheek of the great playwright? She looked around the cavern, for ... something. A rock, maybe. Something she could fight back with, if Mastema, guns first, poked up through Shakespeare's nostril like a whack-a-mole. But there was nothing. The floor was bare chalk.

Distantly, wobbled a little by the wind, came Mastema's mocking tones: 'I know you're here. And I will find you.'

Pu Sto met Alma's gaze, and shook her head.

A minute later Mastema's voice could be heard again. 'I'll blast this whole face from the cliff if I have to!' It was fainter. She was moving away.

Then again, still fainter: 'Don't make me disfigure a national monument! Do yourselves a favour and show a little *dignity*.'

Pu Sto leaned in, whispered. 'She's going in the wrong direction.'

Alma nodded. She put a hand to her face to wipe away the

sweat she had built up in her climb down. It had been as strenuous as it had been terrifying. And it had been *very* terrifying.

Both her hands were covered in chalk. As she wiped her face, chalk went into her eyes, and up her nose.

Oh no.

Rubbing her face with her hands was, in retrospect, a foolish thing to do.

Alma's sinuses trembled, tightened, and then she experienced that dreadful sense of physical inevitability, the one we all recognise as incipient sinus and diaphragm convulsion. She knew she was going to sneeze.

Pu Sto saw the change in expression, read it correctly, and shook her head furiously. No! Don't! But there was nothing Alma could do. She felt the thing – it was like an alien entity, possessing her body and with a will of its own – grow, arch backwards and, then: the sneeze came. She tried to block her mouth and nose with two hands, and a half-strangulated choking cymbal-crash of a sound emerged from her. Trying to block it sent pressure back into her sinuses and her throat caught. She coughed once, twice, tried to stop, couldn't. And following with a direful immediacy upon the footsteps of the first sneeze came another. This one burst from Alma at full volume, unmuted.

Pu Sto had become very still. Alma, wide-eyed, felt the urge to apologise, but of course said nothing. Maybe the ambient noise of wind, waves and gulls had masked her sneeze?

Something hit the outside of the nose, hard and heavy: the chalk shook.

'She's shooting at us,' said Pu Sto, in a low voice.

'I hear you!' came Mastema's voice, gleeful. Coming closer.

'That's,' said Alma, 'unideal.'

'We'll be rat-in-a-trapped,' said Pu, going down onto her belly in the enclosed space and ducking her head down through one of Shakespeare's nostrils. It came back up almost at once, much quicker than it had gone down; and at the same time Alma heard a gunshot squee past their hiding space.

'She's closing.'

'You don't say,' said Alma. She shifted forward and looked straight down through the right nostril. It half-crossed her mind that perhaps it would be possible to jump and splash into the sea. But the view directly downward was of grubby white pebbles,

fifty metres down. To jump would be at best to break one's legs
– which would only make things easier for Mastema – and at
worst to die outright.

'What are we going to do?' Pu Sto asked.

'You're asking *me*?'

'It's at times like this,' said Pu Sto, massaging her wounded
shoulder gently and grimacing, 'when I'm sitting inside Shakespeare's nose about to be shot through the torso – for the *second
time today* – by one of our government's most capable assassins,
that I really wish I'd listened to what my mother told me when
I was young.'

Alma said: 'I ask you what she told you, and you're going to
say you don't know because you didn't listen. Aren't you?'

Pu Sto looked genuinely hurt. 'I would never forget anything
my mother told me. She gave me wisdom by which I have guided
my life – every day of that life.'

'Fair enough,' said Alma.

Mastema's voice cooed from outside. 'Hello in there. Are you
really resigned to the prospect of dying inside a *nose*? Wouldn't
you rather come out and face the inevitable with some dignity?'

'You keep using that word,' Pu Sto called back. 'I do not think
it means what you think it means.'

'Poke your head up a nostril,' Alma shouted, 'and let's have a
chat.'

'*Drôle*,' came Mastema's voice, deadpan. The gulls haw-hawed.
'Believe me, it's only my respect for our national poet that stops
me simply blowing the whole nose off with my yawnbore.'

'Wouldn't want to turn Will S. into an Egyptian sphinx, now,
would we?' shouted Pu Sto. She looked, Alma thought, close to
passing out with her pain. She was as white as the chalk inside
which she was hiding.

'Shakesphinx,' Mastema called back. Her voice sounded mar-
ginally further away. Perhaps she was getting into the best position
to be able to blast with her yawnbore. 'It could become quite
the tourist attraction.' A pause. 'I'm sorry to kill you, Pu Sto. You
taught me a lot.'

'Did I ever get round to teaching you how to evade gravity?
You'll be needing that one in a moment.'

'Enough banter, now, I feel,' said Mastema.

Alma sneezed again. Oh, this was *ridiculous*. What was she

205

waiting for anyway? She onswitched her feed. It flailed, and threw up a bunch of network unconnection warning notices. No network! It was almost physically disorienting. She had never in her life before been in a geographical spot where literally no network at all was accessible. Her feed sent out tendrils, flailed for a moment, and then latched onto something, a half-chance at connection via some coastal facility a dozen miles east.

Her feed booted up. There were about two hundred pokes, messages and parcels which had been left in her feed's porch, but there was no time to go through all of those.

And, right there, she had a choice. She felt the pressure of choice, very acutely. Say she had seconds to live – mere seconds. Say she had time to do one of two things. She could satisfy her curiosity with regard to Derp's package. Or she could throw one of her illegal code keys at the slumbering bot, on the chalk shelf inside Shakespeare's sinus. The latter would surely be a pointless gesture. What good could it do? The bot was not armed, after all, and could hardly overpower Mastema with the sheer elegance of its chalk sculpting.

She might as well satisfy her curiosity with regard to Derp's package.

But she didn't. Instead she tried to stabilise the local network node, lost it for a moment, bounced hard off the firewall – the titanic, towering inferno of a firewall – surrounding the Not Area she and Pu had recently been inside, and reconnected. Then she latched onto the slumbering bot. It was run by a very low-functioning algorithm, which didn't take much to snap open. The whole of its operational protocol was laid bare for Alma to see. This was a mixed blessing: too basic to be able to accept any fancy picklocks, she could only turn it on if she had the encryption key, which she didn't. But she could see the machine's operating parameters. There was a timer up front, ticking down: every two weeks a small part of the bot's rudimentary mind woke, checked the Google Earth realtime of its particular face, and if repairs were needful booted up the rest of the machine. Since repairs were rarely called for, it usually just powered itself down again.

Alma knew she was probably wasting her last moments on a futile task. Still.

The machine was hooked into Google Earth. Alma pulled up a piggyback tool, clipped onto the machine's feed – thoroughly illegal, of course, but since she had mere seconds to live she didn't anticipate getting into any trouble – and took a look. Alma was able to see the outside via Google Earth.

Alma found herself looking at Shakespeare's big white face. There was Mastema, a dark splodge on the far end of Shakespeare's moustache. It was clear enough what she was doing. She was aiming her short-barrelled yawnbore. Then she lowered it, and adjusted her posture.

She was, Alma realised, concerned that she was too close to the nose – shooting it with a yawnbore round would cause perhaps a tonne of chalk to explode in all directions, and Mastema clearly didn't want to get knocked off. She stretched her leg to wedge herself, wiggled her backside a little, and lifted the gun a second time.

The robot stirred. Alma was never entirely sure, thinking back afterwards, if it was her piggybacking its Google Earth feed that force-started its sense that something was wrong with the face it was programmed to maintain. Some kind of dark-coloured excrescence, attached to one side of the sculpted moustache. Scars in the cheek made by their descent. Something. At any rate, it shook itself, buzzed, whirred and scampered straight out through the right-hand portal of the O O Shakespe*her*ian nostril.

Alma watched what happened next, as a real-time spectator. She saw Mastema startled – as who wouldn't be should a creature, big as a child but clearly not human, burst from Shakespeare's gigantic nose and scuttle towards you. The bot was halfway to Mastema when she fired her heavy-calibre gun at it – her wail of surprise clearly audible inside Alma and Pu's little cavern. The blameless robot died then and there, torn into metal shreds that coasted on wings of fire and expanding gas in every direction, and Alma abruptly lost the visual feed.

They waited. The sounds from outside were comprised of seagulls and surf on shingle. The wind shifted its angle again, and played one of Shakespeare's giant nostrils like a kid blowing on a half-filled milk bottle. A low trombone-style moan.

Alma shifted herself, one foot on either side of the circular hole. The pebbles directly below were littered with pieces of the aggressively dismantled robot. And in addition to that inorganic rubble was something else: a human body lying there, unmoving.

10: *Strangers on the Terrain*

The climb back up Shakespeare's face was not an easy one. Alma was overcautious, and the higher she managed the more fearful she became of slipping and joining Mastema's corpse on the shingle below. Pu Sto was an experienced, and trained, climber; but she had lost a lot of blood, and was woozy. She braced herself with her bad arm and hauled with her good, but her feet scrabbled and kicked dust from the chalk frontage, and more than once Alma thought she was going to slide off entirely.

Eventually, though, they reached the top. Alma dragged herself over the lip with tufts of grass as handholds, and then lay on her front, panting. Pu Sto was right behind her. She wriggled round to help pull her up.

For a while the two of them just lay there, beneath the bright blue sky and its shifting fringed blobs of passing white. Every breath Alma sucked in was the most perfectly blissful experience she had ever had in her life.

Alma sat up. She tried her feed, but the Not Area firewall was blocking access to the general web, and with the service robot smashed on the ground there were no other points of even the most limited access. She did at least get a sense of the time. A little over an hour until she needed to be back at R!-town.

'You're checking your feed,' said Pu Sto, still on her back in amongst the wriggling grass. Gulls mocked the croakiness of her voice.

'I have a little over an hour to get home. We need to find a way of summoning help.'

'They'll be here soon,' Pu said.

'They?'

'Come now. You think nobody noticed? The entire Not Area was turned into a battleground, its AI melted from within by industrial-level toxic code. Explosions! Gunshots! Trust me, they're on their way. Minutes.'

'And the chances that "they" will take me back to R!-town are good, yes?'

'I'll tell them to. They will listen to me.'

It was, perhaps, a little cold-hearted of Alma, but her first thought when she heard this was to look closely at Pu Sto and wonder what were the chances of her dying, right there, in the next few minutes. If Pu did die, then what were the odds Alma would be able to persuade whoever arrived to ferry Alma to her flat? Small.

She touched the woman's chest, delicately, up near her left shoulder: it was stickily wet.

'How do you feel?' she asked.

'Thirsty,' replied Pu Sto. 'Don't you worry. I'm not about to expire. Not until I can tell the authorities to hurry you through the sky to your partner in that poky little R!-town apartment.'

'Thank you,' Alma replied, although her inflection somehow turned this into a question.

Pu Sto panted. Panted. 'You could open Babouche's packet now, you know.'

'I thought you wanted it double-firewalled, in case it contains some horrible malware?'

'I'd be surprised,' Pu rasped, 'if Mr Babouche had done anything so destructive.'

'You know what's in his package,' said Alma, staring out to sea. 'Because it was never his package. It was always your package.'

There was a long pause. Finally Pu said: 'Very thirsty. Very thirsty indeed. I wonder if we might—' she stopped, coughed scratchily, then rolled on her side and threw up onto the turf. Sticky strands of something. 'I wonder,' she said, in a smaller voice, 'if it would make sense to go back to the building. Find a tap. Get a drink.'

'I'll help you,' said Alma. But neither of them moved.

After a while Pu Sto pulled herself into a sitting position. She looked very ill indeed. The two women stared out across the wrinkling waves of the Channel. France-EU was visible, hazily: a slender layer of insulation between sea and sky. A seagull swept up like a hoverjet, wings arched, only a few metres away. It opened its insolent beak and brayed at them, before gliding away. Other gulls played tag in the sky of the middle distance.

'He died in my house, you know,' said Pu Sto.

'Adam Kem?'

'He and I were close. Close friends, he and I. And he died spewing up his red and frothy lungs, all over my authentic Safavid-period rug. You wouldn't *believe* the mess he made. Or how long it took him to die. I kept thinking: surely now. Surely now he's gone! Surely there's no lung left! But he gasped on and on. Until, finally, he didn't.'

Alma said nothing. The wind was running its invisible fingers through the grass.

'I didn't kill Adam Kem,' said Pu Sto, eventually.

'But you put him in harm's way, I think,' Alma replied.

The two women were sitting so close their shoulders were almost touching. Alma could have reached round and shoved Pu Sto in the back, pushed her off the cliff. Pu Sto might have been able to do the same to Alma, except that Alma was sitting on the side of her bad arm. Her wounded shoulder. Conceivably, that wouldn't stop her. Alma wondered if they should both move back.

'Inspector Michelangela and I,' Pu Sto said, 'are equally to blame, I think. In that regard. We both underestimated how close the enemy was to – to making its move. Truth to tell, we didn't have a clear enough sense of who the enemy even *were*. I still trusted Mastema, at that point. Just as a for instance.'

'You provoked them?'

'We were trying to flush them out.'

'Job done,' said Alma. 'I would say. Do you think Mastema killed him?'

'Maybe she did. She was a key member of my team, you know. Closer to me than my jugular vein, as the phrase goes. I wonder if she decided Adam was getting too close to *her*, and killed him to keep her cover.' A faint noise on the wind. Alma craned her neck to look back inland. Were those dots in the sky approaching flycars or aircraft? Were the forces of officialdom finally arriving?

'But then again,' Pu added, wheezily, 'nanobiots, chewing up your internal organs – they're not really Mastema's style. She likes *guns*.'

'I would say she's beyond liking and disliking now.'

'Quite right,' wheezed Pu. 'I should say: she *liked* guns.'

'There's no need for me to open Derp's package, I think,' Alma said.

'Who?'

'Mr Babouche. Dave, is he? Is that his real name? I don't think I'll bother with his package. It's going to contain information pertaining to secret developments in teleportation technology, I would guess. I would *guess*' – and she peered at Pu for a moment – 'it's a fat file, carefully forged over years, full of the most convincing detail. That's what I would guess.'

'The plan was for me to put pressure on McA to hire you, supplementary to the police investigation,' Pu Sto said. 'Then Michelangela was to chase you off the investigation – officially, as it were. But only after showing you enough data for you to put two and two together. Punchy's role was to tease you with a drip feed of teleportation data.'

'And Hunter-Colo?'

Pu Stow grimaced. 'Who?' She made gagging noises again, and for a moment Alma thought she was going to throw up again. But she pulled herself together.

'Never mind,' said Alma.

'I didn't realise how ruthless they would be,' Pu said, shortly. 'And I didn't know that Mastema was actually working for them. Once they killed Michelangela, the game changed. Dave too: dead. Poor fellow. They tried to kill me, you know, and came damn close – before this afternoon, I mean. I haven't heard from Prime PA for a long time – I hope he's alright. He may be dead too. High stakes. They're playing for high stakes.'

'They're still playing.'

'They are.'

'I don't understand,' Alma said, 'why you sent Madame Michelangela to take me off the case almost as soon as I'd been recruited onto it.'

'Oh, we wanted you initiated into the mystery,' Pu Sto said. 'But that didn't mean we could let you go running around with carte blanche. We didn't want you questioning the ambulance-woman, for instance. For obvious reasons.'

'For,' Alma nodded, 'obvious reasons.'

'I apologise,' wheezed Pu Sto, 'for getting you caught up in this. Your reputation preceded you, you see. I assumed you would conclude as you *should* have concluded. I assumed you would deduce what we primed you to deduce.'

'I almost did.'

Pu breathed hard for a while. 'How long have you known?'

'There's an adage about eliminating the impossible and considering what remains, however improbable. The only question was whether teleportation was possible or impossible. But realising it was the latter ... well, that clarified things.'

There was no mistaking it now: the faint but distinct sound of approaching aircraft rumbling through the air.

'Here they come,' said Pu Sto. 'Help me up, if you please.'

Alma got up, went round to Pu's other side and helped her up. She put her shoulder into Pu Sto's good armpit. They limped, arm in arm, away from the cliff edge, back towards the Not Area. Three craft – two aircars and an arrowhead-shaped transporter tucked under a vacuum balloon – came closer and closer.

'You see,' Pu said. 'You see, you can't reinvigorate the Real simply by decreeing it. You can't make it happen by fiat. You have to make it more attractive than the Shine. More intriguing to the people who ... Who ...' Her weight slumped away from Alma, and she struggled to continue holding her upright. But she had gone, and Alma was not strong enough. As slowly as she could she lowered Pu Sto's body to the ground. The aircars banked overhead and came down into the turf fifteen metres away.

Pu Sto had fainted.

11: *Topaz*

The transporter contained a medibot and Pu Sto's twice-made wound was dressed by this machine. Alma watched, with a foil cape round her shoulders, as a second medic picked tiny pieces of glass from her bare feet. Pu was put on a micropump drip strapped to the side of her neck, and laid out on a smartcher. It looked as though she wasn't going to recover consciousness, and then she did, opening her eyes and complaining about pain. This led to a brief interaction with the squad commanding officer, who eventually accepted Pu Sto's authority.

Pu then made use of her power to command by ordering the pilot of one of the skycars to fly Alma back to R!-town. 'Have a care,' was Pu's last statement to her. 'This isn't over.'

'But I don't care,' Alma told her. 'I've never cared. Not about this. Not about any of this. All I ever wanted to do was to look after Marguerite.'

'Let's hope for a cure,' Pu Sto said cryptically. 'Medical science can do amazing things nowadays, after all.'

Alma might have pressed her on the implication of this, but she was impatient to get back. The aircar swept her up, over London, and down the other side to land in the street outside her apartment. The drones had dispersed. There was nobody, and nothing, guarding the entrance to her flat. Indeed, since the door had been forced and now neither responded nor locked itself, Alma might even have wished that there had been. Anybody could have walked into the apartment and stolen anything.

Nobody had walked in, of course. In the whole of that populous conurbation called R!-town there was hardly anybody walking anywhere, and most of the ones who did stalk up and down the town's pavements were not conscious as they did so, the whir of mesh-suits giving muscles their needful workout, fighting the body's tendency to atrophy.

Alma took a breath, and onswitched her feed. There was a flurry of new messages, a clutter of packages, and an annoying stampede of while-you-were-away notifications. She swept everything into the tidy margin, and waited.

No drones overflew. There were no police messages.

Alma stepped back into her apartment.

Marguerite, for her part, was starting to come back from her fever. 'There you are,' she said, as Alma came into the bedroom. 'I was starting to worry!'

Alma leaned over and kissed her big face.

'Ugh,' she responded. 'You're filthy! All dirt and grass stains and – is that chalk?'

'Apologies, my love,' Alma replied. 'I'll wash.'

And so she washed, and then she tended to Marguerite's condition as the clock ticked down. A simple fluorescence of microbond histaminoids, easily treated; or at least, easily treated once the pathology recognised the genetic fingerprint of the person doing the treating.

Afterwards Marguerite declared herself super-hungry, and also thirsty. 'Not super-thirsty. Regular thirsty. Let's say a thirsty that has worked out, learned martial arts and designed its own bat-suit. But definitely *super*-hungry.'

'You'll have to wait until after my microshower,' Alma told her.

'To rescue me from the Promethean curse of my pathology,' wailed Marguerite in mock outrage, 'only to watch me literally starve to death! The cruelty!'

'That would be a long watch,' Alma told her. 'Frankly, I'm not sure I'd have the patience for such a vigil.'

'Injury,' said Marguerite, 'with a side order of insult. It's a good job I love you, isn't it?'

'A very good job.'

Alma washed, and put her soiled clothes in the chute. She dressed again in a topaz-coloured all-one that tightened at ankle and wrist, and cinched above her hips and below her breasts. Fetching food to restock Marguerite's feedline made her realise that she was, herself, extremely hungry.

They ate together like old times. Alma even had a beaker of red wine: a rare indulgence. Marguerite was happy to finish the rest of the bottle.

She told her story, and Marguerite nodded, and nodded, and, of course, acted insufferably.

'Did I not say, at the very beginning,' Marguerite declared, lustily, 'that it was prestidigitation?'

'The perfect clarity of your hindsight is a wonder to behold,' Alma said. 'Still, they took a risk. It's possible the whole charade could have fallen apart right at the beginning. If I'd asked the wrong question – which is to say, the *right* question – of FAC-13, on that first viewing of the crime scene.'

'Which one was FAC-13 again?' Marguerite asked.

'Your Mycroft-capacious brain and super-memory not retaining that one?'

Marguerite pulled a doleful expression. 'I've been poorly,' she said. 'You might show a little sympathy.'

'Poorly is the height and breadth and depth of you, my dear,' said Alma, kissing her again. 'And that's a lot of breadth and depth.'

'I suppose FAC-13 is the AI that was running that luxury car assemblage plant?'

'Still is, I suppose. Yes: the factory AI. It *could* be programmed, or more precisely somebody with the high-level government access and legal licence that Pu Sto possesses could *augment* the pre-existing programming. And the fact of that augmentation could be subsumed under the Official Secrets Act, so that it wouldn't show up in the regular feed of the AI. But Pu Sto could not have compelled the AI to *lie*. AIs don't do that.'

'So if you'd asked it...?'

'If I'd asked it the right question. I didn't, though. And maybe it wasn't such a risk, for Pu Sto. I mean, how was I supposed to know what the right question to ask was? At that early stage? I asked the FAC general questions, the sorts of questions anyone would ask. And it answered them truthfully.'

'Press,' Marguerite sang, 'tea – did-she – *tation*.'

'You did say it was a conjuring trick,' Alma conceded. 'As soon as I told you about it. Or rather, as soon as you illicitly eavesdropped on my professional consultation. Then again, you didn't say *how* the conjuring trick had been accomplished. I'm not convinced you knew.'

'Ye of little faith,' wailed Marguerite.

'The machines in the factory build the car, overseen by the

AI, FAC-13. In every respect, the car was assembled like any other car. In every respect but one, because in this case FAC-13 was following instructions from a high-ranking intelligence officer. That was the giveaway – the invisibility of these new commands. McA could have amended the programming of their FAC, of course; but only within the law, and not without leaving a trail. And why would McA do so? There was nothing in it for them. The intelligence agencies, on the other hand...'

'They're called the secret services for a reason,' said Marguerite, diverting a quantity of puréed roseberries down her feed. 'Go on.'

'AIs don't lie, of course. If I'd have asked FAC-13 *Did you 3D-print a lifesize facsimile of Adam Kem's corpse into the car you built?* – then it would have answered: Yes.'

'Yes,' agreed Marguerite.

'It would have said: Yes I did. But I didn't think to ask that question.'

'The question of your questioning remains questionable.'

'Then again, it's simple enough, if only because there's no other way it could have been done. And understanding that leads to the perpetrator, because there are only two classes of person who would have had the legal authority to add commands to the factory AI's assemblage programme. The management of McA could have done it – but why would they? The government could have done it, citing National Security legislation. So there we are. The car is assembled as normal, except that a human-shaped body dummy is 3D-printed into the boot. Adult, curled into a foetal position so that it could fit. It doesn't have to be super-realistic, since it is never going to be examined in any great detail. Although, that said, 3D printing can do wonders, nowadays. Anyway, the car is completed, in plain view of a dozen secure surveillance points-of-view. Then the final human check is made. Not that a human *needs* to check the finished product – that is to say, there aren't any engineering or mechanical reasons. It's all about the marketing. The Quality Control person's name was Chuckie, I believe: and she's looking for mechanical flaws or product malfunction. What she finds is what looks *to her* like a dead body. She is, as you would expect, distraught at this discovery. Encountering a corpse is never a nice thing. So she calls in an ambulance. The ambulance has been primed to be nearest at the completion time of the car: an easy timing to deduce, since the factory timetable is readily available data.'

'And the ambulancewoman, of course,' said Marguerite, 'is one of Pu Sto's people.'

'The surveillance footage is a bit unclear on her,' said Alma. 'I pored over it, but couldn't be sure. Conceivably the ambulance-woman was even Michelangela, in some kind of disguise. Say she joined the ambulance team from an agency, easily done when you can provide any official qualification and references you like. And immediately after this one night she signs off sick – upset and traumatised, it seems, by what she has seen. In and out. Nobody there to interrogate. Loose end, tied.'

'What if you had questioned her, though?'

'I don't suppose I would ever have found her. But if I had done, and assuming she was someone other than Michelangela . . . well, I suppose she would have denied it all. Her ambulance drives up to the factory and it already has Adam Kem's dead body inside it. It probably came directly from Pu Sto's house, having loaded the corpse. Thence to the factory. Ambulancewoman X, whoever she was, stuffs the 3D-printed fake body in the back, to be disposed of later, and drives the actual corpse to the hospital.'

'An elaborate piece of theatre. And for whose benefit?'

'For ours,' said Alma. 'For all of us. A mystery. To catch the attention of the Shine, mostly, I suspect. And that is a job it has done very well. Above all, it's the trailer for a conspiracy – that teleportation is real. How else could the trick be performed, after all? Poor old Derp Throat. I do feel sorry at how fatally out of depth he found himself and how quickly. I think Pu recruited him, discovered him dissatisfied at his dull job and promised him a little excitement. His job was to drip-feed me evidence for actual teleportation. He was, I don't doubt, a small player. It's possible he even believed the propaganda. He was a small part in what was a broad-front set of strategies to persuade as many people as possible that soon we would be able to beam ourselves around the world. Maybe even the galaxy. Something to *intrigue* people about the Real again. To get them thinking, wondering, curious to return. To scare the hospital people into believing their domination was about to end.'

'The ability to beam wherever we want!' sighed Marguerite. 'Like *Star Trek*.'

'To be like Captain Kirk, whose name means church, and Lieutenant Uhura, whose name means freedom,' Alma agreed. 'It's an intoxicating combination, that. *The Church of Freedom*. Science fiction defined in a single phrase, I would say. A beguiling thought, certainly.'

'But false.'

'Stories don't have to be true to be powerful. And as for that, maybe Pu Sto believed that technology would catch up with the story, if enough people wanted it – if there was enough demand, enough pressure on the developers. But for all her grand sermonising about the need to make the Real attractive again, and to diminish the pull of the Shine, that wasn't the reason she put this game in play.'

'Game?'

'The misdirection. Adam Kem's corpse in the boot of the car – she wasn't primarily playing to an audience in the Shine. This must have been something concocted quickly, on the back of Kem's murder. He was infected with nanobiots, and could have died anywhere – he could have lived for minutes or hours or conceivably even days after the contact with the cause of his death. I believe he was infected the same day he died, went to a meeting with Pu Sto unaware of his condition, and collapsed when he was with her. I don't know. She decided, acting quickly, to make a *show* of the death. Not to hide it away, but to shine a light on it. Her real audience was whoever had killed Adam Kem. I think at that point she wasn't sure who they were, but whoever they were they would be sure to notice where their victim ended up. They killed Kem to shut him up, and to send *her* a message. She decided she would knock that back across the net. Send a return message. Like everybody else, the killers would be thinking: *How could that corpse have gotten there?* You poison Adam Kem, and watch him walk away. You know he's going to drop dead. You can't be sure where his corpse will come to light. You expect it to be discovered in a possible place, not an *im*possible one. And so you find yourself thinking: hey, but what if this teleportation rumour is true? What if the people with this technology, the advocates of the Real – what if this is their way of sticking two fingers up at us, at the other side, the people who have decided their best strategy for maintaining power is to herd the complaisant multitudes into the surveillance paradise called the Shine? That would worry you, wouldn't it? If teleportation *is* true, after all, then the whole political game changes. People might indeed come stampeding back from the Shine eager to jaunt through the actual cosmos, to boldly go, to join the new Church of Freedom. People with a grip on power can get pretty ruthless when they feel that grip slipping.'

'Exactly as I deduced,' said Marguerite, with a self-satisfied expression on her face.

Alma ignored this manifest provocation. 'It worked. Indeed, it worked much too well. It provoked panic in the Health cabal – senior people in the Department of Health, in league I presume with the Department of Justice, since hospitals and prisons are basically the same structures now. They launched a de facto coup d'état.'

'*A de facto coup d'état,*' Marguerite repeated. 'Three languages in six words. Well played, madame.'

'They were bounced into it. The coup attempt, I mean. It was hasty of them. I assume it's being played out now, behind the scenes of government.'

'Bloodily, I dare say.'

'I dare say. It's not as if it's likely to register on the mainstream news feeds. They're all clogged with celebrity gossip nowadays anyway. It's all Shine, Shine, Shine.'

'You don't sound very concerned,' Marguerite noted.

'As long as they leave us alone, I'm not concerned in the least.'

'And you're sure they *will* leave us alone?'

'We can't be sure of that,' said Alma. 'I suppose it will depend on who comes out on top of the infighting. And if Pu Sto does lose, we have to hope that the new winners will consider us too low-grade to worry about. There's nothing we can do, either way.'

'Not a very comforting thought.'

'No,' agreed Alma. 'It's not. But it's the best we have.'

After they had finished eating, Alma reflected that she had never felt so exhausted in all her life. She fell asleep on the couch, and plunged straight into deep REM, dreaming a hectic series of vivid dreams. She was flying. Röell figured largely, although Alma, never having met her, had no idea what she actually looked like. In the dream she was a white-faced individual, halfway between male and female: not transgender but, in some complicated way, *alternating* gender. The white god. The white goddess. Her face was a hundred metres high and she boomed out: *I am the master-mistress passion of your task. I am justice. I am law.* Alma ran through a forest whose branches bit at her, threshed and darted like viper tongues. She leapt and banged her head against a hard prong – a finger it seemed, twice as large as life, pointing from the raised hand of a fat-jowled man. You can't go here, said the man, in a slobbery, mouthy sort of voice. When Alma complained, he spoke again. It's all about that, he said. It's all about where you can go and where you can't go.

Pu Sto was in the dream, too. She was inside a car, but although Alma thought it was a large car far away it turned out to be a tiny, toy car close at hand. How could Pu Sto have squeezed herself in such a tiny space? *Let me out*, she squeaked. *Open the boot, and...*

Alma woke, her heart racing. The alarm had woken her. It was time to tend to Marguerite again.

After she had done so, she felt a little better. Colours seemed brighter. The sunset over the factories and roads and accommodation blocks of west R!-town looked riper. Marguerite herself was dozing.

Alma settled down to sort through her feed, and put some kind of order into it.

She ordered some more food, and a drone delivered it.

It took three more sessions tending Marguerite, with naps of various length in between, before Alma began to feel more rested, at least in her mind. Partly it was the growing sense of relief that nobody had come to arrest her.

Her body ached badly the following day, pretty much all over: arms and right leg worst of all. She was covered in little bruises, and several patches on her skin felt somehow scorched, such that even a tepid setting on the microshower felt like washing in scalding water. Marguerite crowed with delight at the size of the bruise on her back. '*That* one looks like a map of Callisto,' she said.

'I'm sure I'm in better physical condition than Pu Sto,' Alma replied.

And the following day she got a message from that very person, or at least from a user with Pu Sto's accreditation, official ID. Alma chased down the legitimation threads, or checked into them as far as she could at any rate, just because. It seemed kosher. The message came without avatar, and simply said: *Your status as a police person-of-interest has been revised. Hopefully you will not be bothered. I cannot say we are winning, my dear; but we are at least not losing. R. has fled.*

Alma replied, but the reply was not collected.

12: *The Meaning of the Ring*

Three more days passed before Alma allowed herself to start believing what Pu Sto's message had intimated. The authorities were no longer pursuing her.

Marguerite, her fever behind her, was a bundle of new energy. 'Did this matter pay?' she demanded. 'We need money. We cannot eat air – or I cannot, at any rate.'

'In the Shine we could live in a vast palace. Command an entire planet.'

'Even people in the Shine need money,' Marguerite reminded her. 'To maintain their earthly bodies. Food and water. Real-world accommodation, be it ever so small. Health. A mesh-suit. And anyway,' she concluded, with a grand roll of her large hand, 'we can't take refuge in the Shine, now, can we?'

'You can't, you mean,' Alma told her. 'But to answer your question: no. It did not pay. I am content to have gotten away with my life. Getting paid as well would have been over-egging the lily.'

'Gilding the pudding,' Marguerite said, nodding. 'Still: we must get money somehow. Somehow!'

'I'll see if anyone wants to hire an investigator, I suppose.'

'You suppose,' boomed Marguerite. 'And I repose.' And she laughed one of her great rolling laughs.

On the next day Alma went for a walk. It took more courage to leave the apartment than she thought it would. The door had been mended and a new AI installed. The elevator had been cleaned. Alma stepped through the building entrance and onto the street and it was another sunshiny morning in R!-town.

She strolled for a while, going nowhere in particular. The streets were empty of real people, although she passed four in-Shine folk stomping along in their mesh-suits.

Of course, it was the same place as ever, familiar to the point of blankness, if not quite invisible. It wasn't that the streets were empty, save for those few people in mesh-suits exercising their muscles and stretching their bones. It was that everything was so *clean*. There were no old bits of paper being blown about, flapping loose newspaper pages turned urine-coloured by time and sunlight, plastic bags expanded by a breeze, old leaves that had survived the winter and were now black like rotten bananas, no cigarette butts and crusts and tin cans. Nothing. Everything was continually cleaned away by tireless bots. It gave the whole place the vibe of a film set. Alma found herself yearning, oddly, for a little honest urban dirt.

Sunlight gleamed on the rhino-horn roof-spike of the Blade Building.

Alma found herself a quiet coffee shop and sat by the window with her drink. All alone, save only for three people plugged into the Shine at the back of the room. It made her think of the last time she'd been in such an emporium. I weep for Derp Throat, she thought: I deeply sympathise.

Still, what Marguerite had said could not be denied. They had to earn money.

She sipped her coffee, readied herself and went into her feed and made a good-faith payment to Lez. Finances did not permit her to quit herself of the whole debt. She needed to earn, fast, and preferably copiously. So she spent a quarter-hour filigreeing a firewall within a firewall within a firewall, to protect herself as well as she could; and then she tunnelled through the overlap and into the dark feed.

Things did seem chaotic, down there. A lot of the shadier middlepeople had gone to ground; the Shine was buzzing with a rainbow of different conspiracy theories. Official news reported only an 'investigation into accounting irregularities within three in-Real government departments'. The dark feed was a tangle of garish stories of arrest and assassination and mysterious disappearance, of government chaos and defection and terror. The army had been deployed. The army had been ordered back to barracks. The EU had activated emergency disaster planning. Impossible to know what was true and what mere rumour.

News of the great swarm of drones over R!-town could not be suppressed, of course: a spokesperson described the assemblage as 'a planned exercise in inter-drone coordination', and told news-feeds that it had lasted less than two hours before the drones had all dispersed back to their points of origin. The spokesperson also insisted that the exercise had passed off 'without incident', which made Alma wonder what they had done with the man who had been battered to death on the Queen's Road.

Of course, she looked into it: surveillance footage from that section of the road at the appropriate time was unavailable: a government interdiction order led Alma down a frustrating maze of tags and authorisations before coming up with a data dead-end that put the absence of footage down to 'malfunction'. So instead Alma searched for recent unusual deaths, and eventually found a story, downsuaded in the toiling newsfeeds, of a Bracknell resident who had committed suicide by fusing the self-drive component of his car and driving the vehicle at high speed into a wall on George Street. Footage for this death was also unavailable: marked sensitive and Coroner's Court Pending.

Alma sat back and took a sup. As cover-ups went it was rushed and clumsy. That fact alone told her a great deal about how much energy was being taken up behind the governmental scenes with fighting, counterattacking and jockeying for power.

It was almost enough to worry a person.

Money, she reminded herself. Then she thought of Lester Hunter-Colo, and his disinclination to be investigated, and his insistence that his mum was a flake who would not pay out. Maybe that was true. But it would be nice to, at least, have an actual invoice she could submit.

She checked on the Ordinary Transport Consultancy. In the few days since she had last looked it up the company had doubled in net worth. That was quite a startling thing. She contemplated wandering over to the company offices to see if there was any-thing to see. But when she tried a preliminary shuffle through the data to see if there was any further news on Lester Hunter-Colo himself, she discovered something very strange.

His name was cached inside something in her spamhole.

Metaphorically levering the lid off the top of her spam folder was never a fun job. If virtual datacontent could smell, this stuff would exhale the mephitic foulness of ten thousand years of com-pacted waste. But the relevant packet had not yet been fractally compressed, which made it easy to pull out and drop in a simple sandbox. The packet was an anonymous, smooth-surfaced datagon, which was why her filters had disposed of it automatically. But when Alma opened it she found a message from Lester Hunter-Colo inside. It was a panda. The panda was wearing an iron crown, like a medieval monarch, but was otherwise not dressed. Each one of its claws had been painted with different colour nail varnish. When she tapped OK, the beast spoke to her: *Wanted you to know*, the panda said, *I appreciate you not following up on my ma's case. It is appreciated. Just wanted to say.* A panda wink. *The kind of player I'm going to become? You did the right thing in terms of staying on my good side.* Then the panda backrolled into a slow burst of purple smoke, and was gone.

The sandbox retained enough of a tagtrail for Alma to extract a sendpoint, and when she checked it seemed to be still active. So she called it. She reasoned Hunter-Colo himself was very unlikely to answer, but she thought she would give it a go.

Hunter-Colo answered. Not such a wily player after all. It was almost endearing.

—Lester, she said, as if they were old friends catching up.

—What? Whatwhat?

—I got your panda. But just so as we're clear, I haven't given up on your mother's case.

—There is no – wait. What?

—I'm having a coffee, she said shunting the address of the coffee shop to him. Come and chat. Off-feed and off the record, and maybe then we can call it quits.

—No.

—Well, in that case I am going to have to make some very public freedom of information requests concerning the OTC. I have friends in the police who can rustle me up an actual warrant, too.

There was a long pause, and finally Hunter-Colo said—Five minutes, in a surly voice.

—Five minutes would be the perfect length for chat-time.

Alma spent the next quarter-hour bringing more order to her feed, and buying a second coffee from the waiterobot, and to accompany that – why the hell not? – a muffin. A chocolate muffin. *With* choc chips. Through the big windows R!-town's striated concrete and blocks of gridwork bricklaying looking almost pretty. Urbanism in place of the pastoral. Earth hath not anything to show more R! she thought; and then tried to remember how the rest of that poem went, and gave up, and consulted her feed for the answer – *dull would she be of soul who could pass by/A sight so touching in its majesty* – and so on. The feed gave her info on Wordsworth. An interesting individual. And his friend Coleridge, too. Both poets and both, of course, men; although one of them was the masculine partner and the other the feminine half of their relationship. Beastly gender essentialism. And yet together they had created a collection called *Lyrical Ballads* that had (the smooth femaleness of the lyric, the manly narrative striding-forward of the ballad) revolutionised poetry. All very fascinating, no doubt.

Lester Hunter-Colo came into the shop. He was wearing goggles and a mouth-mask with Immortan-Joe teeth printed onto it. She smiled at him. After looking around, he took off the mask and the goggles and slipped them into his pocket. Then he stood scowling at her. In the flesh he looked more ill and thinner than he had done in sim. His complexion was carbuncular and the skin around his eyes a mauve-brown colour that did not go nicely with his overall albinesque whiteness.

'Lester,' she said.

He sat. 'Your five minutes starts now. You want to talk, you talk. Talk-talk. I'm not going to say anything. I'm-a just gonna seat, sit on a seat, seat myself and not *say* anything.' He glowered at the table, and then immediately contradicted his last statement by saying: 'I'm up-and-coming, you know? I'm the sort of person you won't daunt.' A sort of spasm of frustration passed over his face, and he tried again. 'I'm the sort of person you *won't* – *daunt* – to, to, gah!'

'Won't daunt is good,' Alma assured him. 'Eloquent, actually.' But it was not what Lester wanted to say.

'I'm the sort of person,' he said, speaking more slowly, 'that you *don't* – *want* – to piss off. Yeah?'

'Yeah,' agreed Alma.

Lester fell silent, and then summoned the waiterobot and ordered a hot chocolate. It arrived and he drank half of it straight away. The sunlight beaming through the window gave a high-definition vividness to the many little yellowhead dots and red blotches on his skin. Corpsey, really. But his eyes, moated by their puckering skin of exhaustion, had a kind of sweetness to them, and the sheer young-man gawky awkwardness of him was oddly endearing.

'Lester,' Alma said. 'I was wrong about you.'

'Oh. Yeah?' He sounded surprised when he said this so he tried again, with a sneer and a *You picked the wrong guy to cross* tone of voice. 'Oh yeah.'

'I thought,' Alma explained, 'that the ring inside your stomach was a kind of crude teleportation device.' As she said this she was amazed at how hokey and false it sounded. Had she ever really believed that?

Hunter-Colo narrowed his eyes. 'You,' he said, '*what?*'

'I know, I know. But never mind that. I have a different theory about the ring, now.'

'Your theory is not worth the paper it is written on.'

'You haven't heard it yet,' she pointed out. 'Besides which, it isn't written on any paper.'

'Good!' said Hunter-Colo, and glowered triumphantly at her as if he had won some kind of victory.

'There's a war coming,' said Alma. 'Isn't there?'

Lester looked at her. Then he gurned. Then he took another sip of his hot chocolate. And then the act all just dropped away. He sighed, and his bony shoulders slumped.

'It's not that I'm scared,' he said. 'Not exactly.'

'I am,' Alma assured him.

'I don't mind fighting. That's what I signed up for. But this isn't fighting. *That's* the worry, see, that we'll never even get the chance to fight. They could be in the air. They could be in the food. They could be in this hot lotta chalk.'

'Chalk,' Alma agreed, nodding.

'This,' he said, pointing a finger at the mug in front of him. 'This hot lotta, hot chotta, lottachotta.' It was fascinating to watch him grow agitated. Little flushes of pink red appeared on his neck; the lines running from the two edges of his mouth up to his nostrils deepened. 'This!' he urged her. 'Hot! Shock! O'Lat!'

'I was investigating the murder of a man named Adam Kem,' Alma said. If she talked for a while it would give him a chance to calm down. 'His lungs had been wholly destroyed, inside his chest. Nanobiots had gotten in there and turned both lungs to red slurry. I don't know if he was infested with them and died straight away, or if, him having breathed *in* the nanobiots, they might then have lain dormant for a time. Maybe for a long time.'

'Nah,' said Lester, gloomily. 'The number they'd need to do

that to a man's lungs – that many, you'd *feel* them going down. 'Course, if you did feel them going down it would be too late.'

Alma said nothing.

'What my boss says,' Hunter-Colo said, in a low voice, 'is that airborne release is not the biggest worry. I mean, they give us the gask and the moggles, and they tell us to wear them, out and about. But if *they* release a big cloud of these things into the air, the death toll would be ...' He let out a long breathy whistle, like McCartney imitating a descending 747 at the start of 'Back in the USSR'.

'Serious stuff,' said Alma.

'It *would* be serious stuff. Serious, endgame stuff.'

'You think the risk is less ... generalised?'

'That's what my boss says. She says food is a more accurate way of targeting the ... the weapons. Maybe not even in your food, you know? Maybe just in the steam coming up off your coffee. But once it's in your stomach, it will eat you alive, inside to outside. V.-dour.'

'Dour is the *mot juste*.'

He shook his head. '*De*vour you. Horrible way to go – see,' he was speaking with sudden urgency, 'I'm no coward, but that's no way to go. You know? Not like that.'

'I entirely agree. And the ring protects you?'

'That's what the boss says. These tiny things are still machines, you know? Each of them has its own access to the cloud, which was how sea rurchers from medi medi *medical* science built them. To to make them responsive to particulars, not blindly programmed to do just one thing. You know why the researchers developed them?'

'Curing disease?'

Hunter-Colo looked at her then, surprised at her denseness. 'Nah, man,' he said. 'Science has that down pat, don't you think? This is for the bodies of people in the Shine.'

'For the bodies,' Alma repeated, finally understanding, 'of people in the Shine.'

'You think you think *clanking* about in them them mesh-suits is the future? That's a real inelegant solution to the problem. Don't you think?'

'That's why these nanobiots were developed,' said Alma in a voice of comprehension. 'The problem of keeping human bodies from atrophy and bedsores when the people whose bodies they are spent months, or years, in-Shine. Makes sense, that does. Oh, that makes sense.'

'That's it. This is the big step. Put some of this in your body and it will tend your muscles fibre by fibre, and keep your bones happy and ... all that. No need for mesh-suits. No need to exercise at all.'

'Well,' said Alma. 'That would make the Shine even more attractive to people.'

'Sure. Not everyone can afford a mesh-suit, you know. Lots of those people tell themselves they'll get out of the Shine before they hurt their bodies but then they get distracting. D-string. Distrac*ted*.'

'It's a very distracting place,' Alma agreed. 'The Shine.'

'So when they *do* come shout of shout shout *out* of the Eye-in, they're crippled, bedsores all that. This technology will change everything. *Out*. Of the. *Shine*.'

'Except that, as technology, it is so easily weaponisable.'

'My boss,' Lester said, 'reckons these rings will keep us safe. Because you can filter the air you breathe, sure, with like a mask and that, but you *can't* filter the food you eat and the daughter you wrink, can you. And you *have* to eat and drink. These rings attract the little nano things and neutralise them. That's what my boss says.'

'Couldn't you scan your food before you eat it? Put one of these rings *in* your food.'

'Nah,' said Hunter-Colo. 'The nanobiots only activate when they're inside you. It's inside you the countermeasure needs to be.'

They were silent together for a while. Then Lester Hunter-Colo added: 'You say war is coming. I reckon it's here. There's two factions and they're sparring, sparring right now. And people don't even notice!'

'Their attention,' Alma agreed, 'is elsewhere.'

Despite insisting that he would only stay five minutes, and that he would say nothing, and that he was a cold-eyed killer and the coming man in the world of organised crime, Hunter-Colo seemed to warm to Alma. In the end they talked for half an hour or more, and he opened up about many of his worries, not just the nanobiot-related ones. It came over him abruptly that he was compromising his toughness. That's when he declared he had to go back to work or he would get into trouble.

After he had gone, Alma put together a report, keeping many of the details opaque but reassuring Mrs Hunter-Colo that her boy was in no danger from the ring in his stomach. She parcelled this up with an invoice for her time and sent the whole to Mrs Hunter-Colo. She did so without much expectation that the old woman would actually pay her. Still, don't ask never gets.

Alma finished her muffin and went through to the café bathroom to rinse her face. Her bruise-speckled face winked at her from the mirror. Cold water gushed from the tap. And there it was, wasn't it? Clear as a stream of liquid diamond. Water from the Thames, or maybe from the Kennet, filtered and cleaned and piped into this establishment. It *looked* clean. It looked good enough to drink. But for all she knew, it could be positively swarming with miniature tech animalcules, ready to go into her stomach and tear her apart from the inside out. Like that old Victorian cartoon of a drop of water filled with horrifying monsters.

Everything that she had lived through had been the preliminary jockeying for position of a much larger war. And that war was now under way. She and Marguerite would not be able to avoid it. She would surely try to keep her head down, and stay out of it. But, with a tingle in her abdomen, Alma finally understood the last thing Pu Sto had said to her, in the flesh, on the south coast. She had been hinting that there might be a permanent cure for Marguerite's pathology. And why would she dangle that in front of Alma's nose, unless she intended at some point to use it as leverage? When the war came, and assuming Pu Sto had survived all the high-level upheavals, she would use the promise of such a thing to draw Alma in. Recruit her. Make her into the last thing she wanted to be: a soldier.

What then?

Alma dried her face and her hands and left the coffee shop, walking out into the warm R!-town sunshine.

Alma returns in...

By the Pricking of Her Thumbs

One of the four richest people in the world may be dead. But which one?

A Kubrickian thriller from one of the world's leading authors of SF.

Turn the page for an extract*

*not final text

1: *The Thumb Itself*

Alma couldn't make sense of it until she met the monkeys. Don't blame her for that. It wasn't a simple business – first the Howdunnit, then the Whodunnit-to, and both together a real tangle, inhospitable to solution. A darker time for Alma than any she had previously known. A confounding puzzle.

Until, that is, she met the monkeys and was finally able to piece the whole thing together.

Well, I *say* 'met'. It wasn't what you'd call a conventional meeting.

Well, I *say* 'monkeys'.

At any rate, first there was the Howdunnit. That was the one with the needle. Then afterwards, as a quite separate matter, was the Whodunnit-to. But first things first. *How* is always primary. *Who-to* has to be a secondary consideration.

It proved easy to be mistaken about such things as who actually was employing her, and to solve which crime. There was a howdunnit in place of the whodunnit, and then a whodunnit-to in place of the same thing.

'Take me through it one more time,' said Alma.

'As many times as you like, sweetheart,' said Officer Maupo. 'The woman is dead?'

'Dead as dial-up,' the officer confirmed.

Maupo was not physically present in the room with Alma, of course, but the latest iteration telephonics were so realistic it would have been easy to think she was. Fact of the matter: Alma was beginning to feel old. They hadn't had this new hyperreal hologrammer, all these creepily precise visualisations of people hundreds of miles away, when *she* was a girl. Back then a hologram looked like a hologram, scratches and blips and all.

Alma cleared her throat. 'And she has a needle in her thumb. Like Aurora.'

Maupo hesitated. 'Aurora? My feed is giving me a disambiguation list as long as my overtime claim sheet on *that* one.'

'*Sleeping Beauty*,' Alma said.

'I see what you— No, though. Because, you see, Aurora got a needle in her thumb and fell asleep, where Alexa Lund got a needle in her thumb and fell *dead*.' Out of nowhere, Maupo grinned. 'Less Aurora, more Aurigormortis.'

Oh, she was a sparky one, this Officer Maupo.

'You are sure the needle in the thumb killed her?' Alma asked.

'Indeed we're not,' said Maupo. 'We're not sure of anything. Which is why Pu Sto has sent me to ask you to assist.'

'Being,' Alma said, 'too busy to come herself.'

'Ah,' said the officer. 'About that. Pu Sto herself asked me to say—'

Alma put her hand up like she was directing traffic in antique times.

'It doesn't matter. Really it doesn't. I'm assuming there's a reason you mention the needle in the thumb? You would hardly bring it up if it were wholly unrelated.'

'We've honestly no idea. No *needle's*-eye, dear.'

Maupo gave Alma the benefit of her loopy grin a second time. It crossed Alma's mind that the policewoman might be flirting with her. She put the notion to one side.

'Let me summarise what you're telling me,' Alma said. 'Just so I'm clear. Ms Lund, a thirty-nine-year-old woman in good health, was found dead in her apartment, and the only thing out of the ordinary about her condition – apart, of course, from the fact that she was dead – is that she had a six-centimetre-long *sewing* needle stuck in her thumb.'

'That's the nub of it.'

'Is there,' Alma prompted, 'anything else I ought to know?'

'That I get off duty at ten?' Maupo offered.

'Anything else I need to know about the case. Surveillance footage?'

'Not that we can find. Normally the apartment would have footage, of course, but it just so happens the program was offline for fifteen minutes, on a diagnostic and rebooting protocol. It doesn't know who ordered the diagnostic and reboot, although whoever it was had good enough bona fides to convince a level-7 AI.'

'Those can be forged,' Alma said. 'Though it isn't cheap.'

'This implies that somebody with a lot of money wanted Lund dead, and was able to sideline the apartment for long enough to make that happen.'

'Or perhaps Lund herself ordered the diagnosis and reboot?'

'Unlikely,' said the officer. 'Why wouldn't she just tell her apartment to undertake the diagnostic? I mean, if it was *her*, then why hide the fact? All we know is that the program recognised valid command codes, and switched itself to diagnostic mode. When it switched back to its regular duties, fifteen minutes later, Lund was dead on the floor.'

'With a needle in her thumb.'

'Through her thumb. Pushed in through the back of the thumbnail, right through the joint and out the other side.'

'Painful sounding,' said Alma. 'But not in itself fatal. And there was no poison, or nanotech, on the tip of this needle?'

'Nothing. Nothing on the needle, nothing in Lund's system.'

'What does your coroner say about cause of death?'

'She says circulatory shock.'

'Having a needle pushed through your thumb would certainly *be* a shock.'

'No,' said Maupo. 'Not that. Circulatory shock is medical terminology. It has nothing to do with common or garden

235

shock. There are four main types of it, each one defined by the underlying cause. It might be, for instance, that your body goes into shock because of a large-scale haemorrhage. Or because the heart stops. Or there's some blockage in the circulation. Or it might be that a massive infection simply overloads your body, or trauma of some kind, allergy – you've heard of anaphylactic shock, I guess. Lots of possible causes, but the same result. The body, in effect, shuts off.'

'Death.'

'Death.'

'Maybe,' said Alma, 'she died of fright. That's a thing, isn't it?'

Maupo shook her head. 'No, not really. Not a thing, generally speaking. And that's super unlikely to have been what happened here, because her adrenaline and cortisol levels would have been way higher. There was evidence of adrenaline residue, so something startled her. But whatever it was had time to settle down, physiologically, before she died.'

'Died,' Alma prompted, once more, 'of?'

'Her circulation went into a specific, medically defined form of shock. Oxygen was not being delivered to her organs. It was probably the cerebral hypoxia that actually killed her.'

'But circulatory shock can't be caused by getting jabbed in the thumb with a needle,' said Alma, who was checking her own feed on the condition. 'Or people would be dropping dead at sewing classes and acupuncturists and tattoo studios in their thousands daily.'

'That is a perfectly accurate summary of the state of play.'

'Why would somebody want to kill her?' Alma asked.

'Why,' Maupo countered, 'does anybody want to kill anyone?'

'You ask that like it's a rhetorical question. Actually, it's not. It admits of quite a straightforward answer. Most people *don't* want to kill other people. When murder happens it's almost always either hot or cold, and if it's cold then the reason is almost always one of two things.'

'Speaking as a police officer,' said Maupo, arching a simulated eyebrow, 'I feel it would be in my professional interest to know what those two things are.'

'Money,' said Alma, as if it were the most obvious thing in the world, 'or psychopathy. Including genocide in the latter category. If it's psychopathy, individual or collective, then the death of Ms Lund will already be, or will soon prove to be, part of a larger pattern of murder.'

'And what about the hot murders?'

'Passion, sex, drunkenness, a flare-up of rage or resentment – all those. Whoever did this took pains to close down surveillance, and left no other clues or pointers. They were meticulous. They knew what they were doing, and planned it carefully. So this one was cold.'

'Money, then.'

'Was Ms Lund wealthy?'

'Not rich-rich. She was well-to-do, I suppose. Worked for a private company, spent most of her time in-Shine, liked classic culture, drank only twentieth-century wine. That level of rich.'

'What was her job?'

'Details are hard to get – it's a privately owned company, and not under obligation to post anything publicly. Owned by a firm that's owned by a firm that's owned by one of the ultra-rich. You know how it is. Best as we can tell she was working on consciousness. Modelling human consciousness.'

'Full AI?'

'That's our assumption. One of those people who hadn't given up on that dream – actual artificial consciousness, the real-deal AI.'

'Maybe she had got close, and was killed to stop the research going any further?'

'Maybe.'

'Or maybe she had broken through, and was tortured to obtain her work, and then killed to cover traces? Either way, actual AI has the potential to generate prodigious amounts of money, and money is a very solid reason to kill.'

'Not much of a torture, though, is it? One pinprick in the thumb?'

'Maybe she had a phobia about such things. Maybe a childhood viewing of the fate of Princess Aurora in *Sleeping Beauty* traumatised her.'

'At any rate, if we get any more details on her employment,' said Maupo, 'I'll let you know.'

'Can I see the body?'

'Pu Sto said you'd ask that. I'll have to get clearance. This is an official police investigation, you know, and however tight you are with Pu, you are not actually police. But I dare say it can be arranged. Maybe tomorrow. Until then, I'm authorised to share all official files and data with you, and any assistance you can render will be—' She broke off. 'There are rules, you know,' she went on, in a different tone of voice, 'rules against police officers entering into relationships with the members of the public with whom they come into contact during the course of their investigations. But you're not strictly speaking a member of the public, are you?'

'I'm not, strictly speaking,' Alma replied, 'single.'

'Oh,' said Maupo. 'I mean, of course.'

'Of course in the sense of OK? Or in the sense that you had previously checked my confidential files and already knew that? And that, given the state of health of my partner, you figured you might have a shot?'

For the first time in their encounter Maupo looked actually uncomfortable.

'You know very well that it's against police rules to go poking around files not immediately relevant to the investigation. Against the rules means against the law. And— Look – this specific thing. This dead person, Lund. I'm police and we have instincts, and my instinct tells me this whole *thumb* thing is surely, surely irrelevant.'

'Either the needle in the thumb is related, in some way, to Lund's death, however hard it is to see how,, or it is *un*related. If it is the latter, the needle is either purely adventitious, which seems unlikely, or else is part of some red herring game, some attempt at distraction. And if *that's* what we're dealing with, then there must be something the killer is trying to distract us *from*. Or I should say, something *from which* the killer is trying,' Alma smiled one of her rare smiles, 'to distract us.'

'And what are you trying to distract *me* from, Ms Alma,' said Maupo, recovering her composure with another of her weird off-kilter grins, and essaying, Alma suddenly heart-sinkingly understood, a waggishly direct form of flirtation, 'with your over-performed hyper-correctness about not ending sentences with a preposition? Could it be that you are a little tiny bit more single than you said? A little tiny bit more open to going on a date with an interested, attentive and, if I may say so without sounding vainglorious, attractive police officer who—'

'No,' said Alma.

Maupo waited for more.

There was no more.

'Goodbye,' said Alma.

'That's … 'That's abrupt.'

'Very much the kind of person I am,' agreed Alma. 'Not just abrupt. *The* brubt.'

Maupo looked blank for a moment, but then, in a manner evidently unconnected with any notion of mirth, moved her facial muscles into a smile. Joining the game was joining the game, after all.

'OK then,' she said, heartily. 'Oh jay, oh kay *and* oh ell – I shall take that,' and she paused, and bowed with old-school courtesy, 'as a definite no-no-maybe. *À tout à l'heure*, Ms Alma.'

She ended the call, and the sim vanished.

It was time for Marguerite's next bout of treatment. Alma went through to the bedroom and settled to the business of determining which fractal iteration her lover's polyform pathology was taking this time. Every four hours and four minutes, without fail. Never quite the same from one appearance to the next, never predictable – designed that way by persons unknown, to torment and likely to kill.

Alma watched the antibodies spread, like smoke through the blood, watched the little spikes run up and down on the toximeter. As with chess, no combination of moves was ever precisely like any previous pattern, but sometimes fell into more broadly recognisable strategies. So absorbed was she in constellating the dosage trifecta and inspraying the antipyre in the right places that she barely noticed how uncharacteristically withdrawn Marguerite was being.

'What's up with you?' she asked, washing her hands afterwards.

Marguerite was staring at a point on the ceiling.

'That young police officer,' she said, in a haughty voice, 'seemed unusually interested in you.'

'And why wouldn't she be?' Alma said, coming to the bedside and kissing Marguerite's cliff face cheek. 'I'm hot.'

'You are so attentive to my physical hurt,' Marguerite replied, affecting a tragic-heroine voice, 'yet so careless of my emotional suffering.'

'Don't be a bloke about this, Rita. 'If you don't trust me by now then you're being seriously stubborn in your insecurity. I'm quite tempted to tell you to get over yourself.'

'Have you *seen* myself?' Marguerite returned. 'You realise what manner of Alpine Hannibal I'd have to be to traverse that?'

Alma kissed her again. 'That's better. And you have nothing to worry about, you know. The flirty copper . . . That was just her manner, I think. I don't think it was anything personal. More to the point, she was bringing me a case – a paying gig, from Pu Sto herself. You were eavesdropping, so you know all about it.'

'A ridiculous case,' said Marguerite, taking a long sip from her straw. 'A trivial case. A waste of your time and my genius.'

'You've solved it then?'

'There was something on the needle, of course.'

'Flirty copper says not.'

'The police officer in question,' said Marguerite, her left eyebrow arching like a willow branch, 'clearly knows nothing, and cares not that this is so. A human being doesn't die of being pricked in the thumb – doesn't die, that is, on account of the prick itself. Ergo there was something on the needle. It injected some lethal toxin into the body. If the toxin hasn't shown up on their post-mortem scans, that means it erased itself, or metabolised into something inert. It means they're looking for the wrong thing. Which means it's not a conventional toxin, or an easily identifiable nanotech agent – so, they need to look again. They need to look harder and look smarter.'

'I shall go see the body, its needle still in situ. Perhaps you could give me some pointers on what this super-subtle, so-hard-to-detect toxin might be.'

'I was adored once too,' said Marguerite, suddenly. 'And more than once, you know? There are *plenty* of people mooning about the world nursing broken hearts on my account, you know.'

Alma waited a moment, to give her a space to expand on this observation. When nothing more emerged, she prompted her, gently enough. 'I don't doubt it for a moment.'

'Maybe *you* are the one who should be touched by

insecurity,' Marguerite said, turning her huge face towards the window. 'Is all I'm saying.'

'My love,' said Alma, kissing her, 'is made perfect in jealousy. There's nobody else in the whole wide web of the world for me except you, dear.'

And, after a short and sulky pause, Marguerite said, 'I do know it,' in a small voice. 'Ignore me.'

'Ignore you? Easier said than done. Have you *seen* you?'

'I should tell you more often that I love you. And say how much I— Oh, *appreciate* is a wormy and underpowered word, a nothing sort of word. But what else can I say? How much I *appreciate* what you do for me. Why is speech so under-adequate to these things?'

'You don't need to say what I already know.' Alma kissed her again, and went through to the front room for a nap.

JACK GLASS

Adam Roberts

Jack Glass is the murderer. We know this from the start.
Yet as this extraordinary novel tells the story of three murders
committed by Glass the reader will be surprised to find out
that it was Glass who was the killer and how he did it.
And by the end of the book our sympathies
for the killer are fully engaged.

Riffing on the tropes of crime fiction (the country house
murder, the locked room mystery) and imbued with the feel of
golden age SF, JACK GLASS is another bravura performance
from Roberts. Whatever games he plays with the genre,
whatever questions he asks of the reader, Roberts never loses
sight of the need to entertain and JACK GLASS has some
wonderfully gruesome moments, is built around three gripping
HowDunnits and comes with liberal doses of sly humour.

Roberts invites us to have fun and tricks us into thinking
about both crime and SF via a beautifully structured novel
set in a society whose depiction challanges notions of crime,
punishment, power and freedom. It is an extraordinary novel.

• • •

TRICIA SULLIVAN

Occupy Me

A search not for who you are but what you are, a stunning revelation about the Universe and our place in it.

A woman with wings that exist in another dimension. A man trapped in his own body by a killer. A briefcase that is a door to hell. A conspiracy that reaches beyond our world.

Breathtaking SF from an Arthur C. Clarke Award-winning author.

• • •

'Occupy Me keeps the pages turning and the wheels of thought whirring. It's a psychedelic experience, a wacky tapestry of an idea' *SFX*

'This is science-fiction at its most surreal . . . the premise is brilliant' The Daily Mail

SOMETHING COMING THROUGH

Paul McAuley

**London is devastated. New worlds are being explored.
And the aliens have arrived . . .**

The Jackaroo have given humanity fifteen worlds and the means to
reach them. They're a chance to start over, but they're also littered
with ruins and artifacts left by the Jackaroo's previous clients.

Miracles that could reverse the damage caused by war, climate
change, and rising sea levels. Nightmares that could forever alter
humanity – or even destroy it.

Chloe Millar works in London, mapping changes caused by
imported scraps of alien technology. When she stumbles across
a pair of orphaned kids possessed by an ancient ghost, she must
decide whether to help them or to hand them over to
the authorities.

And on one of the Jackaroo's gift-worlds, the murder of a man
who has just arrived from Earth leads policeman Vic Gayle to a war
between rival gangs over possession of a remote excavation site.

Something is coming through. Something linked to the visions of
Chloe's orphans, and Vic Gayle's murder investigation. Something
that will challenge the limits of the Jackaroo's benevolence . . .

• • •

'*Something Coming Through* is as tight and relentlessly paced
as an Elmore Leonard thriller . . . interested in gritty Earthbound
near-futurism as William Gibson or Lauren Beukes . . . the
freshest take on first contact and interstellar exploration
in many years, and almost feels like the seed for an entire
new subgenre' Alastair Reynolds

'McAuley's latest is smart, it's challenging, and as an
exploration of the social consequences of sudden
science fictional change, it's very impressive indeed' *SFX*

THE WHISPERING SWARM

Michael Moorcock

**The grand master of fantasy returns to London and the
fantastical for his first independent novel in almost ten years!**

Now return to London just after the war, a city desperately
trying to get back on its feet. And one young boy, Michael
Moorcock, who is about to discover a world of magic
and wonder.

Between his first tentative approaches to adulthood – a job
on Fleet Street, the first stirrings of his interest in writing –
and a chance encounter with a mysterious Carmelite Friar, we
see a version of Moorcock's life that is simultaneously
a biography and a story.

Mixing elements of his real life with his adventures in a parallel
London peopled with highwaywomen, musketeers and
magicians, this is Moorcock at his dazzling, mercurial best.

• • •

'Displaying as it does the full spectrum of
Moorcock's idiosyncratic qualities . . . fusing the
literary approach of *Mother London* with the
generic fun of his earlier work' *Literary Review*

'Fizzes with idea and layers of meaning that
transcend the comic-book plot. Bring on part
two' *The Times*

'*The Whispering Swarm* is fantastically
entertaining . . . Welcome back Mr Moorcock;
nobody else quite has your style' *SFX*

'Inexhaustibly inventive . . . welcome back Michael' *The
Spectator*

'Beautifully written and wonderfully descriptive' *Sci-Fi Now*

IAN McDONALD

Luna: New Moon

The Moon wants to kill you.

She has a thousand ways to do it. The bitter cold of vacuum. The lethal sleet of radiation. Choking dust as old as the Earth. Your weakening bones . . .

Or you you could simply run out of money for water. Or air. Or run foul of one of the Five Dragons.

But you stay, because the moon can make you richer than you can imagine.

Ian McDonald's new novel is a thrilling and violent SF epic of Matriarchs, Machiavelli's and Godfathers. It is also a vivid picture of the dangerous realities of life at the edge of survival.

• • •

'Ian McDonald is one of the very best SF writers in the world' Kim Stanley Robinson

'Provocative, gripping and prancingly adult, it's a stunning example of how good science-fiction can be . . .' *SFX*

**'There's a lot of intrigue, some violence, rather more sex – healthily polymorphous and energetic, this – and all the pleasures of a cut-throat soap opera in space . . .'
Adam Roberts, *The Guardian***

ABOUT GOLLANCZ

Gollancz is the oldest SF publishing imprint in the world. Since being founded in 1927 Gollancz has continued to publish a focused selection of bestselling and award-winning authors. The front-list includes **Ben Aaronovitch**, **Joe Abercrombie**, **Charlaine Harris**, **Joanne Harris**, **Joe Hill**, **Alastair Reynolds**, **Patrick Rothfuss**, **Nalini Singh** and **Brandon Sanderson**.

As one of the largest Science Fiction and Fantasy imprints in the UK it is no surprise we have one of the most extensive backlists in the world. Find high-quality SF on Gateway written by such authors as **Philip K. Dick**, **Ursula Le Guin**, **Connie Willis**, **Sir Arthur C. Clarke**, **Pat Cadigan**, **Michael Moorcock** and **George R.R. Martin**.

We also have a strand of publishing in translation, which includes French, Polish and Russian authors. Gollancz is home to more award-winning authors than any other imprint, with names including **Aliette de Bodard**, **M. John Harrison**, **Paul McAuley**, **Sarah Pinborough**, **Pierre Pevel**, **Justina Robson** and many more.

The SF Gateway
More than 3,000 classic, rare and previously out-of-print SF novels at your fingertips.
www.sfgateway.com

The Gollancz Blog
Bringing you news from our worlds to yours. Stories, interviews, articles and exclusive extracts just for you!
www.gollancz.co.uk

GOLLANCZ
LONDON

BETTWS